NEW BOY

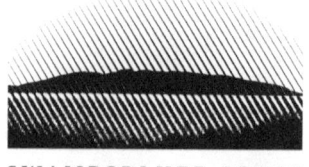

SWAMPSBLUFF PRESS

MURPHY EVANS

BOOK AND COVER DESIGN BY ROB DAY AND GIN EVANS

CONTENTS

With love and thanks to Anna,
My best friend, my love, my inspiration

ARRIVAL

MOVE-IN DAY

HENRY PALMER WAS HANDSOME, graceful, and from the right sort of family — the kind of fair-haired, blue-eyed boy so often beguiled by good fortune — but as he stared up at the words engraved over the front doors of The Randolph School he wondered, perhaps for the first time in his fifteen years, whether he might be someone other than the person everything had told him he was.

"Ye enter a boy, confused and alone, and leave a Brother endowed with Spirit and Honor."

Henry sat down on his duffel bag. What is this "Ye" crap, he wondered, and if he was "confused and alone" it was only because his father was forcing him to leave all his friends in Raleigh and go to this stupid boarding school in the middle of Nowhere, Virginia, with three hundred and fifty strangers — all of them boys for god's sake! "Endowed with spirit and honor" — that rang a bell. Where had he heard that?

Just then a driving, repeating pounding of double organ notes rang out above his head. Henry knew that riff. Hopefully, expectantly, eagerly, he looked up to the dorm room windows above the front doors — sensing some relief or even rescue — but before he could locate the source of the music, it disappeared, and as his gaze fell back to the words above the front doors, Henry remembered. Motherfu—! Last Spring, after he'd been sent home for drinking beer at his junior high school, Henry's father had corralled him in the study, and while standing over him and affecting his best Gregory-Peck-as-Atticus-Finch impersonation, which was pretty spot-on, full of probity and arched eyebrows, until he ruined it by droning on about how disappointed he and Henry's mother were — all the normal parental bullshit — his father had suddenly paused, cleared his throat in that annoying, underlining way grownups had, and said the weirdest thing. "You're a lost boy, Henry. Not the young man endowed with spirit and honor that your mother and I expect you to be." 'Endowed with spirit and honor'. At the time, Henry thought his father was maybe quoting the Bible, which was sort of weird and over the top, seeing how the only thing Henry had done was sneak a 40-ounce can of Schlitz Malt Liquor into the janitor's closet at Josephus Daniels, take a few sips, then spit it out when the foam and the bitterness of the thing surprised him. That was how he got caught. Mrs. Emerson was walking past, heard his sneeze and opened the closet door. The whole thing was just a stupid prank, Henry thought, but his parents — or his dad, rather — treated it like a come to Jesus moment and announced that Henry would be following his older brother, Gordon, to boarding school in the fall. And from then on his dad acted like Henry's two-day suspension from the Raleigh public schools was the best thing that could have happened, because it had led to this moment: Henry stepping through the doors of the Randolph School like Gordon Palmer Sr., Gordon Palmer Jr., and a dozen of Henry's uncles and first cousins had done before him. Until this very moment Henry would have chalked his father's "endowed with spirit and honor" comment to some kind of Presbyterian God-speak that Henry had managed to ignore for most of his life. But now, seeing those words above the Randolph School's front doors, Henry realized that his father had not, in his moment of parental crisis, channeled the words of Jesus, Apostle Paul or the Revelator but instead had simply recalled the inscription over the entrance to his alma mater. Now it all made sense. All that talk this summer — "You're going to meet people who will be your friends for the rest of your life" "You're going to meet people you'll go to college with and pledge" "You're going to meet the people whose weddings you'll attend, whose sisters you might marry" — to Henry it had sounded like a cult, only without girls. He'd tried to say as much, but his father had chalked up Henry's misgivings to a reluctance to leave home. "Don't worry," he'd said. "Gordon will show you the ropes." Henry's brother Gordon was a chip off the old block. Mr. Perfect. A senior, or sixth former as they called it here. Gordon had inherited not only his father's name but his temperament — dutiful, reliable, sensible. Gordon never got into trouble, never disappointed his father, and always thought Henry had screwed up somehow. A place like The Randolph School was perfect for Gordon, who looked for rules to follow and people to impress. The last thing Henry wanted was for someone like Gordon to "show him the ropes." As Henry looked up at the inscription over the front doors, he realized that his father had sent him here not in accordance with some Biblical injunction; his father had sent him here to become a Randolph man. A 'Gordon.' A 'Brother.' "Fuck," he muttered to himself. This was going to be harder than he thought.

Before his parents drove off to search for parking, his father had said, "We'll meet you in the lobby. Find Gordon. He'll take care of you." With a sigh Henry stood up, pushed his way through the front doors, and entered a high-ceilinged room that buzzed with the over-loud laughter of men in Jos. A. Bank button downs and mini-men in Izod polos. Fearing that at any moment his own father would walk in and motion him over to meet an old classmate, or worse, that Gordon would appear and start introducing him as his baby brother, Henry made a beeline for the broad staircase at the far end of the room. Hastily, he dragged his duffel bag, bumpity bump, up the steps and through a heavy metal door onto B Dorm.

The door clanged shut behind him and smothered the sounds below. In contrast to the wide, elegant sweep of the lobby, B Dorm was a narrow hallway running the length of the building, with rooms on either side and a well-worn carpet the color of dead squirrel. Henry's assigned dorm room was 222. He checked the metal tags nailed above the doors and headed down the hall. Fluorescent lights cast a ghastly blue pallor, and the smell of bleach failed to mask the odor of adolescent boy. A God-awful noise blared from the open doorway of Room 220. Henry peered in and saw two large speakers ranged along one wall, and books everywhere — on the dresser, on the desk, on top of the speakers, in piles on the floor. Taped to the walls were posters of various men and women, none of whom Henry recognized: a man in a red wig who appeared to be dressed like a showgirl, a painting of a long, thin woman lying naked on a bed, a pen and ink drawing of peasants who appeared to be tied together and running across a field blind-folded. Henry's eyes passed from one object to another and finally came to rest on a thin, irritable-looking person with narrow shoulders, pale complexion, and stringy, unkempt hair, sitting in front of the room's only window. He had a book propped open on one knee, and a frown on his face. Henry read the slogan on the boy's yellow t-shirt: "Never Mind the Bollocks." The boy put his book down on the windowsill and lowered the volume on his receiver.

"May I help you?"

"Oh. I'm Henry Palmer. I've been assigned Room 222."

The boy pointed straight ahead. "Next door over, mate."

Henry detected what he thought might be a vaguely British accent. "What does 'bollocks' mean?" he asked.

The boy cocked his head and considered Henry from head to toe. "Are you friend or foe?"

Henry fidgeted. "Can't say. I just met you."

"So you reserve rights to hate a person do you?" The boy nodded at Henry with approval. "Until you decide, the word means a castrated bull."

Henry thought about this. "Isn't that a bullock?"

Now the boy smiled. "Ah. I see we have a logophile. That's a rare breed in these parts. Perhaps you deserve better. 'Bollocks' means balls."

Henry laughed.

"But don't share that information with a master. You can tell Nightingale — he knows about bollocks anyway — but don't tell someone like Mackie. I plan to do an experiment on Mr. Mackie. See how long it takes a graduate of the Virginia Military Institute to open a dictionary."

"Nightingale's my advisor," Henry said.

"Well then you hit the jackpot!"

"And Mackie is going to be my English teacher."

The boy grimaced and shook his head in commiseration.

"You don't like Mackie?"

"He's the Dean of Students. The master in charge. The beadle. The beak. The rules grinder. A regular Marley's ghost," the older boy said, again with that strange accent. "You'll meet him tomorrow morning when he inspects your room."

Henry turned to leave but hesitated. He pointed to the turntable in front of the boy's armchair.

"Were you playing *Teenage Wasteland* a little while ago?"

The boy smiled. "*Baba O'Riley.* How'd you know?"

"I thought I heard it out on the patio."

The boy slapped his knee. "All's not lost!"

"What does that mean?"

"I wanted to warn you newcomers to wake up."

This pleased Henry. "I only heard the opening riff."

"Yes. I got Mackie'd. He barged in right when I put it on and made me take it off and shut the window." He rapped the glazing next to his armchair.

"That sucks," Henry said.

The boy nodded soberly. "You'll soon learn that Mr. Mackie's got an evil genius for showing up when he's least wanted."

Henry noticed that the boy was no longer speaking with that British accent. He had some kind of accent, but Henry couldn't place it.

"I'm Ken Bright by the way. What did you say your name was?"

"Henry Palmer."

"Palmer? You're no relation to that tool, Gordon Palmer, are you?"

Henry smiled. "He's my brother."

"Poor bastard."

"It's not so bad, really."

"Not you. Your brother."

Henry laughed. He started to ask 'How so?', but before he could get the words out of his mouth, Ken waved him on.

"Away with you, lad."

Henry turned to go, and as he left the room Ken Bright gave the boy his nod of approval, then cranked up the volume to his speakers and returned to his book.

Next door, the first thing Henry saw as he entered his room was a poster of a nude, large-breasted brunette in high heels with a terrifyingly alluring come-hither smile pinned to the wall. "Hello?" he stammered.

A pasty, freckled boy peered around a dresser. He held a football in one hand and spun it casually toward the ceiling in an affected demonstration of nonchalance, but when Henry extended his right hand in greeting, the ball fell to the floor.

"I'm Henry."

"Bob. Bob Wembly."

Bob was at least two inches shorter and fifteen pounds lighter than Henry, and when the two boys came together Bob rose up onto the pads of his feet and puffed out his chest in an effort to match Henry's stature.

"My dad drove me up this morning but had to get back to Greensboro. I went ahead and made up the bottom bunk, but we can flip for it if you want."

"That's okay. You take it." Henry looked around the rest of the room. In the corner was a red director's chair emblazoned with the N.C. State logo, and on top of one of the dressers were bottles of vitamins and a can of Barbasol. Henry did a double take of his roommate's baby soft chin.

Bob picked up the football and began spinning it again. "You gonna try out for J.V.?"

"Football?"

Bob nodded.

"Probably not."

Henry looked at his corner of the room. There was space for a small desk or an armchair but not for both. Gordon had offered his old desk, but Henry didn't like taking Gordon's hand-me-downs. Maybe he could find a decent chair somewhere.

"I'm going out for quarterback," Bob said.

"Really?"

Bob did not notice the skepticism in Henry's voice. He gripped the ball in his right hand and feigned a pass. "Got wicked arm strength."

Henry nodded. "Good for you."

"You should go out for wide receiver. We could be like Roman Gabriel and Fred Biletnikoff."

Henry noted the N.C. State reference. "I'm kind of tired of football to tell you the truth."

"Aw man. It would be awesome. We could be like the kings of fourth form."

"I'm good," Henry said. He eyed the centerfold. "Is that Miss August?"

"Miss May," Bob said. "Isn't she awesome?"

"Where'd you get it? Your dad's?"

Bob shook his head. "Found it."

"Poking around ditches?"

"Damn right! Won't believe what you can find on the side of the road."

Henry laughed. He had no trouble imagining Bob biking around his neighborhood, his head on a swivel, looking for dirty magazines. "You think they're going to let you hang that on the wall?"

"Hell yes!" Bob said. "It's my room, ain't it?'

"Yeah. But I bet they got some pretty strict rules about stuff like that."

Henry unzipped his duffel bag and began pulling out clothes and placing them in his dresser.

"I'd like to see them try to take it down. There's freedom of speech, ain't there?"

Henry was pretty sure that didn't apply to hanging naked pictures in your dorm room. "Maybe —"

"They'll have to come through me first!" Bob pounded his chest with a clenched fist.

Henry smiled. "You know my mom's gonna be here like any minute."

As if on cue there was a knock at the door, and panic overtook Bob. "Uh no, right. What should we do?" he stammered.

"Just a second!" Henry called out, and he motioned for Wembly to take down the centerfold.

Bob reached up for the poster and in his haste ripped it into two pieces as the door to the room swung open.

"Whoa there, little fellow. Careful with that."

Bob dropped the centerfold at the sight of a sixth former walking through the door. It was Gordon, who laughed when Bob fell to his knees and tried to push the pieces of the centerfold under the bunk bed.

"Jesus, Henry. Five minutes on campus and you've already committed a major infraction."

Gordon watched his brother's face go blank in disbelief then pulled him close in a bearhug. "Where you been, man? I was downstairs looking all over for you."

"I didn't see you when I came in." Henry stepped to one side to make room for Wembly as he stood up. "This is Bob. He's from Greensboro."

"Bob Wembly," the boy said, extending a hand.

Gordon bumped the boy's hand with his fist. "Gordon," he said, and turned back to his brother. "How was the drive up?"

"It was okay."

"Mom and dad fight about Sand Hill?"

"Not so much. Dad mostly talked about Randolph. And you," Henry said sourly.

Gordon laughed. "Sounds like you had a blast."

Gordon was only a little taller than Henry but outweighed him by forty pounds. In his khaki pants and Oxford cloth button down he already bore a striking resemblance to the middle-aged men Henry had seen in the lobby. Indeed, for as long as Henry could remember Gordon had looked — and acted — like an old fart.

"Where're mom and dad?" Henry asked.

"They're talking to Mr. Endicott."

"Big surprise."

Gordon punched his brother in the arm. "Jesus, man. Give it a chance."

"Already talking to the headmaster, and I haven't even unpacked."

Gordon smiled. "I don't think they're talking about you."

"What then?" Henry asked.

Gordon looked away and picked up the can of Barbasol on Bob's dresser. Weighed it with his hand. Noted that it was full. Pointed it at Bob. "Expecting a growth spurt, Wombley?"

"Wembly." The boy rubbed his chin with thumb and forefinger. "Maybe," he squeaked.

Gordon gave Bob an encouraging nod and replaced the shaving cream. "That's the spirit."

"What then?" Henry repeated.

"What then, what?"

"Mom and dad. And Mr. Endicott."

Gordon looked out the boys' windows. "I don't know .... Wow. Lucked out on the view. You can just make out the East Gate."

Henry could tell his brother was hiding something. "What, Gordon?"

"I don't know. Me maybe. Mr. Endicott knows a lot more about me than you. You couldn't even hang around long enough for Dad to introduce you?"

Henry turned aside and continued unpacking his duffel bag. "Forget it."

Gordon glanced at Bob, who made a show of re-taping the two halves of Miss May to the wall. Gordon shook his head. "Not a chance, Wombley."

"It's Wembly," the boy said. "Like the stadium but without an 'e' at the end."

Gordon studied the boy. Not much to look at. Weak chin. Scrawny.

But he stood up for himself. Gordon gave him that much. "Sure thing, Wobbly."

For a split second Bob asked himself, 'Is the guy deaf, or stupid?' Then his mouth fell open as he realized he'd just been nicknamed. Wobbly? He didn't like the sound of that. Hoping to shrug it off, he snorted, but the sound that came out of his mouth was so pathetic that Gordon, who had already turned to Henry, looked back, confirmed Wobbly's discomfort, nodded to himself, and committed the nickname to memory. Wobbly was screwed.

Gordon Palmer Sr. appeared in the hall outside Henry's door, erect as usual and taciturn. Seeing Henry standing in his room with his shirt tail already out gave Mr. Palmer pause. He knew from experience how important first impressions were at places like this and like Princeton, which he hoped Henry would one day attend. He himself was neat and tidy by nature, qualities which had served him well. Strange that Henry had turned out so much different from himself, and different from Gordon too. A free spirit, 'More Wilson than Palmer,' as his wife, herself a Wilson, liked to say. Spirit was all well and good, but making a good impression counted more in Gordon Palmer Sr.'s book. Now that Henry was at Randolph his father thought that Henry might fall in line. Be more like Gordon. A little less Wilson and more Palmer. He worried about Henry but told himself that Randolph would straighten things out. He cleared his throat and walked in.

"We looked for you in the lobby."

"Oh, hey Dad."

"You were supposed to wait for us there."

"I know," Henry said. "It was crowded, and I had my duffel bag, so I decided to come up here and get unpacked."

His father cleared his throat again. "But that's not what we agreed."

Gordon, who'd witnessed several rows between his father and brother over the summer, jumped in. "Hey Dad, this is Bob Wobbly, Henry's roommate."

Mr. Palmer's manner immediately softened, and he stepped forward and extended a hand to the freckled boy. "Nice to meet you, Bob. I'm Mr. Palmer. Henry tells me you're from Greensboro."

"That's right. And it's Wembly."

"Very good. Do you know Dave Burns? He's the editor of the

Greensboro newspaper and was one of my roommates at Princeton."

Henry looked to Gordon — was their father actually name-dropping to his roommate? — but Gordon didn't seem to notice.

"I don't think so, but my mom probably does."

"Well, he's a fine man — "

"Where's mom?" Henry interrupted.

"I didn't think it was a good idea for her to come onto B Dorm," Mr. Palmer said.

Gordon laughed. "Naked things everywhere!"

"She's going to meet us in the Reading Room."

"What's the Reading Room?"

"It's a place where you read books, dumb-dumb." Gordon punched his brother in the shoulder in an effort to lighten the mood.

"I figured, but why meet there?" Henry saw Gordon and his father exchange looks. "What? What is it?"

His father and Gordon exchanged glances again. "There's something there that I want to show you," his father said. He hesitated.

"I know what books look like," Henry said.

Gordon laughed. "There's this thing. It's kind of corny — "

"It's history," Mr. Palmer objected. "It's tradition."

"Sure," Gordon said, nodding to his father. "But it's actually cool," he said, turning to Henry.

Henry looked to Wobbly and would have rolled his eyes, but Wobbly stood transfixed; it was like Wobby thought he was about to be let in on some super secret shit.

"What is it?" Henry asked.

"It's the names of all the Head Boys. In chronological order," Gordon said, and with his right hand he drew an imaginary line above their heads. "Printed just below the ceiling, all around the room."

Now Henry understood.

"Dad's name's up there — "

"Got it," Henry interrupted.

"Really," Gordon insisted. "It's pretty cool."

"Uh-huh." Over the summer Henry had heard all about how his father was once Head Boy at the Randolph School. Henry turned his back on Gordon and his father and resumed unpacking his duffel.

The awkward silence that followed was broken by the sound of someone whistling in the hall. Mr. Palmer turned around in time to see an elderly black man in a gray striped shirt and blue canvas pants walk by.

"Is that really you?" Mr. Palmer called out, as though hailing him.

The man stopped, took two steps back, and peered into the room. His close-cropped hair was speckled white, and the whites of his eyes were honey-colored.

Mr. Palmer started at the second sight of him. "It *is* you."

The man raised his right hand, held it palm out toward Mr. Palmer, and said "Hi-i-i-i-i-i-i," and the sound of his I's petered out like the air from a deflating balloon. He stood there, framed by the door and stock still, waiting for Mr. Palmer to say something. Finally, out of embarrassment, Mr. Palmer waved him away.

"Sorry. I was speaking to my sons."

The man nodded, lowered his hand, and continued down the hall, and his whistling picked up where it had left off.

Mr. Palmer turned to Gordon. "I'd swear that man was here when I was a student."

"What's his name?" Gordon asked.

"I don't remember."

"Uly," Henry said.

"That's right!" Mr. Palmer pointed at Henry and smiled. "How did you know that?"

Henry pointed to his chest. "It was stitched on his shirt."

"The man's Methusaleh," Mr. Palmer said. "He was old when I was a New Boy."

"They say it's hard to tell how old a black person is," Gordon commented.

"They?" Henry asked. "Who's 'they'?"

Gordon rolled his eyes. "Way to go Brando."

Mr. Palmer gestured towards the hallway. "Let's go. Your mother's waiting."

"I'll meet you there," Henry said. His father started to object, but Henry pointed to his duffel bag. "I want to finish unpacking."

Gordon nodded to his father and stepped to the door. "It's just down there and to the right. Above the dining hall."

Henry nodded and took a deep breath once his father had left the room. He turned to Wobbly. "That's my family," he said.

"Pretty cool that your dad was Head Boy," Wobbly said.

"Sure." Henry turned his back on his roommate. This was not something Henry wanted to talk about, but it seemed inevitable — what with his father's name up on a wall. Didn't seem to bother Gordon, even though Gordon shared the name. He seemed to love it. 'Be proud of your family,' he'd say. But Henry couldn't help but feel that everyone now would expect him to act like his father.

On the other side of the room, Bob thought about this nickname. *Wobbly.* Sounded weak-kneed, cowardly even. It won't stick, he told himself.

Soon there was a knock at the door, and a red-haired chubby kid with wet lips and narrow slits for eyes stepped into the room. He wore a white t-shirt with a long, horizontal X across the chest. He said nothing but grinned.

"Nice t-shirt," Bob said after an awkward silence.

"It's the Alabama state flag."

"You're from Alabama?" Henry asked.

"Nope. Charlotte. Just like the flag."

Another awkward silence ensued. The two roommates looked at one another. Bob raised his eyebrows nervously, as if to ask, 'What now?' "

"What happened to the pinup?" the boy said finally, pointing to the pieces of centerfold in Bob's hands.

"He tore it by accident," Henry explained.

"You don't want it?"

Henry looked to Bob, who was staring at the red tuft of whiskers on the older boy's chin; Bob shook his head.

"No," Henry said.

"I'll take it."

Bob was strangely immobilized, so Henry retrieved the scraps and handed them to the boy. "Are you going to put it up?"

"No."

"What are you going to do with it?"

"Look at it. What do you think?"

Henry considered the boy's eager, panting expression and decided not to tell him what he thought.

The boy held the scraps at arm's length, fitted the pieces together, and a charge of pleasure whooshed through his nervous system. He thrust a hand into his pocket in a belated attempt to conceal his not-so-secret boner.

"Thanks!"

"What's your name?" Henry asked.

"Ned. But everyone calls me Bone."

The boy grinned. Henry didn't ask about the name's provenance. "And you?"

"Henry Palmer."

"Gordon's brother."

"Yep." Henry turned to Bob. "This is — "

"Wobbly," Bone interrupted. "Gordon told me."

Wobbly's heart sank. Henry recognized his roommate's disappointment but only offered him a shrug. He turned back to Bone. "You live on B Dorm?"

"Yep. Just down the hall. Across from Mongo."

"Mongo?"

"The big hairy mountain."

Henry and Wobbly looked at each other.

"You'll know him when you see him," Bone said, and he gave them a quick salute and jogged happily, higgledy-piggledy down the hall.

Henry turned to Wobbly, who was running a thumb and forefinger along his smooth chin, searching for solace in his one whisker.

"So long Miss May," Wobbly mumbled wistfully.

"Hello B Dorm," Henry answered.

MACKIE'S CLASS

A DOZEN WOODEN ARMCHAIR DESKS flanked three walls of the classroom, and a long slate chalkboard ran the length of the fourth. In front of the chalkboard was a double-pedestal oak desk whose top was bare, save for a tidy stack of notebook papers folded lengthwise. Behind the desk, at a window in the corner farthest from the door, stood a man with his back to the room. He was tall and lean with narrow shoulders and dark, straight hair. As the boys filed in, he remained motionless except for his right hand, which held a red marking pen that he used to slowly tick the time against the palm of his hand.

The bell rang just as Henry entered the room. He stopped briefly to consider the two remaining empty chairs then took the one farther away from the teacher's desk, next to a pudgy, round-faced, black kid whose right leg bounced nervously up and down.

Mackie continued to stare out the window, keeping time as Henry put his backpack under his seat and pulled out his notebook.

"Palmer, you're late."

Henry started. He had no idea Mackie had seen him, let alone that he knew who he was.

"Sorry—"

Mackie held up his red pen and slowly rotated his head, owl-like, in Henry's direction. His two large, brown eyes—already magnified by the pair of thick-rimmed glasses that sat on his great, curved beak of a nose—seemed to bulge with anticipation as they came to rest on Henry Palmer.

"When the bell rings you are to be in your seat—not inside the door, not on your way to your seat, but sitting down—*sessio*—eyes forward and poised to tackle the English language. You have ten minutes to get here from Mr. Theobald's World History class. That's plenty of time, isn't it Palmer? Ten minutes? Does it take you that long to walk from the lobby of the Carolina Country Club to the first tee?"

"Sir?" Henry didn't play golf, but how did Mackie know his family belonged to the country club? Or that he was from Raleigh? Or that he'd just had history class?

"No more free passes, boys. No more pats on the head. No more A's for effort or sincerity. We are here to learn to write a proper English sentence, and by sentence I mean a subject and a verb, and by proper I mean spelling according to Merriam Webster and grammar according to Warriner's. You can have the noblest sentiments in the world, but in this class if you express them with five or more grammatical mistakes you will get an F."

Mackie stepped to the front of his desk while he let the threat of an 'F' sink into the skulls of these coddled boys.

"I suspect many of you do not know what an F means, but I can assure you that at some point during this year—and sooner rather than later, I hope — you will become acquainted with that letter and its meaning. It means 'fail'," and Mackie slapped the top of his desk with his hand, "and 'flunk'," and he slapped it again, "and oh my God what am I going to tell my 'father'." One last slap. "Well, you're going to tell him that you still have a lot to learn in English. Now, I have your summer reading assignments here, and if you would be so kind as to come forward as I call your name."

Mackie picked up the papers on his desk and read the names he had written on the back pages. "Jobe ... Cutbert ... Basset ...." As he read each name another boy shuffled forward to receive his mark. "Wales ..." The black boy sitting next to Henry got up from his desk, and when he returned, Henry stole a glance at his paper and saw written on the back page an "A-" in red pen. Henry breathed a sigh of relief — the man gave A's after all.

"Palmer." Henry stepped forward and reached for the paper in the teacher's hand, but before he could grasp it, Mackie pulled the paper back, caught Henry's eye, and said, "The sand and surf days are over, Mr. Palmer." Then he placed the paper into Henry's hand and called the next student's name.

Henry turned the paper over and written on back was, "F — Over 5 grammatical errors." Henry felt like the floor had fallen out from under him. He'd never received an F in his life. When he got back to his seat he slipped the paper into his notebook as casually as he could manage then glanced around the room to see if anyone else looked devastated. What are 'sand and surf days'? Henry thought to himself.

Mackie stepped to the opposite side of his desk and wrote 'The Sick Rose' on the blackboard then faced the class.

"I want everyone to open his book to page 272. Please read the poem to yourself, and then we will discuss it."

Henry rummaged through his backpack and found a copy of *Sense and the Imagination*. It was a used copy. Gordon had given it to him before he'd left home. There were underlined passages and notes written in the margins. At the time, Henry had taken one look at the book and handed it back to Gordon.

"No thanks," he'd said.

Gordon had pushed the book back on his brother. "I had Mackie in tenth grade. This has everything we talked about."

Henry had opened it at random and read his brother's comments next to a poem called, "Ozymandias". "Nothing lasts," Gordon had written. Henry wasn't impressed. He'd handed the book back to his brother. "I'd rather read it for myself."

"Just take it, Henry. Do you really want to make mom and dad buy you a new book?"

Henry thought he'd managed to put his brother off, but he'd found the book when he'd unpacked his bag yesterday. He suspected Gordon had somehow snuck it into his things yesterday, but he couldn't be sure that his mother hadn't put it there. Maybe they did want to save some money on books? God knows, the school cost a fortune — at least that's what Gordon told him.

"Henry Palmer, what does the author mean by 'the invisible worm' in the first stanza?"

Henry looked up and found Mackie seated behind his desk but leaning forward and pointing the red pen directly at his nose.

"Pardon?"

"The first stanza. 'The invisible worm'. What does it mean?"

Henry looked around the room and saw the other boys had their books open.

"I'm sorry. What page did you say it was?"

"What is a worm, Palmer?"

"Pardon?"

"A worm," Mackie said.

"It's a bug or an insect thing that lives underground."

"Is that the kind of worm the poet is writing about here."

"I s'pose."

"Do worms 'fly in the night'?"

"A flying worm?" Henry asked.

"That's what the poem says."

That didn't make sense to Henry. He looked at the kid's book next to him to try to figure out where they were. He felt Mackie's attention bearing down on him. He felt the blood rushing to his face. Any second now and he was going to start sweating.

"What page did you say we were on?"

"We are on page 272. Try to keep up, Palmer, will you? What about you, Wales? Can you help Palmer out?"

Wales had kept his head down in hopes of not being called on. Now the blood rushed to his face, and his cafe au lait cheeks turned reddish brown. Wales's head dipped lower towards his book. "Worms don't fly," he said, without looking up.

"Thank you for that bit of scientific information about the invertebrate phylum, but I was hoping for something that bears a relation to this poem."

Henry opened his book to page 272 and found *The Sick Rose* by William Blake.

> *O Rose thou art sick.*
> *The invisible worm,*
> *That flies in the night*
> *In the howling storm:*
> *Has found out thy bed*
> *Of crimson joy:*
> *And his dark secret love*
> *Does thy life destroy.*

Gordon had circled the word 'worm' and written 'penis' in the margin. Henry closed his book quickly.

"Do you think, Mr. Wales, that William Blake did not understand that worms — the same worms that appear on sidewalks on rainy days and that robins pull from the ground in the spring — don't fly?"

"Everybody knows that worms don't fly," Wales offered weakly.

"Even poets writing in the 18TH Century?"

"Sure. He probably knew."

"Then why did he write, 'The invisible worm / That flies in the night'?"

"Maybe he meant some other kind of 'flies'," another boy piped out.

Mackie swiveled his attention to the other side of the room where a dough-faced boy with long ears and a sweet, unintelligent expression, gazed back at him.

"Well that's interesting. What 'other kind of flies' might he have meant, Mr. Grimes?"

"Green flies …. Bottle flies …. House flies …. You know, flies." Bobby Grimes spoke the words like it was the simplest thing in the world, and he was happy to be of use.

Mackie smiled at the boy's demonstration of stupidity.

"Now that is very helpful, Mr. Grimes. I thank you for that, because your comment raises a fundamental question of English grammar. And as I said at the outset of class, grammar — or I should say the proper use of grammar — will be our main focus this year. Unlearning the bad habits that you've all grown accustomed to and in their place learning good, proper, American English, the sort that will distinguish you from the common, lowbrow know-nothing that you will find yourself surrounded by when you leave these hallowed grounds. Can anyone here tell Mr. Grimes how we know that William Blake did not mean a blue-bottled house fly when he wrote 'flies' in this poem?"

Mackie looked around the room, and finding no volunteers he called on Bob "Wobbly" Wembly, who was holding his book up in front of his face in a pathetic effort to conceal himself. Wobbly slowly lowered the book to his desk, and as he lowered his book he also lowered his gaze, to avoid making eye contact with Mr. Mackie.

"Well, Mr. Wembly?" Mackie repeated.

"Because they didn't have those kinds of flies back then?"

His words were spoken more like a question than a declaration, and they seemed to send a jolt of electricity through Mackie, and his right forefinger shot up to the heavens then suddenly struck down hard onto the open page of his book. "From this poem, Mr. Wembly! What in this poem tells us that William Blake wasn't talking about horseflies or deerflies or houseflies when he wrote 'flies'?"

Wobbly looked back down at the page in front of him and then across the room at Henry. His lips moved, and Henry imagined that he was asking for help, but Henry dared not say anything. Finally Wobbly looked back at Mackie and shrugged his shoulders pathetically.

Mackie smiled cruelly. He relished that look of abject surrender. "I'll give you a hint," he said. "Grammar."

"Grammar?" Wobbly asked.

Mackie nodded, but Wobbly said nothing.

"I'll give you another hint. Parts of speech."

Wobbly stared at him but said nothing.

"Do you know what a verb is, Mr. Wembly?"

Now Wobbly felt that Mackie was making fun of him, and his spirits rallied. "Yeah," he said with a slender note of defiance.

"What is it?"

Wobbly hesitated. It occurred to him that this might be a trick question. Then he wondered whether he actually knew what a verb was. Mackie waited. "It's an action, like kicking or eating," Wobbly said finally.

"Correct. And what's a noun?"

"It's a thing, like a book or a table."

"Very good. And what's a housefly, Mr. Wembly?"

"It's a black bug that rubs its legs together and washes its face."

Mackie hesitated long enough for Wobbly to realize that something bad was about to happen.

"Spent some time staring at houseflies, have you Wembly?"

Several of the boys laughed, and Mackie smiled because he felt like the boys appreciated that he had pinned Wobbly to the wall like a specimen.

"I meant as a part of speech. What part of speech is a housefly?"

"Noun," Wobbly said, uncertainly.

"Correct. And in this poem" — Mackie again poked the page in front of him — "what part of speech is 'flies'?"

Wobbly looked down at his book and read over the poem. "It's a verb," he said finally.

"Right. So was Mr. William Blake talking about houseflies or about the act of flying when he wrote 'flies'?"

"The act of flying."

"Correct. So Mr. Wembly, I ask you, do you think that our poet here failed to understand that earthworms don't fly?"

"No. I think he knew they don't fly."

"So why do you think that he wrote, 'The invisible worm / That flies in the night'?"

"He meant a different worm?"

Again, Wobbly spoke the words more as a question than an answer, but this time Mackie greeted his answer with enthusiasm. He pointed his red pen at the nose in the middle of Wobbly's face and jabbed the air twice. "Exactly!" Mackie said. And he turned his attention away from Wobbly and toward the rest of the class.

As soon as Mackie looked away Wobbly exhaled. He congratulated himself for handling Mackie's questions so well and glanced around the room to see who else had admired his performance.

Meanwhile, Mackie had decided he'd played with Wobbly long

enough, and he looked about the room for his next mouse to torture.

"Does anyone have any idea what sort of worm Mr. William Blake meant?"

"A flying worm?" one of the boys said.

Mackie rolled his eyes. "Literally, yes. That is what he wrote. And what, pray tell, is a flying worm?"

Mackie looked around the room, but there were no takers. Henry kept his eyes down. He wasn't going to say the word written in the margins of his book, and he didn't understand how that could fly, anyway.

"Wyrm," Mackie said. "W-y-r-m. Wyrm. Have any of you worms read The Hobbit?"

Wales raised his hand in an unfortunate reflex of enthusiasm — he was an avid fan of Tolkien — then quickly tried to lower it before Mackie spotted him, but he was too late.

"Mr. Wales. What is called "Worm" in The Hobbit?"

Wales nervously tilted his head sideways and rolled his eyes toward the ceiling. "Go — "

"Not Gollum," Mackie interrupted. "It flies, like this 'invisible worm'."

"The dragon," Wales said.

"Excellent. The dragon, Smogul, flies. Thank you, Mr. Wales."

Wales decided that Mackie's thanks were sincere this time, and he acknowledged the thanks by nodding to his teacher — all the while making a mental note to himself to suppress all enthusiasms in the future.

"The ancient word, wyrm — W-y-r-m," Mackie said, "is another word for dragon in Olde English. Now do you think, Mr. Wales, that the author meant a dragon?"

Wales looked back at the text and tried to imagine an invisible dragon flying through the night. "Possibly?"

"Really?" Mackie arched his eyes and looked at the boy skeptically.

"Or not," Wales said. He tried to feign indifference in order to mask his fear — Wales had already learned that fear stimulated Mackie's attention. Maybe if Mackie thought he was bored, Mackie would leave him alone.

"Great big Smogul flying to a bed? Smogul is quite large, isn't he Mr. Wales?"

No such luck, Wales thought. He nodded. Yes, Smogul was large. That was a safe answer.

"Bigger than this room, wouldn't you say? About the size of half this building?" Mackie raised his arms and pointed at the walls and ceiling of the room.

"About," Wales muttered, sensing some trap being laid.

"It's hard to imagine something that big flying to a bed, isn't it, Wales?"

Wales nodded miserably, fearing the inevitable.

"Or being invisible for that matter — the poem does say that the worm is 'invisible', doesn't it?"

Wales looked down at the page. He already knew the answer, but maybe if he acted like he didn't understand what Mackie was talking about Mackie would move on to another boy.

"How can a dragon be 'invisible' Wales?"

Wales now had the sinking feeling that Mackie had latched onto him and none of the other boys was going to come to his aid.

"Magic?" Wales said reluctantly.

"What in this poem suggests magic to you, Mr. Wales?"

Wales again looked down at the page. "The dragon?" Wales asked.

"But is the worm really a dragon?" Mackie asked slowly, and the sound of his voice grew quieter, more menacing.

Now Wales felt sure that misfortune was about to strike.

"I don't know," he said carefully. "You said — "

"A dragon wouldn't fly to a bed, would it? Did Smogul seem to be the romantic type to you, Wales?"

Wales shook his head, and a bead of sweat dripped from his hairline, down his forehead, to the tip of his nose.

"A bed is a bed, is it not, Mr. Wales?"

"I s'pose," he said quietly.

"And what is 'thy bed'? Whose bed does the worm fly to?" Much to Wales's relief Mackie looked around the room, but none of the boys showed any sign of recognition. Mackie frowned.

"Help them out, Wales. Whose bed is the author talking about?"

"Rose's?" he muttered.

"Exactly!" Mackie exclaimed. "And who is Rose?"

Wales looked down at the poem then back up at Mackie. That, he thought, was a stupid question. How was anyone to know who Rose was from the poem?

"I have no idea," Wales said, with some spunk finally.

"Well of course we don't know who Rose is." Mackie seemed to laugh at the thought with Wales. "The poem doesn't provide us with any biographical information, does it? But what do we know about Rose?"

"She has a bed," Wales said.

"Yes. And that's she's a 'she' — a girl or a woman — which do you think, Wales, girl or woman?"

"I don't know," Wales said.

"Really? No idea?"

Wales shook his head.

"What about 'crimson joy'?"

"What about it?"

"Help him out, Palmer."

Henry jumped at his name and looked up from the book. "What?"

"What is her 'crimson joy'?"

Mackie's eyes were getting bigger again. Henry looked back at the text. Gordon hadn't written anything there. "I don't know," he said.

"It's in her bed, right?"

"Whose bed?"

"Palmer, you need to try to keep up," Mackie said dismissively. "Whose bed are we talking about, Wales?"

Wales groaned inwardly. "Rose's," he said softly.

"Right. And what is her 'crimson joy'?"

Wales looked down at the floor and his blush deepened, revealing a flush of acne down the back of his neck.

"Wales? 'Crimson joy'?" Mackie said.

There was silence in the room as all of the boys seemed to share in Wales's embarrassment. Mackie let the silence linger and the discomfort grow. Several of the boys stole glances at one another as if begging for someone to break the silence and come to Wales's aid.

"'Crimson joy', 'dark secret love,' 'thy bed'. Obviously, gentlemen, the poet is writing about coitus, sex, and its bloody aftermath."

There was a low murmur as several of the boys struggled to suppress their laughter. Mackie pretended to ignore that.

"Which takes us back to 'the invisible worm', Wales. Have you given that any more thought?"

Wales was paralyzed with embarrassment. He stared at the floor and could not lift his head.

"Come now, Mr. Wales. Surely you've figured that out by now."

Wales clinched his teeth and shook his head.

"Anyone?"

Henry avoided eye contact. Wobbly had his book up in front of his face again. Grimes stared absently out the window.

"Obviously, the 'worm' is a penis—"

"Aaaaahrrg!" At the word a shout rang out, a desk crashed to the floor, and Tom Wales ran out of the room.

There was silence as all of the boys turned to Mr. Mackie to get a read on his reaction. He stood in front of the window with his head turned to the door. At first he appeared genuinely surprised by the turn of events, and he held the red pen to the tip of his chin as he contemplated the discomfort that must have prompted Wales to flee the room. Slowly his lips stretched into a narrow, unpleasant smile, and a sharp cackle burst from the sides of his mouth as he glanced from boy to boy with a look of genuine amusement. "A bit melodramatic, don't you think?"

Most of the boys laughed as all their pent up anxiety of the last several minutes suddenly released. Several of the boys sat quietly with a sense of relief that the ordeal was finally over. Others, like Henry, felt sympathy for Wales and anger towards Mackie, thinking an injustice had been done. Still others, like Wobbly, concerned themselves only with self-preservation and were already considering how best to parry their next encounter with the man, who seemed likely to become more vicious as the year progressed.

Mackie returned to his desk at the front of the room. "For the remainder of the period, I want you all to read *The Rocking Horse Winner*," he said "It's at page 83 of your textbook. And please come to class tomorrow prepared to discuss why Paul rides his horse."

When the bell rang, all the boys fled the classroom. Henry leaned down and picked up Wales's backpack—maybe he'd see the boy in the cafeteria. As he walked out he looked back at Mackie, who now had his back to the door and was staring out the window at a giant Chinese chestnut tree.

CUB FOOTBALL PRACTICE

THE GROUNDS OF THE RANDOLPH SCHOOL were roughly 2,000 acres of rolling hills and bottomland in the foothills of the Blue Ridge Mountains. The school's classrooms, dormitories and faculty houses were clustered along the top of a broad ridge running through the center of the property. Along one side of the ridge — the backside of the campus — was the Rapidan River, which formed one long, meandering and wooded boundary of the school property. On the other side of the ridge were the school's golf course, athletic fields and pastureland. The athletic fields were numerous. There was a baseball diamond, a football stadium, a fieldhouse, and practice fields used for football, lacrosse and soccer depending on the season. In the fall, most of the fields were taken up by football — the sport with the longest history and the greatest support at the school. The Varsity team used two fields. The Junior Varsity team used a third field, and the Junior Orange team — which was made up primarily of third and fourth formers who aspired to play one day on the Varsity squad — used a fourth. These four fields, each of them regulation length and width and immaculately maintained, were located side by side, with the varsity practice fields closest to the main campus.

Set apart from these four fields — in the most distant reach of the inhabited portion of the campus — was the practice field for the Cub football squad. Along one side of this field was a plot planted in corn that was used to feed the school's small dairy herd. Along another side was a pasture with a field pond and one scraggly persimmon tree whose trunk had been rubbed smooth by the rumps of cows. The practice field itself was uneven, as if it had been disked and harrowed but not properly rolled before being planted in grass. The field naturally drained toward the pasture pond and along that edge was a minefield of molehills. The Cubs themselves were indifferent to the lack of care that had been shown their sod. These were the boys least likely ever to play Varsity football, but because the school required every boy to play a sport in every season, and because the only other fall sport was cross country — which required every member of the team, even the most determinedly sedentary, to run at least five miles a day — the least athletically inclined students were Cubs by default and found themselves on the field in shoulder pads and helmets, bumping into one another reluctantly and in a somewhat random fashion.

Henry Palmer was on one knee on the sidelines of this unpromising corner of the Randolph campus, picking crabgrass out of the turf. Beside him sat Tom Wales, whose shoulder pads had rolled forward onto his chest. Apparently, no one had shown Wales how to buckle the pad straps underneath his armpits. Henry and Wales had been banished to the sidelines by the Right Rev. Frank Deemer, the Cub football coach and school chaplain, who'd caught them playing air guitar during one of his addresses to the team. Technically, Wales hadn't been playing air guitar; he'd been fingering Bach's Prelude and Fugue in C major from The Well-Tempered Clavier, which he was supposed to have memorized before his first piano lesson tomorrow. As for Henry, he had been daydreaming about a slow dance with Karen Butler at the Raleigh Y and hadn't realized that he was drumming the beat of "Stairway to Heaven" on his knee pad. Deemer had ordered them to the sidelines where they watched as the rest of the team performed tackling drills.

"Ever play football before?" Henry asked.

Wales smirked. "Do I look like I've played football before?"

"Not so much," Henry reached over and straightened Wales's shoulder pads. "Did you buckle these?"

"Buckle what?"

"Your shoulder pads. There's a strap that goes under your arm and buckles in the front." Henry pulled up the front of his own jersey and revealed the breastplate of his padding. "Look here. Is it buckled?"

Wales lifted the front of his jersey and saw the slots where the buckles went. He reached behind his back, found the straps and buckled them. "What about you?"

"I hate football," Henry said.

Wales laughed. "Why are you playing then?"

"I promised my dad. He thinks I'm going out for J.V."

"Ha! I told my mom I'd go out for Varsity piano."

"Why didn't you?"

"It's not an option. My advisor told me, 'Every Randolph boy plays a sport every season. No exceptions!'" Wales wagged a finger in the air as he spoke those last words.

"Who's your advisor?"

"Mr. Bloodstone."

"Colonel Bloodstone? The Latin teacher?" Henry asked.

Wales nodded. "Is he really a Colonel?"

"No," Henry said. "I'm pretty sure that was the name he was born with."

"Am I supposed to call him Colonel Bloodstone?"

"Only behind his back," Henry said.

"He did say I could get out of playing a sport if I was in the school play. Only problem is, New Boys aren't allowed to be in the Fall play."

"I thought you guys like to play sports," Henry said.

Wales gave Henry a mortified look, and Henry shoved Wales's shoulder pads and accidentally knocked him on his butt. "I'm kidding, man!"

Wales scrambled back to one knee. "Oh, I'm hella good at basketball. Football's just not my thing."

"Really?"

Wales looked at Henry like he was an idiot. "Come on, man," he said shaking his head. He pointed at himself. "Trust your eyes."

They both laughed and resumed watching their teammates, who stood in a circle and stared at two boys grappling on the ground in front of them. Rev. Deemer blew his whistle and then picked up one of the boys by the shoulder pads and stood him upright.

"You got to keep your chin up and explode into the ball. Like this." Deemer crouched in a low squat in front of the boy then lunged forward and knocked the boy back to the ground. "See how it's done?"

"I can't believe I missed out on that," Wales said sarcastically.

"It's actually a fun game when there's no grownups involved."

"Yeah?"

"Yeah. Making up plays. Knocking the crap out of your best friend."

Wales looked at Henry like he was crazy. "Who can say no to that?"

Henry smiled. He gripped an imaginary football in his hand and made a passing motion.

"Throwing the perfect pass downfield. Finding that one receiver who's open and putting the ball right there where no one but him can catch it. Running as fast as you can with the ball tucked under your arm and no one can catch you."

"Sounds like you miss it."

"I'd miss it if we could play without coaches yelling at you."

They looked at Rev. Deemer who was now on the ground in front of the boys, on all fours, moving back and forth like an angry crab.

"What position did you play?"

"Quarterback." Henry looked at Wales, and thinking that Wales might really be as ignorant as he looked, added, "That's the guy who throws the ball —"

"I know what the quarterback is," Wales said with some indignation. "What're you complaining about then?"

"I'm not complaining. I'm just saying. They take all the fun out of the game."

Deemer finished the tackling drills, then blew his whistle at Henry and Wales and waved them over. As the boys took a knee in a semi-circle in front of him, Deemer paced back and forth, clenching his left hand behind his back and rubbing his right hand against his chin. He wore white tube socks pulled up over his calves and tight polyester shorts that gripped his butt and stopped halfway down his thighs. He was broad and muscular up top. His biceps stretched the sleeves of his polyester shirt, and he had a thick neck and shoulders that were slightly humped from too much weight lifting. By comparison, his legs were smallish and undeveloped, as if he'd spent too much time bench pressing and not enough time running. He had gold, wire-rimmed glasses that were squarish, like his face, and his hair was parted on the side, with bangs running straight across his forehead. Everything about him was tidy and in place except for his nose, which turned awkwardly to starboard halfway down its length, as if it had been smashed in a boxing ring by a thundering right hook. It was the one thing that betrayed him — that showed that in his former life his college education had come at the price of playing football.

"I know most of you have never played this game before. My job is to teach you the fundamentals. How to block. How to tackle. How to recognize your assignments and carry them out. I'm going to do my job, so that when game time comes around you will know what you have to do and how to do it. That's my job — giving you the knowledge and training about how the game is played. Your job is to play the game. That means knowing the fundamentals of the game. That means knowing your assignment on every play. That means knowing that unless you do your job, the team cannot win. We cannot succeed.

Look around you. For us to succeed, everyone on this team has to do his job. At practice, when we run a tackling drill or a blocking drill, it will be my job to make sure not only that you learn those skills but that you help your teammates learn those skills. That means trying to fight through that block so that your teammate learns how to keep his feet and maintain contact. That means you running through that tackle so that he learns how to hit low and wrap up. Games are not won or lost on Saturdays. The games are won or lost out here, on the practice field."

Two boys raised their hands. Rev. Deemer nodded to one of them. "What is it?"

"Do we play on Saturdays or Fridays?" The other boy lowered his hand. He'd also wanted to make sure that his Saturdays were free.

Deemer frowned. "Fridays. My point is we have to make every practice count. That means giving me your complete attention and giving 100 percent effort. Anything less than that and you are not only letting yourself down. You're letting the team down. Does everyone understand that?"

Most of the boys nodded. Henry picked at the grass beside his shoe.

"I said, does everyone understand that?" Deemer repeated in a louder voice.

All the boys looked up. Several boys muttered "yes."

Deemer placed his chrome whistle between his lips and blew loudly. Henry, who had his head turned to Wales who was saying something, looked up and saw that Deemer was looking directly at him. When Deemer had everyone's attention, he pulled up the elastic waistband on the front of his polyester shorts so that it was once more parallel to the ground, clasped his hands behind his back, and began pacing back and forth in front of them again.

"Gentlemen. Let's get one thing straight here at the outset. When I speak, I'm speaking to you. When I ask you a question, I'm not being rhetorical. Football is not a field of rhetoric. Football is a field of action."

He paused, and looked sternly at the boys.

"Indeed, in case you haven't already noticed, it is the closest thing we have here to a field of military action — at least as wars were once fought, on a field of battle. Like those old battles, it's a game of field position. When you are on defense, you are protecting your homeland.

When you are on offense, you are attacking enemy territory. It's no surprise, then, that the best football is played in the states of the old Confederacy, where the memories of those battles are still alive."

He stopped in front of his charges, and held his left hand in front of him with the palm up, and began striking it with his right fist.

"So when I speak to you on this field"—BANG!—"it's as if I am your general and you are my troopers."—BANG!—"And when I ask you a question"—BANG!—"you must answer, 'Yessir' or 'No sir,' "—BANG!—"And you must speak loudly,"—BANG!—"because you are soldiers preparing for war."—BANG!—"Do you understand?"

"Yessir."

"Again. Louder."

"Yessir!"

"That's better. Now I want everyone who wants to play quarterback or receiver to come with me, and the rest of the team hit the showers."

As Wales and most of the team headed up the hill, Henry and six other boys followed Deemer to the far end of the field where Deemer had placed half a dozen footballs and three cones to mimic a line of scrimmage.

"Gentlemen, it's time to find our starting quarterback," Deemer said gravely, as though announcing a sacred rite. He turned to Henry. "Gordon tells me that you have a pretty good arm. Let's start out with some post patterns."

"I'd rather not play quarterback," Henry said.

Deemer looked at him like he was being insubordinate. "What's that son?"

Henry twirled a football on his middle finger. "I've always played quarterback. I'd rather play tight end."

Deemer looked Henry up and down. "You're not much built like a tight end. Tight ends need to be thick across the middle." He pointed a football at Henry's waist, which was slim, like a sprinter's.

"I'm big enough for Cub football," Henry said stubbornly.

"We're not here to settle for the adequate, Palmer. We strive for excellence."

Henry shook his head. "I really don't want to play quarterback anymore."

Deemer smiled, but Henry knew from the way that the reverend's eyes bore into him that Coach Deemer was not happy. This was his mean smile.

"We're not here to figure out what you want, Palmer. We're here to put the best team on the field. I'll call the patterns. You throw the ball on a five-step drop."

Henry had played enough football to know that he'd reached the end of any discussion with the coach. The school said he had to play a sport, so he couldn't quit. He pulled his facemask down and stepped to the mark, but he didn't buckle his chin strap.

"Post," Deemer said.

Henry called the signal, ran back, planted, turned, and threw a rope downfield. The ball hit the receiver in the chest but he wasn't able to pull it in. Deemer nodded.

"Nice pass. Flag," Deemer said.

Again, Henry ran back, planted, and hurled the ball downfield. Again the ball hit the receiver in stride but the receiver wasn't able to pull it in.

Deemer smiled. "Out," he said.

Henry ran back, turned, and threw the ball before the receiver had made his cut. The ball arrived at the right spot just as the kid turned and hit him in the facemask.

"Go route," Deemer said.

Henry kicked at the ground with his cleats in frustration. These receivers are garbage, he thought. I put the ball there every time and they drop it. I can't catch the ball too. I got to give them time to see the ball, he thought.

He snapped his chin strap, stepped to the line, called the signal, but this time, he didn't sprint back. Instead, he ambled back, turned, and when the receiver looked back over his shoulder Henry lofted the pass high downfield. This time the receiver watched the ball from the moment it left Henry's hand to the moment it landed in his arms. A catch.

Deemer blew his whistle and looked back at Henry. This time his smile was for Henry. "I think we found our quarterback," he said.

Henry shrugged. He had to admit it did feel good to complete a pass like that. "I guess," he said.

ASSEMBLY

AFTER DINNER HENRY AND WOBBLY joined the flood of boys that spilled out of the dining hall and flowed down the brick pathway to Randolph Auditorium for the school's Opening Assembly. Henry had tracked down Gordon before supper. He'd wanted to tell him about Mackie's class and what a dick he was, and about Coach Deemer and what a dick he was — except that he was going to be the quarterback for the Cubs, which was kind of cool, after all — but Gordon had cut him off.

"I can't talk right now. I have to meet somebody."

"Who?" Henry asked.

"Don't worry about it," Gordon said.

"Then I'll meet you after supper, at the assembly thing."

Gordon had laughed, which seemed weird to Henry. He said they couldn't sit together.

"Why not?"

"I don't have time to explain. Just sit with the fourth formers," Gordon had said. "I know it sounds weird, but it's not. Trust me. Just sit with the other fourth formers, and we'll get together after the assembly. You'll understand why later."

When he thought about it now, walking in a thick cluster of older boys, none of whom he knew, the whole thing made him homesick. It was like this place could make even his own brother seem like a stranger. And Wobbly, blathering on and on about JV football practice, only made matters worse.

"Coach said he wanted out-patterns, but I thought he said in-patterns. I can throw out-patterns all day if that's what he wants, but because he said I threw inside when he wanted outside he told me to take a knee, and by the time he remembered I was on the sideline practice was over. So I guess it's back to square one tomorrow, but I'll show him for sure then. He'll see what arm talent really is …"

And so on and so forth until they walked into the auditorium, and the sight and sound of the entire school in one place and talking all at once shut Wobbly up. The faculty was seated in a section close to the stage. Beyond them, boys quickly filled the rest of the auditorium. And up on the stage, seated alone, was the headmaster, Edwin Endicott. Henry had been hearing stories about Mr. Endicott for two years — ever since Gordon was a new boy — but this was the first time he'd seen him in person. He recognized the bald head from photographs, but the man himself was older, shorter and tubbier than Henry had imagined.

Henry and Wobbly hastily moved towards two seats in the middle of the room, but a group of fifth formers waved them off with, "Up front new boys." Henry then got the gist of what Gordon had told him earlier. By now the auditorium was almost full, and the only adjoining seats available in the new boy section were on the front row, directly below the podium on stage. As Henry and Wobbly made their way down, Henry noticed Gordon enter and take a seat in the faculty section to his left. Gordon had changed into a jacket and tie, and as he took a seat Henry saw Gordon and Mr. Endicott exchange words. Once they were seated, Wobbly elbowed Henry and pointed at Gordon.

"I know," Henry said, and he wondered why Gordon was sitting with the faculty, not to mention talking to Mr. Endicott.

Edwin Endicott had been hired in 1941 to coach the school's basketball team on the strength of his reputation as a scrappy defender and capable floor general for the Hampden-Sydney College Tigers. For twenty years he'd diagrammed backdoor cuts and preached the virtues of the full court press while teaching four sections of U.S. History and Rhetoric and slowly working his way up the Randolph School administrative ladder. Then one day in 1961 the school's headmaster abruptly ran off with his secretary, and the board of trustees appointed Endicott to the big chair in the corner office. For seventeen years Mr. Endicott had run the school on the cardinal coaching principles of repetition, discipline, and if it ain't broke, don't fix it. Endicott firmly believed that proper conduct, like accurate foul shooting, had to be drilled into a boy; that all hell would break loose without strict discipline; and that so long as repetition and discipline were maintained, everything at The Randolph School would proceed according to plan.

Endicott had long seen the Opening Assembly as an opportunity to set the tone for the school year. As he gazed out at the room he acknowledged and approved of the seating arrangements: the sixth formers had taken possession of the back of the auditorium, just like every sixth form class before them; the fifth formers occupied the middle of the room, like all fifth formers before them, and the third and fourth formers, most of them new boys, had been relegated to the seats closest to the stage and to the faculty. A proper pecking order, he thought, and he was the cock of the roost.

Endicott leaned forward in his chair and pointed at Terrence Mackie, his Dean of Students, with the rolled up copy of his prepared remarks. "I have a good feeling, Terry. This is going to be a fine year."

Mr. Mackie managed to smile but said nothing. He did not share his headmaster's optimism. To his way of thinking discipline was less about maintaining school order than it was about punishing the wrongdoer, and there were always wrongdoers.

While Endicott waited for the last stragglers to take their seats, he looked at Gordon, who sat in the front row of the faculty section staring down at his own printed remarks. Much would depend on this boy, he thought. Last spring when Terrence Mackie had brought him the tally of the faculty and students votes for prefect, Endicott had crossed out the names of two of the top vote getters, whom he would not permit to be prefects because they were suspected pot smokers, and had circled Gordon Palmer's name. This was the boy he wanted for Head Boy. He did not know Gordon well, but the faculty spoke well of him, the students supported him, his grades were good, and he looked the part. Most important was the boy's father. Endicott knew the father well. He was a good man, a stalwart supporter of the school, and he, the father, had been Head Boy himself. Like father like son, Endicott believed. This boy would do, he'd told himself. This boy would do very well.

Endicott waited for Gordon to look up from his paper, and when he did, Endicott gave the boy his *'Are you ready to go in, son?'* nod. Gordon nodded back, *'I'm ready, coach,'* and Endicott pushed himself to his feet and waddled across the stage. The room grew quiet as Mr. Endicott gripped the sides of the podium and glowered at the boys like a disapproving patriarch. He cleared his throat, then launched into his Welcome Address, the same one he'd been giving, with little variation, for seventeen years.

"One hundred years ago this week, J. Taylor Randolph opened the doors of his home to ten boys, two of them his own sons and eight the sons of neighboring families, and started Randolph Academy. It was his vision then that this school should be dedicated to three things: the improvement of a boy's mind through the study of math, science and the liberal arts, the improvement of a boy's body through regular exercise, and the improvement of a boy's character through moral instruction and community living. That was his vision then, and that has been this school's vision ever since."

Endicott's voice was deep and rich and retained much of the Tidewater accent of his youth. To many of the boys — those from Virginia — the sound was familiar and reassuring, like the voices of their grandparents, but for Henry and others who lacked connection to the Old Dominion it sounded uncanny, as if from a distant time and place.

"For the last one hundred years, on the last Monday of August, this school has opened its doors and invited a new group of boys to participate in a radical experiment — " Mr. Endicott paused and surveyed the auditorium — "to see if together we can create a better place not just here on campus — " Endicott pointed out at the boys — "and not just here in the larger world — " Endicott pointed to the heavens above — "but also here — " and now Endicott poked himself in the chest — "in our hearts, where, as the prophet says, the still speaking God speaks to us, everyday, if only we can hear Him."

With a flourish Endicott took the reading glasses out of his jacket's breast pocket, placed them on his nose, and leaning forward peered out — not just at all of the boys altogether, but seemingly at each of them, one by one. As his eyes passed from boy to boy, almost every one of them, from the most sullen sixth former to the most timid new boy, sat silent, face uplifted, as he was counted. Whether it was simple herd instinct, or an inherent respect for authority, or an inchoate understanding that the privileges of sitting in this room, attending this school, and enjoying their place in the world carried a price, the boys submitted to the accounting without protest. Only among the older boys, who'd seen all this before, were there a few small pockets of resistance — boys who refused to be entirely cowed. But Mr. Endicott saw none of that, if only because the strength of his reading glasses made it darn nigh impossible to make out faces, especially in the back of the auditorium.

Gordon, sitting to the side, recalled the awe and reverence he'd felt during his first Opening Assembly, two years ago, when he'd witnessed Mr. Endicott's conquering gaze overtake the room for the first time. He remembered also that Mr. Endicott had introduced the school to its new Head Boy shortly after his accounting. Soon Mr. Endicott would summon him to the podium and present him to the school. He felt a jumble of emotions stirring about in his chest: pride for everything he had accomplished; happiness that he had fulfilled his own dream and his father's; humility about the challenges of living up to what would be expected of him and what he would expect of himself. All of this and other emotions that he could not identify rumbled through his heart and head as Mr. Endicott once again overawed the room. What a great year this was going to be, Gordon told himself. What a momentous year.

After what seemed like an eternity, Endicott released his grip on the podium and stood up straight, removed the glasses from his nose and returned them to his pocket. He nodded to the room as if to confirm that his accounting was complete, and there was a sudden stirring as the boys shook off his spell. Endicott gave no outward sign, but inwardly he was pleased. He'd performed the ritual and put things in order. Now the school year could begin. He looked to Gordon and gave the lad a nod as if to say, 'I'm putting you in Palmer. Don't disappoint me.' then turned back to the hall and cleared his throat.

"Every year, on the night before school opens, the prefects meet and choose one boy from among them to serve as Head Boy. This year that boy is Gordon Palmer."

A murmuring passed through the hall, and Henry's heart skipped a beat. Of course Gordon had been named Head Boy — he'd been talking about this for as long as Henry could remember. Good for Gordon, he thought, and he heartily joined the applause offered by other boys.

Endicott nodded with approval to the room, then turned to Gordon who was seated below him. "I have asked Gordon to say a few words to you tonight about the Honor Code."

As Henry watched Gordon solemnly ascend to the stage, he wondered why Gordon couldn't at least look happy. He knew this was like a dream come true for him, and their Dad was going to flip! Henry watched his brother walk across the stage with that dogged, indomitable gait of his. When he saw Gordon take Mr. Endicott's hand, and the two of them exchange nods of such identical serious matter-of-factness — as if they both had known all along that this was going to happen; that it was fated by the gods! — Henry was reminded of his father, who also never seemed to be either surprised or particularly happy about the way things turned out, even when they turned out exactly as he'd hoped.

Wobbly nudged Henry and looked at him as if to say, Is everything all right? Wobbly was clapping, and Henry suddenly became aware that most of the student body was also clapping but he was not. Henry joined in as Gordon stepped past Mr. Endicott and up to the podium. Gordon glanced down at Henry and winked, and Henry gave Gordon a big thumbs up. Ah, Henry told himself; he is happy after all. Gordon smiled, then addressed the room.

"'On my honor, I will neither lie, steal, nor cheat.' For one hundred years Randolph students have pledged their Honor with those simple words, and for one hundred years those words have helped to make this place what it is today. Why do we have an Honor Code? Because Randolph has always had an Honor Code, it's part of our history, it defines us, not only here at Randolph but in years to come. Randolph men know they can trust one another, because they share this bond."

Gordon went on to describe how the Honor Code worked. A boy caught lying, stealing or cheating would be turned over to the Prefect Board, who would determine whether an honor offense had occurred and if so what punishment would be levied. He noted how the letter of the school's Honor Code had not changed in decades; it was the same now as it was when Gordon's father had been a student. The prohibition on lying, stealing and cheating was the same. The pledge that was signed to every test and paper was the same. The makeup of the Prefect Board — twelve seniors elected by the faculty and the students — was the same. This continuity, Gordon said, was proof of the Honor Code's enduring value and relevance.

What Gordon didn't describe — because he was unaware of it — was how the administration of the Honor Code had become narrower and stricter over the course of Mr. Endicott's tenure as Headmaster. Although nothing in the words of the Honor Code defined the punishment for any honor violation, Mr. Endicott made it clear that he considered any violation, however small, to constitute grounds for dismissal. Over time, Endicott's one-strike-and-you're-out preference had become the de facto rule, and while Gordon's speech painted an admirable picture of the Honor Code's place at the moral center of the school, the underlying threat of Endicott's construction of the Honor Code lurked in the minds of many of the boys in the audience.

Henry, though as of yet uninitiated, had heard stories about

Randolph from his father and cousins since childhood, and he'd heard Gordon talking to his father about honor while home on vacation. Like the words over the school's front entrance, this droning on and on about honor gave Henry a stomach ache. He didn't think Gordon would cheat on a test, but he had no doubt that Gordon would let people say untrue things if it helped him get ahead. In the last twenty-four hours how many lies had he heard Wobbly tell about his football prowess or his success with girls? And what did the Honor Code have to say about the way Mackie or Deemer had bullied the students today? How was telling a lie worse than that? And what about just being a good person? You could follow the Honor Code but still be a horrible person. No one got kicked out of Randolph for being a dick—just look around!—while a good guy might get kicked out for cheating on a quiz? That seemed upside down.

Henry looked at the other New Boys sitting near him. They stared up at Gordon, wide-eyed and nervous, drinking it all in. Farther to his left, were the faculty members. There was Mr. Mackie, staring at his fingernails and pinching the creases in his khaki pants. What did Ken Bright call him? Rules grinder? Most of the other faculty seemed bored—like Mackie, not really paying attention, waiting for the assembly to end—but one of them, an older man with striking white hair and horned-rim glasses, sat with his legs crossed and his head cocked slightly to one side. He was paying attention. Was he smiling a little? Henry was almost positive this was Mr. Nightingale—he'd seen his photograph. Gordon loved Mr. Nightingale, and his father had talked about having him as a teacher on the drive up. The man looked old enough to have taught Henry's father, but there was also something ageless about him—not just his smile but also his attentive good humor. He remembered Ken Bright saying how lucky he was to have Nightingale as his advisor, and seeing him now Henry felt for the first time something akin to genuine excitement about being here. Maybe he would learn something here that he couldn't learn elsewhere.

David Nightingale was smiling because he found Gordon's performance endearing; just as he'd found his old friend Edwin Endicott's performance—a variation of which he'd seen seventeen times—endearing. David Nightingale did not laugh at life; he laughed with it, and there was much that he still found amusing at The Randolph School, even after twenty-nine years on the faculty. While many of his fellow faculty members groaned inwardly and looked away during Mr. Endicott's accounting, Nightingale had turned toward the room to observe the boys. He'd especially sought out the misfits and oddballs — boys who managed to express their personality in the face of so much tradition. There was Ken Bright, one of his favorite students, slumping and scowling in his seat; Nightingale chuckled to himself when he saw Ken cross his eyes at Endicott. Seated not far from Ken, in the farthest back row of the room, was Bob Coogan, otherwise known as "Mongo" by the boys. Mongo was a head taller than everyone around him, and even from his seat near the stage Nightingale was able to make out the white wire of a transistor radio ear plug dangling from the boy's ear. Mr. Nightingale happened to know that every Monday night WTJU, the student radio station at the University of Virginia dedicated two hours to the music of The Grateful Dead. Nightingale knew this not because he was a Deadhead himself, but because he sometimes proctored Study Hall, and Mr. Coogan, who was not among the brightest lights in the student body, was a frequent inhabitant. On one occasion last Spring, while reading *The Pickwick Papers*, Nightingale had noticed a peculiar humming coming from the far end of the room. One look at Mongo's smiling, bobbing, closed-eyed face and Nightingale had his culprit. Signaling to the other Study Hall denizens to keep quiet, Mr. Nightingale walked down the aisle until he stood directly in front of Mongo's chair. Mongo kept grooving to the music until the song was over, and when he opened his eyes and found Mr. Nightingale standing there, he said, "Hi Mr. Nightingale."

"Mr. Coogan. May I inquire what you were listening to?"

Mongo smiled. "That was *Box of Rain*. Phil Lesh's song. It's awesome."

"I can see that, Mr. Coogan. Now would it be asking too much for you to turn off your radio during Study Hall?"

"No. No. No. No. Sorry about that. Could y'all hear it through my ear plug?"

"Actually we heard you humming. And would you mind letting me hold onto your radio until Study Hall is over?"

Mongo had gladly handed over his transistor radio and ear plug, and as Nightingale turned to walk back to the Proctor's Desk, he'd offered, "The show runs until nine. Every Monday. Check it out." And he'd let out a high-pitched infectious laugh that broke the room.

Mr. Nightingale had no doubt that Mongo was checking it out right now, and when he saw the boy raise a hand and wave at Edwin when the headmaster's gaze passed by, Nightingale had almost burst out laughing himself.

When Gordon spoke, Nightingale caught sight of Henry sitting in the front row. He recognized him, not so much from his similarity to Gordon as from his similarity to Grace Palmer, whom Mr. Nightingale had enjoyed meeting at several school functions that she attended with her husband. Nightingale saw that Henry appeared to be happy for his brother; this pleased him immensely.

After the assembly was over, Henry caught up with Gordon outside. Gordon was surrounded by fifth and sixth formers who congratulated him. Henry recognized some of the boys from parties his parents had dragged him to over the years. He hung back and watched Gordon shake their hands, thank them, and give each of them the same smile. When Gordon had finished with the last boy Henry stepped forward and shoved his brother in the chest.

"Good job, man. Did you tell mom and dad?"

"I called dad two nights ago, after the vote."

"Two nights ago? They didn't say anything on the drive up."

"I told them they couldn't tell you. It was a secret. No one was supposed to know until the assembly."

"Even mom didn't say anything."

"I know. I told dad not to tell her, but he said he had to tell mom. I was sort of worried about that."

"Dad must have been in heaven."

"I thought he was going to cry. Look what he gave me." Gordon pulled a pocket watch from the watch pocket in his pants.

"What is it?" Henry asked.

"It's Papa's pocket watch."

Henry took it from Gordon and turned it over in his hand. It was a heavy, gold conductor's watch with Roman numerals and a second hand that ticked loudly as it circled the face. Henry remembered sitting in his grandfather's lap and pulling it out of his pocket by its gold chain. He turned it over and found the engraving on the back, 'G.A.P.' Gordon Augustus Palmer, their grandfather's father. He handed it back to Gordon.

"Dad gave it to you?"

Gordon nodded. "Yesterday. He said Papa would be proud, and he knew he'd want me to have it."

Henry watched Gordon stuff it back into his watch pocket. "You going to carry it?"

"I thought I might. See how it feels."

Henry laughed. "Feels like you're somebody's grandfather."

The sun had gone down and a group of bats, hunting gnats and moths, swooped overhead. Crickets chirped in the pasture behind the auditorium, and Henry heard mourning doves calling in the trees down by the river. They headed back up the hill, towards the Randolph Building.

"What does it mean?" Henry asked.

"What does *what* mean?"

"You being Head Boy."

Gordon put his arm around Henry's neck and pulled him closer in a mock headlock. "It means that for the first time in your life you got to do what I tell you."

Gordon put his hand on the top of Henry's head and rubbed it roughly. Henry gave his brother a hug. He felt proud of him.

BACK ON B DORM

WHEN HENRY GOT BACK to his room, there was no sign of Wobbly, but the stereo was cranked up so high that the clanging chords of multiple synthesizers collided against Henry's eardrums like pinballs. Henry stuck his head into Ken Bright's room and found Ken standing on a milk crate, hammering nails into the wall. When Ken saw Henry, he took three nails out of his mouth.

"Styx? Really?"

Henry shrugged. "Not mine. I don't know it."

"I suspect that will change soon." Ken stepped off the milk crate and hung up a photograph of a skinny and oddly attractive man dressed like a woman. The man bore a slight resemblance to Ken.

"Who's that?" Henry asked.

"That would be Ziggy Stardust."

"Ziggy what?"

"Perhaps you know him as David Bowie."

Henry shook his head.

Ken frowned. "Where did you say you were from?"

"Raleigh."

"Really? I'm sorry. But don't worry. Music is an acquired taste. What did you think of your first assembly?"

Henry wasn't ready to admit that he found the experience uncomfortable. "Okay, I guess."

"Congrats on Gordon."

"Thanks."

Ken got back up on the milk crate and picked out another spot on the wall.

"Endicott gives the same speech every year," he said, "and every year his eye passes over each of us, and we all succumb to it like sheep at a slaughterhouse."

Ken placed the nail and hammered it into place.

"The question I have is, 'Are you afraid or are you amused?' My guess is that ninety-nine percent of the boys there are afraid that they've been spotted."

He waved the hammer about in the air like a conductor's baton.

"That their shallow, shriveled souls have been espied for the first time, afraid and ashamed that the truth of their paltry existence has finally been uncovered, that they're a sham and a fake and good for nothing other than whatever their fathers tell them to do."

Ken pointed his hammer at Henry.

"It's the ones that are amused that I want to know. The ones who see through that hocus-pocus-light-and-mirrors claptrap about ultimate truth, who know the answer lies without and not within. So which are you?"

What the hell is this guy talking about, Henry wondered, and he laughed out of embarrassment. Ken waited for Henry's answer.

"I got to say, Mr. Endicott scared the hell out of me," Henry said finally.

Ken stared at him for a full five seconds, then let out a high shrill laughter. He hadn't expected Gordon Palmer's little brother to be so candid. "Take solace, Pip. You may spot landfall yet." Ken eyed Henry slyly hoping that he'd recognize the allusion. Alas — too much to expect of any Palmer, he told himself. "What about Mackie?" he asked

"Mr. Mackie?"

"You've been to your first English class, haven't you?"

"Yes."

"Let me guess, *The Rocking Horse Winner.*"

"No. We talk about that tomorrow — how did you know?"

Ken gave a theatrical yawn. "I had the privilege of Mackie's English class two years ago."

"We discussed *The Sick Rose* — "

"Of course you did! Ee-gads, a 'flying worm'!" Ken shrieked in mock horror.

"Exactly! He said it was a penis."

"It is a penis!" Ken said emphatically.

"It's like he thinks it's all about sex."

"Maybe not all, but most of it is about sex!"

"You think about sex all the time?" Henry asked.

"YOU think about sex all the time!" Ken responded.

"But we're at an all boys school."

"Tell me about it. Makes it harder, doesn't it?"

Henry hesitated — was he making a joke? Then Ken laughed, but Henry wasn't sure if he was joking.

"Don't worry," Ken said. "You'll get the hang of it. By the end of the year Mackie will have you feeling guilty about your mother and seeing penises everywhere!"

Henry had no idea what Ken meant by 'feeling guilty about your mother' but seeing penises sounded hilarious. He still had to read that short story, and so he waved good night and stepped next door. Ken finished hammering in the nail for his Lou Reed poster, and he smiled at the thought of becoming friends with Gordon Palmer's little brother.

HALFWAY BETWEEN THE RANDOLPH BUILDING and the East Gate, stood Faison Chapel, a modest Victorian brick structure with a slate roof, tall stained glass windows, and a white interior trimmed with thick, dark moulding. A long central aisle with straight-backed wooden pews on either side led to a raised platform at the head of the sanctuary. A simple wooden cross hung behind the communion table, and the depictions of various saints, most of them martyrs, peered down from the stained glass windows around the sanctuary. Small brass plates mounted at various places carried the names of alumni who'd been killed in various wars. On the wall just inside the front door was a large brass plaque that read:

Thomas Swift Faison, Class 1946,
February 21, 1928 — November 1, 1950.
Scholar — Athlete — Soldier
Died at the Battle of Unsun, Korea.
Dedicated in his honor, November 1, 1964.

Hanging beside the plaque was a photograph of Thomas Faison, taken in front of the East Gate of the Randolph School in 1945, And standing in front of that photograph, staring intently, was Lawton Faison, the nephew of the deceased. There was a strong family resemblance between the live boy and his dead uncle, the same wide-set eyes, the same long slender nose, the same high cheekbones, the same piercing, blue eyes. Lawton was almost too beautiful — untouchable, like a Botticelli painting or his Uncle Thomas. Lawton caught his own reflection in the glass of the picture frame, and he adjusted his stance so that his face aligned with his uncle's. The soaring arch of the East Gate that framed the subject of the photograph now appeared like a crown on Lawton's head, and Lawton recalled the words his father had spoken, many years ago in Charleston, while standing before his uncle's tomb. "He was as beautiful and valiant as the saints of old." Lawton had never forgotten those words. They'd served as a kind of touchstone, something for him to strive for, something for him to live up to, and now here he was, a sixth former, at the school his father and his uncle had attended, standing before his uncle, pledging his troth and assuming the mantle. Lawton bowed his head, summoned to mind the marble angel that graced the roof of his uncle's tomb, then kissed his fist and blessed himself. "Thy will be done," he muttered, then strode down the center aisle of Faison Chapel and joined three other sixth formers, also scions of wealthy Southern families and the sons of Randolph graduates, for the inaugural meeting of the Chapel Council.

"Gentlemen!" Lawton called out.

"You made it!" answered Billy Richardson.

"Of course I made it. I wouldn't miss our first meeting."

"Mr. Endicott said if you didn't make it to school by Friday he was going to expel you," said John Gillespie.

"I missed him too. Terribly."

Lawton joined the other boys on the platform at the head of the sanctuary, and he and Richardson and Gillespie bumped chests. The fourth boy, Ned Claiborne, stood to one side. "When did you get here?" he asked.

"Plane touched down at 4."

"Where were you?"

"I missed the train in Charleston."

Gillespie slapped his friend on the back. "That was a week ago."

"Then I missed the train in New Orleans."

"What were you doing in New Orleans?" Ned Claiborne asked.

"Visiting TU-lane." Lawton pronounced the name as they do in New Orleans, drawing out the emphasis on the first syllable.

Ned looked at him quizically. "Are you going to apply to tu-Lane?" he asked, using the more prosaic Northern pronunciation.

Lawton shook his head. "It's not tu-LANE," he said. "It's TU-lane."

"Whatever," Claiborne said.

"And no. I have no intention of going to Tulane, but the girls are pretty." He winked at Richardson and Gillespie, and they both laughed. "Then I missed the train in Chattanooga."

"U-T-C?" Claiborne said doubtfully.

"Hell no!" Lawton scoffed. "The University of the South. Sewanee. V-E-R-Y cool. Upholding all the ancient traditions. The smartest students get to wear gowns to classes." Lawton brushed the sleeve of his hunting jacket as if he were admiring the gown. "And they have a mace dedicated to Nathan Bedford Forrest."

"A mace?" Billy Richardson asked.

"It's like a club, for bludgeoning the enemy. But this one has a huge blue diamond on top."

"Who's Nathan Bedford ... whoever?" Richardson asked.

"A real bad-ass. Started the Ku Klux Klan."

Ned Claiborne rolled his eyes at Lawton. "Please."

"I'm just saying," Lawton said.

"So you applying to Sewanee?" Claiborne asked.

"No. Nice school, but no. Princeton." He paused and nodded to each of his friends. "I'm applying early admission."

The other boys huzzahed, but Claiborne crossed his arms and looked at Lawton with concern. "Where else you applying?"

"Nowhere."

Claiborne, like Lawton, had come to Randolph as a third former. Like Lawton, he was a third generation Randolph Lion. And like Lawton, Claiborne had been disappointed when he was passed over in the prefect election last spring. But Claiborne had never really expected to be elected a prefect. He was small and lousy at sports, his grades were average, and his best quality — fidelity — was vastly underappreciated. Claiborne had worked through his own disappointment, but he suspected that Lawton still nursed a grudge.

"It doesn't hurt to apply to SC as a backup."

"SC — gawd. My grandfather would roll over in his grave if I went to SC." Lawton's family had settled in South Carolina two hundred years ago, but not a single member of his family had ever attended the state university. "Stop being a girl, Claiborne. I'm in."

Lawton smiled at his two minions, and they laughed.

"Let's get started." Lawton put his palms on the communion table, hopped up and took a seat. "I hereby call the Chapel Council to order."

"What the hell are you doing?" Claiborne was aghast.

"Calling the meeting to order."

"On the communion table? Man, that's not right!"

Lawton glanced at Gillespie and Richardson, who were withholding their approval. "Okay. Maybe you're right. Sorry about that." He hopped down.

Claiborne continued to shake his head.

"Anyway," Lawton said, ignoring Claiborne. "Like I was saying. The first order of business is selecting new members. We need four more sixth formers and four fifth formers. Any nominations?"

Lawton turned to Richardson and Gillespie, but Claiborne spoke first. "I nominate Gordon Palmer."

Lawton rolled his eyes for his buddies before facing Claiborne. "His qualifications?"

Claiborne scrunched his mouth in an expression of disbelief. "He's Head Boy."

"So I hear." Lawton continued to stare at Claiborne. "And?"

"Give me a break, Lawton. He's perfect for Chapel Council."

"Because?"

Claiborne ignored Lawton and directed his comments to Richardson and Gillespie.

"Because he's probably respected more than anybody else in the school. He's a Christian. And he cares about setting the right example."

"Second," Gillespie said.

Lawton shot his friend a withering glance, then held up his hands to the group.

"Before we vote on Gordon, I think I should share some news with all of you. I don't think this is general knowledge, and I wouldn't want it to come out before the school addresses it openly, so what I am about to tell you needs to remain secret — at least for the time being. Agreed?"

"What the heck, Lawton?" Claiborne protested. "What are you talking about?"

"I'll tell you in a minute. Does everyone agree to keep this secret until I say it's okay to talk about it?"

Lawton didn't bother to look at Richardson or Gillespie; his gaze was trained on Claiborne.

"Give me a break," Claiborne protested. "Are we going to nominate new members or not?"

"In good time. But I have information that could, shall I say, shift our emphasis this year. This is top secret stuff. Do you promise, on your honor, not to share this with anyone outside this room?"

Lawton did look at his friends now, and they both nodded. "On my honor," they both said. Claiborne grimaced and nodded.

"On your honor?" Lawton asked.

"Sure. On my honor."

Lawton smiled smugly. "I have reason to know that Mr. Endicott is going to announce that this is his last year at Randolph."

All three boys expressed alarm. No one actually liked Mr. Endicott, but he did represent a comforting status quo. Lawton assured them it was true.

"Obviously, this means that there's going to be a search for a new headmaster, and as part of that some members of the Board of Trustees want to make some fundamental changes."

"Like what?" Gillespie asked.

"Like going coed."

"Wha'?"

"No way!"

"That's fucked up!"

Lawton nodded. "I agree. It's probably not going to happen, but they're also talking about hiring a Jewish faculty member."

Richardson and Gillespie looked at each other doubtfully. Neither was sure how to react. But Claiborne piped up.

"So what?"

"'So what?' Look around you, Claiborne." Lawton pointed to the stained glass windows around the chapel. "Randolph was founded as a Christian school, and it's always been a Christian school."

"That doesn't mean we can't have Jewish teachers."

Lawton shook his head. "Every teacher who's ever taught here has been a Christian."

"Give me a break." Claiborne waved a dismissive hand.

"I'm serious. Every single one."

"If that's true — which I doubt — it's stupid."

"It's not stupid! This is a Christian school. You can't have a Jew teaching at a Christian school."

"Why not? Jesus was a Jew."

"Don't give me that bullshit. The Jews killed Jesus."

Claiborne paused. "I don't think that's right, Lawton."

"You took Deemer's class last spring."

Claiborne nodded. He had indeed taken the class, and he'd hated it. "You want to take a stand against hiring Jews?"

"I want to take a stand for keeping Randolph Christian."

This was not what Claiborne had in mind when he joined Chapel Council. A curious and gentle soul, Claiborne had daydreamed about doing more than meeting now and then with Rev. Deemer and straightening the church pews after service. He was thinking he might try to start a Bible study group or even suggest a ministry at a nearby nursing home. Protesting Jewish teachers didn't even sound Christian to him.

"Who put you in charge?" Claiborne asked.

Lawton smiled. "You're right. We need to elect officers. Do I hear any nominations for head of Chapel Council?"

Lawton looked at his friends. Richardson and Gillespie grinned back.

"We're cool, Lawton," Richardson said.

"Your family, like, bought the chapel," Gillespie said.

"I hear a nomination for Lawton. All in favor?"

Richardson, Gillespie and Lawton all raised their hands. Lawton turned to Claiborne.

"Looks like I'm Head Boy this year."

"Gordon's Head Boy," Claiborne corrected.

"Duly noted," Lawton nodded. "Now, I suggest you offer your resignation."

"Why?"

"You can't be loyal to this council."

"Are you kidding me?"

"If I told you that this council was going to keep Randolph a Christian school would you support it?"

"No. I think it would be a complete waste of time."

"Then you need to resign."

Claiborne looked at Richardson and Gillespie in disbelief. "Council hasn't voted on anything," he said.

"Ah. But we have."

"When?"

"Just now," Lawton said.

Claiborne looked around at the others expecting one of them to offer him support. "You're going to go along with this crap?" No one denied it. "All right. Fine, I quit." Claiborne picked up the hunting jacket draped across the back of the nearest pew and stormed out of the chapel.

As the door slammed behind him, Gillespie asked, "Are we going to vote on Gordon now?"

"God no!" Lawton said. "We don't want that prick on Chapel Council."

"Remind me why you wanted Claiborne to resign," Richardson asked.

"I don't trust him. Now that he's out of the way let's talk about Ichthys."

"Icctus?" Gillespie asked.

"The Sign of the Fish."

"I didn't think that was going to be part of Chapel Council," Richardson said.

"It's not. Right now it's just the three of us."

ENDICOTT AND GORDON MEET

EDWIN ENDICOTT SAT IN HIS CORNER OFFICE smoking a Cuban cigar, a *Romeo y Julieta* — an alum he'd taught twenty years ago had smuggled him a box out of Havana. The headmaster took particular pleasure in this brand, knowing that it had been Winston Churchill's cigar of choice. A photograph of the prime minister, cigar in mouth, his right hand holding a cane, his left holding a V aloft at a campaign rally, hung on the wall beside Endicott's desk. Below the photograph was a reproduction of Churchill's painting of Chartwell, his home in Kent. Endicott often thought that he might take up watercolor painting once he retired and paint the places he loved: the school's sweeping boulevard with the tall boxwood hedge on either side framing the Randolph Building. The view of Faison Chapel from the front patio with that fine Pin Oak. The Lawn with its towering oaks and elm trees and the Manor at the far end. And the Seventh Hole with its tricky green just below the headmaster's house. But Endicott worried that his glaucoma, which was encroaching on his peripheral vision, might ultimately prevent him from taking up paintbrushes. If so, he'd still have his historical fantasy novel based on the idea that Stonewall Jackson had survived Chancellorsville.

Endicott took a contemplative puff on his cigar and centered his gaze on Gordon Palmer, who sat on the leather sofa across from Endicott's polished oak desk. He paused to let the full weight of the moment register with the boy. When he was sure he had Gordon's complete attention, he began talking, expelling smoke and using his cigar to punctuate his words, like the way he imagined Churchill had done in the War Rooms.

"The crucial thing is to keep your nerve! Don't lose your nerve!"

Endicott insisted.

"Yessir."

"The day will come, and it's coming soon, when you will be tested like the boys at Dunkirk, with your backs to the sea, or the wall if you will, and nothing to do but face the adversary and do your duty!"

Endicott had stabbed the air above his head three times as he declared those last three words — "DO — YOUR — DUTY" — and Gordon had dodged a stub of ash that shot out in his direction.

"Yessir."

"There will be no way out. You can't turn and run. There'll be no door to open and walk through. There'll be no help from sea or sky, no cavalry rounding the hill, no tank division, no reprieve from the governor's office, no 'Father come help me'. It will be up to you, and you alone, to hold the line, to make sure that duty is done, and the unjust are punished!"

Endicott's voice grew louder as his metaphors piled up. His cigar struck with fury above his head. His face grew redder. And Gordon felt himself strangely moved by the man's passion, his conviction, his rectitude, his mania. He felt like he was witnessing the greatest halftime speech of his life — and Gordon had heard plenty of them.

"Yessir," Gordon said, but in his heart he thought, 'Hell yes!'

Endicott stuck the cigar back into his mouth and took two deep puffs. The smoke calmed him as it hit his lungs, and when he continued to speak, now in a lower voice, the smoke petered out of his mouth.

"Every year I have this same talk with my Head Boy, and I hold it as one of my most sacred duties to communicate to you, just as I have communicated to all the others, just how important, how necessary, how critical, how crucial, how pivotal-to-the-life-of-this-school it is that we get it right. That you get it right. That you make sure that the other boys get it right. To uphold our honor."

Gordon, who had heard about the honor code practically his entire life, already felt that sacred obligation to safeguard the school's tradition.

"Yessir," he said.

Endicott considered the boy. Satisfied that Gordon shared his conviction, he leaned forward and began speaking in a low, slow voice, but the longer he spoke the quicker and louder his voice became.

"The temptation is always to let the boy off with a warning, a stern rebuke, a strong condemnation only, thinking that he'll learn his lesson, he'll become a better person, that next time he won't glance at the other boy's paper, or steal a book from the shelf, or tell a little lie, but what does that say about the Honor System? It says that it only applies to a second-time cheater or liar or stealer, that we only have to live with honor after we have been judged to have acted with dishonor at least once, that honor is like a mulligan on the golf course, something that we can pick up and ignore — it doesn't count, it didn't happen, no one's keeping score anyway. That we don't live with its burden always but only after we have failed it once, that we are willing to look the other way, to sacrifice honor in order to give a fellow a break, a fellow who has acted with dishonor, no less."

"Yessir."

Endicott leaned back in his chair and looked at the portraits hanging on his wall. There was Churchill. There was Lincoln in a photograph taken shortly before his death, careworn and haggard. There was Teddy Roosevelt, from a portrait painted shortly after McKinley's assassination. And there was Stonewall Jackson, from a photograph taken in 1863, not long before he died. Endicott, an old history teacher, felt a connection to all of them. Mostly, he felt an obligation to the past — to that better, nobler time.

"What does that do to the Honor System," he said, returning his attention to Gordon, "when we look the other way? It degrades it, because how can you honor something that you won't uphold? That you won't protect? That you don't cherish? You can't! You say there are other considerations, and pretty soon you're like every other school in the country — you have an Honor System in name only."

"Yessir." Gordon agreed. Unless you were willing to pay the price, the thing was worth nothing.

"You have to think of those who came before you. Your father — he was Head Boy."

"Yessir." His father was the first thing Gordon had thought about after Mr. Endicott announced to the prefects that Gordon had been elected Head Boy.

"He knows the cost of honor — its price as well as its reward."

"Yessir." Gordon and his father had actually talked about how hard the job was. How lonely it could be. How lonely it would be.

"And so when that day comes and you are faced with hearing your first honor violation, you must remember him and all the others who came before you, and make sure your prefect board understands what must be done."

"Yessir."

"Its sacred duty."

"Yessir." Gordon was sure that he was up to it.

"To uphold the Honor System."

"Yessir." He believed that it was a just cause.

"Against all the clamor and claptrap calls to 'Take care of the boys'. Take care of the boys indeed," Endicott said dismissively. "The boys can take care of themselves!"

"Yessir." He believed that he would serve with distinction.

"So long as we give them clear, unyielding, absolute clarity about what is right and just in this world."

Endicott took a long drag on his cigar and then smashed it with emphasis into the crystal ashtray on his desk.

"You're a good boy, aren't you Palmer?"

"Yessir." He was a very good boy! He was the Head Boy!

"You know your duty?"

"Yessir." He knew his duty.

Endicott once again fixed Palmer in the center of his tunnel vision and considered him. Not a bad sort of boy, he thought. Eager enough. Sober-minded. Not the brightest boy in his class, but above average. Fair to middling on the football field. Better at lacrosse. Not the best Head Boy he'd had, but not the worst either. He'll try to do his best and not bother me with too many questions, Endicott thought. He motioned to the door.

"Off to bed with you then. It's lights out."

And Gordon left the headmaster's office, feeling like he had received a benediction. He was finally Head Boy, and he'd just had his first meeting with Mr. Endicott. Some of that had been weird, a little over the top, maybe, but he felt righteous, like he could accomplish almost anything.

INITIATION

CUBS GAME

AT THE FARTHEST EDGE of the campus, under a clear, cerulean sky, beside a cow pasture where a solitary Holstein lazily rubbed her bottom against the trunk of a persimmon tree, the Cubs were about to lose their third game in a row when a mad howl bellowed from the bottom of a dogpile in the middle of the field.

"OWWWWW! GET OFF! GET OFF! GET! OFF!"

The referee blew his whistle, stopping the clock, and motioned to Coach Deemer on the Cub sideline. Legs and arms untangled from the pile, and the boys from both teams stood up on either side of No. 57, who lay writhing on his back. Henry bent down to look inside the player's facemask.

"Are you okay, Grimes?"

Bobby Grimes opened his eyes wide and screamed up into Henry's face, just two feet above his own. "NO, GODDAMMIT!! I'M NOT OKAY! I BROKE MY FUCKING BUTT! MY BUTT IS BROKEN GODDAMMIT!!!!"

Henry looked to his bench and saw Rev. Deemer jogging over.

"What's the problem, Palmer?"

"Grimes says he broke his goddamn butt."

Deemer shook a finger at Henry. "That's two demerits, Palmer."

Henry pointed down at Grimes, who had closed his eyes again and was still screaming. "That's what he said."

Deemer took a knee next to Grimes and placed a hand on the boy's shoulder pads. "Grimes. It's Rev. Deemer. Can you stand up?"

Grimes opened his eyes and stared up wildly at his coach. "No. I can't. My butt's broke."

Deemer motioned to the sideline for two players to come onto the field. He leaned back over Grimes. "We'll help you off the field."

Grimes shook his head. "No. Uh-uh. I don't want to move. It hurts!"

Deemer patted him on the shoulder pads. "It's going to be okay. We'll help you up, get you back to the locker room, put you in the whirlpool and you'll be fine."

"I don't want to get up! I need a stretcher!"

Deemer patted his shoulder pads again and motioned the two boys over. "You're going to be fine."

Grimes cast a frightened and bewildered look from Deemer to Henry. Henry shrugged his shoulders.

"I can't get up! Get a stretcher!"

Deemer continued to pat his shoulder pads, until Tom Wales and Bob Wobbly arrived from the sideline. "Wales, you get on that side, and Wobbly you take this side, and on three we'll lift him up." Deemer stood above Grimes's head and bent down to lift him up by the shoulders.

"No!"

"One."

"NO!"

"Two."

"NOOOO!!!"

"Three."

"OWWWWWWWWWWWW!!!!!!"

Henry watched them lift Grimes up off the ground as Grimes screamed. Once Grimes was upright, Deemer pulled Wales and Wobbly away so that Grimes was left standing under his own power. Grimes staggered, caught himself, took a couple steps forward, and looked at Deemer in surprise. Deemer pointed to the sidelines.

"Off you go. Wales, tell McMullen to take Grimes's place at center, and you take McMullen's place at tight end. Wobbly, you walk with Grimes up to the locker room and make sure he gets in the whirlpool."

As Wales trotted over to the offensive huddle, Henry watched Wobbly walk off the field with Grimes. In the last three weeks Wobbly had been demoted from J.V. to J.O. to Cubs. When he broke the news to Henry that he was joining the Cubs, Wobbly had acted apologetic, as if this meant that Henry would be losing his job as starting quarterback. But after one practice, it was clear to Henry and everyone else that Wobbly was a sorry excuse for a football player. He had no arm strength, and no amount of padding could induce him to throw his body in front of anything moving. He made a lot of noise on the blocking shed; he made even more noise when he was the tackling dummy. So far he hadn't seen any action — not even on special teams — and Henry couldn't help but notice that Wobbly's spirits seemed to lift when Deemer told him to accompany Grimes to the showers rather than take his place on the field.

Deemer placed an arm over Henry's shoulder. "It's fourth down, and we need a little more than a yard. We're out of timeouts. So let's go with Bulldog twenty-one, get a first down, then throw outs to Nelson. If time's running out, send everyone to the end zone and throw a Hail Mary. Got it?"

Henry nodded. Deemer slapped the top of his helmet and jogged back to the bench. Henry checked the scoreboard. The score was 17-12 and there were 0:31 seconds left. They were on the 40 yard line and down five points. Bulldog 21 was a dive play off-center, and Henry knew that McMullen would be a disaster at center. The entire line was a disaster. The entire team, for that matter, was a disaster. They hadn't gained more than 15 yards on the ground the whole game. The only reason they had twelve points on the scoreboard was that Henry had been able to scramble to buy time for Jack Nelson to get open down the field for two lucky touchdowns. Everything else was a catastrophe.

Henry took a knee in the middle of the huddle.

"Okay. Listen up." Henry looked around at the ten faces staring down at him. "This is our last chance, so let's make it count. Ward," Henry looked at his fullback, "we're going to fake Bulldog 21. And Jack," Henry looked at his wide receiver, "you run an out, and I'll fake the throw to you. And Wales," Henry looked at Tom Wales, the slowest kid on the team, who'd never played a game of football in his life, who was only in on this play because he'd come out to help get Grimes off the field, "I want you to fall down as soon as the ball is snapped, and then get up and run as fast as you can to the end zone. When you get there stop, turn around, and I'll put the ball in your hands. Got it?"

Wales's eyes grew wide, his mouth fell open, and he nodded solemnly as he comprehended the majesty of what Henry described. The rest of the team broke out in protest.

"Henry what ... Wales's never played ... What play is this ...?"

"Quiet! Quiet! You think they don't expect me to throw to Jack? This is our only chance. Just hold your blocks as long as you can, don't go downfield, and pray to God for a miracle. On one."

Henry slapped his hands, and the squad broke the huddle and walked to the line of scrimmage. Henry nodded at Jack, who was lined up on his left. Jack nodded back, and the cornerback and safety on that side took two steps backward and to Jack's side of the field. Henry bent down and placed his hands under McMullen's butt.

"Hut." McMullen's snap was short and only hit the tips of Henry's fingers. Henry bobbled the ball but managed to get a grip. The nose tackle who was lined up over McMullen exploded forward and knocked McMullen backwards into Henry. McMullen's left foot stepped onto Henry's left foot as he fell backward, and when Henry tried to pull back from center he almost tripped, but he gripped the ball with his left hand, put his right hand down on the ground to steady himself, and managed to pull his left foot out from under McMullen's and take a step backward, but the timing was now off, and Ward Carter, who was faking a dive off left center, collided headfirst into Henry and spun him around, clockwise, a full rotation. Henry bobbled the ball a second time, it toppled out of his hand and up into the air above his head, but as he spun around he managed to catch it with his trailing left hand and regain his balance, now two yards behind the line of scrimmage. He looked down. McMullen had fallen onto his butt but had managed — whether by accident or by design Henry couldn't tell — to grab hold of the noseguard's facemask and pull him down on top of himself, so that there was now a small pile of bodies thrashing in front of Henry, and the thrashing tripped a defensive tackle who had been fast approaching on his right. Henry turned his back on the defense and retreated five steps. When he spun around, the other defensive tackle, who appeared to have broken through the line unblocked, lunged at Henry's face. Henry did not have time to lift his right arm to fend off the tackler but managed to spin to his left. He felt the tackle brush against his shoulders, and not knowing whether he was down or still pursuing, Henry ran to his left and looked for Nelson, who had by now broken to the left sidelines. Henry pulled back his right hand and pumped his arm in Nelson's direction. Both defensive backs broke towards Nelson. Henry looked back over his shoulder to see who was pursuing, but the tackle had fallen to the ground five yards behind him and was only now getting up to his feet.

Henry looked for Wales, and saw a small, solitary player in a clean white jersey running alone, surprisingly quickly, towards the end zone, with no one in pursuit. Henry scanned the field in front of him, and saw two linebackers who, now sensing that someone far downfield might be open, charged forward as fast as they could towards Henry and the ball. Henry stopped, saw that Wales was now five yards from the end zone with no one closing, and planted his feet. He held the ball a moment longer, hoping that Wales would look back, make eye contact, acknowledge that the ball was on the way, but Wales kept going, and with the two linebackers now only two strides away, Henry stepped forward and released a perfect spiral towards the end zone.

The ball flew high and far downfield, up into a cloudless and windless blue sky, spiraling, spiraling over the heads of twenty boys. The linebackers turned, and Henry lifted himself up onto his tiptoes to watch it fly. When Wales reached the goal line, he spun around and looked back for Henry. He saw a crowd of boys back at the line. He heard the shouts from his sideline. He saw that he was all alone, and there was Henry, looking at him, standing on tiptoes with his right hand by his side and no football. Wales looked up. There was the football. Falling, falling down through the sky towards him. It was like a bird falling from the sky, a duck getting bigger as it fell, as if it had been shot out of the heavens in order to fall to him, directly to him, a gift for him. Wales lifted his arms and reached out with both hands toward the ball that was now hurtling faster and faster downward, towards the very spot where he stood. He closed his eyes and thought about his mother back at home, sitting beside him at the piano when he was six years old, showing him how to hold his wrists at the keyboard, and guiding his fingers through the scales. He thought how happy she would be if she could see him now, standing at the goal line, reaching out for the ball, that fell. Fell. Fell. Fell down. Straight down into ... and out of his hands. Down onto the ground. Rolling. Rolling out of the end zone and coming finally to a stop at the base of a persimmon tree laden with bright fruit.

Wales blinked, and Henry fell to his knees. The two linebackers gave each other high fives and shoved Henry to the ground. Wales tugged once at his facemask, stamped his foot, and trudged towards the sideline. McMullen helped Henry get back onto his feet.

"Nice try, Henry." McMullen patted Henry on the helmet.

"Thanks, Fart."

They walked off the field together as the other team celebrated.

Coach Deemer met Henry on the sideline. He had that mean smile on his face when he grabbed Henry by the bicep and squeezed.

"Oww!"

Henry tried to pull away, but Deemer had latched on. He leaned closer until his crooked nose was inches from Henry's facemask.

"This is not a game for hot dogs, Palmer. We win as a team and we lose a team. We don't lose on half-baked sandlot plays, understand?"

Henry nodded, and Deemer let him go. Henry turned away and joined the rest of the team on its long walk up the hill to the locker room

"Asshole," Henry muttered to himself.

GRAND ILLUSION

AFTER THE CUBS' LOSS Henry stopped by the room before heading to supper. Wobbly was already there, sitting in the corner, tossing his football into the air and listening to Styx on the stereo.

"How'd it turn out?" Wobbly asked.

"We lost."

"Well yeah. Coach should have put me in instead of Wales."

"Uh-huh." Henry decided not to mention Wales dropping the pass in the end zone. That would only add fuel to Wobbly's 'what might have been' fantasies. "Grimes okay?"

"Yeah. He's fine. I tried to get him to get in the whirlpool but he wanted to leave before Coach Deemer showed up."

Just then Ken Bright turned up the volume on his stereo next door so that it could be heard over Styx. Wobbly responded in kind.

"D'you hear about Tim Radley?" Wobbly yelled.

"No."

"Grimes told me he got expelled. Sent home today."

"What for?"

"Cheating on a quiz."

"What class?"

"Moser's."

"Trig?"

"Yep. Grimes said he was the smartest kid in the class."

"Why'd he cheat?"

"Don't know. But one strike and you're out."

Radley was a new boy from West Virginia. Henry had a couple classes with him — Classical History and Public Speaking. He was a little kid. Didn't say much in class. Roomed with Tom Wales.

Ken Bright turned up the volume on his stereo again so that the lyrics from Bright's room drowned out Wobbly's beloved *Grand Illusion* album.

> *There's a starman waiting in the sky*
> *He'd like to come and meet us*
> *But he thinks he'd blow our minds*

Wobbly took this as a personal affront and again turned up the volume on his own receiver.

"What the hell is that guy listening to?" Wobbly said. "Sounds like fag music. That guy's weird. Have you seen the stuff he has hanging on his walls? He has boys dressed up like girls. I can't believe they let him keep that up. I can't hang up Miss May but he gets to hang up a bunch of queers? No wonder he couldn't get a roommate."

"Maybe he didn't want one," Henry said.

"I don't believe that. Who'd want to room with the guy? Half the school would think you're a fag."

Henry grimaced. 'Fag' was a generic insult, like 'girl' or 'baby', used whenever a boy did anything out of the ordinary or expressed too many scruples. Wobbly, though, seemed to be using the word in its other meaning, which was unusual because everyone knew that no one at Randolph was gay.

"Dude. Relax," Henry said. "Ken's not a bad guy."

"He called me a mulatto just now."

"A what?"

"A mulatto. Half nigger and half white."

The ugly word jumped out at Henry, and he laughed out of embarrassment. He knew Wobbly was from Greensboro, but he hadn't realized he was such a redneck. "I think you probably misunderstood him."

"No I didn't. That's what he said. That's how I know he's an asshole. You could say he called my momma a nigger."

"Or your daddy," Henry said.

"Or my daddy. Either way, he's an asshole."

Wobbly was speaking so loudly that Henry was sure that Ken could hear him — not that Wobbly cared.

"Seems like a nice guy to me," Henry said.

"He didn't call you a mulatto, did he?"

"No. He didn't. But I don't believe he said that to you either."

Wobbly pointed in the direction of Ken's room. "You go ask him. See what he says. Ask him if he called me a mulatto."

Wobbly was clearly angry, but Henry couldn't tell if he was mad at Ken or mad at Henry for doubting him. Either way, Henry didn't want to hang out with him.

"Okay. I will."

Henry stepped into the hallway and closed the door behind him. It was a relief to have a door and a little distance between himself and Wobbly and Styx. The fluorescent tube outside their door was flickering and the hallway smelled like B.O. Henry felt a sudden pang of homesickness.

He knocked on Ken Bright's door and opened it without waiting for an answer. Ken was sitting in his leather armchair looking at a large picture book, *The History of Art*. He turned down the music when Henry walked in.

"Apologies for the volume, mate. I'm not trying to listen to Bowie. I just can't stand to hear any more Styx. Does your roommate have another album?"

"Not that he plays at the moment," Henry said.

Ken was wearing a Jimi Hendrix t-shirt and had a pair of scissors in his lap. Henry was about to ask him about the mulatto comment when Ken held up a finger to his ear, then pointed in the direction of Wobbly's room and spoke the words of the song in time with the music:

> *So if you think your life is complete confusion*
> *Because your neighbor's got it made*
> *Just remember it's a grand illusion*
> *And deep inside we're all the same*

"Sadly," Ken said, "it does get worse than that."

Henry smiled. "That's not really so bad, is it?"

Ken nodded with what Henry thought was a trace of condescension. "It's not America, I grant you, but let's just say it's paint by numbers. Rock opera by pre-adolescents."

He waved a dismissive arm in the direction of Henry's room. "I tried to speak to him about his Styx fever. I thought if I pointed out to him how predictable the lyrics are he might hear them in a new light. No such luck. I fear your Wobbly is musically deranged. When I questioned his taste for *Grand Illusion* he turned red in the face, pointed at my shirt and said, 'Who's the hippie nigger?' Not a nice person, your roommate."

Henry shook his head and laughed. Sounded like Wobbly. "He says you called him a 'mulatto'."

"I did."

"Why?"

"I said, 'That, my mulatto friend, is Jimi Hendrix.' I thought he was going to lose it then."

"I think he did," Henry said.

"Yes. He would. He's a bigot after all."

"I guess he is. But why?"

"Why what?"

"Why call him a 'mulatto'?"

"Why call Jimi Hendrix a 'nigger'?"

"Well ... "Henry's head bobbed and his weight shifted from one leg to the other as he tried to think of how best to put it. "He is black," he said finally.

"Whatever does that mean?"

"The color of his skin. He's black."

Ken put both hands up to his chin and looked at Henry as if he couldn't decide whether Henry was ignorant or racist or both.

"Not really black," Ken said. "Brown maybe. But what does that have to do with the word 'nigger'?"

"Well. I mean. I'm not saying I like the word, or use it," Henry said defensively.

"No, really. What does the color of his skin have to do with the word 'nigger'? Absolutely nothing. That word does not describe the color of his skin. That word describes his race. It's not a statement of personal color preference. It's a statement of racial hatred—the white race's hatred of the black race. It's as simple as that. One must have a very strong racial identity to use it. So I called him a 'mulatto' in hopes of muddying his waters, so to speak."

Henry was at a loss for words. He'd never heard anyone speak like this before. If Ken noticed his confoundment he didn't acknowledge it.

"It would appear that my efforts have borne fruit."

"Not at all," Henry said. "He hates your guts."

"Ah, but don't you see? I've pricked a nerve. One must prick a nerve to get anywhere with these people. I must be cruel to be kind."

Henry thought Ken was fooling himself. There was no way he was getting through to Wobbly. That kid's self-regard was impregnable.

"You obviously don't know Wobbly very well," Henry said.

"Tilting at windmills, am I?"

"Huh?"

"Well." Ken shrugged. "Sometimes you just have to fight the good fight."

Ken picked up the scissors and continued cutting out a picture from the book in his lap.

"What are you doing?" Henry asked.

"Adding to my gallery of images." He held up the cutout for Henry to see.

"What is it?"

"It's Gustave Dore's illustration of Charon transporting Dante to the Underworld. I'm going to post it on my wall in honor of you and the mulatto—or the mulatto mostly."

Ken handed the cutout, a little bigger than a postcard, to Henry, who held it up to his face to get a better look. Two lonely figures standing in what looked like a lifeboat surrounded by drowning men to whom they offered no aid. It was horrifying.

"And what does that have to do with Wobbly?"

"You do know who Charon is?"

Henry shook his head.

"Acheron?"

"No."

"He's the Greek demi-god who ferries the souls of the dead across the river to Hades in the Underworld. And you do know the name of the river?"

Henry shook his head again.

"Oo-la-la, *mon frère*, what have you been reading all of your life? In the classical world the River Styx separates the land of the living from the land of the dead. If any living thing touches it they die, and even the gods cannot break an oath made on the river."

The beauty of the myth pleased Ken greatly, and he looked at Henry and smiled, hoping to find some sign that he also saw its beauty.

"So you can understand on how many levels Wobbly's music offends me. It's not simply un-listenable; it's a sacrilege. Greek mythology re-duced to drivel. It was painful — literally — to listen to at first, but Dore has made things bearable. Now, when The Mulatto plays *The Grand Illusion* I can look at this illustration and imagine Wobbly being ferried to the Underworld."

Henry and Ken both laughed — Henry at the thought of Wobbly exploding with indignation if he ever learned the secret meaning of the picture, and Ken at the feeling that in Henry he might have found a kindred spirit.

The music next door stopped, and Henry heard Wobbly open and close the door. It was 6 o'clock and the doors to the dining hall were opening. Henry turned towards the door to leave but Ken stood up and caught his arm.

"Listen to this one song before you go."

Ken switched the album on his turntable and placed the needle down on another Bowie track. Ken watched Henry's face closely. He watched Henry's head nod with the opening drumbeat of *Changes,* and then his sly smile at the barely sung, spoken opening words that turned into a broad smile at the chorus. Such a lovely smile, Ken thought, warm and open and innocent — not naive so much as pure — and Hen-ry's blue eyes sparkled with happiness. Such a beautiful, glorious boy. A fair companion? Probably not, Ken thought. In his seventeen years he'd not yet met one. When Bowie sang of 'strange fascinations' Hen-ry looked Ken fully in the face, and Ken's heart leapt at the possibility of recognition. But Henry's glance was fleeting. He watched Henry's head bob as he hummed the closing chorus and the song tapered off with a plaintive saxophone, Henry stopped moving and stopped hum-ming and looked at Ken matter-of-factly. Ken waited expectantly for his response to the music, and Henry, sensing an awkward silence, said simply, "That's good."

Ken's heart settled back into its familiar rhythm of disappointment, but when Henry leaned down to lift the needle off the record, Ken slapped his hand away. "Don't touch! That's holy script."

Henry watched Ken carefully lift the needle off the record, return the tonearm to its rest and sit back down. "I like it," Henry said, and sensing that Ken had expected more of a reaction, he added, "but what are the 'strange ch-ch-changes'?"

Ken's face brightened instantly. "Exactly right!" he said. He leaned forward. "And who is this 'different man'? That's what he's telling you to figure out."

Ken leaned forward and pointed to a black and white photograph of a man's face or a beautiful woman's face — Henry wasn't sure which — on his wall. The hair was combed back from the forehead and was wet, as if the person had just come out of a swimming pool.

"That's David Bowie you've just been listening to."

"That's what he looks like? Isn't that the same guy in the red wig?" Henry pointed to the photograph of Ziggy Stardust.

"That is he, *mon cher.*"

Henry blushed, but he wasn't sure why he felt suddenly embarrassed. Ken speaking French maybe? He pointed to an album cover that was tacked to Ken's wall. "Who's that?"

"Lou Reed. The Transformer album. David Bowie produced that."

"You like men with heavy eye shadow?"

Ken gave him a funny look. "Maybe."

Just then Gordon stuck his head in the door. "Henry?"

Henry jumped at the sound of his brother's voice. "What? How long have you been standing there?"

Gordon frowned. "I just got here. Wobbly said you were up here so I came to get you. Come on. Let's go to supper."

Henry pointed at Ken. "You guys know each other?"

"Oh yeah," Gordon said. "How's it going Bright?"

"Oh Jim Dandy." Ken slumped back into his chair.

This was the first time Ken had seen them together. He noted the family resemblance — the same broad forehead, the same al-mond-shaped eyes — but Gordon's nose was thicker, his shoulders were broader, and he was altogether heavier than Henry. Self-importance weighs him down, like chain mail, Ken thought. He took the Bowie album off the turntable and slipped it into its sleeve and album cover.

Gordon pulled the pocket watch out of his pocket and made a show of checking it. "It's five after six," he said. "Let's go eat."

"What you got there?" Ken asked, nodding at the watch in Gordon's hand.

Gordon twisted his hand so that the watch faced Ken. "Pocket watch."

"Nice."

Gordon thought he heard a note of contempt in Ken's voice, but Ken nodded approvingly.

"Come on," Gordon said to Henry. "Let's eat." He nodded to Ken, then grabbed Henry's arm and practically pulled him out of the room.

"See you later," Henry said to Ken. He jerked free of his brother's grip as soon as they were in the hall. "What's your problem?"

Gordon leaned closer to his brother as they walked down the hall and lowered his voice. "I came up here because Wobbly told me you were in Bright's room. You shouldn't spend too much time with that guy."

"What is he? A leper?"

"He's got a reputation, if you know what I mean. The last thing you need at the start of school is to be known as someone who hangs out with Ken Bright."

Henry stopped short as Gordon continued to walk down the hall. "What sort of reputation?"

Gordon hesitated, and his mouth twisted into a grimace. That was hard to explain. Ken was smart. He was opinionated. He liked art. He was captain of the drama club. He wore weird clothes. He grew up in New York City. He was Jewish. He hung out with stoners. He hated Jimmy Buffett. He sometimes affected a British accent. He wasn't a jock. He didn't care what jocks thought. He didn't care what Gordon thought. He made Gordon feel stupid. Needless to say, Gordon didn't like him. But it was more than all of these things that had prompted Gordon to retrieve Henry from Ken Bright's room.

"He's a druggie," Gordon finally muttered, for want of anything more specific.

"A druggie?"

Henry didn't lower his own voice, and Gordon motioned with his hand for him to be quieter. "He smokes pot."

Henry didn't buy it. Lots of kids smoked pot. Even some of Gordon's friends smoked pot, he was sure. That wouldn't disqualify anyone from being your friend. But Gordon was Head Boy now, so maybe it was suddenly a big deal for him?

Henry held his palms out at his waist and nodded at Gordon in a condescending kind of way. "I'm pretty sure you know this, Gordon, but lots of people smoke pot at this school."

Gordon looked around. Although there was no one else in the hallway, he stepped closer. "Keep it down. It's not so much that he smokes pot as that he's a stoner. That's his reputation, and, you know, as far as you're concerned that's enough."

"What's that supposed to mean?"

"That means you don't want to get a reputation as a stoner."

"Does it matter whether or not he really is a stoner?"

Gordon frowned. This was so like Henry — standing up for the little guy — but Gordon knew how these things worked.

"Look. You're a new boy. Take my word for it. You don't want to get a reputation from the get-go that you hang out with Ken Bright."

"Because he's a stoner?"

Gordon looked down at his feet and rubbed the top of his head. "It's more than that," he said.

"Like what?"

Henry waited for some kind of explanation but Gordon couldn't think of how to put it into words.

"I can't say," he said finally.

"Oh, for Christ's sake, Gordon. Give me a break!"

As Henry started down the hall, Gordon grabbed his arm and pulled him closer. "He's a weird guy. I'm telling you."

Henry shook loose of Gordon's grip. Gordon was acting just like their father, always trying to control what he did, even what he thought.

"I don't think he's weird," he said defiantly. "I think he's interesting to talk to. He's got cool ideas. And he's funny."

Gordon threw up his hands in exasperation.

"All right! Forget it!" he burst out, then catching himself, he leaned closer and lowered his voice to a hiss. "Forget that I've been here two years already, and I know how this place works. Forget that I'm trying to help you out. Forget that if you get a reputation the next thing you know you're spending half the school year trying to prove to people you're not who they think you are."

"I don't care what people think I am." Henry's voice cracked as he said this. He wanted to believe what he said, but he wasn't sure.

Gordon hated it when Henry got on his high horse like this. He knew he was right, but he also knew that no matter what he said Henry wouldn't listen.

"Yeah right. You say that but just wait and see. I know."

And this was exactly what Henry hated most about his brother. Always looking over his shoulder. Always worrying about what people were saying about him.

"You don't care about my reputation!" he barked. "You care about your reputation! You don't want a brother who has a 'reputation' for hanging out with 'druggies' or 'weirdos'. That's what this is about. You're worried that I'll make you look bad."

Gordon shoved his brother against the wall. "Stop being such a dickwad!"

Henry bounced off the wall, and for a moment he imagined throwing himself at Gordon and wrestling him to the floor. He shook the thought from his head and glared at his brother angrily.

"You're the one who comes to my room and the first thing out of your mouth is stop hanging out with Ken Bright because he's 'weird,' when as far as I can tell you have no idea who Ken Bright is and don't care to find out."

Gordon had a feeling of *deja vu*. When would he learn that there was no point in trying to help his brother? He brushed his palms together as if to wash his hands of Henry.

"That's right. Forget I said anything. Do whatever you want!" Gordon turned and stormed off.

Henry watched his brother thunder down the stairs to the dining hall. He wondered, what just happened? And what was Gordon's problem with Ken Bright?

AFTER STUDY HALL, Henry walked to Tom Wales's room on the third floor of Mortimer Hall, one of the student dormitories that fronted on the Lawn. It was dark outside and the temperature had dipped into the 50s, but most of the dorm windows were open, and the air was filled with a heady mix of Bozz Scaggs, Jimmy Buffett, Marshall Tucker Band, and — thankfully to Henry's ears — Allman Brothers. Henry knocked on Wales's door and opened it without waiting for an answer. He found Wales sitting up in bed reading sheet music with a pair of headphones on. Wales quickly closed his music binder and removed the headphones. Before Wales turned the music off, Henry made out the sound of a piano through the headphones.

"Who's that? Mozart?" Henry asked.

"Bach."

"Nerd."

Wales smiled. "Moron," he retorted. Had the insult come from anyone else, he might have been embarrassed, but he and Henry had hit it off since that first day of Cub football. Their shared dislike of Rev. Deemer had broken the ice and sealed their friendship.

Henry looked around the room. The other single bed was already stripped to the mattress; the desk beside the bed was empty, the dresser opposite the same.

"I heard about Tim. What happened?"

Henry took a seat on the empty bed, and Wales told him how he and Radley had been sitting next to each other during the quiz. "There were ten questions and an eleventh question for extra credit. Mr. Moser always makes the extra credit question tricky, which Tim liked, because he's good at math, and he figured what's the point of extra credit if you just give the points away? It's like you and football — "

"I'm on the Cub team," Henry reminded him.

"You know what I mean. Or like me and piano. It's the one thing we do better than other people. He knew it and other people in the class knew it. It was his thing, so he wanted to get the highest grade in the class, maybe more than he should have. So we're taking the test, and I'm like halfway through and look over, and I can see that he's finished with everything but the extra credit question. No surprise. He just flies through the thing, prestissimo—"

"Presstissi-what?"

"Very fast. But when I get to the extra credit question, Tim's still stuck, and I see why, because the question involves cosecants which we really hadn't gone over. I'm able to figure it out because I'd looked ahead in the textbook—"

"Really?" Henry pretended to be surprised. Wales really was a nerd.

"—so I write down the solution and Tim looks over at my paper. I really don't think he did it to cheat so much as he was irritated at himself for not being able to figure it out, but one look at my paper and 'presto' he sees the solution and writes it out, probably finished before I did. When we turned in our quizzes Mr. Moser asked to see us after class. He told Tim what he'd seen, and Tim admitted that he'd looked at my answer to the extra credit question because he didn't remember going over cosecants in class. Mr. Moser asked me if I'd shown him the answer. I said, 'No.' And he said he was going to have to turn Tim in for an honor offense."

"Damn." Henry shook his head.

"Thing is, I don't think he was trying to cheat. I think he just wanted to get the answer right."

"Isn't that true of any cheater?"

"Well yeah, but the difference is he wasn't doing it to get a better grade. I'm sure he got 100% on the quiz. If Moser had gone over cosecants he would have gotten the extra credit question too. It wasn't like he was cheating anybody else."

"I don't think that's an excuse."

"That's easy for you to say."

"What's that supposed to mean?"

"Your nickname's 'Chosen' for god's sake, and I'm 'Worm'. You're the starting quarterback, and I'm the last person in—"

"Almost scored a touchdown!" Henry interrupted.

"Very funny! Your brother's the Head Boy—your father was Head Boy, for Pete's sake. Tim Radley is from Welch, West Virginia. His dad works for the post office, and his mom's in a wheelchair. He was here on scholarship. He was going to be the first person in his family to go to college."

"He shouldn't have cheated."

"He didn't do it to cheat! He did it to prove he belonged!"

Henry understood that Wales was trying to make a point about Radley's intent, but he didn't think the Honor Code said anything about that. "Did you tell that to the prefects?"

"I didn't talk to the prefects."

"You didn't go to the hearing?"

"No. Tim said it was just him and Mr. Moser. Said it lasted like fifteen minutes, then they told him he was expelled."

"That's fucking nuts!" Henry said.

"Tell me about it. Then he had to call home and tell his parents."

Henry imagined calling home with the news he'd been expelled. His father would kill him. Or die himself. Brutal. And he imagined Gordon in a room being Head Judge with little Tim Radley sitting in front of him, terrified. What was he thinking when he voted to kick Tim out? What did he think now, afterwards? He might have thought to ask Gordon about Tim himself if Gordon hadn't gone off on Ken Bright. He suspected Tom might want to ask him about Gordon now, so he changed the subject.

"What about you?" Henry asked.

"About me what?"

"What do your parents do?"

"My mom's a music professor," Wales said.

"Where?"

"Winston Salem State University," Wales said with evident pride.

"Oh yeah?"

Wales nodded.

"And what about your dad?"

Wales glanced out the window and then back at Henry. "He's not much in the picture, I guess you'd say."

"Oh, shit, man." Henry mumbled in embarrassment.

"Naw, it's alright." Wales waved his right hand in Henry's direction to reassure him. "Just not something I care to talk about."

Henry stood up from the bed, thinking maybe this was a good time to leave. "So do you get to keep the room as a single now?" he asked, looking around.

"They said I'd probably have to move once a single opens up."

"That sucks," Henry said.

"Not really. To be honest I wouldn't mind moving."

"How come?"

"Lawton Faison's a dick." Wales described how during the first week of school Lawton and Billy Richardson, his roommate, had hanged Radley by his belt loop on a coat hook after Radley refused to swear allegiance to all sixth formers.

"Is Lawton's room here?"

"You know him?"

"A little. Our families are friends."

Tom pointed in the direction of the Lawn. "The Prince of Darkness lives at the end of the hall."

"Prince of Darkness?" Henry laughed. He wasn't surprised that Lawton could be a dick, but comparing him to Satan seemed a little dramatic.

Instead of answering, Tom opened his desk drawer and pulled out a spiral notebook. He flipped through the pages until he found what he was looking for, then handed the notebook to Henry. It was a pen and ink drawing of a devil with horns and a tail, wearing a white, button-down shirt, topsiders and an LL Bean hunting jacket. On the breast of the hunting jacket was a pin with the letter P in an old English font. Henry recognized the P from his father's Princeton swag. The caption at the bottom of the drawing read, "P is for Prick". Henry laughed.

"This is really good," he said.

Tom put the notebook back in his desk drawer. "Prince of Darkness," he repeated.

AP ENGLISH

ON A FINE MORNING IN EARLY OCTOBER, David Nightingale stood in front of the desk in his classroom on the top floor of Jackson Hall. He wore khaki pants, a white Oxford cloth shirt with the sleeves rolled up, and a blue polka dot bowtie. He was tall and broad-shouldered, and maintained an athlete's build even now, at 60. A shock of prematurely white hair fell gracefully over the tops of his ears and the back collar of his shirt.

Nightingale was the Lion of the faculty—both widely liked by the boys and revered by the alumni. He had graduated from the school in 1937. Legend had it that he had been one of the greatest athletes in the school's history. During college the St. Louis Cardinals had offered him a minor league baseball contract, but the war intervened and he nearly lost his life at Omaha Beach. During his long recovery he met an English nurse named Jane Storey. She sat by his bed and read him poems by John Donne and George Herbert while he swam in and out of consciousness, and later, while helping him to learn to walk again, they read Wordsworth and Tennyson together. At the time of his discharge, they were discussing *Paradise Lost*, and on their honeymoon they read aloud *Midsummer Night's Dream*. Later, in graduate school, Nightingale absorbed the poetics of Brooks and Warren, but to the end of his life he credited Jane Storey for giving him his religion, which was literature.

A grave rubbing he'd taken himself from Shakespeare's tombstone hung above the classroom door, and the walls were decorated with some of Nightingale's favorite images and quotations, all handsomely framed. There was Peter Breughel's *Fall of Icarus* and beside it Auden's poem, *The Musee de Beaux Arts*. There were the opening lines from the General Prologue of *The Canterbury Tales*. There was an illustration by Gustave Dore from *Paradise Lost*. There was a portrait of a lady. And there was a small photograph of a storefront somewhere in Europe. His students affectionately called his classroom, room 301, 'Nightingale's Perch'.

On that day a dozen students sat at desks around the room. This was the sixth form AP English class, widely regarded as the crucible and capstone for the school's best students. Some of them were indeed lovers of literature. Others had no patience for poetry but had enrolled in the class in hopes of bolstering their academic record and, by extension, their chances at admission to an elite college. One was there simply because his father had told him Nightingale was the best teacher he'd ever had. Nightingale tapped his yardstick against the blackboard where he had written a quotation in his elegant hand:

> *Rightly to be great*
> *Is not to stir without great argument,*
> *But greatly to find quarrel in a straw*
> *When honor's at stake.*

"Here we have Hamlet encountering Fortinbras' army on the plain, about to go to war against the Poles for a worthless piece of land that no one cares about, and yet Hamlet cannot bring himself to avenge his father's death or his mother's dishonor. Why, Mr. Faison, do you think Hamlet hesitates to kill the king?"

Lawton had his notebook open and was sketching a picture of Nightingale standing at the front of the room. Nightingale could see that Lawton was drawing but couldn't make out the subject. Lawton often drew sketches during class. At first Nightingale had suspected that Lawton was daydreaming, but he had quickly learned that the boy was actually more engaged with the class material when he drew, that drawing helped him to think.

"He's a coward, obviously," Lawton said, and he glanced up quickly to get the measure of Nightingale, then returned his gaze to the drawing.

"Why do you call him a coward?"

"Because he won't kill the king, even though he knows the king killed his father."

"But he hasn't exactly run away from the fight, has he?"

Lawton continued drawing without looking up. "No. He dicks around talking to Horatio, talking to Ophelia, talking to Polonius. Talking to himself mostly — like he's talking himself out of killing the king, like in that scene when Claudius is bowing down right there in front of him and he finds an excuse not to kill him by talking."

Gordon Palmer, who was sitting next to Lawton, felt the back of his neck grow hot. It irritated him that Nightingale let Lawton draw pictures during class. Gordon could see that the drawing was of Nightingale at this very moment — a remarkable likeness, in fact — and he assumed Nightingale could see Lawton's subject, but he just let it pass like he was taking notes or something.

"So is someone who thinks too much a coward?" Nightingale addressed the question to Lawton.

"He is, if thinking is his excuse not to act," Lawton said, still not looking up.

Nightingale left the blackboard and began circling the room as he talked. Gordon watched to see what his reaction would be when he looked at Lawton's notebook.

"And is that what we have in Hamlet, Mr. Bright? A person who thinks in order not to act?"

Ken was sitting several desks away from Lawton and Gordon. He wore his *Night at the Opera* t-shirt to which he had pinned a white collar in order to comply with the school's classroom dress code. "Weirdo," Gordon thought.

"No. I think Hamlet doesn't kill the king because he has a conscience."

"Exactly," Lawton said, still drawing and not bothering to look at Ken. " 'Conscience makes cowards of us all,' he says so himself."

Ken turned in his seat and directed his comments to Lawton.

"Yeah, but that's Hamlet beating himself up because he has to wrestle with his conscience — he can't just murder his uncle the way Claudius murdered King Hamlet." Ken's voice grew louder as he continued to address Lawton and Lawton continued to ignore him. "Claudius is the coward — he killed King Hamlet in his sleep. But Hamlet has a conscience so he has to weigh the consequences. And the actions aren't trivial — like Prufrock, 'Do I dare to eat a peach?' — they're heroic actions, and they carry great consequence — killing the king!"

Lawton still didn't look up. Ken turned his focus back to Nightingale, abandoning his attempt to breach the ramparts of Lawton's arrogance.

"Hamlet's not a coward because he has a conscience; he's a human — not a monster — because he has a conscience. It takes courage to take stock of things. 'To be or not to be.' How many people ask that?"

Lawton smirked, and he quickly sketched the back of Bright's head, wearing a yarmulke, into his drawing.

"You make it sound like he's more heroic because he thinks more," Lawton said, as he made tiny hatch marks to indicate shadow behind the image of Ken's head. "The opposite is true. He only kills Claudius by accident, by mistake, practically. Like he has to trick himself into killing Claudius. And when he finally thinks he is killing Claudius — in Gertrude's bedroom — he kills Polonius by mistake. It's pathetic, really."

"A pathetic hero," Mr. Nightingale said. He smiled. "I don't think I've ever heard it put quite that way before."

Nightingale now stood in front of Gordon's desk. Gordon saw his eyes flicker in the direction of Lawton's notebook, but he registered no reaction. Nightingale had noticed Gordon's irritation with Lawton's drawing, and he'd chosen to ignore it. Lawton was one of his advisees, and he knew Lawton's parents were having marital problems and he'd heard rumors of financial difficulties. He suspected drawing helped Lawton process his feelings about home, and he knew from experience that it helped him think in class. As for any discomfort this might cause Gordon Palmer, Nightingale thought it a useful practice in toleration for the Head Boy.

"Is that what we have in Hamlet, Mr. Palmer? Not a tragic hero, but a pathetic hero?"

Gordon had not managed to finish reading Hamlet before class—he'd only made it to the end of Act III—and he was at a loss to respond. Rather than fess up, he bluffed.

"I have a question about Polonius, if that's okay."

Nightingale chuckled to himself. He recognized a bullshitter when he encountered one, and it amused him to think that the Head Boy was about to use Polonius as cover. Rather than correcting Gordon, he decided to let him hoist himself with his own petard. "Go ahead," he said.

"Polonius always gets a bad rap, but a lot of what he says makes sense."

"Go on."

Gordon flipped back in his book to a passage that he had marked. "So right here in Act III he says to Laertes,

'Give every man thy ear, but few thy voice;
Take each man's censure, but reserve thy
judgment.'"

Gordon read Polonius's lines in a monotone, with little inflection and no characterization. "And a little further down,

'Neither a borrower, nor a lender be;
For loan oft loses both itself and friend,
And borrowing dulls the edge of husbandry.
This above all: to thine own self be true,
And it must follow, as the night the day,
Thou canst not then be false to any man.'

Who can argue with any of that? I kind of admire Polonius."

Gordon looked up from the text, pretty sure that he had covered for himself nicely. Several of the boys rolled their eyes, and Ned Claiborne, who sat in the back of the room, put his fist to his mouth and coughed, "Bllsht!"

Ken Bright scoffed. "Admire him? He's a total tool."

Gordon shifted uncomfortably in his seat. "What do you mean?"

"He prostitutes his daughter to serve the king."

"But that's his job! He's doing his job."

Ken guffawed. "Prostituting his daughter?"

"Serving the king." Gordon shifted his weight again. His neck felt tight. As a general rule he avoided arguing with Ken if he could help it.

"And the king is corrupt. A drunk. A murderer."

"No one knows he's a murderer." Gordon felt confident in this fact.

"We know. We've seen King Hamlet's ghost."

"But Polonius hasn't. And no one has even told him what the ghost said. How is he supposed to know that Claudius is a murderer?"

Gordon looked to Nightingale, hoping for some sign that he was in the right ballpark, but Nightingale remained on the sidelines. Lawton, meanwhile, laughed to himself and drew a caricature of Gordon in overalls like some hick store clerk.

Ken smiled. Gordon's plodding argument had helped him to forget Lawton's earlier snub. Magnanimous in his victory, his voice grew gentle, almost as though he were talking to a child. "We know he's a tool, because Shakespeare tells us he's a tool."

"What is that supposed to mean?"

Ken flipped through his copy of the play, found the passage, and using different voices — a teasing, patronizing tone for Hamlet, and a dull, monotone for Polonius, he read:

> Hamlet: *Do you see yonder cloud that's almost in shape of a camel?*
>
> Polonius: *By the mass, and 'tis like a camel, indeed."*

Several boys laughed at Ken's Polonius voice, because it sounded very much like Gordon's earlier reading voice.

> Hamlet: *Methinks it is like a weasel.*
>
> Polonius: *It is backed like a weasel.*
>
> Hamlet: *Or like a whale?*
>
> Polonius: *Very like a whale*

The boys laughed again.

"Polonius says whatever he thinks the powers that be want to hear," Ken concluded. "The very definition of a tool."

Nightingale waited for Gordon to respond, but Gordon kept quiet. He knew that he'd been licked. To his credit, Gordon tipped an imaginary cap to Bright, and Ken acknowledged the gesture with a nod and a smile.

Nightingale had worried that he'd made a mistake by letting Gordon take the class on his little frolic and detour, but when he saw Gordon's gesture to Ken he told himself it was worth it — maybe Gordon had learned something. He returned to the front of the room.

"So we have two theories on the table so far: Hamlet is a coward, and Hamlet has a conscience. These are by no means the only theories for Hamlet's refusal to kill Claudius. The theories are legion — this is, after all, the central mystery of the play."

"What's your theory?"

"I don't have one theory. There are lots of theories — that's the richness of the play. Whatever your life experience or biases, it speaks to you. There's Hamlet as melancholiac, Hamlet with Oedipal issues — "

"What's your favorite theory?" Ken asked.

Over the last few years Nightingale's interpretation of Hamlet had shifted in the direction of a man coming to terms with his mortality. At the beginning of the play he's haunted; at the end he caresses Orrick's skull and leaps into Ophelia's grave. He finally kills Claudius by playing a game: the swordplay. It seemed to Nightingale that Shakespeare was saying that although man cannot control his fate, he can play with Death. Make the best of things: 'the readiness is all.' Nightingale smiled, because he recognized that his interpretation of Hamlet was an old man's theory.

"One of my favorite interpretations is Hamlet as the artist."

"How does that theory go?" Bright asked.

Nightingale smiled; he knew that one would pique Ken's interest. "It goes something like this. For Hamlet, killing the King is like fulfilling his destiny — his debt to his father, his duty as the Prince, clearing the way for him to become the rightful King. But Hamlet doesn't want to be King; he wants to be an artist. That's his identity. To be the King is to define conformity — after all, what the King says is the Law — which is the opposite of being an artist, who always struggles against conformity. So Hamlet is stuck between fulfilling his destiny, which is to kill the King and be the King, or being true to his identity, which is to be an artist. And when your destiny and your identity are that contradictory, you're powerless to act."

Gordon and several other boys furiously scribbled notes. Ken Bright applauded. Lawton smirked as he added the words "Pvt. Hamlet" to the blackboard behind Nightingale in his sketch.

"Sounds like another excuse for cowardice," Lawton said. "Hamlet wouldn't be a Colonel, let alone a king in Charleston."

Ken Bright laughed. "I don't think Hamlet would care to be a colonel in South Carolina."

For the first time Lawton redirected his attention from his notebook. "Who cares what you think?" he said angrily, and in an undertone he muttered, as if to himself, "mongrel".

Nightingale, who was standing at the front of the room, had not heard the insult. He continued to address the class. "The question is whether he is worthy to be king. Whether he is fit for the throne. And clearly he is not. You can't be an artist and play the king. You must be the king or renounce the birthright."

"What did you call me?" Ken said.

Lawton ignored him and stabbed his drawing with his pen.

Nightingale now recognized Lawton's anger. He'd seen him flash it before — finding some slight where there really wasn't one. His father, whom Nightingale had taught, had the same temper. He worried about the boy. A strange rigidity seemed to be creeping into him. More talk about kings and the call of duty wasn't going to be helpful.

"I think we've traveled far enough with Hamlet for today," Nightingale said. "In the little time that we have left, let's look at another lyric poem."

Nightingale turned and ran his finger across the top of a dozen books on the shelf behind his desk, and there was an audible groan among the boys as they began stuffing their notebooks and paperback Hamlets into their book bags. At least once a week Nightingale made a point of reading a lyric poem aloud to the class. He'd invite the boys to imagine themselves as the speaker of the poem. What was the person feeling as he or she spoke or thought those words? What had happened to give rise to those feelings? Nightingale lifted a battered green volume from the shelf and flipped through its pages until he found what he was looking for. He scanned it once then smiled at his students.

"Let's try this one," he said, and he lifted the book and read the words slowly, in his rich Southern accent.

As Adam early in the morning,
Walking forth from the bower refresh'd with sleep,
Behold me where I pass, hear my voice, approach,
Touch me, touch the palm of your hand to my body
as I pass,
Be not afraid of my body

He lowered the book and gazed at his students. "What are we to make of that, class?"

"Not Rumi again," Claiborne muttered.

"Nope. Not a bad guess though," Nightingale said. "This is Walt Whitman. Can anyone tell me anything about Mr. Whitman?"

Ken Bright raised his hand.

"Mr. Bright?"

"He's America's greatest poet."

Ned Claiborne rolled his eyes. Such a brown-nose, he thought.

"I would not argue with you on that point but I was looking for something more biographical," Nightingale said. Nightingale looked at Lawton, who, to his surprise, had his hand raised.

"Mr. Faison?"

"He's a fag."

"Pardon?" Nightingale looked at Lawton with disapproval; he did not tolerate slurs in his classroom.

"Ho-mo-sexual," Lawton said slowly.

Several of the boys who had largely tuned out — Nightingale's poems of the day were never tested — sprang back to attention.

"That is probably correct, Mr. Faison, although some people believe that he was celibate. Anyone else?"

Ken started to raise his hand but changed his mind. Nightingale looked at him, and Ken shook his head no.

"Whitman published *Leaves of Grass* in 1855 and then reissued the book several times until his death, adding new poems and sometimes editing old ones. He wrote in a form and a style that had never been seen before, long lines, almost always unrhymed, often confessional, often like Rumi — Mr. Claiborne's favorite — mystical, always in celebration of the connection between all people, calling for the connection in all people, which was remarkable, given that he lived through the most violent, chaotic and divided period of our nation's history."

"Did he fight in the Civil War?" Lawton asked.

"No. He probably was too old to fight, and he certainly would have been a terrible soldier if he had. He did serve as a nurse in a hospital for wounded soldiers."

"Easier to preach about connections when no one's shooting at you," Lawton said sarcastically.

Ken jumped in. "He would say it's harder to shoot other people if you see them as your brothers."

"What about the text of the poem?" Nightingale asked, to get the boys back on track. "I'll read it again."

And Nightingale did. This time the boys played closer attention.

"Who's he talking to?" Lawton asked.

"Very good question," Nightingale said. "Who do you think he's talking to?"

"I think he's talking to another man," Lawton said.

"And who is it?" Nightingale asked.

"Sounds like another gay guy," Lawton said, and several boys in the room laughed.

"Why do you think the person's gay?"

"Because he says — what was the last line?"

Nightingale looked down at the page. " 'Be not afraid of my body.' "

"Why else would the person be afraid?" Lawton said, as if it were obvious.

"If they're both gay, they wouldn't be afraid," Ken Bright said.

"You should know," Lawton said in a stage whisper, and the same boys laughed.

Ken closed his eyes and tried desperately to think of something to distract himself, or anything that would keep his face from turning bright red at that moment, but all he could think of was his hatred for Lawton Faison.

Nightingale had heard Lawton's comment this time, and he saw Ken's discomfort. He briefly considered correcting Lawton but decided against bringing more attention to the comment. "I think Mr. Bright is right," he said. "Who is Adam?"

"No idea," Lawton said.

"Anyone?"

"Adam and Eve?" Gordon offered doubtfully.

"All right. And what does that tell you, Mr. Palmer?"

"No idea," Gordon said.

"Was Adam gay, Mr. Faison?"

"No."

"So could the two people in the poem just as easily be heterosexual as homosexual?"

Lawton didn't answer. He looked at Ken, and Ken felt like Lawton was gloating that he'd silenced him.

"I don't think it's about sex," Ken Bright said defiantly.

"Interesting. If the subject is not sex, then what is the fear of the body that the poem is talking about?" Nightingale asked.

"Intimacy," Ken said. "Between a man and a man or a man and a woman or a woman and a man or a woman and woman. Doesn't matter. It's the fear of being close to another person, man, woman or child."

Nightingale glanced at Lawton as Ken spoke. He worried about the boy. Lawton still had his notebook open and was looking down at his drawing, but Nightingale could tell that Lawton was listening to Ken, because Lawton's lips were moving as if he were speaking to himself. Nightingale wondered what he was thinking, and whether any of this had sunk in.

Just then the class bell rang, and the boys began stuffing their notebooks back into their book bags.

"Please come forward as I call your name and receive your papers."

Nightingale took the stack of papers from the corner of his desk and distributed them one by one. When Lawton took his paper, Nightingale made a point of saying, "Thank you for your comments and your close attention today, Lawton."

The last boy to step forward was Ken Bright. He took his paper from Nightingale and read the comment on the back page. He nodded. "Fair enough," he said, and placed it carefully inside his spiral notebook. He glanced over his shoulder to make sure that all the boys had left the room.

"Do you mind if I ask you something, Mr. Nightingale?" he said quietly.

"Of course not."

Ken hesitated, looked down at his feet, then at Nightingale, then looked down again. "Do you know whether Walt Whitman and Oscar

Wilde ever met?" he asked finally.

"I believe they did," Mr. Nightingale said, matter-of-factly. "At Whitman's home in Camden, New Jersey."

Bright looked up, his eyes considerably brightened. "I wonder what they talked about."

"I don't think anyone knows," Mr. Nightingale said. "Though each of them complimented the other in the newspapers at the time."

"It was in the newspapers?" Ken asked.

"I'm pretty sure. Whitman had been a journalist, and he rarely missed a chance at publicity. And at that time, Oscar Wilde was perhaps England's most famous man of letters."

Ken hesitated again and slowly rubbed the tip of his chin with his finger. "So that was before he went to prison?"

Nightingale nodded. "Yes. It was."

Ken looked at Mr. Nightingale. "Crazy, right?" he asked softly.

Nightingale smiled at him reassuringly and nodded. "And very sad. Still. Even today. But remember the words of Walt Whitman. 'Be not afraid.'"

Ken smiled brightly then and gave his favorite teacher a friendly wave as he left the room. "See you tomorrow, Mr. Nightingale."

SMOKEHOUSE

KEN RAN INTO HENRY outside of Jackson Hall. It was lunchtime, and they walked together to the dining hall along with dozens of other boys who'd just gotten out of class. It was a crisp, fall day. The sky was light blue with no clouds, and the oak trees on the Lawn were turning.

"What did you just have?" Ken asked.

"Mackie's English."

"How's that going?"

"Not so good. I got an F on my first paper, and a C-plus on my second."

"Mackie is a dick. He tries to make you feel like you're an idiot in the beginning. He'll ease up after a while."

"I've never gotten a C in my life," Henry grumbled. "Let alone an F."

"Half my class had F's going into their final exam first term. They all passed."

"That makes me feel better, I guess." But it didn't make Henry feel better. 'Passing' wasn't what he was hoping for. Plus, he suspected that Ken had gotten an A his first term with Mackie.

In the distance Henry saw Wobbly, Wales and some of the others from Mackie's class walking up the steps to the dining hall. When they reached the doors Wobbly and Wales looked back for Henry. Wobbly groused at the sight of Ken but waved to Henry and motioned inside, as if to ask whether he should save Henry a seat; Henry gave Wobbly a thumbs up. Tom Wales didn't wave or walk into the dining hall with Wobbly; he only watched. Henry knew what Wobbly thought about him hanging out with Ken; he wondered what Wales and the other new boys thought.

"I just had Nightingale's AP English class with Gordon." Ken said.

"How's that?"

Ken tapped his chest with both fists and then raised them briefly to the heavens in praise. "Nightingale's awesome. You definitely want him senior year."

"He's my advisor."

"I know. I saw you sitting with him last Sunday."

"He's kind of formal."

"He just has style." Ken thought about the bowtie Nightingale had worn to class that day and smiled to himself. "The main thing about Nightingale is he's smart as hell but he doesn't treat you like an idiot."

Opposite of Mackie, Henry said to himself. "How's Gordon doing?"

"Eh." Ken shrugged. "He's like a whetstone."

Henry looked at Ken curiously. "What does that mean?"

Ken smiled. "Good for sharpening your wits on."

Henry laughed. "You know he warned me about hanging out with you."

Ken stopped walking and looked at Henry sharply. "What did he say?"

"He said you're a stoner, and that you hang out with stoners."

Ken's expression suddenly darkened, and Henry smiled, thinking that Ken was only pretending to be upset. But Ken abruptly turned away and strode towards the dining hall at a quicker pace than before.

"You're kidding, right?" Henry said as he caught up to Ken.

Ken said nothing for several strides, then suddenly stopped and looked Henry full in the face. "I don't smoke pot," he said angrily.

"What?" Ken's sudden temper confused Henry, and he wondered if he'd offended him somehow. "I don't care if you smoke pot or not," he said.

"That's not the point," Ken said. He pressed his fists against his chin in consternation. "I hang out with stoners because they're funny. Who else am I supposed to hang out with? The jocks? Please." Ken shook his head, then looked up at the sky as if to seek counsel before he continued walking. "That cracks me up. Warning you about stoners. Half the prefects smoked before their election."

Henry blinked. Half the prefects? he wondered. "How do you know that?"

"I hang out with stoners, remember? Where do you think those boys get their stuff?"

Not far from the dining hall they crossed paths with Uly, who had a brush broom slung over his shoulder. Walking beside him was a small dog, a mutt, that looked like a cross between a terrier and a chihuahua.

"Hey Uly!" Ken yelped.

Uly looked up and waved his broom in the boys' direction. "Hi-i-i-i-i."

"I love that man," Ken said.

"Do you know him?" Henry asked, surprised.

"Not at all." Ken looked at Henry, expecting him to make some cutting remark, something about claiming to love someone he didn't even know. Something like what Ken himself might say. When Henry offered nothing, Ken added, "And that's a damn shame, isn't it?"

Henry watched Uly walk in the direction of the outer dorms. He noticed that every now and then Uly would look down, smile, and say something to the dog, and the dog was always looking up at Uly, listening.

"Does everyone call him Uly?" Henry asked.

"That's his name. What are they supposed to call him? 'Boy'?"

"No. No. I mean does everyone call him by his name?"

"Everyone who's not an asshole," Ken said.

Henry tried again. "What's his last name?"

"Good question," Ken looked at his young friend and smiled. "You are full of surprises for a Palmer, aren't you?"

Henry laughed. "Only if you have low expectations."

They continued on until just before they reached the steps to the dining hall, when Ken stopped at the junction to a pathway that led to the brick courtyard behind the Randolph Building.

"You got a free period?" Ken asked.

"Yeah."

"Then why don't you come with me."

"Where're you going?"

"To The Smokehouse. I'll introduce you to my stoner friends."

"But I don't smoke," Henry said.

"You don't have to smoke to go to the Smokehouse. You only have to have your parents' permission to smoke."

"I don't have my parents' permission."

Ken shrugged. "Then don't smoke."

"Do you smoke?" Henry asked.

Ken reached into his jacket pocket and pulled out a pack of filtered Camels. "It was the last thing my parents agreed on before the divorce. Takes me back to happier times."

The Smokehouse wasn't a house. It wasn't even a structure. It was simply a wooden bench and a trash can in the corner of a brick courtyard surrounded on three sides by the Randolph Building. Ken and Henry joined a cluster of five boys who stood around the bench underneath a cloud of tobacco smoke. All of them were fifth or sixth formers. Henry recognized John Gillespie from Goldsboro. His father owned tobacco warehouses and had attended Randolph with Henry's father; they'd met at an Episcopal game years ago. Most of the other boys he knew by reputation. There was Billy Richardson, whose father was some kind of hotshot banker in Charlotte. There was Tom Coker, whose father was an orthopedic surgeon in Atlanta and a member of Augusta National. There was Jeff Lando, whose family was said to own a large chunk of the Mississippi Delta. And then there was Bob Coogan, a huge kid from the mountains of Virginia that everyone called "Mongo".

Altogether the Smokehouse gang was an unlikely mishmash of boys, but they did have three things in common: a taste for cigarettes, a distaste for football, and a lust for the stinky weed. Ken stepped into the circle and got a light from Richardson. "Guys, this here's Henry Palmer, Gordon Palmer's little brother, that I told you about. He lives next to me on B Dorm and he's all right — despite the brother."

Henry nodded to the group.

"You know everyone here?"

"Yeah. I think so. I mean we haven't met — I've met John before, but the rest of you ... Yeah."

Ken pointed at Mongo, who was smoking a clove cigarette. The boy was a colossus, a full head taller than Gillespie, who was forward on the basketball team. Even more remarkable was his beard, thick and bushy, like a full grown man's.

"You've met Bob?"

"I thought his name was Mongo," Henry said.

Everyone laughed, and Coker punched Mongo in the shoulder. "MONGO!"

The colossus himself giggled.

"No, Grasshopper," Ken corrected, indulgently. "He's Bob to you."

"Sorry," Henry said. "Someone told me your name was Mongo."

"You can call me Mongo," Coogan said. "I just don't like it when people I don't know call me Mongo."

"Mongo have deep feelings!" Coker said, and all the boys laughed.

Everyone knew of Mongo — the strongest boy on campus and its biggest stoner. Before the Blazing Saddles moniker stuck, he'd gone by Bear, because practically every inch of him was thick with muscle and hair. Legend had it that he'd started shaving in Sixth Grade, and he could lift anything — vending machines, boys two in each arm, fallen trees, the rear end of Mr. Mackie's Volkswagen van.

"I wanted Henry to meet all of you, because Gordon warned his little brother not to hang out with stoners."

"Palmer can kiss my ass," Billy Richardson said.

"Gordon's been kissing ass his entire life," Gillespie said. "No offense, Henry."

"Then I take it back," Richardson said. "I don't want just anyone to kiss my ass."

Ken turned to Henry. "Billy has Gordon issues."

Henry didn't say anything, but he now wished he hadn't mentioned Gordon's comment to Ken. He didn't like Gordon telling him who to hang out with, but he also didn't like people tee-ing off on his brother. Fortunately, Mongo changed the subject.

"Oh — oh!" Mongo said, bouncing up and down on the toes of his feet and pointing to the sky to locate his thought. "You got to hear this bootleg tape I got!"

"What is it?"

"The Dead at Fillmore East."

"Which show?"

"February 13, 1970."

"No way!"

Coker and Lando high-fived each other, and sparked by their enthusiasm, Mongo did a pirouette. Henry took a step back to avoid Mongo's spinning elbow.

"Way dude!"

"Where'd you get it?"

"I met this chick in Blacksburg over the summer. She's been traveling with the Dead for like five years. She said she had bootlegs of all their shows. Said she was at the Fillmore East show. Said she plugged into the soundboard and had her own tape and everything. I gave her twenty bucks for it."

"Twenty bucks? Dude!"

"Are you kidding me? It's Fillmore East, February 13."

"Some hippie chick you met at a Dead show?"

"Yeah, but man, she was awesome! She was, like, better than awesome! She was, like, the coolest chick I ever met in my life!"

"Mongo, you're from Deep Gap and go to an all-boy's school," Ken said.

"Naw, man, I'm telling you. She told me I should get on the bus."

"Be a Deadhead?"

"Fucking-A!"

"With her?

"Fucking-A!"

"Why didn't you?"

Mongo fell silent. His hands drifted to his sides, and his shoulders slumped. He stared first at the boys, then at the school building around them. Tears welled up in his eyes. "I don't know, man. I don't know. I think I fucked up."

Jeff Lando put an arm around Mongo's shoulder and shook him. "No, man. You did the right thing. We need you here, Mongo."

"Yeah, dude. You bring the buzz," Richardson added.

Ken reached across the circle of boys and patted Mongo on the shoulder. "What does Jerry tell you?"

Mongo blinked the tears from his eyes and stared at Ken for a moment as he searched his brain's vast archive of Grateful Dead songs. Soon, he began to sway, first his shoulders back and forth as if in prayer, then his feet, one step up and then the other, one step back and then the other.

"There is a road, no simple highway," Mongo said in a hushed tone, "between the dawn and the dark of night." And his voice grew slowly louder as he grew more confident in his choice. "And if you go, no one may follow," and he smiled as he recognized just how appropriate his words were for himself, standing here, in a courtyard of The Randolph School. And his voice rang out, "That path is for your steps alone." And then he was singing:

> Ripple in still water,
> When there is no pebble tossed,
> Nor wind to blow.

All of the boys laughed, both out of embarrassment and out of happiness, and Mongo wiped the tears from his cheeks and let loose a deep guffaw.

"You guys gotta hear Jerry on *Dark Star*. It's like, man, twenty minutes of jamming bliss, like, man, nothing you've ever heard before."

Mongo closed his eyes then and started twirling, colliding with Gillespie and Richardson and knocking them backwards. He twirled in the midst of them, round and round like a dervish, all the while singing a song that Henry had never heard before. Something about a nightlight, or a lovelight—Henry couldn't quite make out the words. And as Mongo continued twirling, Ken waved so long to the others, and he and Henry left the group and walked into the Randolph Building.

As they stepped into the hallway that ran the length of the ground floor, Henry moved closer to Ken and lowered his voice. "Is he high?" Henry asked.

"He's Mongo."

"Does that mean, yes?"

"That means if he's not high right now, he soon will be."

Henry laughed and tried to imagine what Gordon would say if he saw him talking to Mongo. "Do you listen to the Dead?"

"Only when I have to."

"Not your cup of tea?"

Ken arched one eyebrow and nodded to Henry in confidence. "Let's just say a little too much weed in the bowl."

They walked past the phone room and turned up the steps leading to the dining hall. Henry could hear the hum of boys ahead and smell the hamburgers and french fries. He knew that he'd be joining his friends at the new boy table and Ken would join the drama kids at theirs and so he spoke hurriedly.

"I like *Ripple,* but I've never understood what it means."

Ken stopped just outside the doors to the dining hall and gestured to Henry with the first two fingers of his right hand like a cleric. "You're paying too much attention to the words. Forget about the words. Just listen to the sound and feel the feeling. That's the music. That's the Grateful Dead."

Henry nodded excitedly. "Mongo makes it sound like some sort of religion."

Ken laughed. "You're getting it. For him, it's sailing into the mystic."

He patted Henry's arm, and they stepped into the dining hall and went their separate ways.

LAWTON MEETS DEEMER

HAD KEN AND HENRY LOOKED UP while they were still standing at the Smokehouse, they would have seen a solemn figure dressed in a black shirt and clerical collar at a window roughly twelve feet above their heads. The Rev. Frank Deemer's office overlooked the Smokehouse, and this afternoon Rev. Deemer surveilled the gathering with predictable disapproval.

"Does Gordon Palmer know that his brother, Henry, is hanging out with the smokers?" The question was posed to Lawton Faison, whom Deemer had summoned to his office.

Lawton joined Deemer at the window and looked down. "Probably not."

"I think it might be very good of you to let him know."

"Sure thing," Lawton said, but he had no intention of telling Gordon anything—Gordon could go to hell. He was pleased, however, to see Henry Palmer straying from the narrow path.

Deemer checked out the faces of the other boys, most of whom had been his students in New Testament class, which was mandatory for fifth formers. "What are John Gillespie and Billy Richardson doing with that group?" Deemer asked, alarmed that two of his Chapel Council officers were smoking cigarettes with the likes of Bob Coogan.

"They smoke," Lawton said matter-of-factly. "I'm sure they have their parents' permission. Henry Palmer not so much."

"He's a fourth former—not eligible for permission."

"And his father wouldn't give it even if he could."

Deemer nodded. "Rightly so," he said. He lifted a finger to the windowpane and pointed at Ken Bright. "Who's the skinny boy in a t-shirt?"

"Ken Bright," Lawton said.

Deemer frowned disapprovingly at the boy's pinned collar. "Fifth former?" he asked.

"Sixth former," Lawton said.

"Why hasn't he taken my New Testament class?"

"Don't know."

"He's not Jewish, is he?"

"Probably," Lawton said.

Jewish students were sometimes given exemptions from attending Deemer's class. In the case of Ken Bright, however, a scheduling conflict—AP Physics—had thus far spared him Deemer's particular brand of hellfire and damnation; he was set to take New Testament in the spring.

"What is Bob Coogan doing?" Deemer asked Lawton.

They watched Mongo spin round and round and round.

"He's twirling," Lawton said.

"I can see that."

"It's a Grateful Dead thing."

Deemer snorted. "That makes sense." Among the faculty, Mongo was the student most suspected of smoking marijuana; Rev. Deemer considered him beyond redemption.

Deemer turned away from the window and walked back to his desk, which was bare except for a single file folder. "Have a seat, Lawton." He gestured to the wooden armchair across from his desk.

As a fifth form member of the Chapel Council, Lawton had not had occasion to visit Rev. Deemer's office last year. Now that he was head of the Chapel Council, Lawton would be meeting with the reverend once a week to review the upcoming service, to confirm the hymn numbers that were to be posted in the chapel, and to assign the readers for the scripture lessons. He and Deemer had agreed to meet every Wednesday for this purpose, and he'd been surprised to find a note from Deemer in his box this morning — Tuesday — requesting a meeting today.

Deemer waited for Lawton to take a seat, then sat down himself in his plush, leather office chair. "I wanted to see you to share some very good news." He tapped the folder on his desk and smiled at the boy. "Yesterday the school received the final commitment from the Class of 1946, and we can now move forward with installation of the stained glass window."

Some years ago the school had commissioned a stained glass window to be installed in honor of Lawton's Uncle Thomas Faison, based on assurances from the Faison family that they would provide any and all necessary funds for the project. Although often late with their installments, the family had paid the initial deposit and all of the progress payments up until three years ago, when Lawton Faison Sr. had informed the school that the family now preferred that the window be styled as a gift from the Class of 1946 rather than from the Faison family per se. In order to fulfill their contract with the manufacturer, the school had been forced to solicit funds from Uncle Thomas's surviving classmates, whose ardor for the project had proved to be less keen than expected.

Rev. Deemer, who had not been on the faculty when the project was first commissioned, had played no role in either ordering the window or overseeing its manufacture. Although he had his suspicions about the reasons for the Faison family's change of heart, neither Mr. Endicott nor anyone in the development office had shared with him any details relating to Mr. Faison's communications about their financial commitment. Nor had they asked Rev. Deemer for his opinion on the subject. Nevertheless, when Mr. Endicott had informed him yesterday that the school had finally secured the funding necessary to move forward with the installation, Rev. Deemer had sensed an opportunity to be of additional service to the school. He asked Mr. Endicott if he himself might not break the news to Lawton, noting that Lawton was head of the

Chapel Council and suggesting that he was a sort of spiritual advisor to the boy. "Go ahead. Tell the scoundrel," Endicott had responded. "Maybe the son will receive the news with greater grace than the father." Rev. Deemer did not expect Lawton to confide in him, but he did hope the boy might display some emotion that would provide a clue to any change in the family's fortunes.

Lawton yawned. "Dad told me last night," he said.

"I know this has been a long time coming for your family."

Lawton nodded.

"Your father must have been pleased."

"Dad wanted the commission to include his classmates," Lawton said, and brushed a piece of lint off his pants leg.

"Isn't it wonderful when your classmates come through for you?"

Lawton put the back of his hand to his mouth. Deemer watched him closely. What was he hiding, he wondered. A smile? A grimace? Then Lawton yawned again.

"Sorry," the boy said. "Late night last night."

Deemer decided to move on. "I couldn't agree with your father more. Mr. Endicott has sent a copy of the final design to your father, but I thought you'd like to see it yourself."

Deemer opened the folder and passed a color photo of the stained glass window across his desk. The window depicted Jesus standing in a resplendent red cape and wearing a golden crown of glory. His left hand held a scepter, and his right hand pointed to the heavens.

"It's Christ the King," Deemer explained.

Lawton leaned over to get a closer look. "What's he doing with his fingers?"

Jesus's right forefinger and middle finger were pointing up, and his other fingers were crossed in a peculiar manner.

"He's blessing us and pointing the way."

"Why are those fingers crossed?" Lawton pointed to the little fingers.

"It's spelling out his name."

"What?"

"It's abbreviated," Deemer explained. "In Greek. Jesus is IC, and Christ is XC. The fingers pointed up are Jesus. The crossed fingers are Christ."

Lawton looked again. Now he saw it. Just like Ichthys, he thought. He almost said something but thought better of it.

"Gotcha. … The scepter's cool." He pointed to the bottom of the color photograph. "Why's he barefoot?"

Deemer wondered if the boy had learned anything in his New Testament class. "Because he's Christ, who died on the cross."

Lawton didn't bother to decipher that. "Dad said they wanted to show Jesus on the cross."

"I think that was the original design," Deemer said.

"This is better. He was a soldier. Not a martyr."

Deemer looked at Lawton for clarification. "What?"

"Uncle Thomas. He died at Busan."

"Right," Deemer pointed at the stained glass figure. "This is Christ, the King over Heaven and Earth."

"Sure," Lawton said.

Deemer took a black and white photograph out of the same folder and handed it to Lawton. "Your father gave us this. I believe it was taken shortly before your uncle shipped out."

The photograph showed a group of three soldiers in uniform, their arms around each other's shoulders.

"That's him." Lawton pointed at the soldier in the middle, who, like Lawton, had fine features, striking good looks, and a cocky expression. "Dad says he would have been a general."

"What was his rank?"

"Captain, I think. … I'm not sure."

"West Point?"

"Princeton," Lawton said.

Deemer pointed to the two photographs. "It's a good likeness, isn't it?"

The face of the stained glass Jesus was very much like the face in the photograph, only bearded. Lawton recognized himself in the face of the stained glass Jesus and smiled.

"When's it going to be finished?"

"They plan to begin installing it in February. We'll have a dedication ceremony in the spring."

Deemer put the two photographs back into the folder and placed the folder in his desk drawer. Once again his desktop was empty, and the light from the window reflected off its high gloss. Hanging on the wall behind Deemer were his undergraduate diploma from Campbell College, his MDiv. from Southern Baptist Theological Seminary, and a signed portrait of Billy Graham. On the wall beside the window over-looking the Smokehouse was a framed copy of the Cadet Creed from the Army ROTC. Before seminary, Deemer had fulfilled his ROTC obligation by serving four years as a lieutenant in the U.S. Army. Those years had been the happiest of his life. Deemer had a passion for chain of command and loved rules and order. Sometimes he worried that he'd made a mistake by not re-enlisting, but his job here carried its own opportunities for promotion. Deemer didn't want to be a school pastor forever. His plan was to move up the administrative ladder, either here or at another prep school, and one day assume full command. Headmaster Frank Deemer. Not as good as Lieutenant Colonel, perhaps, but not bad for a ROTC kid from China Grove, NC. Deemer was a long way from China Grove, and he was proud of how far he'd come. But people like Lawton Faison and his family could help him go even farther.

"You know, Lawton, I also wanted to talk to you about your college plans."

The change of subject surprised Lawton. "Pardon?"

"Your choice of college," Deemer repeated. "My good friend, Major Gingrich, is the head of admissions at The Citadel. I would be happy to write to him on your behalf if that's something you'd be interested in. I served under him from 1970 to 1972."

As a new boy, Lawton had caught a whiff of Deemer's low-born origins: the broken nose, the rectangular, gold-framed spectacles, the polyester, sansabelt shorts at football practice. Now that he was sitting in Deemer's office and getting a gander at his Campbell College diploma, the portrait of Billy Graham, and the ROTC creed, Lawton had sized Deemer up. Here was a man from the other side of town, who'd made it this far by dint of hard work, and who probably knew how lucky he was. Lawton could tolerate Deemer's having gotten this far — pluck has its privileges — but Lawton could not tolerate Deemer's presuming to offer him a place at The Citadel like it was a favor.

"I'm going to Princeton," Lawton said. "I had my interview last month. I'm applying early admission."

Deemer had taught Lawton last spring, and he still remembered how surprised he was when he read Lawton's first paper and realized that the boy had done none of the reading and had paid virtually no attention to his lectures. At the end of the term, Deemer had given him a C, which was generous. Princeton seemed beyond his reach.

"I'm just saying. If it would be helpful."

The man is a fool, Lawton thought. "My great-grandfather went to The Citadel and has a building named for him. If I wanted to go to the Citadel I would not need help from your Major Gingrich."

Lawton made no effort to conceal his disdain, and as he said, 'your Major Gingrich' he tossed his right hand into the air as if he were shooing a servant from the room. He stood up.

"Are we done?" Lawton asked. "I have to grab some lunch before next period."

"All done."

Deemer stood up quickly and extended his hand to the boy. He thought that they should congratulate each other on the stained glass window. Lawton seemed to be in a hurry to leave, and for a second Deemer feared that Lawton might refuse to shake his hand, but Lawton recovered himself and even mustered a smile, one very much like his Uncle Thomas's smile in the photograph.

"Thank you, reverend. I'm sure my family is very pleased that the stained glass window will finally be installed."

Deemer watched Lawton walk out of his office. He opened his desk drawer and took out the photo of the stained glass window. He felt some scruple about the school putting Thomas Faison's face on Christ the King — what if the uncle was anything like his nephew? — but his predecessors had agreed to the commission years ago, so the matter was out of his hands. It was a good family, he told himself. It would be fine. He thought about his friend Major Gingrich. He'd re-enlisted. He'd done well for himself, advancing on merit. He rubbed his hands together and cracked his knuckles to comfort himself. Surely he could advance on merit here.

"MAJOR GINGRICH," LAWTON MUTTERED to himself as he stepped into the hallway outside Deemer's office. The presumption that he'd ever need that man's help! Or accept it. Or that he would even consider going to the Citadel! Stupid man! He consoled himself with the photograph of the stained glass. How awesome would that be? There would be his likeness captured in a stained glass window at the head of the chapel, behind the communion table, now and forever. Had his father seen a photograph of the stained glass? He hadn't mentioned it last night. He'd call him. His dad would be happy about the news. And Christ the King!

Lawton didn't go to the cafeteria. He had a free period and walked to the Mess, the student lounge in the basement of the Randolph Building. The Mess was decorated like a hunting lodge with dark wood paneling and wainscotting. There was a large fireplace and mantlepiece along one wall, and mounted above the fireplace was the head and shoulders of a large, six-point, white-tail buck. Legend had it that the deer had been shot on the grounds in the 1930s.

Lawton spotted Tom Wales and Troy Lindsey at one of the foosball tables. "How 'bout a game of foosball?" he called out, motioning to John Gillespie, who had been waiting for him to show up.

Lindsey was a new boy, like Tom, and black, like Tom, but the similarities pretty much ended there. He had grown up in public housing in Clarksdale, MS, where his father gutted catfish for a living and his mother cleaned other people's houses. The husband of his mother's employer was a Randolph graduate; he had helped the boy land a scholarship to the school.

Lawton stepped directly behind Wales and brushed his knee against the back of Wales's leg. Tom lurched forward and bumped the table.

"How's it going, Worm?"

Wales glanced nervously over his shoulder, surprised that Lawton hovered so close and irritated at the nickname — courtesy of Mackie's class. "We're almost done," he said. He shifted his weight away from Lawton then quickly moved his right hand to the goalie handle but not in time to block Lindsey's shot.

"Yes!" Lindsey gloated.

Wales rolled his eyes and thought about demanding a playover. As he bent down to retrieve the ball, Lawton moved forward so that when Wales stood up he bumped against Lawton.

"Sorry," Wales said. He sidestepped toward the center of the table, away from Lawton. "It's 10 to 3, game point for Troy."

"Troy?" Lawton said.

Lindsey lifted a hand and gave Lawton and Gillespie a quick wave, then rocked back and forth, shifting his weight from one foot to the other.

"You don't have a nickname yet, like Worm?" Lawton asked.

"Friends back home call me Bug-eye," Lindsey said nervously.

Lawton considered the boy's big-eyed, hyperthyroidic expression. "I don't think we can improve on that, huh John?"

Gillespie laughed. "Definitely not."

Wales placed the ball in the service hole and started to spin it to his midfield when Lawton took a step forward and pinned him against the table. Wales dropped the ball and grabbed the edge of the table to steady himself. Lawton drove one of his thighs into Wales's buttocks and the table lurched as Wales tried to move away from the pressure. Lawton prevented Wales from escaping by grabbing the table with his left hand and blocking Wales's way with his left arm. Lawton laughed.

Lindsey stepped away from the table, and when Gillespie moved forward, he threw out both hands. "Don't touch me! Don't! Don't!"

Gillespie didn't take another step when he saw the terror on the boy's face. He held his hand to try to calm him. "Settle down. I ain't going to hurt you."

Wales was not so lucky. As he struggled to push himself away from the table, Lawton drove both hands down the back of his pants, grabbed his underwear band and lifted him off the ground.

"— down! down! down!" Wales cried, and he flailed about like a frightened child tossed into the air.

Lawton pivoted and dropped Wales on the floor. Wales's hands broke his fall and he scuttled sideways with his underwear hanging out of his pants.

"Off you go, Worm," Lawton said.

Gillespie motioned to Lindsey, who gave him a wide berth as he walked around the table to Wales's side. Lawton picked up the foosball and dropped it through the service hole.

"We told them we wanted to play foosball," Lawton said. "Some new boys won't learn."

Lawton and Gillespie casually knocked the ball back and forth, neither of them with any enthusiasm.

"Let's go eat! We got to get out of here!" Lindsey grabbed Wales by the wrist and dragged him towards the door. Wales looked back at Lawton, staring daggers.

Wales and Lindsey passed Gordon Palmer as they walked out. Gordon had just come from lunch where he'd made the mistake of putting raw onions on his hamburger bun. He had AP U.S. History with Mr. Endicott next and needed a roll of Certs to cover his breath.

'Hi'ya John, Lawton," Gordon called out on his way to the vending machines. "You got a free period?

"Free as rain," Gillespie said, smiling at Gordon.

Lawton violently spun the handle that controlled his forwards and knocked the ball into Gillespie's goal. "Get your head in the game, John." Lawton retrieved the ball and prepared to serve again.

Gordon noticed that Lawton was ignoring him. Ever since the prefect selection last Spring, Lawton had avoided him. Ned Claiborne had told him about Lawton blocking his nomination to Chapel Council. Gordon wondered just how hostile Lawton now was. He leaned down and grabbed the breath mints. "How'd you do on your Hamlet paper?"

"A-minus," Lawton said. In fact, he'd received a C, but he wasn't going to tell Gordon that. For the same reason, he wasn't going to ask Gordon how he'd done. He figured Gordon must have done well; otherwise, he wouldn't have brought it up.

"Damn," Gordon said. "Good job. I got a B-minus."

"Tough break," Lawton said.

"He said my thesis was weak."

"Not as weak as your Polonius thesis." Lawton smiled at the memory of Gordon's bumbling performance in Nightingale's class. He placed the foosball into the service cup and spun it to his midfielders.

"Thanks a lot," Gordon said.

"Don't you hate Bright?" Lawton asked. He moved the foosball handle back and forth, passing the ball between two midfielders, then expertly flicked it past Gillespie's defenders and knocked it into Gillespie's goal.

"Nice shot," Gordon said. He joined them at the table. "I hate it when he shows me up in class."

"Typical Jew crap."

Gordon frowned. He didn't like Ken, but using a slur was uncalled for. He started to object but stopped himself, because he didn't want to sound sanctimonious. But then saying nothing made it seem like he approved. Finally he equivocated. "What's that supposed to mean?"

"Trying to prove he's the smartest person in the room."

"He probably is the smartest person in the room," Gordon said.

Lawton detected the mild censure in Gordon's voice. What a prick, he thought.

"'Cept for Nightingale."

"Well yeah. There's that."

Lawton looked to the glass doors leading outside and was able to make out his reflection and Gordon's. He stood up straighter and noted the fine figure he cut — lither than Gordon's and lighter. He smiled to himself, retrieved the foosball from the cup underneath Gillespie's goal and tossed it up and down in one hand. "I met with Rev. Deemer just now."

"Oh yeah? What about?"

"We meet once a week, because I'm head of council."

"Lucky you."

Lawton ignored the sarcasm. "He had an interesting piece of news. The school is going to install a new stained glass window in the front of the chapel."

"That'll be cool," Gordon said.

"And the Jesus is going to look like my uncle."

"What's that supposed to mean?"

"It means what I said. The window company or whoever the hell makes these things is making Jesus look like my Uncle Thomas."

"That seems weird," Gordon said.

"The chapel is named for him."

"Yeah. I know, but —." Gordon paused to consider why exactly it seemed weird to him…. Making Jesus look like a Faison. That was it, but he decided not to say that.

"It has to look like somebody," Lawton said. "You can't make a convincing Jesus that looks like a made up person."

"Don't want a velvet Jesus," Gillespie chimed in.

"Exactly," Lawton said.

"I guess so." Gordon sounded skeptical.

"The funny thing is," Lawton said, and he faced Gordon to be sure to see his reaction, "my uncle looks just like me."

Gordon made no effort to hide his reaction now. "You mean like he stepped out of a goddamn L.L. Bean catalog?"

"No, dipshit. I mean we have the same face. My mother always said I was his spitting image. Like I'm his resurrection."

Gordon laughed. "Don't you mean reincarnation?"

"You know what I mean," Lawton said.

"Right on!" Gillespie held up his hand, and Lawton gave him a high-five. "Praise Lawton!" Gillespie said in a fake preacher's voice.

Gordon watched Lawton and Gillespie congratulate one another and decided against sharing his thoughts on the subject. He popped two Certs into his mouth. "Off to class," he said.

"What you got?" Gillespie asked.

"A.P. U.S. History with Endicott."

"Damn," Gillespie said. "You don't know how to take a rest, do you son?"

Gordon smiled. He liked Gillespie. He gave them a wave and walked out.

"Arrogant prick," Lawton said.

"He's all right. What do you have against Gordon?"

Lawton recalled something his father had said about Gordon's family over the summer. 'The Palmers made their money foreclosing on farmers a hundred years ago. Shitty kind of business, but it explains why Gordon acts like a banker. Dull. No style.'

"He reminds me of Levin."

"Who the fuck is Levin?" Gillespie said.

His mother had given him *Anna Karenina* to read over the summer, and he'd hated it at first. It was boring, but his mother swore that it was her favorite book. So he'd kept reading. For her sake. And then he'd fallen in love with Count Vronsky, the dashing cavalry officer. He despised Levin, whom he'd identified as Gordon. None of this was worth explaining to Gillespie. "Nobody," he said. "Nevermind."

Lawton looked again at his reflection in the glass doors behind the foosball table. Slim. Erect. He liked the lines of his hunting jacket. He could be a catalog model if he wanted — unlike Gordon, who was all blocky.

The really irritating thing about Gordon was that he was also applying to Princeton, and being Head Boy he was almost sure to get in. That didn't help Lawton's chances. Nightingale wanted him to have backups. He'd even suggested SC — Fuck that! Lawton thought. Gordon goes to Princeton and I go to SC? Dad would love that! Funny how doing what daddy wants seemed to be working out for Gordon but not for me, Lawton thought. Mr. Palmer might be dull as a banker but at least he's not a class A prick. "It's going to be a huge disappointment if you can't get into Princeton, son," his father had told him. Sorry I didn't turn out like Gordon, dad, Lawton thought. From the look of things at the Smokehouse, Gordon's little brother's not turning out like Gordon either, he thought.

"What's Henry Palmer like?" Lawton asked Gillespie.

"Seems like a good kid."

"I saw him standing around with you and Billy in the Smokehouse today."

Gillespie laughed. "Yeah. Bright brought him by. He said Gordon doesn't want him hanging around with stoners."

"Bright said that?"

"He said Gordon told Henry that."

"Prick. What did Henry say?"

Gillespie shrugged. "He didn't deny it."

Lawton smiled. "Didn't you say Richardson scored some Panama Red off Mongo?"

"Yes I did." Gillespie put his thumb and forefinger together to the edge of his mouth and took an imaginary toke.

"I think we should invite young Henry Palmer to join us on the golf course tomorrow night," Lawton said.

"You sure?" Gillespie asked.

Lawton nodded. "I have a feeling he might be perfect for Ichthys."

THE RANDOLPH SCHOOL SAT ON A HILL surrounded by miles of wood-
lands and rolling pasture. The Blue Ridge Mountains shaped the west-
ern horizon in the distance while the eastern horizon was defined by a
nearer wooded hillside behind the far bank of the Rapidan River. During
daytime the campus was a remote, sun-kissed garden, but when night
came darkness swallowed it like Jonah's whale.

Earlier that day, John Gillespie had sidled up to Henry in the lunch
line and whispered, "You wanna get high tonight?" Henry had never
smoked pot in his life and at first wasn't sure what Gillespie was talking
about, but when Gillespie said, "Mongo scored some Panama Red," Henry felt like his heart would leap out of his chest.

"Sure," he muttered and looked around to see if anyone was
watching.

"Okay. Meet me at the post office at 9 o'clock and we'll walk to the
golf course."

The rest of the day Henry had trouble concentrating. At first, he worried that someone might have overheard Gillespie and that he would be
pulled out of class for questioning. Then he worried that Gillespie had
told someone else and that person had told someone and on and on until the words fell into the ear of a master, like Mackie, that Henry Palmer,
Gordon Palmer's brother, smoked pot. Next he worried that he might be
one of those people he'd heard about who have a bad reaction to pot
and do something crazy like jump out of a window or run in front of a
car. (He'd comforted himself with the reminder that he'd be standing
in the middle of a golf course with no one and nothing nearby.) Finally,
he was left with the thought that he really had no idea how to smoke
pot and that when the time came he'd probably do something stupid
and the upper formers would laugh at him. He didn't want to look like
an idiot when someone passed him a joint. He'd almost gone to Ken's
room between supper and Study Hall to ask him how it was done. But
then he didn't know if it was supposed to be a big secret and if telling
Ken would violate some doper's code that he didn't know about. In the
end, Henry decided that it was better to keep the pot smoking plan to
himself. That way, if things turned out badly, Ken wouldn't be involved.

The post office was located in the basement of the Randolph

Building. Henry arrived there a little early and pretended to read a copy of The Washington Post that someone had thrown away. Gillespie arrived a short time later, wearing a down jacket and a toboggan cap. He tossed a bag of potato chips to Henry. "Munchies," he said. "Let's go."

They walked out into the darkness. Gillespie led him along a box-wood hedge toward the chapel then turned right through a break in the hedge and headed downhill onto the golf course. At first Henry kept looking over his shoulder to see if they were being followed. The lights from the dorm rooms made the Randolph Building glow in the darkness, and Henry could hear music and voices coming from that direction. But as soon as they passed through the hedge and headed downhill they lost sight of the building and were cast into an outer darkness that forced Henry to speed up in order to keep sight of Gilles-pie. There was no moon that night, and Henry had trouble seeing more than a few yards in any direction, but Gillespie knew where he was headed. He never slowed down as they traversed the fairway, down the hill, towards a small band of cedars. Suddenly, Henry could hear voices, and in the flash of a lighter he made out a group of five or six boys standing in a circle.

"Boo-yah," Gillespie called out.

"Boo-yah," several of them called back.

Henry and Gillespie joined the circle. All the boys except Henry wore dark caps. Even at close quarters Henry was only able to make out the face of Billy Richardson when he flicked his lighter and held it to the bowl of the short wooden pipe in his mouth.

"This weed is righteous," someone said.

The pipe bowl brightened as Richardson drew in a long breath. He removed the pipe from his lips, took in a short breath and straightened up, as if the smoke had struck him between the shoulder blades. He held the pipe out to Gillespie. Henry watched Gillespie closely as he first checked the flame by placing one hand over the bowl and then took in a long deep breath through the pipe. Henry took the pipe from Gillespie and watched him lift his chin and exhale the sweet smoke into the night sky.

"Don't let the bowl burn out," someone said.

Henry quickly put the pipe to his lips and drew in, but no smoke came through.

"Aw man, you're wasting it."

"It's out. I killed it," Gillespie said. "Here, give me the pipe." Gillespie took the pipe from Henry and tapped it against the palm of his hand to empty the bowl. "Who's got the bag?" he asked.

A boy across the circle handed Gillespie a plastic baggie. Gillespie rocked it up and down in his hand to weigh it. "Nickle bag?" he asked.

"You wish. Paid Mongo twenty bucks, but it's the real stuff. Panama Red!"

Gillespie removed a pinch of weed and stuffed it into the bowl with his finger. He handed the pipe back to Henry and pulled a lighter out of his pocket. "I'll give you a light. Breathe in nice and slow."

Henry put the pipe to his lips and watched Gillespie flick his lighter and hold the flame to the end of the pipe.

"Start dragging," Gillespie said.

Henry pulled in his breath and felt the hot smoke hit the back of his throat and then his lungs. The sudden burn surprised him, and he coughed violently and dropped the pipe on the ground."

"Shit!" someone said.

Henry's eyes welled up with tears which he wiped away with the back of his hand. He dropped to his knees to look for the pipe. He reached for a small burning clump beside his foot, thinking that it was the end of the pipe, but instead it was the burning nub of weed that had fallen out of the bowl. The nub burned his fingers and he dropped it again onto the ground.

The person standing to Henry's left bent down, flicked on a lighter and found the pipe. He reached across Henry for the baggie Gillespie was holding, tamped some more weed into the bowl and handed the pipe to Henry. He flicked his lighter and held it out for Henry. When Henry leaned over to light the bowl he saw Lawton Faison's face in the light of the flame. Henry pulled back.

"What are you doing here?"

Lawton laughed. "Don't worry. I won't tell Gordon. I told John to bring you. You know John and Billy," Lawton pointed to Gillespie and Richardson. Henry knew Gillespie through his family, and he'd met Richardson at the Smokehouse. "And that's Willis and Jackson." Lawton pointed to the two boys standing directly across the circle from Henry. "What's it been, two years?"

"Something like that."

Lawton flicked the lighter again. "Take it easy this time. If it's too hot, take the pipe out of your mouth and suck in the night air."

Henry nodded. He watched the bowl as he sucked in, and he stopped sucking as soon as he saw the bowl glow red. He held his breath and handed the pipe to Lawton. Lawton took a long drag and passed the pipe around the circle. Henry waited for Lawton to exhale, then exhaled himself.

"First time?" Lawton asked.

Henry nodded.

"First time I smoked pot was right here as well. Gordon and I came down with Jim Cooter and smoked a joint."

"Gordon smokes pot?" Henry asked.

"Fuckin' A," Richardson said. "I betcha I got stoned with Gordon half a dozen times new boy year. Then last year he decides he wants to be Head Boy, and it's like I'm a leper. We go from best buddies to 'we can't be friends anymore.' Your brother's a two-faced bastard."

"Gordon's wanted to be Head Boy since he was probably ten years old," Henry said.

"Dream big," someone said sarcastically.

"But it took him 'til last year to figure out he couldn't have friends," Lawton said. He turned to the other boys in the circle. "This little punk comes down to Sullivan's Island with Gordon and says to me, 'I wanna water ski.' I said, 'Okay. Have you ever water skied before?' He says, 'Nope.' Like it's the simplest thing in the world. So I decide I'm going to teach him a lesson and take him out on a choppy day, and goddammit if I can't get him to spill. By the end of the day he's getting up on one ski."

"Mr. Natural," Gillespie said and toasted Henry with the pipe.

"Fuck that Mr. Natural shit," Lawton said. "That's for hippies and potheads."

"Isn't that what we're doing here?" Gillespie said with a laugh.

"We're not potheads. We just smoke pot sometimes."

"And the difference is?"

"We're not hippies. Right Henry?"

Henry, who was already starting to feel the eerie effects of the weed, nodded. He wasn't agreeing with Lawton necessarily; he just didn't want to try to talk right now.

"So our fathers used to be like best friends, right Henry?"

Henry nodded. That was correct.

"They were like roommates here and at Princeton, right?"

Henry nodded again.

"Used to be that me and Gordon were buddies too, but like Billy said, once Gordon decided he wanted to be Head Boy it was, 'Sorry, Lawton. I don't have time for you anymore.'"

"It's not like we're dying to hang with Gordon," Gillespie said, pointing to the lit pipe in his right hand.

"My point is that just because me and Gordon don't get along anymore, there's no reason why you and I shouldn't."

"Sure," Henry stammered. He was surprised and flattered. Lawton was definitely one of the big names on campus, and though he knew their parents were friends he had expected Lawton to ignore him the way all sixth formers ignore new boys, except to harass them.

"Is it true you got kicked out of school for drinking?" Richardson said.

"Where did you hear that?" Henry said.

"Lawton told us."

Lawton laughed. "Gordon told me last year that you'd been caught drinking and your parents were sending you here."

"I didn't get kicked out," Henry said. "It's a public school. I just got sent home."

"What was it?" Jackson asked.

"What was what?"

"What were you drinking?"

"Schlitz Malt Liquor."

The boys erupted in laughter and congratulated him. Two of the boys, who'd gotten an earlier start, continued giggling for no apparent reason.

"Righteous!"

"The Champagne of Beers!"

"That's Miller."

"Whatever."

"How would you like to join us?" Lawton was looking at Henry.

"Us?" Henry asked.

Lawton pointed to the circle of people around him.

Henry was confused. Did he mean now, or later, or what? "And do what?" he asked. "Smoke pot on the golf course?"

Gillespie handed Henry the pipe, which had made its way around. Lawton watched Henry hold the pipe with the burning bowl. Henry looked at Lawton. Lawton looked at Henry. Suddenly, Lawton laughed at what Henry had said.

"No," Lawton said. He motioned at the burning pipe in Henry's hand. "Don't waste the cherry."

Henry stared at Lawton, unsure of what he'd heard and what it meant.

Lawton nodded. "Take another hit."

Henry cupped one hand over the bowl, just like he'd seen Billy do, and took another drag. This time he alternated between keeping his lips on the pipestem and taking them off to control the burn.

"We got a secret society called the Sign of the Fish," Lawton continued. "D'you know about 'sign of the fish'?"

Henry shook his head and exhaled. "Nu-uh." He handed Lawton the pipe.

Lawton said something about "early Christians." Henry watched him take another hit then hold up one hand and with the pipe draw an arc on his palm. Henry laughed, and Lawton laughed at Henry laughing. Lawton said, "If you're a Christian you draw another arc," he said, or something like that, and then drew another arc on his hand with the pipe until one of the other boys said, "Stop wasting the weed, Faison!" and Lawton laughed, and Henry laughed, and Richardson stepped forward and took the pipe out of Lawton's hand.

Henry had a sudden dizzy spell and he reached out to Lawton and Gillespie to steady himself. Gillespie grabbed him with both hands.

"Whoa there big fellow," Gillespie said.

Henry stood as still as possible, until his equilibrium vibrated back into place and the people around him stopped spinning. He wondered whether he'd passed out. Lawton was talking, but his words slipped through his mind like seasurf on the sand.

"... not enough rules ... the right sort of person ... tradition matters ... God willing ..." At some point he took Henry by the elbow and turned him so that they were facing each other. "Can I count on you ... can we count on you ... can we count you in ... can you count ...?"

And then suddenly everyone was walking back up the hill toward the Randolph Building in order to get back to their dorm rooms before lights out. Henry kept his head down and concentrated on keeping his feet moving and not bumping into the person in front of him. The group split up outside the Randolph Building. Lawton grabbed Henry's arm and said, "We'll talk more." Henry nodded. Most of the boys headed off to the outer dormitories, and Henry found himself walking up the back staircase to B Dorm, then stumbling along the hallway and into his room. Wobbly stood at his dresser with a toothbrush and a towel. Henry suddenly worried that he reeked of pot.

"Where have you been? I looked for you at the Mess."

"I walked to Lauderdale to see Gordon."

"What happened to you? You look terrible. Your eyes are bloodshot."

Henry stepped into the closet to get away from Wobbly; he pretended to look for something. "Allergies," he mumbled.

"Did you finish your paper for Mackie? I wrote three pages, and it's pretty good stuff."

"Uh-huh." Henry remembered working on a paper. He thought he'd finished it. He pulled the front of his jacket up to his nose and smelled it. Definitely reeked. Then he tried to remember the question Wobbly had asked. Nevermind. Wobbly was talking again.

"The ego is what we want to happen. It's the choices we make, controls our behavior, right? The superego keeps us in line. And the id is like all the crazy shit that we do sometimes for no reason. Am I right?"

"Sounds good," Henry mumbled. That was the Freud paper. Henry remembered now. He'd written something about the unconscious that night in the library, but he couldn't remember a thing about it.

"Mackie is going to love it!" Wobbly walked out of the room and down the hall to the bathroom.

Henry went to the dresser and stared at his eyes. They were bloodshot. He felt the room spinning. He opened the top drawer to Wobbly's dresser. He didn't find anything to eat, but he did find a photograph of a girl with Farrah Fawcett wings that Wobbly had cut out of his junior high yearbook. There was a red heart around her head. This must be that Bridget girl Wobbly was always talking about — not as pretty as Henry had imagined.

Henry remembered his mother had mailed him a care package, and he went back to the closet to find the cookie tin containing his mother's homemade peanut brittle. As he bent down to open the box he lost his balance and fell into the closet, knocking the clothes rack off its hook and tumbling the shirts and jackets onto the floor. He thrashed about, and by the time he managed to roll over, Ken was standing in the closet doorway looking down on him.

"Look what the cat drug in," Ken said.

Henry held out his hand. "Help me get out of here," he mumbled. The walls of the closet were falling down on him.

Ken pulled Henry to his feet and looked him over. "You need some Visine, and you need to stash that coat. It reeks."

Ken guided Henry out of the closet and into his own room and closed the door. He sat Henry down on the bed and found a bottle of eyedrops. Henry reached out for the bottle, but Ken pushed his hand away. "Better let me," he said.

Ken sat down beside Henry and put a hand to Henry's chin to tip his head back. Ken watched Henry's eyes open wide and his lips part in anticipation. At first, Ken thought Henry might say something, but Henry was only waiting for the drops to fall, and Ken squeezed the bottle slightly and watched two drops fall into one of Henry's eyes. Henry blinked and his head moved. Ken touched his chin to steady him, and Henry looked up again and received two drops in the other eye. Ken smiled as he watched Henry blink and tears roll down each cheek.

"How do you feel?"

"Like I just stepped off the Zipper," Henry said, referring to a particularly nauseating carnival ride. He made several kissing motions with his mouth. "You got anything to drink?"

"Cottonmouth?

Henry nodded.

Ken handed him the mug that was sitting on his desk, and Henry drank its contents.

"What is that?" Henry asked.

"Chamomile tea."

"Huh." Henry had never heard of it. He handed the mug back to Ken.

"Mongo's stuff?" Ken asked.

"That's what they said."

"Head still spinning?"

Henry nodded.

Ken clicked his tongue against his teeth. "You need counter-rotational therapy."

"What?"

"The whole room is spinning one way, right?" Ken held up his finger and rotated it one direction in the air.

Henry nodded.

Ken now rotated his finger in the other direction. "We got to get you spinning the other way."

Ken picked up the headphones on the receiver across from the bed and started to put them on Henry, but Henry held out his hands.

"No-no-no-no!" Henry felt like he would throw up if he heard loud music.

"Relax." Ken smiled at him. "This will stop your world from spinning."

Henry let Ken put the headphones on his head.

"Now close your eyes."

Henry closed his eyes. At first he heard nothing. Then he heard the needle drop onto the album, and then the clear, melodic line of Debussey's *The Girl with the Flaxen Hair*. Henry followed the simple solitary notes up and down, sometimes quickening, sometimes slowing, through a small stand of trees to a fresh meadow at daybreak or dusk, either one, and the buzz in his head diminished, diminished, slowly diminished, until it finally disappeared. When the music was over Henry stood up, handed the headphones back to Ken and, without saying a word, slipped back into his room and climbed into bed. Wobbly was there and almost surely babbled something, but Henry paid it no attention. He simply closed his eyes, went to sleep, and dreamed that he was far, far away from The Randolph School.

NIGHTINGALE AT HOME

DAVID NIGHTINGALE CARRIED a plastic container out the kitchen door and walked toward the old walnut tree in his backyard. He looked up into the morning sky and, not seeing anything, gave out a "Yawp! Yawp!" A short while later, there was an answering call, and from the direction of the Lawn he saw two crows flying towards him. He emptied two pieces of potato onto the ground — leftovers from yesterday's supper — and placed the container upside down on top of them. He heard a rustle of wings, and two crows landed on a branch ten feet above his head. They stared at Nightingale for a moment, then screamed, "Caw! Caw! Caw!"

Nightingale walked to his back stoop, took a seat on the top step, and pulled a pipe out of his shirt pocket. He tapped the pipe against the side of the stoop, stuck it into his tobacco pouch and filled the bowl. He tamped down the tobacco with his thumb, pulled a kitchen match out of his shirt pocket, struck it against the brick step, took several drags to light his bowl, then leaned back on his elbows and watched the crows. They stared back at him.

"Caw. Caw. Caw," Nightingale yawped. He tapped the bit to the pipe against his yellowed bottom teeth and laughed.

"Caw. Caw. Caw," the crow on the lower branch replied.

"Don't look to me, Bottom. I won't help you. You have to figure it out yourself."

Bottom was a juvenile crow — maybe ten months old — who was often outside Nightingale's door in the morning. He was a bold bird — not aggressive, but loud and self-important, like the Shakespearean clown for whom he had been named. Nightingale had little confidence in Bottom's puzzle-solving. The companion crow was a newcomer. He'd only seen the crow in the company of Bottom — usually in this very tree at this time of day. The crow always waited for Bottom to take the initiative then followed. Had Nightingale not already named another crow Falstaff he would have renamed Bottom and named this new crow Ned Poins or Bardolph, but things being as they were, Nightingale was waiting for the right name to present itself. "Lower groundlings," Nightingale said to himself.

"Caw. Caw."

From a distance there was another crowing, and Nightingale watched as a third crow landed on the ground just a few feet from the cottage cheese container. He bowed his neck, thrust his head two times in Nightingale's direction and uttered a low croak.

"Nice to see you, Mr. Emerson," Nightingale said. "Please demonstrate your native intelligence for the boys."

Mr. Emerson walked around the container — he could smell the potatoes inside — and pecked at the container's rim. It wobbled but did not tip over.

"Caw. Caw. Caw," called Bottom.

Mr. Emerson uttered another croak, this time in the direction of Bottom.

"Thou art a boil, a plague sore," Nightingale translated. Mr. Emerson was among the oldest crows on campus. Nightingale had named him last year when he taught Forster to his fifth form class. His feathers were not as shiny as Bottom's and his standing posture no longer as upright, but he walked with self awareness, like an old man among school children.

Mr. Emerson reminded him of Mr. Bennet. Mr. Bennet reminded him of Miss Elizabeth. Miss Elizabeth reminded him of his wife Jane. He often thought of Jane. So many things reminded him of her. Not just the poems and novels that he taught, but the music he listened to, the food he liked, the places he loved …. Anything, really, that made him happy. Last night, he'd listened to Brahms' clarinet quintets — he loved the sound of late Brahms, so melancholy and ruminative — and now the opening line of the second movement of the B Minor quintet meandered through his mind. There was a time, long ago, that too much Brahms would put him in a grey funk and keep him up at night, knocking about between light dreams of what might have been and dark memories of what was, and he would have to be careful not to drink too much, lest he miss a class or, worse, show up reeking like a painter's rag. Edwin Endicott had looked the other way once. He had lost his balance in the kitchen, struck his head on the counter on his way to the ground, and opened a wound three inches long just above the ear. Uly had found him lying there when he'd come by to do the cleaning. He'd picked Nightingale up off the floor, set him in a chair, washed the blood from his hair, then wrapped his head in a towel. Nightingale told him to find Edwin, and Uly had walked straight to Endicott's classroom in Jackson Hall and knocked on the door, hat in hand. Endicott had dismissed his class early, telling his students that he was needed at home, and had rushed directly to Nightingale's. As he checked the wound, Endicott told Uly, "You did good. This is just as it should be, clean and tidy. Thank you, Uly. No one could have done better."

"Now listen to me, though. No one must hear of this. You understand?

You mustn't tell anyone what you found here. Not a soul. You understand? Not Johnny. Not Luther. Not James. Nobody. You understand? If people hear about it, then bad things will happen to Mr. Nightingale and to me, and we don't want that to happen, do we Uly? This will be our secret. I'll not talk about it, and Mr. Nightingale won't talk about it, and you won't talk about it."

"Right Uly? Are we clear? You understand?"

Uly looked down at David Nightingale and nodded. "You got my word. You got my word, Mr. Nightingale. It'll be our secret." And Uly had never told a soul. And he'd never spoken of it again. Not to Mr. Nightingale. Not to Mr. Endicott. Not to anyone.

Edwin had made calls to make sure Nightingale's classes were covered and then taken Nightingale himself to a doctor to have him checked out. At Edwin's suggestion the doctor had kept Nightingale in the clinic overnight, and when Nightingale returned to the school the next day he learned that Edwin had told colleagues that David had tripped on a squash ball and concussed himself, and the doctor had insisted on keeping him overnight to make sure things weren't worse than they seemed. Later that day he'd met Edwin in his office to thank him and to apologize.

"Is this the anniversary?" Edwin had asked.

"Yes. Didn't realize it, until just now. Right before you said it."

"Strange how things sneak up on you. Do you need help, David?"

"I don't think so. I mean, obviously, yes, but not the kind that anyone can give me."

Endicott had nodded and touched his friend on the shoulder.

"I just have to know that this isn't a problem that's likely to repeat itself, because if it does I won't be able to look the other way again. You know how I feel about you, and how the school feels about you, but this is as far as I can go. You understand that, don't you?"

"I do. And you have my word it won't happen again."

"Very good."

And he and Edwin hadn't spoken of it again. For a while he'd been careful with himself, and if he felt a storm approaching he would put on his '78s of Louis Armstrong and His Hot Five and Hot Seven to dispel the clouds. But as the years went by he found that his deep sorrow had ripened into melancholy, and now when he listened to Brahms or the second movement of Beethoven's Seventh Symphony, he was no longer overwhelmed by grief but instead was tenderized by his remembrance of things past.

There was a sudden commotion in the backyard. Mr. Emerson had managed to flip over the cottage cheese container and had wolfed down one chunk of potato before the two younger birds dropped down to claim the second. The bell in Faison Chapel chimed the three-quarter hour; his Friday morning class would begin in fifteen minutes. Nightingale knocked his pipe against the back stoop and bid adieu to the crows. He picked up the stack of graded papers off the kitchen table and placed them in the outer pocket of his jacket. And as he did every morning, he kissed the tips of his fingers, pressed them against the faces of Jane and their infant son in the photograph that hung beside his front door, and left for class.

HENRY GETS A MUSIC LESSON

KEN SAT IN HIS GREEN ARMCHAIR wearing a Dark Side of the Moon t-shirt and faded jeans. He pointed to the pictures on his wall, and his long, slender fingers fluttered as he spoke.

"This is my Holy Trinity." He pointed to the album cover for *Transformer* on his wall. "That's Lou Reed. He's the darkness." He pointed to the poster for *Changes*. "That's David Bowie. He's the light." And he held up the album cover for *Some Girls*. "And the Rolling Stones are everything in between."

Henry sat on the single bed beside Ken's chair. Study Hall was over. Henry had poked his head into Ken's room hoping to get some help with a Mackie paper he was struggling to write, and Ken had insisted that he sit down and listen to *Some Girls*.

"When'd you get it?" Henry asked.

"Last weekend at the BandBox." Ken pointed to a photograph pinned to his wall of an Alice-in-Wonderland caterpillar and a large, mushroom-shaped hookah. "It's a record store and head shop near VCU. I go there to get away from my dad."

Ken's father lived in Richmond. The son of a prominent Jewish family in a Richmond enclave that traced its roots back a hundred years, he'd fallen in love with Ken's mother while he was an undergraduate at Columbia and she at Barnard. To please her he'd tried to recast his destiny as a willing denizen of the wider world by taking a job on Wall Street after graduation. Ken's fondest childhood memories involved bagels from Zabar's on the Upper West Side and playing hide and seek with the doorman at their co-op. But Daniel Bright had struggled to ground himself in the vast anonymity of New York, and eventually he'd dragged his little family back to the Old Dominion, where his place in the spheres of commerce and civic influence had been secured by previous generations. For Esther Bright the transition from the footloose freedom of Broadway to the encoded expectations of Monument Avenue presented challenges that soon became overwhelming. As the years passed Ken's vivacious, funny, artistic mother became more anxious and even hysterical, and his always enigmatic father grew more stone-faced and distant. Ken spent three unhappy years at a private day school in Richmond, but when the marital relations reached their inevitable crisis, his parents shipped him off to Randolph in order to spare him the crossfire of their breakup. The divorce had been finalized last June, and Ken's mother had moved back to New York City to live with her mother in an apartment near Lincoln Center.

"What about you?"

"What about me, what?" Henry asked.

"Who makes up your Father, Son, and Holy Ghost?"

"I don't know if I have three like that. I'm definitely not as into music —"

"No. Let me guess," Bright interrupted. "Styx."

They both laughed. "Definitely Styx," Henry said.

"No for real. Boz Scaggs?"

"He's okay," Henry said.

Ken frowned. "Jimmy Buffett?"

"Can't stand him."

"Thank God!" Ken said. "Fleetwood Mac?"

"They're okay."

Ken shook his head in disapproval. "Marshall Tucker Band?"

"I like them better."

"Dan Fogelberg."

Henry blushed. "I have to admit, I used to listen to a lot of Dan Fogelberg."

Ken watched the pink flow across Henry's cheek to the edge of his ear. He noticed the light brown fuzz of a future sideburn on Henry's cheek and smiled.

"I thought I'd heard his dulcet tones. Chalk it up to the innocence of youth," Ken said. "I don't know. I'm not getting any hell yeahs. 'America'?"

"Hell no!"

"That's good. All right. I give up. You tell me."

"Like I said, I don't listen to a lot of music, but I like The Who."

"That's good."

Henry pointed to Ken's t-shirt. "Pink Floyd."

"Now we're talking."

"Led Zeppelin. The Allman Brothers —"

"You listen to a lot of music."

"Not a lot. But I know what I like."

"Top album of all time?" Ken asked.

"I really like *Blood on the Tracks*. 'Tangled up in Blue' is awesome."

Henry looked to Ken for affirmation. Ken admired the blue of Henry's eyes, which reminded him of cornflowers.

"An old soul," Ken said.

"I don't know about that. What about yours?"

"For pure rock and roll it's got to be *Let it Bleed*. But my personal favorite is *Ziggy Stardust*.

"Bowie?"

"The light."

"Have you ever tried to write songs?"

"Oh hell yes," Ken said. "Are you kidding? Look at my pantheon." He motioned to the posters on his wall.

"And?"

Ken made an emphatic thumbs-down gesture. "All garbage."

"Didn't make any sense?"

Ken shook his head. "Made too much sense. Problem is no 'music'."

Henry drummed the bedspread on Ken's bed with the fingers of both his hands. "Couldn't find the tune?"

"That's part of it. Maybe most of it. I don't know."

Ken's room was warm and close. It was smaller than Henry's room, and Ken had the radiator open full bore. Henry pulled off his sweatshirt, and Ken noticed the darker spots of perspiration at the underarms of Henry's t-shirt.

"You hot?"

"I'm okay," Henry said.

Ken turned to the window and cracked it open several inches.

"I'm a word guy," Ken said. "I can put what I'm feeling into words — I am pretty good at it, damn good, relatively speaking — but I can't find the music for a song. It's weird."

Henry pointed to a scrap of paper with several lines of handwriting that was thumbtacked to the wall, next to the *Ziggy Stardust* poster. "What's that? One of your songs?"

"That's a poem Nightingale read to us in class a few weeks ago."

"Oh yeah?"

"It's Whitman. I liked it, and ...." He hesitated before going on. " — what the hell."

"What's it about?"

Ken pointed at the scrap of paper with some embarrassment. "See for yourself."

Henry stood up and read *As Adam Early in the Morning.*

> As Adam early in the morning,
> Walking forth from the bower refresh'd with sleep,
> Behold me where I pass, hear my voice, approach,
> Touch me, touch the palm of your hand to my body
> as I pass,
> Be not afraid of my body.

He turned to Ken. "Be not afraid of my body?"

"It's about friendship," Ken said.

"Touch me?" Henry asked.

"It's not what you think," Ken said.

Henry didn't know what he thought. He was still trying to under-stand how the poem was about friendship. "Like I was saying," Ken said, picking up their prior thread, "It's like it's a different part of the brain. The words and the music. As much as I listen to music, and like music, I am not musical."

Henry had never thought about writing songs, but he thought about writing stories all the time. He could imagine a plot — easy. He could hear the conversations — easier. His problem was describing the people and the places. The setting. The smells. The sound and look of things. It seemed like maybe he was missing the music as well.

"I think about writing all the time," Henry said.

"What kind of writing?"

"Stories, essays — "

"Poems?"

"No. Not so much poems."

"And?"

"I'm terrible at it."

"What's the problem?"

Henry threw up his hands. "I don't know!"

The plaintive note in Henry's voice and the look of bewilderment on his face communicated the intense frustration that he felt about not being able to explain the problem. This candid expression of dumbfoundedness touched Ken.

"You have nothing to say?"

"No. It's like I have too much to say! But I can't sort it. Or make sense of it."

"You have trouble framing your argument?"

"No…. It's hard to describe." Henry tapped his fingertips against his forehead. "It's like I know there's an answer, and I can almost grasp it, but the harder I try to put it into words the farther I get away from it. It's like trying to catch a chicken. It's right there at your feet, but when you reach down it won't let you touch it."

"Hmm. I'm not too good with barnyard metaphors. Do you have an example?"

"Yes!"

Henry had wanted to show Ken the paper he was working on for Mackie's class, and he pulled three pieces of notebook paper covered with handwriting out of his pants pocket. Words, lines and entire paragraphs had been XX'd out, and other passages written in the margins or between the lines, with arrows pointing here and there, and asterisks and double asterisks marking where the marginalia fit into the body of the paper.

Ken looked it over. "Holy shit! What is this rabbit hole?"

"Right? I start off with too many ideas, and by the time I'm halfway through none of them make sense anymore. I keep writing and rewriting until I'm completely lost."

Ken was surprised. Writing came so easily for him that he assumed Henry, with whom he felt such affinity, shared his facility. Obviously, there were some obstacles — Henry sprang from the same household and gene pool that had created Gordon after all — but he was still young, and he was asking for help. There was hope for the boy; perhaps he was a late bloomer. He handed the paper back to Henry.

"Don't try so hard," Ken said.

Henry frowned. "How's that supposed to help?"

"It sounds like you're trying to find the answer to everything and ending up with nothing."

"That's about right."

Ken shrugged and cocked his head to one side. "Maybe there isn't an Answer with a capital A to anything?"

Henry looked at Ken like he'd just said something slightly obscene. "What's that supposed to mean?"

"Maybe all there is is whatever it is you," — and Ken pointed his finger at Henry's chest — "Henry Palmer, have to say."

"But I'm not saying anything! I keep trying and nothing comes out."

Henry was exasperated and a petulant pout appeared on his face. Ken found the look adorable but suppressed a smile.

"Don't be afraid to be yourself, Henry."

"Huh?"

Ken was aware of the irony of his advice, since for as long as he could remember he had desperately harbored a secret.

"You are who you are," Ken said. "Don't be afraid that people won't think you're interesting, 'cause there's nothing less interesting than a person who's afraid to be himself."

Henry waved the pages of his paper at Ken. "Jesus! How is this supposed to help me write my paper?" He needed advice on how to write a paper — not how to be a better person.

"Okay. Forget what I said." Ken threw up his hands. "What does Mackie say?"

"He says I need to outline my argument, have an introduction, then at least five paragraphs, each with a topic sentence, followed by the conclusion. When I tried to talk to him about my rough draft, he said" — Henry cocked his head and mimicked Mackie's imperious, disapproving tone of voice, — "'Look to Warriners, Mr. Palmer. Spare me your navel gazing.'"

"Fuck Mackie! He's a tool. You might as well ask a deaf person about the *Moonlight Sonata*. Go see Nightingale. He's your advisor, right? Ask him how to find your way out of the wilderness."

"But he's not my English teacher."

"He's your advisor! What could possibly be more important than getting advice about how to write?"

Henry stuffed his paper back into his pocket. He was disappointed that Ken hadn't had any good ideas, and a bit chagrined that he'd opened up as much as he had.

"Well. See you tomorrow I guess." Henry tossed his hand into the air and walked out.

As soon as Henry left the room, Ken noticed the sweatshirt on the bed. He picked it up and was about to call Henry back when he caught the smell of Henry's body. He put the sweatshirt to his nose and thought he could feel the warmth coming off the fabric. He breathed in the body aroma and closed his eyes. Such a beautiful boy. Just beautiful. He decided not to give the sweatshirt back to Henry that night.

HENRY REJECTS LAWTON

ON THE WAY TO SUPPER the next day, Henry checked his student box for assignments or messages and found a folded piece of paper that read, "Meet me at the big Oak behind the Chapel at 9:30." It wasn't signed, but there was a drawing of two intersecting arcs at the bottom of the paper. He remembered Lawton had talked about that on the golf course. Henry smiled to himself and stuffed the note into his pocket.

After Study Hall Wobbly asked him if he wanted to play foosball, but Henry made up an excuse, mumbling something about having to meet Gordon. He knew that if he mentioned Lawton Faison, Wobbly would ask him a bunch of questions he didn't want to answer. He wasn't going to tell Wobbly about the fish thing, because Lawton had made it sound like some big secret. At 9:15 Henry walked out of the Randolph Building by a side entrance, skirted past the gym and cut across the golf course towards the break in the hedge below Faison Chapel. As he walked he remembered the story Wales had told him about his encounter with Lawton at the Mess, and the story about hanging Tim Radley from the coat hook. Lawton had a bad reputation for bullying new boys, but he had already singled Henry out once for favor. Plus their fathers were friends. Henry didn't think Lawton would summon him to the chapel to mess with him or do something crazy. He assumed it had something to do with the fish thing — hence the drawing on the note. From what he could remember, Lawton had wanted him to be part of some group made up mostly of sixth formers. This made Henry nervous but also excited him. He was sure Gordon wouldn't approve, which made it even better.

The sky was clear, and the moon, which was almost full, cast a cold light over everything. When Henry cut through the opening in the hedge below the chapel he spotted Lawton in his hunting jacket beside the large oak tree. At first Henry thought he saw someone standing beside Lawton, but as he moved closer he realized Lawton was alone, and what he had mistook for a human figure must have been Lawton's moon shadow.

"You got my note," Lawton said as Henry approached.

"Yeah."

"I wasn't sure you'd remember the sign of the fish. You were high as fuck." Lawton laughed and clapped Henry on the back.

Henry shook his head and laughed too. "Yeah, I was."

"I probably should've taken you to your room. You were on roller skates out there."

"I made it back all right — "

"But I figured it would look fishy if I showed up with my little novice."

Lawton laughed again and punched Henry's shoulder. Henry was flattered. He liked the way Lawton carried himself, and he liked the whole hunting-jacket- with-khakis-and-white-Oxford-cloth-shirt thing. Lawton was definitely cool.

"Just think. What if we'd run into Gordon?"

"Gordon lives on Lauderdale — "

Lawton put his hands on Henry's chest and pushed him away

playfully. "You think I don't know where Gordon lives? That sack-cloth-wearing eunuch!"

They both laughed. Henry had to admit, Gordon was a bit of a prude. He looked around and didn't see anyone else behind the chapel or approaching from the Randolph Building. "Is anyone else coming?" Henry asked.

"Nope. Just me. Thought it'd be easier to talk if no one else was around."

Henry liked the sound of that. "Okay. What's up?"

Lawton waved in the direction of the golf course. "Do you remember talking about ICHTHYS?"

"Out there?" Henry asked.

Lawton nodded.

"Um. Well, no. Not really." Henry grinned, apologetically.

"Not surprising." Lawton held up his hands and twinkled his fingers. "Mongo's Panama Red!" He laughed. "Anyway. Quick story. The early Christians —" He stopped to make sure Henry was following his drift.

"Right," Henry said.

"Had to meet in secret. So they'd draw the sign of the fish." Lawton held out his hand and drew two arcs on the palm. "To find each other." He nodded to Henry, and when Henry didn't say anything he shrugged his shoulders. "You with me?"

"Yeah. Yeah. Not high now," Henry joked, but to himself he wondered why Lawton was giving him a Sunday school lesson.

"And do you remember why it was a fish?" Lawton asked.

"Because they were fishermen?"

"No. Because ICHTHYS means fish."

Henry blinked. "What's ICHTHYS again? I don't remember that."

Lawton held out his left hand, and with his right hand spelled out the letters on his palm. "Jesus — I — Christ — ch — God's — th for theos which means God — and son — ys. ICHTHYS is the Greek word for fish, and it spells Jesus Christ the Son of God." Lawton held out his hand as if it held the heavenly host. "How cool is that?"

"Um. Yeah. That's pretty cool," Henry said, but still he wondered where on earth this was going.

"So we're calling ourselves ICHTHYS, because we're a secret society."

Lawton stepped closer, and it suddenly felt like Lawton was looming over him.

"I thought you were the Chapel Council," Henry said, trying not to sound too baffled.

Lawton shook his head. "This isn't about Chapel Council. This is a separate thing. It's a secret society like the early Christians."

This didn't make sense to Henry. Seemed like the Chapel Council wore their Christianity on the sleeves of their button-downs. "Why's it secret?" he asked.

"I'll tell you. But first I got to know whether you're with us or against us."

Henry didn't like the sound of that. It reminded him of something unpleasant. What was it? Something his mother had once said. He took a step back, away from Lawton. "How am I supposed to know that if I don't know what you are?"

Lawton pulled a large silver coin out of his pocket and started spinning it in his right hand. Around and around, across the top, then under, then back over the top of his fingers, and back again. It was like a magic trick, and Henry couldn't help but stare at it.

"We're the old school," Lawton said. "Tradition. The ones who understand why things are the way they are."

The spinning coin gave Henry an uncanny feeling, and a dark timbre in Lawton's voice made it sound like he was reciting verses from the Old Testament or something. "Okay," he mumbled.

"Your father and brother went to Randolph, right?"

Henry looked up at Lawton, who was studying him closely. "Yeah. And like every boy in my family."

'Exactly," Lawton said.

"Exactly what?"

Lawton stopped spinning the coin and swept his arm in a wide circle above his head. "This place is your heritage. Like mine. And that means something —"

"Okay," Henry muttered.

"That's worth preserving —"

"Okay."

"And fighting for."

Lawton's eyes widened, and he edged closer. Henry felt like Lawton was waiting for him to say "Amen", but Henry didn't like where this sermon was headed.

"For what?" Henry asked.

Lawton lifted his eyebrows.

"Fighting for what exactly?" Henry repeated.

Lawton smiled, as if he'd anticipated the question — or even prompted Henry to ask it. "To keep Randolph Christian," he said triumphantly.

Henry's general unease switched to misgiving. Did he mean *more* Christian? That sounded dreadful. Henry suddenly felt an unfamiliar longing to be with Wobbly, at the foosball table. He pointed at the chapel. "Isn't it already Christian?"

"Always has been."

"So what's the point?"

"*That* is the point."

"To keep it the way it is?"

Lawton nodded. "To keep it from changing!"

Henry surprised himself by laughing. "Like this place will ever change."

Lawton took a step forward but checked himself when Henry moved away. Spit the hook this time, Lawton thought.

Henry felt the hair rise up on the back of his neck, and he remembered Tom Wales' describing how Lawton had pinned him against the foosball table.

"You know they're talking about hiring a Jewish teacher next year," Lawton said, and he resumed spinning the coin in his hand.

"Really?"

"Reverend Deemer told me the board of trustees wants to hire Adam Ginsburg to teach Latin because Colonel Bloodstone is retiring."

"And he's Jewish?"

"You think?" Lawton said sarcastically. "He was valedictorian like seven years ago."

"So he went to school here."

"Yeah. Then Yale. And was a Rhodes Scholar."

Henry nodded. "Wow. Impressive."

"Don't you read the Alumni Magazine?"

Henry smirked. "Duh, no. I go to school here, remember?"

"Anyway, Randolph has only ever had Christian teachers."

"So it'll take Jewish students but it can't have Jewish teachers?" Henry asked.

"Teacher's totally different," Lawton said.

"Because?"

"Because he has to set an example."

"Like Deemer."

"Exactly."

Henry started to roll his eyes, but stopped, fearing that Lawton would notice, even in the dark.

"Or Mackie?" Henry said, as a test.

Lawton caught Henry's drift. "Mackie's okay," he said. "People complain about him, because he's a hardass. But you have to draw a line and keep it. That's what this is about."

Henry felt a gust of wind against his cheek and shuddered. Deemer? Mackie? He started to say, 'Give me a break!' but stopped himself for fear of Lawton's reaction. Now he felt ashamed at not standing up to him. He wasn't afraid of Lawton, he told himself. He folded his arms.

"I think that's stupid," Henry said resolutely.

Lawton resisted the impulse to grab the punk and shake some sense into him, but he did edge slowly to his right until Henry was standing between himself and the oak tree. "Well aren't you the godless hippie," he said.

Henry tensed, anticipating a blow, but Lawton only laughed, a short, mirthless laugh. The guy's bonkers, Henry thought. Was his dad like this? He knew his father and Mr. Faison were friends.

Lawton spun the coin in his hand. Too full of himself for a new boy, he thought. Basking in big brother's glory. "So what do you say?" he asked. "Are you with us or against us?"

There it was again, only this time Henry remembered. It was the first day of second grade. He'd come home in tears because most of his friends weren't at school. They'd fled to the new private school on the outskirts of Raleigh. His mother had tried to explain to him the school desegregation order. He'd asked her why he couldn't be with his friends. Go to the new school too. "Because we don't believe in us against them," she'd said, in tears.

"Yeah. I don't think so," Henry told Lawton.

Lawton moved closer. "Why not?"

Henry started to move away but stood his ground. He refused to let Lawton bully him. "I don't see the point," he said.

"What don't you understand?"

Henry looked up at the perfect white teeth in Lawton's malicious smile. Henry felt his heart beating like a caged bird inside his chest.

"I think I understand. I just think it's embarrassing we don't have a Jewish teacher already, or worse, that we don't because of some stupid tradition."

Lawton's throat tightened. He's worse than Gordon, Lawton thought. He was pretty sure Gordon would have no problem with having only Christian teachers, but this little prick would be happy to burn the whole thing down.

"It's not stupid if it's the way it's always been," Lawton said through clenched teeth.

"Well then I guess it sounds lame."

Lawton tossed the coin into the air, and when Henry's attention shifted, Lawton slapped him hard across the mouth and wrestled him face down to the ground. Henry tried to free his arms but Lawton had one arm pinned behind Henry's back and the other arm pinned beneath Henry's stomach. Lawton sneered into his ear. "Not feeling so high and mighty now are we?"

Henry smelled the pot on Lawton's breath. He threw his head back and struck Lawton's face.

"Oww! Cocksucker!" Lawton twisted Henry's left hand up toward Henry's neck and drove Henry's face into the ground with his right forearm. Henry yelled out in pain.

"You're breaking my arm asshole!" Henry thrashed back and forth as best he could but Lawton pinned him to the ground.

" 'It sounds lame'," Lawton said in a sing-song voice. "You're just like Gordon. Think you're smarter than everyone."

"Get off'a — !" Henry tried to yell but Lawton pushed his face into the ground with his elbow.

"It's not lame if it's true. You really want the boy who mows your lawn to be governor?"

Henry tried to roll over but Lawton held him fast. He put his mouth next to Henry's ear. "I thought you'd want to stand for something, new boy, but it sounds like you'd rather take a seat in the back of the bus to New Town."

Henry went limp. What was he talking about?

Lawton felt Henry's arms relax, and he felt his own body sink as Henry's torso also relaxed.

"That's better." Lawton pushed against Henry's body to see if there was any resistance. Finding none, he released his grip on Henry's arms but remained on top of him. He laughed then put his lips to Henry's ear and said loudly, "Anyone who says things have to change is trying to drag you down to their level. Remember that, new boy."

Then suddenly Lawton was no longer on top of him. Henry pulled his right arm out from under himself and gingerly moved his left hand to the ground beside his face. He pushed himself up. His shoulder ached but everything was working. He got to his knees. Lawton stood in front of him and put out his hand to help him up.

"The Force is strong with this one," he said, laughing.

"Fuck you, Lawton," Henry said.

"Eh, eh," Lawton stepped forward and pushed Henry back onto the ground. "Why make life so hard for yourself, Henry? I offered you a hand to help him up."

Henry didn't say anything. Lawton stood over him for several seconds, waiting for Henry to do something, but Henry kept his eyes on the ground.

"Not so proud now, are we?"

Henry saw Lawton's hand reach down and pick his silver coin up off the ground. Then he saw Lawton's feet move, and he heard him walk away. Henry got up and rolled his neck and shoulders to make sure everything was okay. He saw Lawton's dark-backed figure disappear around the corner of the chapel. His body shook involuntarily as if to wake itself from a nightmare. "Sick fuck," Henry muttered. He brushed himself off and limped back to the Randolph Building.

HENRY REJECTS KEN

BY THE TIME HENRY MADE IT BACK to B Dorm it was 10:15 and some of the boys, mostly third and fourth formers, were making their way to the common bathroom for showers. From the glances cast in his direction, Henry surmised that he looked a little worse for the wear. He put a hand to the top of his forehead, just above the hairline, and found he was bleeding. He ducked into Ken Bright's room in order to avoid Wobbly's inevitable questioning. Ken had his headphones on and was reading when Henry entered, but one look at Henry and he tossed off the headset and hurried to shut the door behind his friend.

"What happened to you?"

"Lawton Faison."

"Lawton Faison what?"

"Lawton punched me with an elbow."

"Looks like he did more than that." He led Henry to the bed. "Sit down and let's have a look at you."

Henry took a seat on the bed as Ken crouched in front of him and brushed the hair back away from his face. "You're bleeding there." He pointed to the damp spot at the hairline above Henry's right eye. "Does it hurt anywhere else?"

Henry leaned forward and touched his lower back, where Lawton had used his knee to drive him into the ground. "Here," he said.

Ken grabbed the towel hanging from a hook in his closet. "I'm going to go wet this towel to clean up the blood. Take your shirt off, and I'll take a look at your back."

Ken left for the bathroom as Henry winced and started unbuttoning his shirt. When Ken got back Henry was sitting on the edge of the bed shirtless, with the headphones on. Ken eased down beside him and heard Queen's "Love of My Life" through the headphones.

"Why don't you, ... um ... let me ... no."

The song disconcerted him. Truth be told, he'd lately begun to think of Henry whenever he listened to the song. He shook his head to collect himself.

"Why don't you turn around and let me see your back."

Henry got up with a groan and stood with his back to the bed while Ken remained seated. Henry was about the same height as Ken and, like Ken, his torso was smooth except for some light, downy hairs on his belly and back, just above the waistband. Unlike Ken, whose arms and chest were soft and lacked definition, Henry's body had the long, lean muscles of an athlete. His body was as beautiful as Ken had imagined. In the small of his back was an ugly red mark, the size and shape of a chicken's egg. Ken reached out to touch it with his finger but hesitated.

He could feel the heat of Henry's body on his face.

"What do you see?" Henry asked, craning to look down at Ken over his right shoulder. The headphone cord stretched taut.

Ken touched the red mark, first with the tips of his fingers, then with the palm of his hand.

"Ouch!"

"Sorry. I ... um ...... It looks like a bruise," Ken mumbled. He took a breath then continued. "But it's not swollen. Turn back around."

"What?" Henry pulled the headphones away from his ears.

"I said turn back around."

Henry turned around so that his belly was just inches from Ken's face and the headphone cord coiled around Ken's shoulders. Ken felt his face grow hot. In confusion he rose abruptly and Henry took an awkward step back.

"Careful," Ken said, as Henry instinctively grabbed Ken to steady himself and Ken at the same time reached out to prevent Henry from falling. In that instant, face to face with their hands on each other's shoulders, Henry saw the look of tenderness in Ken's eyes, and a shock of recognition ran up his spine. This is what Gordon had tried to warn him about.

Henry took the headset off his head and thrust it at Ken with such force that the plug pulled out of the receiver. Suddenly the song filled the room.

Love of my life
Love of my life

"Jesus!" Ken cried and lunged to turn off the volume.

When Ken turned back around he started to lift the wet towel to Henry's forehead like nothing had happened, but Henry grabbed the towel out of his hands.

"I got it," Henry said. He quickly daubed the towel against his forehead, checked it for blood, then dropped the towel to the floor. He turned his back on Ken and began putting on his shirt.

"Let me help you—"

"I got it," Henry said, and he stepped away before Ken's hand could touch him again.

Ken tried to think of something to say. He bent down to pick the towel up off the floor. He hadn't done anything. Henry wouldn't think twice about it, he told himself. By the time he stood back up, Henry was already moving towards the door, still buttoning his shirt.

"Don't you want me to —"

Henry didn't let him finish the sentence. "See you later," he mumbled, and walked out without looking back.

Ken kicked the table across from his bed, and the needle skipped across the record album.

"Goddammit!"

He threw himself down on the bed and covered his face with his hands, while the record spun around and around and around, and the needle scratched the innermost groove.

THE FISH AND THE OWL

THE AFTERMATH

KEN DIDN'T GO TO BREAKFAST the next morning. He waited at his door until he heard Henry and Wobbly leave their room then headed to the Smokehouse for a cigarette. He'd lain awake for much of the night worrying about what Henry was thinking. He'd replayed the encounter over and over in his head, like a record on repeat. He hadn't really said or done anything untoward; he'd simply let himself hope. Foolish hope. He never should have let his guard down. He could not explain how it happened, except.... Damn. He needed a cigarette bad.

Normally the brick courtyard was empty at breakfast, and so Ken was surprised to find Mongo sitting on the bench. Mongo wasn't smoking; he was reading a book—this was also a surprise. Had it been anyone else, Ken would have skipped the smoke and walked to his first class early, but the sight of Mongo reading cheered him up a bit. Maybe Mongo was the trick to take his mind off things.

"How's it going, Mongo?"

Mongo looked up from his book. "I'm good man. Did you see the sunrise this morning?"

Ken had been awake when the sun rose, but he hadn't bothered to look out his window. "Missed it," he said.

"Aw man. It was awesome. Like seventeen different shades of blue and purple—a perfect tie-dye!"

Ken nodded. "Cigarette?" He held out his pack of Camels.

"Naw, man, I'm good. I don't do cigarettes anymore."

"What're you doing here then?"

"Reading!" Mongo held up a slim paperback with a drawing of a mushroom on its cover. The book was entitled *Psilocybins Everywhere.* "Did you know magic mushrooms grow right here at Randolph?" Mongo's eyes got big.

"Is that what the book says?"

"Says they're everywhere, especially pastures with horses."

"Lots of cows around here," Ken said. "Not so much horses."

"Cows, horses — same thing," Mongo shrugged.

"I don't think so." Ken put a cigarette in his mouth, struck a match, and leaned over to light.

"Have you ever ridden a cow?" Mongo asked.

Ken wondered if Mongo was high. "Do I look like someone who's ridden a cow?"

Mongo glanced at Ken, blinked, then boomed with laughter. Once the laughter subsided, he leaned back and casually took the full measure of his friend. "To be honest, man, you look like shit."

"Thanks, Mongo." Ken took a deep drag on his cigarette and exhaled.

"Naw, seriously man. Your auras're all out of whack." Mongo waved his arms at invisible rays of energy. "Crazy reds and yellows!"

"I'm not surprised." Ken took a second drag and felt himself relax. Maybe it was partly the nicotine from his cigarette, but talking to Mongo always put things in a new perspective.

"Let me ask you something, Mongo."

"Shoot."

"What do you do when you're having a really shitty day, when you're in a total bind — a complete clusterfuck — and it feels like there's nothing, absolutely nothing, you can do about it?"

Mongo rubbed the rough whiskers on his chin. "Bong hits help." He smiled and held up the paperback. "I'll let you know about liberty caps."

"Other than drugs. Let's say you don't have any drugs," Ken knew this was hard for Mongo to imagine. "What do you do?"

Mongo's head swayed, his eyebrows twitched, and his mouth convulsed in cockamamie directions. Ken could almost hear the rusty gears turning in Mongo's brain.

"I call my grandma," Mongo said finally.

"Your grandma?" That was unexpected. "Why?"

Mongo slapped his knees and rocked back and forth like a six-year-old. "She's the nicest person in the world, and I always feel better after I talk to her."

Ken laughed at the sight of Mongo's overflowing happiness. "Thank you, my friend. You've actually made me feel better. I only wish it were that simple."

Ken had a grandmother, but not one that he'd call about this. He couldn't even talk to his mother about it. He'd lived almost his entire life with a secret, and he saw no other option than to keep quiet and prepare for the worst. How had he been so stupid? He hated feeling helpless, but try as he might, he could not resist the fear that Henry might say something — anything — to someone that would cause him to be downgraded from mere drama nerd to full pariah. He took one last drag on his cigarette, snuffed it out against a red brick paver, said goodbye to Mongo, and walked to his first period class.

Henry was not so lucky in his choice of companions that morning. Wobbly had accompanied him to breakfast, regaling him with tales of his purported sexual exploits. From the sound of things, Henry very much doubted Wobbly had ever drifted beyond first base and suspected that Wobbly's apparent command of certain tumid details sprang from a combustible imagination set ablaze by too much Playboy and Penthouse.

"And then she, like, pulled off her t-shirt and her tits were huge, I mean HUGE." Wobby cupped both hands in front of his chest to demonstrate the mammary magnificence. One of his hands held a fork that he'd used to spear an improbably large piece of french toast, and a sticky stream of syrup oozed onto his breakfast tray as Wobbly dandled his imaginary paramour. "And I said, 'Whoa Nelly—'"

"Whoa Nelly?" Henry watched his roommate stuff the entire dripping slab into his mouth. "What are you, a mule driver?"

"Djwulp," Wobbly garbled in response, and his eyes grew large as he struggled to choke down his French toast. Henry shook his head as Wobbly swallowed the wad and chased it with a slug of milk. The guy was a freaking moron.

"Jesus, Wobbly, show some home training."

Wobbly was unfazed. "No, dude, you gotta hear this. I mean it was a-mazing." He took another gulp of milk and wiped his mouth on his shirt sleeve. "So I've got her tits in my hands, right? Like, unbelievable. And she says to her friend, 'You hold him down 'cause I'm gonna suck until he turns inside out ...'"

Although Henry in principle had no objection to talking about girls, Wobbly's pornographic phantasmagoria was a bit much for breakfast. At least his roommate's preoccupation had prevented him from noticing the odd, Prince Valiant-like way Henry had combed his hair across his forehead. Hopefully, no one would notice. Otherwise, Henry would have to come up with some story to explain how he'd managed to cut himself just above the hairline.

While Wobbly rattled on, Henry kept an eye out for Lawton and for Ken — especially Ken. He knew how things stood with Lawton; that was clear. But he was at a loss for what to do about Ken. He was almost sure that he had read his friend's gesture correctly. If he'd been wrong then surely Ken would have said something or called him out, but he hadn't. He'd just looked at him in that way that was … What was it? Henry had trouble putting it into words, but he knew what it meant. Or did he? What if he'd misread the whole thing? Ken hadn't said anything. He hadn't tried to kiss him. He hadn't tried to hold his hand. It was just that look in his eyes …. A look in marked contrast to Wobbly's antic display on the opposite side of the table. Wobbly's eyes practically rolled back in his head as he continued his breathless description.

"… 'You think you can get it up again, big fellow?' her friend asks me …."

"Sounds like one hell of a wet dream," Henry interrupted, pushing back his chair and grabbing his tray with an abruptness that stopped Wobbly cold. "Wash your sheets, Wobbly. Room's getting rank, if you know what I mean."

As Henry left the dining hall, he spotted Ken across the Lawn outside Jackson Hall. Only yesterday he might have called out a greeting; now he looked away to avoid Ken's glance. For Henry, fortune's fair-haired boy, this sudden furtiveness was strange. What did he have to be afraid of? It made sense for him to be afraid of Lawton, but Ken? It wasn't like Ken had grabbed him or would grab him. Then again, he'd never had a gay friend. Everyone he knew was straight — until now. How were they supposed to be friends if Ken had those kinds of feelings for him? It felt weird. Was there something between straight and gay? Was there a place where straight and gay people could actually be friends? He wanted to talk to someone about it, but who? He didn't want people to find out about Ken. To be honest, he was kind of worried about what might happen if it got out that Ken had made a pass at him and he'd done nothing about it. What would happen to him? Or to Ken? Or to both of them? It was a muddle. For the time being, he decided to plod along and keep Ken at a distance.

PREFECT ROOM

TWO DAYS LATER, after football practice, Henry was walking with a clutch of Cub teammates from the gym to the dining hall when he spotted Gordon up ahead. He separated from his friends and ran to catch up with his brother.

"Hey Chosen! We'll save you a seat!" Wobbly shouted.

Henry cringed. Wobbly had never called him that. When Gordon turned around, Henry put a hand to his forehead to make sure that his bangs covered the scab at his hairline. He was struck by how perfect Gordon's hair was; he must have spent like five minutes combing his hair in front of the locker room mirror. Henry had simply given his head a rubdown with a wet towel; his hair was a damp, tangled mess.

"Chosen?" Gordon asked, with a wry smile.

"That's Wobbly trying to impress you."

Gordon cocked his head. "I don't get it."

"I'm 'Chosen' because you're the Head Boy and dad was Head Boy, so ...." Henry let his voice trail off.

Gordon nodded then smiled. "So you're going to be Head Boy too." He slapped his little brother on the back.

Henry shook his head. "Like that'll ever happen."

"You might be surprised," Gordon said. "You've always been a leader. You're the quarterback, right?"

"Of the Bad News Cubs," Henry said sarcastically.

"Don't sell yourself short."

Henry smirked. "I wouldn't want to be Head Boy."

Gordon laughed. "Why not?"

Henry frowned. "Because I don't want to have to kick out my friends."

Gordon waited for Henry to laugh. Then he realized that his brother wasn't joking. What a jerk, he thought. And typical. Henry had always thought he was the cool Palmer.

Henry had not meant the comment as an insult; he was just being honest. Being a prefect seemed like a complete pain in the ass, and Head Boy? Forget about it.

"Hey. I wanted to ask you something. You got a second?"

"Sure."

Henry glanced over his shoulder and saw his friends were in earshot. He turned back to Gordon. "Somewhere private."

Gordon suggested they go to the Prefect Room. It was off limits to everyone but the prefects, and he needed to check his box for messages there anyway. They entered the Randolph Building on the ground floor along with everyone else, but instead of heading upstairs to the dining hall they continued down the hallway, past the phone room, where the boys placed their long distance calls to home.

"Have you talked to mom lately?" Gordon asked.

"A couple days ago."

"I talked to her last night."

"She's coming for Parent's Weekend, right?"

"Yeah." Gordon wagged a finger at his brother. "To see you."

Grace Palmer hadn't made much effort to disguise her dislike for the Randolph School. She'd attended Parent's Weekend Gordon's new boy year, but had found an excuse to stay home last year.

"Did she sound upset?" Henry asked.

"About dad?"

Henry nodded. "She told me he's been going to Sand Hill like three days a week."

Sand Hill was a mostly forgotten town in a sandy corner of North Carolina. Gordon Sr. had grown up there and lately had been spending more and more time there in an effort to salvage various family enterprises.

"Well of course he is," Gordon said. "What does she expect him to do? Let the whole thing fall apart?"

"She doesn't think there's much dad can do," Henry said.

"That's 'cause she's never had faith in dad."

Henry let the matter drop. He didn't want to get into another argument about Sand Hill. He wanted to talk about Ken, and possibly Lawton. At least he'd thought he did. But hearing Gordon leap to their father's defense reminded him of how pig-headed Gordon could be. If he told him what had happened with Ken, wouldn't he just say 'I told you so', or worse, say nothing and smile in his condescending way?

When they reached the Prefect Room, Gordon unlocked the door and walked to a side table at the far end of the room, where there was a wooden box with papers that Gordon looked through. Henry took in the rest of the room — a long walnut table, its finish buffed to a high gloss, twelve high-backed chairs, one for each prefect; and a bank of tall windows overlooking the Lawn. A thirteenth chair was set against the wall at one end of the room — the end opposite the side table where Gordon was standing. The walls were painted white and had no photographs, no paintings, and no clock. The only decoration was a reproduction of the school's honor code printed on a plain sheet of white paper and hanging in a black wooden frame.

Henry watched Gordon fold a piece of paper and put it in his pocket. "What's that?" he asked.

"Prefect stuff."

Henry wondered if another boy was being brought up on honor charges.

Gordon took a seat at the head of the table, and motioned for Henry to pull up the chair against the wall and take a seat next to him. "What's up?"

"Are you sure it's okay for me to be here?" Henry asked.

"Yeah. Sure. We meet here once a week on Sunday. Otherwise, it's pretty much empty."

"Is this where the honor hearings happen?"

"Yep." Gordon felt a sense of fraternal pride that he was able to show Henry the ropes. "I sit here." Gordon pointed to the place he was seated. "And the student charged with the honor offense sits there." He pointed to where Henry was seated.

Henry thought of Tim Radley and shuddered. "That's crazy," he said.

"Didn't you want to talk about something?" Gordon asked.

Henry remembered the way Ken had looked at him — that sort of frightened, generous, searching look he had — but sitting in Randolph's version of the Star Chamber, he got cold feet. Even if Gordon could get past his basic dislike of Ken, he'd never be able to see the situation as anything other than some sick pervert preying on his younger brother.

But Henry knew it hadn't been like that. Not even close. Plus, Henry didn't want to tell Gordon anything that he might repeat out of context, or insinuate later on — something negative about Ken or even about himself. He didn't think Gordon would violate his trust maliciously, but he could imagine Gordon telling himself some bullshit about it being an older brother's prerogative and spilling the beans to their dad or, worse, to his prefect buddies. No, he decided, he wouldn't talk about Ken. Or Lawton. Or any of it.

Henry touched his bangs to make sure they were still covering his forehead. "I was, um, wondering what you'd decided to do about college applications. Deadlines are coming up, right?"

Gordon eyed his brother suspiciously. "Really? You brought me here to talk about college?"

"Yeah. I heard some seniors talking about it and realized I didn't know what you were going to do."

Gordon held up a hand and made an exploding motion from the side of his head, mimicking a random thought escaping Henry's brain. "Since you asked, I just turned in my college essay for Princeton today," he said.

"You applied already?"

"No. I gave Nightingale a copy to get his feedback. It's not due for a couple weeks."

"Can I read it?" Henry asked.

"My essay?"

Henry nodded.

Gordon laughed. "No."

"Why not?"

"It's personal!"

Henry shrugged. "That's why I want to read it."

Gordon shook his head. "Sorry."

"What's it about?"

Gordon tapped the top of the table with his finger. "It's about our first honor case."

"Tim Radley?"

Gordon nodded. "Yeah."

"I've been wanting to ask you about that." This was true — ever since his talk with Tom Wales.

"What about it?"

Henry imagined Tim sitting where he was seated, with twelve prefects around the table and Gordon right there; the prospect was terrifying.

"Tim was like thirteen, wasn't he?"

"I'm pretty sure he was 14."

"He skipped a grade."

"No idea."

"But he was young."

"Sure," Gordon said. "And he was a new boy, but what difference does that make? It's not like it's hard to understand the concept, 'You cannot cheat'."

"Yeah, I know, but was it cheating?"

"He got help from his neighbor's paper."

"I know."

"On a quiz."

"But it was extra credit! He already had like a 100. Tim was a whiz. He didn't need extra credit. He probably just wanted to show off."

Gordon looked at Henry curiously. "How do you know so much about it?"

"He was Tom Wales' roommate. On the Cub team."

"The black kid?"

Henry nodded. "From Winston-Salem."

"Okay." Gordon placed his palms on the table in front of him. "What do you want me to tell you?" Gordon asked.

"He was on scholarship. His dad was like a mailman or something."

Gordon shook his head. "What does that have to do with anything?"

"What if he just wanted to impress everybody?"

"What do you mean?"

"He's from some podunk town in West Virginia. His mom's like in a wheelchair."

"So?"

"He's not like us."

"What do you mean 'not like us'?"

"He was trying to catch up. For Christsake we're like royalty. You're Head Boy. Dad was Head Boy. They call me Chosen."

Gordon bristled. "I was elected Head Boy by the other prefects." He placed a special emphasis on the word 'elected'.

"And if dad was a mailman and mom was in a wheelchair you think that would have happened?'

"Yes I do!" Gordon said emphatically.

Henry was reminded of a story their grandfather used to tell, at family dinners, about their great, great grandfather walking home from the Civil War, penniless, and starting a general store, then a bank, then a railroad, then textile mills, and on and on until he owned a huge swath of eastern North Carolina. He'd heard that story so many times, but as his mother had pointed out, they always left out the part about him already owning a farm when he got home, and marrying a girl who inherited a second farm, and both farms were built on slavery, and those slaves that were freed by the War just became tenants after the War, working the same land and being paid with scrip that they could only redeem at the man's general store. What had his mother told him? 'The Palmer men forget where their money came from. Makes it easier to ....' something .... He couldn't remember the rest. Henry could see that Gordon was mad; the muscles in his jaws were clenching. There was no point arguing with Gordon about it.

"Nevermind," Henry said.

Gordon nodded, satisfied that he'd won the point. "You know you could be Head Boy if you wanted."

Henry grumbled.

"I'm serious. I've seen how boys follow you. They already call you Chosen."

"Like I said, I don't want to be 'chosen'."

"You were born to it. Dad and I talked about it. You're a natural leader."

"No thanks."

"Opens a lot of doors," Gordon said.

"To what?"

"Look at dad's friends. Paul Turner's a top corporate lawyer in the state. Jimmy Johnson probably owns more interstate exits than anyone in America. Charlie Battle's a big-time insurance broker."

"Lot of good it's done dad."

"You sound like mom!"

"Well she's right. Don't you get tired of hearing the same stories over and over? Dead governors, dead senators, and the great old man who lies dead in the ground. Do you really want to visit those cemeteries for the rest of your life?"

Gordon laughed. Henry really was just like their mother. He's just a new boy, Gordon thought. He'll figure it out. Give him a year. He pulled the gold watch from his watchpocket. "Dining hall's open."

Gordon stood up and motioned for Henry to follow him to the door. As Gordon turned off the lights, Henry was relieved that he hadn't brought up Ken and Lawton. Gordon would have ended up lecturing him about the right sort of people and the wrong sort of people. He knew which basket Gordon put Ken in, and he suspected Gordon put Lawton in the other one.

MONGO AND THE PERSIMMON TREE

THAT SATURDAY MORNING MONGO, wearing headphones, cut-off jeans, torn sneakers and a Hokie Love t-shirt, jogged past the athletic fields toward the school's west entrance. He had an awkward, lumbering gait, like a giant toddler's, and the Walkman clipped to his waistband played another bootleg tape of a Grateful Dead concert. Truth was, Mongo was teaching himself to jog, and the music helped. Made it less boring. But occasionally he'd forget himself and twirl.

At the beginning of the year, Coach Boney, the football coach, had happened upon Mongo and another boy playing rock-scissors-paper in the parking lot behind Jackson Hall. Playing "paper" only, Mongo won two rounds and collected a dollar bill from the other kid. On the third round, the other boy threw down "scissor", and Mongo slapped his thigh. "God-dawgitty," he'd cried out as the other boy laughed, but instead of handing over a dollar bill, Mongo had lifted the back end of the Volkswagen van parked next to them two feet off the ground. Coach Boney thought he'd died and gone to heaven. Rather than giving Mongo demerits, the coach had ordered him to report to football practice that afternoon. After watching Mongo push the blocking sled across the practice field by himself and knock down ball carriers with one arm, Coach Boney had visions of a conference championship. At the end of practice he'd told the boy that in his 25 years of coaching he'd never seen anyone with so much raw talent. Mongo had thanked him politely and then handed him the uniform and pads.

"You put that in your locker. You'll need that tomorrow," Coach Boney had said.

"No thank you, sir."

"What do you mean, 'no thank you'?"

"I'd rather not, sir."

Coach Boney tugged at his pants and straightened the bill of his sun visor. "Now son, you have to play a sport. Why not football? I'm telling you, you're a natural. What else you going to do?"

A big smile had spread across Mongo's face. "Guess I'll just keep trucking on."

Randolph did require every boy to participate in a sport every season; the only exceptions were students who were cast in the school play. Mongo had no desire to be on the stage, and Mongo had no interest in team sports. So, after turning in his pads to Coach Boney, he'd signed up for Special X, or special exercises. During the winter and spring quarters, when Rev. Deemer was in charge, Special X involved excruciating workouts utilizing ropes, peg boards, medicine balls and free weights. But in the fall Mr. Nightingale took the helm, and the boys who took Special X in the fall fondly referred to it as Exercise for Poets. Each boy developed his own exercise regimen in consultation with Mr. Nightingale, and when Mongo met with Nightingale he'd told him that he wanted to run a marathon. Mr. Nightingale asked him what was the longest distance he had ever run. Mongo told him that the previous year he had tried to run from his dorm room on Mortimer Hall to Hayes Pond, but he'd only made it as far as Faison Chapel.

"So, a quarter mile, maybe?"

"Sounds about right," Mongo said.

"Did you jog or run?

"I ran."

"Okay. What about jogging? What's the longest distance you've ever jogged?"

"I don't jog," Mongo said.

"What's the longest you've run slowly?"

Mongo looked at Mr. Nightingale like he didn't understand the question. "I either run fast or I walk. I don't run slow on purpose."

For a moment, Nightingale suspected Mongo was pulling his leg, but one look at his guileless face convinced him otherwise. "Why do you want to run a marathon, Mr. Coogan?"

The honest answer was that Mongo only wanted to be able to run all the way from his room on B Dorm to the river — or a little over a mile — but he decided not to share this with Mr. Nightingale, since everybody knew boys went to the river to smoke pot.

"I think it would be cool," he said.

"Very well," Mr. Nightingale said, and he'd devised a running schedule that had Mongo taking short runs three days a week and progressively longer runs on the weekends, culminating with a 10-mile run just before Thanksgiving. During the first week Mr. Nightingale showed Mongo some stretching exercises and joined him on two runs to make sure he got the hang of jogging. After that, he'd left Mongo to his own devices.

On this Saturday morning, Mongo jogged past the Cub field, he noticed the persimmon tree at the edge of the pasture. The tree was laden with orange fruit, almost ripe. He remembered hearing somewhere — maybe from his grandma, or maybe from a Deadhead — that persimmons make a fine beer. He'd never made beer before, but how hard could it be? He imagined himself drinking homebrew in his room on B Dorm and a smile spread across his face. He was about to walk to the tree to start picking the fruit — and while he was there he might as well poke around in the pasture for little brown mushrooms — when he heard a car honk.

Mongo turned around and saw Mr. Mackie in his idling Volkswagen van. Mackie had rolled down the driver's window, and his unblinking eyes stared at Mongo. Mongo noticed a boy sitting behind Mackie on a booster seat. The boy looked to be six years old and wore a deadly serious expression. He held a toy six-shooter that he aimed at Mongo. A mini-Mackie, Mongo thought.

"Hello, Mr. Mackie." He gave the master a friendly wave.

"What the hell are you doing out here in the middle of the road by yourself, Coogan?"

Mongo removed his headphones. "Pardon?"

Mackie frowned and said more loudly, "Why are you out here alone?"

"Just hangin'," Mongo said, and he twirled around on one foot as if to demonstrate the varieties of hangin'.

Mackie was not amused. He bore a grudge against Mongo and kept his name at the top of his list of likely transgressors. He sniffed the air for traces of marijuana. "Tripping the light fantastic, are we?" he said, pointing to the headphones.

"Sir?"

Mackie rolled his eyes. "Just taking in the fresh air?"

"Mr. Nightingale's teaching me how to jog."

This sounded fishy to Mackie, but he was aware that Nightingale often allowed his Special X students to pursue independent exercises — a practice he disapproved of. He made a mental note to fact-check this detail when next he saw the chairman of the English Department.

"When you're running on the road I suggest you not wear headphones. And move your feet!"

Mongo watched Mackie roll up the window and put his van back into gear. Mackie waved at him to get out of the road, and Mongo stepped aside. Mini-Mackie stuck his tongue out as the van rolled past, and Mongo responded in kind. When he noticed Mackie checking his rearview mirror, Mongo waved. The man seriously needed to chill. He decided to come back that night, after dark, with a garbage bag and pick the persimmons. He put his headphones back on and thought of a present for Mr. Mackie.

ADVISEE DINNER

HENRY HAD MANAGED TO AVOID Lawton since his battering on Wednesday night, but there was no avoiding him on Sunday, because every Sunday night the students had a sitdown dinner with their advisors in the dining hall, and both Henry and Lawton were advisees of Mr. Nightingale — Lawton because his father had insisted on it; Henry because fortune favored him. Henry was later than usual because he had waited for Ken to leave his room before coming down. Mr. Nightingale was already seated towards the middle of the table; Lawton was seated at one end; Henry took a chair across from Mr. Nightingale and purposely ignored Lawton. As he sat down Henry accidentally made eye contact with Ken Bright, who sat facing him three tables away. Had Henry not been so intent on avoiding Lawton he would have located Ken before selecting his own seat, but now it was too late. He nodded to Ken, and Ken nodded back. Before he looked away, Henry was pretty sure he saw a smile pass across Ken's face.

Mr. Nightingale looked around the table at the fresh white faces, all the same age, all the same features, all the same background as most of the boys who had come before them. Nightingale had made peace years ago with the fact that his students always remained the same age while he continued to grow older, year after year after year. He did not fear death; the photograph of Jane and Joey beside his front door was his *memento mori,* that and the memories of the accident and its aftermath. But in recent years, as he'd started teaching the sons of former students — like Henry Palmer and Lawton Faison and Johnny Taylor, to name only the ones sitting now at his advisee table — he had begun to ask himself if he'd perhaps remained too long at Randolph. It wasn't that the boys made him feel old — though he could now almost be their grandfather, for god's sake — it was that they made him wonder if he'd made any difference. Nothing seemed to change. The son of the father is the father of the son, Nightingale thought. Sometimes he wondered if he'd become like the Ulysses in Tennyson's poem, telling himself that he still had the strength "to strive, to seek, to find, and not to yield" but going nowhere.

Rev. Deemer delivered a predictably dreary blessing over the dining hall's sound system, foregoing a simple prayer of gratitude in favor of an admonishment to pray for the Lord's forgiveness. Nightingale did his best to dispel the gloom by loudly declaiming, "Amen," then merrily remarking on the prodigious bounty before them as he passed the platters of roast beef, mashed potatoes, brussel sprouts and salad around the table. He took stock of all the boys while they served themselves. He noticed that Lawton appeared to be glummer than normal and wondered if he'd received bad news from home. Noticing that several of the boys didn't fancy their brussel sprouts, he motioned for the kitchen staff to bring more salad. He noticed the small bruise at the top of Henry's forehead and assumed it must be football related.

"How did the Cubs fare, Henry?"

"We lost."

"Close game?"

"Not really. 22 to 6."

"How'd you play?"

"Not very well. Threw an interception that they returned for a touchdown."

"That's the worst, isn't it?" Nightingale commiserated. "Happened to me once. We were up by four points, had the ball with less than three minutes to play. Coach said whatever you do, don't turn the ball over. Had a little screen pass in the flat—didn't see the defensive end. He intercepted the ball and ran for a touchdown. Lost the game for us."

"Was that when you played here?" one of the boys asked.

"Nope. That was in college. Coach told me afterward, 'We learn more from failure than from success'. And he was exactly right. So I congratulate you, Henry, on your interception."

Nightingale smiled at Henry so warmly that Henry had no choice but to thank him. Henry caught a glimpse of Lawton scowling at the end of the table. He remembered his snarling, 'Not feeling so high and mighty now are we?' and looked away.

"Angus," Nightingale said, turning to the large, freckled, red-headed boy sitting to his left. "What news of the world do you bring us?"

This was a common refrain at Nightingale's table, and by this time of year most of his advisees knew to come armed with some morsel to share in case they were called on. Somehow, Angus Yelverton had failed to read that memo, and his eyes grew bigger as he chewed his cud.

"There's going to be a new silver dollar," Yelverton said finally, before swallowing. He'd heard that very thing in his civics class on Friday.

"Yes, there is. A new dollar coin," Nightingale gently corrected.

Yelverton beamed, and breathed a sigh of relief.

"And what can you tell us about Ms. Susan B. Anthony?" Nightingale inquired.

Shit, Yelverton thought. How was he supposed to know that? Mr. Nightingale waited for some spark of recognition to register on Yelverton's bovine expression. Finding none, he turned to the other boys at the table.

"Anyone?"

Most of the boys avoided eye contact, but Lawton piped up to Nightingale's right. "She wanted to give women the right to vote," he said.

"Exactly so," Nightingale said, surprised that Lawton had known the answer and pleased that he cared to share it. "You have the floor, Mr. Faison."

Lawton put his fork down and made a show of looking at the paneled ceiling overhead. A smile rose to his lips as he glanced around the table. "This one's for Henry," he said.

Nightingale saw Henry wince. "We'll all play," he said to Lawton.

Lawton nodded. "That's fine. Henry just made me think of it."

"And what is that?" Nightingale asked.

"I'm thinking of a poet,"

"Very good!" Nightingale exclaimed, but sensing the table's lack of enthusiasm, he asked, "And is this poet American or English or something else?"

"American."

Nightingale looked around the table, hoping for someone else to engage. Finding only empty looks, he asked, "Male or female?"

"Male, obviously," Lawton said, with a bored expression.

Nightingale laughed. "Well, I don't know about that. Consider Emily Dickinson or Elizabeth Bishop or Sylvia Plath."

Lawton stared at him mutely.

"Living or dead?" Nightingale continued.

"Dead."

Nightingale turned to the other boys. "So, Lawton has a dead, American, male poet. Does anyone have any guesses?"

"Walt Whitman," Henry said.

Lawton frowned at him. "Please. I wouldn't touch that fag."

"Lawton!" Nightingale said sharply.

Lawton glanced at Nightingale. "Sorry," he said, without conviction, and turning back to Henry, said, "Homosexual."

Several boys at the table perked up. Buddy Jeffries, a sixth former from Mount Airy, asked, "When did he die?"

"Eighteen hundred and something."

"Before or after the Civil War?" Jeffries continued.

"Not sure," Lawton said.

Jeffries stroked his cheek thoughtfully. Nightingale waited. "Well, Buddy, who do you think?"

Buddy shook his head. "I got nothing."

Nightingale looked around the table. "What other questions do you have about this dead, American, male poet from the 19th Century."

"What school did he go to?" Joey Wilson asked.

"University of Virginia," Lawton said.

"Ah!" Nightingale brightened. "That's a great clue. Good job, Joey. Who do you think that might be?"

Wilson shook his head.

"Oh! Oh! Oh!" exclaimed Johnny Taylor, the small, apple-faced third-former sitting next to Henry.

"Yes, Johnny?"

"I know this," the boy said to Nightingale, then turned to Lawton. "William Faulkner."

Lawton groaned, but before he could say anything, Nightingale interjected, "That's a good guess. William Faulkner was an extraordinary writer who did live in Charlottesville, briefly, but he did not go to school at UVa." In deference to Johnny's youth and enthusiasm, Nightingale decided to leave it at that.

Nightingale scanned the faces. "Anyone else?" Blank stares. He turned to Lawton again. "Might I ask, was this poet born in Richmond?"

Lawton shrugged his shoulders. "I guess so?"

"I think he did," Nightingale said, and he turned to Frank Holden, a sixth former who himself had grown up in Richmond."

"Well, Mr. Holden? Can you think of any poets from Richmond?"

Holden shook his head. "I don't know any poets."

Nightingale had taught Holden last year. He resisted the temptation to rattle off the names of two dozen poets with whom they had spent time together, because he knew from experience that the boy suffered from an incurable form of poetry blindness.

Sensing that the table's interest in Lawton's poet was flagging, Nightingale asked Lawton, "Is it fair to say that the poet you are thinking also wrote short stories, one of which, I know, is read by the fourth formers in the spring."

Lawton nodded. Nightingale again glanced around the table. Still no takers.

"And would you agree that among his most famous lines are, " 'Once upon a midnight dreary, while I pondered weak and weary, Over many a quaint and curious volume of forgotten lore—' "

"Poe," Henry blurted out.

"Very good, Mr. Palmer," Nightingale said. "Do you know what comes next?"

Henry shook his head.

Lawton chimed in. "While I nodded nearly napping, suddenly there came a tapping, As of someone gently rapping, rapping at my chamber door."

"Very good, Mr. Faison," Mr. Nightingale said, with genuine enthusiasm. "How do you come to know the lines?"

Lawton shrugged. "My mother used to read it to me before I went to bed," he said.

"Really? Did she read you other poems?"

"By Poe?"

Nightingale nodded.

"She read 'To Helen.'"

"And do you remember any of that?"

"I remember, 'The weary, way-worn wanderer bore To his own native shore' and 'To the glory that was Greece And the grandeur that was Rome.'"

"The best parts! So you like Poe?"

Lawton stabbed his roast beef and cut it in two. "I hate Poe."

Nightingale laughed. "Too Romantic?"

Lawton shook his head. "God no. What's romantic about sleeping with a corpse?"

Jeffries poked Wilson in the ribs, and Wilson dropped his fork.

"I mean Romantic in the literary sense. The individual's experience of the sublime."

"I don't know about that. All I remember was death and disgust."

"The brooding air, the maudlin tale, the morbid longing for the past." Mr. Nightingale said. "That's what makes him a Southern writer."

"What's that supposed to mean?" Lawton said defensively.

"The Lost Cause. The chivalric code. But with Poe it didn't matter whether that past ever existed. What mattered was that he could imagine it."

Nightingale turned to Henry. "Well, Henry," he said. "I think you're up. What do you care to tell us? Current events? News from home?" From experience, Nightingale knew that was a longshot—the last thing a boy wanted to do was say something that might sound like he was homesick — but he always enjoyed hearing the boys tell stories about their families. "Or the guessing game again, though maybe not a poet this time," he added in deference to the less-lettered at the table.

Henry gave it some thought. He remembered when he and Gordon snuck into Aunt Ine's chicken coop and Gordon got flogged by the rooster. 'You got to keep a rooster if you want to get the eggs,' his great great aunt had explained to his mother. Henry said, "Okay. I got one — "

"He was a head, wasn't he?" Lawton interrupted, looking at Henry.

"What?" Henry asked.

"Poe," Lawton said, still looking at Henry.

"I have no idea — "

"Do you mean, was he brilliant?" Nightingale had observed Lawton's strange fixation on Henry, and he tapped his glass, seemingly by accident, to draw Lawton's attention. "Yes, quite."

"No — no — " Lawton said.

"And his head was quite large," Nightingale added.

Several boys at the table laughed nervously, but Lawton didn't. "Seriously?" he asked Nightingale. Even Holden and Yelverton shifted their attention from the roast beef to the drama at the other end of the table.

Nightingale smiled. "You mean drugs?"

Lawton nodded, and several of the boys at the table exchanged excited glances.

Unlike most of his colleagues, Nightingale had no qualms talking about drugs with his students so long as it was germane to the subject at hand. "May have," he said. "The record is not entirely clear."

"Didn't he die of an overdose?" Lawton insisted.

Nightingale pursed his lips. "We don't know exactly. Opium. Alcohol. Rabies. Suicide. They're all candidates."

"Rabies?" one of the boys piped up.

"Some people say. He may have gone insane."

"Death. Insanity. Rabies," Lawton rattled off. "This is why I don't like Poe."

"And yet you can quote his poetry," Nightingale gently chided.

"Blame my mom for that."

"I'll do no such thing!" Nightingale protested. "I will congratulate her."

"For what?"

"For adding music to your life."

There was a loud clattering sound of dishes falling in the kitchen.

"Music with meaning," Mr. Nightingale added.

"That's the definition for poetry I've been looking for," Wilson interjected.

Nightingale laughed. "What a wonderful thought — to search for a definition of poetry."

Joey Wilson noticed several boys at the table rolling their eyes. "It's an assignment from Mr. Mackie," Wilson said, more for the benefit of his classmates than for Mr. Nightingale.

"We've talked about some definitions of poetry in class this year, Lawton. Do you remember any?"

Lawton shook his head.

"'What oft was thought but ne'er so well expressed'," Nightingale prompted.

Lawton shook his head again.

"That's Alexander Pope," Nightingale said, addressing the rest of the table. "How about, 'Poets are the unacknowledged legislators of the world'," he said, turning again to Lawton.

Lawton frowned.

"That's Shelley — "

"Name one poet in the U.S. Senate," Lawton scoffed.

Nightingale smiled. "Point well taken. Hence 'unacknowledged'. We would never elect a poet to the U.S. Senate — alas — but Shelley believed that poetry was an expression of the new and the possible, and hence a guiding light for the future."

"Try turning that into a law," Lawton said.

Nightingale surveyed the table hoping to find another student to invite into the conversation. Most of the boys avoided eye contact with him, either because the topic bored them or they didn't care to get crosswise with Lawton Faison, but Henry appeared to be engaged.

"Henry," Nightingale said, "what do you think? Can poetry get a law passed?"

Henry, like the other boys, had noticed the storm clouds growing at Lawton's end of the table and had not intended to offer any comment, but he couldn't say no to Mr. Nightingale.

"I think he's saying it's bigger than a law," Henry said. "It's a new idea."

Nightingale smiled. "Exactly! 'An invasion of armies can be resisted but not an idea whose time has come.'"

"Napoleon," said Buddy Jeffries, who recognized the heightened tone that came into Mr. Nightingale's voice whenever he offered a quotation.

"In principle, yes," Nightingale said. "In actuality, Victor Hugo."

Lawton watched Henry's face brighten as he followed Nightingale's generous bursts of thought. He remembered how he himself had marveled at Nightingale's erudition when he was a new boy. His enthusiasm, however, had curdled, when he soon discovered that eloquence was not his natural birthright but instead was a skill that he could only possess with much effort and humility.

"*The Count of Monte Cristo!*" Henry said.

"Close," Nightingale said. "*Les Miserables* and *The Hunchback of Notre Dame. The Count of Monte Cristo* was written by his contemporary, Alexander Dumas."

"*The Three Musketeers —*"

"Dumas was black, wasn't he?" Lawton said, interrupting Henry.

Nightingale was surprised by Lawton's apparently angry countenance. "I suppose that depends on how you define black, Mr. Faison."

"His dad was a negro."

"No," Nightingale said. "His father, I believe, was the son of a French nobleman and a black slave in Haiti —"

"So negro," Lawton said.

"— and a general. I suppose, by blood, that could be correct," Nightingale said. "But isn't it funny, and tragic really, that Dumas was able to become a literary hero in France, and one of the great writers of the world, but had he lived here, he almost certainly would not have had the opportunity to write anything, and might very well have ended up a slave?"

Nightingale smiled at Lawton in a way that Lawton suspected was condescending.

"The white man's burden," he responded, his voice acid with sarcasm.

"Quite the opposite," Nightingale retorted. "That would be the white man's guilt."

"I don't buy that." Lawton tossed his head dismissively.

"Guilt's not something you buy and sell, Lawton," Nightingale said still more sharply. "In this case, it's inherited."

Lawton grimaced. Who was Nightingale to lecture him about Southern history? His family went back over two hundred years. His great-grandfather had been a United States senator and governor.

"I refuse to feel guilty," Lawton said defiantly.

"I can see that," Nightingale said. And suddenly, Nightingale had an uncanny experience of *deja vu*. He remembered being at the Lincoln Memorial with the baseball team after a game against Episcopal. Lawton's father was there — Lawton Faison Sr. — so it must have been around 1952. Nightingale had been staring up at Lincoln's statue when he heard Lawton Sr.'s voice.

"My great grandfather didn't fight for slavery."

Nightingale thinks Lawton is talking to his teammates until he hears another voice. One he doesn't recognize. An older voice. A man's voice.

"So you think both sides were right, and both sides were wrong?"

When he gets there he finds Lawton and three other boys standing opposite a black man, in his 50s. He is trim and wears dark slacks, a white shirt, and a tie.

In the dining hall Lawton began stabbing his forefinger into the tabletop. "Slavery wasn't some monstrous crime," he said.

All of the boys at the table stopped eating and looked nervously from Lawton to Nightingale, who was caught in a reverie. Most of the boys waited for Nightingale to say something, but Henry did not give that a second's thought.

"You're defending slavery?" Henry asked.

"Actually no," Lawton Sr. says. "I think my side was right, but your side had more gunpowder." And he smiles at his buddies, like he's scored a point for their side.

"My grandfather was a slave," the older man says. "We didn't have a side."

He sees that Lawton is irritated — at himself for responding and at the coolness of the man's response.

"My grandfather was a senator," Lawton Sr. says. "His great-grandfather was a nobleman."

In the dining hall, the blood rose to Lawton's cheeks as he turned on Henry. "It was a different time. You can't judge it a hundred years after the fact."

"It was judged a hundred years ago."

"By abolitionists!" Lawton said with a sneer.

"And the Union Army," Henry said.

"The Civil War wasn't about slavery." Lawton spat out the words.

"That's crazy!"

"It was about politics. And tyranny. And states' rights." Lawton's eyes darkened and he felt the cold heat of that dismal fire that still burned among an ever-dwindling number of Southern families.

Lawton Sr. turns his back on the man as if to dismiss him, and the man crosses his hands in front of himself, and Nightingale sees now that he is holding a Bible.

"I don't know who my grandfather was or his great-grandfather." The man speaks calmly and resolutely, as if Lawton still faces him. Lawton spins around and with sudden fury spits,

"My people didn't sell your people into slavery!"

"You mean the rights of slave owners in South Carolina to own slaves," Henry said.

"Nigger lover," Lawton muttered.

"Lawton Faison!" Nightingale snapped. "If you cannot behave in a civilized manner you will leave this table at once!"

The sudden outburst—by Mr. Nightingale no less—quieted not only everyone at Nightingale's table but the voices in half the dining hall. Henry felt a sudden thrill at Lawton's comeuppance, but he dared not look over to see its effect. Lawton felt like the eyes of the entire room were on him and kept his head down. He hated Nightingale's sanctimonious crap, and he hated Henry for baiting him.

Nightingale surprised himself with his sudden loss of temper, and he paused to take account. He knew he'd humiliated Lawton, but he didn't regret the outburst. The boy needed to be called out. He looked over at him—pushing mashed potatoes around his plate. Might Lawton apologize? No. Too much like the father, Nightingale thought, only now forlorn, as if the music had fled. The boy needed help, but he was at a loss about how to reach him. He had to hope he had a conscience. *The Agenbite of inwit.* Suddenly, he heard the silence at the table, and he looked about and found most of the boys staring at him. He sat up straighter in his chair.

"'That all men are created equal'," he said, and looked from face to face. "'All men are created equal'," he repeated. "Those are sacred words. They appear in the Declaration of Independence, in the Gettysburg Address and in Rev. King's *I Have a Dream* speech. They describe why this country was founded. Why we fought a Civil War. And all the work left to do. Heed those words, gentlemen. Let us not forget those words."

Nightingale nodded to each of the boys, and all of them acknowledged him. All of them except Lawton, who sat with his head down in grim solitude. Nightingale wondered whether any of this would make a difference with Lawton. He could only hope. After a moment of silence, Angus Yelverton raised his eyebrows to Frank Holden, and Buddy Jeffries coughed as he reached across the table for the bowl of mashed potatoes, and Nightingale smiled.

"Did you watch the World Series yesterday, Mr. Taylor?"

The little third former perked up. "Dodgers were robbed," he said.

"Jackson definitely got in the way of the throw," agreed another boy.

And soon the boys resumed their familiar pitter patter, and the paddleboat started up again. But Lawton ruminated darkly. He thought about Charleston and his father. He thought about Ichthys and tradition. He thought about the school losing touch with its history. He didn't expect boys like Henry to understand — they wanted everything to change — but he'd thought Nightingale would. Nightingale, who'd been such a big part of the school for so long. The fact that Nightingale was against him only proved the stakes. Something must be done. Something drastic. He was sure there were other boys like him who hungered for the old and the pure. Something lasting. Some boys like the early Christians, looking for a sign.

FOR SEVERAL DAYS, Henry had actively avoided Ken. He'd listened at the door to make sure the coast was clear before leaving his room. He'd kept an eye out in the dining hall. He'd avoided the routes that he and Ken used to take together between classes. Gradually, his embarrassment grew less keen, and he became less vigilant. He still avoided running into Ken outside his door, as best he could, but he no longer surveyed the dining hall or looked over his shoulder between classes or out on the grounds. After a week, Henry found that his life had pretty much returned to normal; the only thing missing was that certain lightness of being that he'd experienced in Ken's presence unawares.

It was one week after their encounter before Henry finally exchanged words with Ken. Henry had just gotten out of Mackie's class in the basement of Jackson Hall and was climbing the steps to the second floor on his way to football practice. His book bag with all his books for all of his classes was slung over his right shoulder, and he leaned forward with his eyes down as he climbed the steps. When he got to the landing on the second floor, someone rushing down the steps from the third floor brushed against him and knocked his book bag to the floor.

"Sorry," Henry said automatically. When he looked up, he saw it was Ken and he was momentarily flummoxed.

"Young Henry Palmer. What you got in there? Mount Parnassus?"

"How's it going?' Henry answered awkwardly.

Ken nodded. "All good. And you?" Ken examined him closely, hoping for some sign that he might be willing to parley, but Henry sensed the entreaty and did not look up.

"I'm good," Henry said.

Ken waited a beat, hoping for something more — a look at least — but Henry kept his head down and pretended to study the floor tile next to his book bag that was engraved with the words, "Dedicated to the Memory of those who came before us. Class of 1946"

"Gotta run," Ken said finally. "Dress rehearsal for *Inherit the Wind*. See you around?"

Ken spoke these last words in the form of a question, hoping for some acknowledgment. When Henry nodded, Ken felt a touch of optimism that rapprochement might be possible. But he didn't press the matter and left for the theater.

Henry looked up in time to see Ken rush out the front door, then he himself headed for the gym to change for football practice. As he walked, he took solace in the facts that he had not blushed, Ken had not barked, and no one else had taken notice of their meeting. For the first time since that awkward moment in Ken's room, he knew they could share the same oxygen without decompensating. That was a start, he thought. What came next was still clouded by his apprehension.

Halfway to the gym he heard footsteps clip-clopping behind him, and when he turned around he found Tom Wales out of breath.

"Didn't you hear me call your name?" Wales said, and he leaned forward with his hands on his knees.

"Sorry," Henry said. "Must have spaced out." He stared down at the top of Wales head. "Cub football has done wonders for your conditioning."

Wales stood up and pointed back toward Jackson Hall. "I ran practically all the way from Mackie's class," he said.

Henry laughed. "What's your hurry?"

"Guess who's moving to B Dorm after Christmas?"

"No way!"

Wales beamed. "Mackie just told me."

Henry clapped Wales on the shoulder. "No more Lawton?"

"No more Prince of Darkness," Wales said.

Henry held up a palm, and Wales slapped it. They continued walking toward the gym.

"You know, I got into a fight with him last week," Henry said.

"With Lawton?"

"Yeah. Behind the chapel."

"You're kidding! What happened?"

"He jumped me. Drove the back of my head into the ground with his elbow and cut my forehead." Henry pushed back his hair and showed Wales the pink line where the scab had been.

Wales stopped walking and rocked back on his heels. "Jesus! Doesn't sound like much of a fight."

"Wasn't. He stomped me."

"I thought you said your families were friends."

"We were ... or we are. I don't know."

Henry shrugged and continued walking. He hadn't told Gordon or his parents about the incident. He didn't need Gordon's help, and he didn't want to seem like a tattletale. But he was curious what his father would say if he knew. His father had always laughed when he told his own stories about getting hazed as a new boy. He knew his mother wouldn't like it.

"What was that all about Sunday night?" Wales asked.

"What?"

"At the advisee dinner."

Henry had had no qualms about relating the incident to Wobbly after chapel, but he hesitated now. He looked away from Tom and noted their distance from the gym. "What about it?" he asked.

"When Mr. Nightingale blew up at Lawton. What was that about?"

"Oh yeah." Henry nodded and continued looking straight ahead. "That was crazy. Nightingale was pissed."

"About what?" Tom insisted.

Henry stole a glance at Tom. "You didn't hear?"

"Hear what?"

"Hear what Lawton said."

"How am I supposed to hear that from Bloodstone's table?"

"No one told you?"

Tom shook his head. They continued walking, and after an awkward silence Tom finally asked, "What did he say?"

Henry stopped and turned to his friend. "He called me a 'nigger lover'."

Tom continued walking towards the gym. Henry waited for him to say something, but Tom just kept going, with his head down.

"I couldn't believe it. You saw how Nightingale reacted."

"I can," Tom said without looking up.

Henry waited for Tom to continue. "You can what?" he said finally.

"Believe it. Why?" Tom said.

"Why what?"

"Why'd he say it?"

"I don't know. We were talking about Alexander Dumas, of all things, the guy who wrote *The Three Musketeers*, and out of the blue Lawton says that he was a black guy, and it turns out that he was black, or his grandmother, I think, was a slave or something, and Nightingale says if he'd lived here he probably would have been a slave but because he lived in France he became one of the greatest writers that ever lived, and Lawton for some reason takes offense to this, and says he doesn't feel guilty about slavery and pretty soon we're arguing about the Civil War, and the next thing you know Lawton calls me … that."

Tom stopped walking and faced Henry. He waited until Henry had stopped walking too.

"What?" Henry asked.

"What did you say?"

Tom's manner and tone of voice was matter of fact, and yet Henry suddenly felt accused. He remembered being so shocked that he hadn't thought of anything to say. Then Nightingale had exploded and there was no need for him to say anything, but he wasn't sure he would have said anything if Nightingale hadn't spoken up. In fact, he doubted he would have said anything. He blushed. "I don't think I said anything," Henry admitted. "I should have, but then Nightingale blew up and there wasn't any need for me to say anything…. Or maybe there was."

He looked to Tom for some kind of acknowledgement, but Tom didn't say anything.

"I'm sorry," Henry said finally. "I should have spoken up too."

Tom nodded and resumed walking in silence. Just before they got to the gym he said, "I'm going to be so glad to be off Mortimer."

Henry breathed a sigh of relief. "It'll be good to have you on B Dorm."

They changed into their football gear and walked down the hill to the Cub field together. It was the last week of Cub football, and neither of them was in any hurry. Henry kicked the umbrella flowerheads of the Queen Anne's lace that grew beside the road, and Tom let his helmet bump against his knee pads as he lazily clip-clopped alongside. Before they reached the Cub field they passed the varsity football practice. The varsity players were already divided into position groups, and Henry looked for Gordon among the receivers and defensive backs. The practice jerseys didn't have numbers, but Henry was able to pick out Gordon by the way he ran, upright, with a stiff upper body and his elbows close to his sides. Henry laughed. It occurred to him that Gordon ran just as he imagined Ken Bright would run — kind of prissylike. He thought about telling Gordon how much he reminded him of Ken Bright, just to see him get all butt-hurt. Then he remembered Gordon talking about what good friends he was with Lawton Faison during their Sullivan's Island trip two years ago. How could anyone be friends with that jerk? Even at Sullivan's Island Henry could see Lawton was an asshole. At least Ken told you what he thought about things and didn't act like he was doing you a favor when he treated you like a human being.

Henry looked ahead. They were still two hundred yards from the Cub field, and most of the Cubs were already there. Henry looked behind. There were no other stragglers; he and Wales were bringing up the rear. Henry leaned closer to Tom and lowered his voice.

"Have you ever had a dude make a pass at you?"

"Like a gay dude?"

"Yeah. I guess."

"No," Tom said.

"What would you do if someone did?"

Tom looked at Henry with a mixture of surprise and alarm. Was this some kind of test? Henry didn't look like he was trying to trick him. There was no sly grin, no arched eyebrow, no canny reserve behind the eyes. Lest he betray his own nervousness, Tom took a sudden interest in a pile of varsity players across the road engaged in some kind of sadistic drill with two boys on one side of an imaginary line pulverizing a third boy on the other side. That was the sort of boy that Tom found himself surrounded by at Randolph. Willing pulverizers. Was Henry that sort of boy?

"Why're you asking?"

Henry inched a little closer and lowered his voice even more. "'Cause it happened to me."

The toe of Tom's right foot clipped the back of his left heel, and he stumbled a bit before catching himself. Henry grabbed his elbow.

"Don't hurt yourself." Henry laughed.

"Stupid foot," Tom muttered, and he made a show of stomping his foot against the ground while he tamped down his excitement. "Really? Who?"

Henry shook his head. "Doesn't matter."

"What happened?"

Henry tried to think of how to describe it. "He looked at me funny," was all he could muster.

Tom waited for something more, but when Henry just continued walking he asked, "And that's a 'pass'?"

"Yeah."

"What did he say?"

Henry shrugged his shoulders and kicked a grasshopper that had landed nearby. "He didn't say anything."

Tom shook his head. "And that's a 'pass'?"

"Yes! Look, I just know that's what was going on," Henry snapped with sudden irritation.

"But how do you know?"

The two boys glanced at each other. Henry bit his lip. "By the way he looked at me."

Wales slowed down. "How was that?"

Henry remembered the look on Ken's face and blushed. "I can't do it."

"Here at school?"

"I'm not saying."

"You're not giving me much to work with," Tom said.

Henry shrugged.

"Was he a stranger or a friend?" Tom persisted.

"A friend."

"Good friend?"

"Yeah."

"What did you do?"

Henry picked up a rock and threw it at a pair of crows twenty yards away. They squawked and flew up into the air. "To tell you the truth I kind of freaked out."

"Did you yell at him?"

Henry glanced at Wales, saw his skepticism, and turned to the Cubs players gathering on the field in the distance. "No. I didn't say anything. Just got out of there as fast as I could."

"Have you seen him since?"

"No."

"Did he say anything?"

"Not really."

Tom studied the side of Henry's face and could still see the blush high up on his cheekbone. He was pretty sure he knew who Henry was talking about. He'd seen Henry walking with Ken Bright to class and standing with him at the Smokehouse. He remembered hearing Lawton

Faison complain about "Queen Bright" to Billy Richardson.

"Have you said anything to him?"

"No." Henry shook his head.

They walked on in silence. Tom waited a bit, expecting Henry to look over, but Henry kept marching straight ahead.

"I don't know," Tom said finally. "It's not like he tried to kiss you. Seems pretty harsh that you can't still be friends."

Henry glanced over nervously and was relieved when Tom simply shrugged, like it was no big deal. Henry had wanted to think as much himself. Ken really hadn't done anything more than look at him in that weird way. Henry was sure that Ken was at least as uncomfortable about the way things turned out as he was. He wasn't ready to spend as much time with him as he had before, but they could still be friends. To be honest, Henry didn't think they'd stopped being friends. They'd just stopped hanging out.

"Maybe," Henry said.

There was a sudden whistle up ahead, and they heard Rev. Deemer shouting. They were still fifty yards from the Cub field, and the other Cubs were lining up for calisthenics. If they didn't get there before jumping jacks started, Deemer would make them run laps. They put their helmets on and started running toward the back of the warm up lines. Wales ran as fast as he could, and Henry jogged beside him. If Deemer made Wales run laps, Henry would run with him.

ON THE LAWN AT NIGHT

A FEW DAYS LATER, Henry lay on the grass of the Lawn staring up at the stars in the night sky. He'd picked a spot in front of Mortimer Hall, where there was a large opening in the tree canopy overhead. He found the belt of Orion. He found one of the dippers hanging upside down. Was it the Big Digger? He looked for the North Star. That must be it — the bright star at the tip of the handle. The Little Dipper then. Where was the Big Dipper? It must rise later, he thought.

He remembered sitting in his mother's lap, looking at a book about Greek gods, with the faces of Zeus and Hera and the other gods outlined by the stars in the night sky. Used to be he could look up and see a menagerie of gods and animals and creatures of his own imagination. Now he could only make out the two dippers and Orion's belt. He tried to make out the rest of the Hunter, but he wasn't even sure which star was Beetlejuice. It was better when he made shit up.

Henry could hear music coming from Mortimer and Lauderdale halls, and boys calling to each other on their way to the Mess. Somewhere there was a whistle. Then, "Hey Ned! Grab me a Nutty Buddy on your way back!" that sounded like Gordon, but Henry didn't sit up to look. He didn't want to be seen. No one walked out into a night like this to be seen, and not much chance of that anyway. He was too far away from the dorms and there wasn't much of a moon — hence the stars.

As he stared up at the galaxies, he thought he saw a dark shape flitter at the edge of his line of sight. He turned his head; it was gone. Then there it was again. Something swiftly careening in three directions almost all at once, a dark, ping-ponging lump. Too heavy and too late to be a swallow, he thought. A bat! He followed it briefly with his eyes then lost it in the confusion of tree branches. He looked back at the stars, hoping to catch it again, or its partner, or partners, in his peripheral vision. Was there more than one? There it was again, ten feet off the ground, swooping down towards him. Henry gasped, and it flipped back up into the air, ricocheting off invisible surfaces until he lost sight of it in the darkness.

A solitary bat, Henry thought. Hunting moths? Maybe a hatch of flies from the dairy. Henry thought he heard a whistle. He listened, with hope but little expectation, for the high chirrups it used to locate insects. He loved bats. Such fierce, ferocious creatures, half bird, half fox, impossible to fix in place, their sharp teeth snapping the night air. Little monsters. Defiant of anyone's opinion. Like Ken maybe?

"I should be friends with Ken." He said the words aloud, to see how they sounded, not loud enough for anyone else to hear, but spoken, not just thought, to make them real. That sounded right. He'd been thinking about it for days, and what Wales had said rang true. "It's not like he tried to kiss you." Henry spoke Wales's words aloud too, and it felt like he'd gone on record to the world. Wales was right. He'd been stupid. They could still be friends. He didn't need to be afraid.

He heard the sudden sound of footsteps to his left, coming from the direction of Mr. Endicott's house, and when Henry turned his head, there stood Lawton Faison.

"Palmer? What the fuck!" Lawton was dressed entirely in black. Black pants, black sweatshirt, black cap. Another step and he would have tripped over Henry.

"Lawton?"

"What the hell are you doing out here?"

Henry looked beyond Lawton, hoping someone else was also there. No one. Only the water tower looming in the distance. There was that whistling again.

"Looking at the stars."

"My little nemesis," Lawton snarled.

"Your what?"

Lawton bent closer, his hands on his knees, and Henry saw the grim smile on his face.

"Funny how I was just thinking about you, and here you are," Lawton said.

Henry rolled over and pushed himself up onto his hands and knees. He hobbled backwards to give himself room to stand up, but Lawton advanced.

"Bet you wish you had Nightingale's skirts to hide behind now."

Henry tried to stand up, but Lawton charged and bowled him over with his knees.

"My little John Brown thing," Lawton hissed.

Henry scuttled backwards with his hands and feet underneath him, keeping his eyes on Lawton as he advanced. He heard the whistling again, closer now and behind him.

Lawton heard it too, looked over Henry's shoulder, and stood up, suddenly surprised. "Mongo?"

Henry looked back and found Mongo in shorts and a tie-dyed t-shirt with some sort of necklace around his neck.

"Hi-ya Henry. Wha-cha' wallowing on the ground for?" He put a hand out to Henry and pulled him up.

"Get lost, Mongo," Lawton said.

Mongo ignored Lawton as he brushed off Henry's backside. "Lawton playing Ring around the Rosie?"

"Shut up, Mongo!"

Mongo smiled as he patted Henry on the shoulder. "You alright?"

Henry nodded. "Thanks, Mongo."

"Are you deaf? Go the fuck away!"

Mongo took a step towards Lawton.

"I said, 'Get lost'!"

Mongo took another step forward and loomed over Lawton like a storm approaching the shore. He poked Lawton in the chest with a finger.

"Don't touch me, hippie scum!"

Mongo smiled at the attempted insult and took another step closer. Lawton backed away.

"I said get the fuck away!"

Mongo didn't move, so Lawton bent his knees, placed both hands against Mongo's chest, and pushed with all of his strength. Mongo barely budged, but Lawton's topsiders scrabbled against the ground and he had to catch himself to keep from falling.

"Motherfucker!"

Mongo grabbed Lawton under the armpits and lifted him off the ground. Lawton's legs dangled as he groped the air with one hand to steady himself and swung wildly at Mongo with the other. Mongo extended his arms and held Lawton at bay.

"Feisty little fellow," Mongo said. Lawton reminded him of an opossum he'd caught once, only without the threat of teeth. He tossed Lawton onto the ground.

Lawton immediately sprang to his feet. For a moment Henry thought he might charge Mongo, but Lawton knew better. He dusted himself off then brushed his hands together in a show of mock disgust.

"You two mongrels deserve each other!" He spat on the ground, then turned and walked quickly toward Mortimer Hall.

Mongo had his hands on his hips as he watched Lawton rush away. "I never liked that guy," he said calmly, then stared intently at his hands as he brushed them together in imitation of Lawton. He laughed, then started whistling again. Henry thought he'd heard the tune before — the Grateful Dead maybe?

"Thanks, Mongo. I owe you."

Mongo poked Henry in the arm, knocking him off balance. "You don't owe me a thing."

Henry wanted to give the big bear a hug. "What are you doing out here?"

Mongo pointed towards the far end of the Lawn. "I was going to check on the cows."

"At night?" Henry asked.

Mongo nodded. "I like to look at them while they're sleeping."

"In the barns?"

"Naw!" Mongo laughed as if Henry had said something ridiculous. "They sleep standing up in the field."

Henry imagined Mongo staring at a field of sleeping cows and laughed himself.

"Where's Ken?" Mongo looked around, as if he expected Ken to walk up.

"In his room, probably."

Mongo stared at Henry for a long time. At first Henry figured Mongo must know all about what had happened between him and Ken; he probably thought it was stupid that they weren't still friends. Then he thought Mongo was just stoned and not thinking about anything, except maybe sleeping cows. Was the guy a saint or just a stoner? Wasn't there a word for people like him?

"Well thanks again, Mongo," Henry said. "I guess I'll see you back on B Dorm."

Mongo lifted his right hand, gave Henry a gentle wave, and walked in the direction of the cow fields. Henry watched until the darkness swallowed Mongo up. Then he looked back up at the stars and listened for Mongo's whistling.

PARENTS WEEKEND

PARENTS WEEKEND FELL on the last weekend of October when the fall colors were on the hills and long chevrons of sounding geese flew south overhead. Henry was excited to see his parents, especially his mother. At 4 p.m. on Friday, he sat in his room looking down the school's front drive for the family's blue Mercedes. When it finally appeared he ran downstairs to greet them, and he was waving at them from the railing of the front patio when his parents looked up from the parking lot.

"Henry!" his mother called out, and Henry ran down the steps and gave her a big hug.

Henry's father waited two steps behind, and when his wife released the boy, Gordon Palmer Sr. held out his hand. "How are you, son?"

Henry shook his father's hand. "I'm good." His father nodded, and Henry turned back to his mother. "I've been waiting over an hour for you to get here."

"I'm sorry, dear. Your father's meeting in Richmond ran longer than expected." Henry heard more than the usual irritation in his mother's voice, and by the set of his father's jaw Henry guessed that his parents had been arguing again. "But we're here now," she said.

Henry's father looked at his watch. "Darling, we should drive to the Manor and get dressed. The reception starts in half an hour."

The Randolph School had been built on the grounds of an old plantation; the Manor was the former plantation home at the far end of the Lawn. Legend had it that Thomas Jefferson had had a hand in designing the house for Thomas Randolph, the patriarch of patriarchs. No longer a residence, it now hosted trustee meetings, visiting dignitaries, fundraising dinners, and graduation ceremonies.

Henry's mother fixed her smile on her son. "I'm not going to the reception," she said pointedly, without looking at her husband. "I'm taking Henry to dinner."

Mr. Palmer ran his thumb and middle finger along the sides of his jaw until they met at the tip of his chin. "Grace, we discussed this already. Henry is invited to the Trustees' reception. He can come too. We'll take Henry and Gordon out for supper tomorrow night."

Grace Palmer put one hand on Henry's shoulder and turned to face her husband.

"I told you I don't want to go to the reception, and I'm sure Henry doesn't want to go either."

"For heaven's sake, Grace. You know the Board members are expected to be there." Henry heard the familiar strain in his father's voice.

Mrs. Palmer pursed her lips and nodded in condescension. "I understand that, Gordon, and you should do what you have to do. But I'm not on the Board. Furthermore, I don't care to spend another evening talking about the Madison Bowl or the color of the trees in Linville. I want to eat dinner with Henry. I haven't seen him in over two months, and I don't care if I never eat another dinner with the Board of Trustees."

It went without saying that Grace Palmer was not fond of the Randolph School. Over the last several years, as the stress in her marriage had gradually increased, she had come to regard Randolph men as being both smug and oblivious to change. She hadn't opposed Gordon Jr.'s enrollment at the school, because Gordon was clearly desperate to follow in his father's footsteps. But when Henry objected to her husband's announcement that he should follow Gordon, Grace Palmer had taken her son's side. She told herself and her husband that she liked having Henry at home. What she didn't tell her husband — or even herself — was that she worried about Henry turning into another Palmer. Eventually, Mr. Palmer had gotten his way by arguing for family tradition — blah blah blah — and now Mrs. Palmer wanted to make sure that her deference had not been too dear a sacrifice.

"You go with Gordon," she said. "He likes those things, and the Board loves talking to the Head Boy. You'll have a better time if Henry and I aren't there with you."

This was not a wholly unfamiliar scene for Henry. Over the summer Henry had noticed that little things his father had always done — like leaving his dishes on the table or his overcoat on a chair in the hallway or an unfinished game of Patience on the coffee table — had started to irritate his mother, and his small peace offerings like a hug or a kiss on the cheek were barely tolerated or even rebuffed. Henry had passed it off as a rough patch and ignored it more or less, but now that his parents' apparent stalemate was on display at the front entrance to the Randolph School for all of his classmates to behold, he felt alarmed. He turned to his mother.

"It's all right, mom. We can all four go out to dinner tomorrow night after the game."

Mr. Palmer pointed at his son. "See Grace? Even Henry — "

"Henry's right," Mrs. Palmer interrupted. "We don't need to spend another second arguing about this. You and Gordon go to the Trustee reception. I'll find you when we get back from supper."

Even Henry recognized the steely timbre in his mother's voice. His father slowly shifted the balance of his weight from his left foot to his right and clenched his teeth. He cleared his throat and started to insist on his wife's company, but then his natural discretion got the better of him.

"Henry, I'll see you tomorrow." He nodded to his son, retrieved his suitcase from the back of the car, and left without so much as looking again in his wife's direction.

Once her husband was out of earshot, Grace Palmer leaned into Henry and in a lower voice said, "That wasn't too painful, was it?"

When Henry shook his head, she smiled brightly and looped one arm through her son's. "Where shall we eat?"

Henry only knew of two restaurants nearby — one Italian, where everything was smothered in mozzarella, and the other German, where everything smelled of boiled cabbage. Neither appealed to his mother.

"There's a French restaurant I'm dying to try," his mother said. "How would you like to drive to Charlottesville?"

Henry agreed and started to walk to the passenger side of the car, but his mother stopped him. She held out the car keys. "I mean, *you* drive," she said.

Henry grinned. He had his learner's permit, but he had not driven a car since August. "Are you sure?"

"How are you going to learn if you don't drive?" His mother gave him a peck on the cheek and crossed to the passenger side.

Henry got behind the wheel, located the clutch on the floor, depressed it with his left foot and practiced shifting gears.

"You remember how to drive a stick shift don't you?" his mother asked.

Henry nodded. His dad had taken him out several times in the diesel Mercedes, and he'd almost gotten to the point that he could pull forward, uphill, in first gear, without stalling. He didn't tell his mom that. He turned the key in the ignition.

"You have to wait for the glow plug lights to come on," his mom said.

That's right, Henry thought. He scanned the front panel for some kind of indicator light. "What does the glow plug look like again?"

His mom pointed to a little yellow light below the speedometer. "Now turn it on," she said.

Henry pulled the starter knob, and the engine gave a loud cough and the car lurched forward.

"Put in the clutch," his mother said patiently.

"Oh right! Right" Henry looked down at his feet and found the clutch pedal. "Sorry. Stupid." He pulled the starter knob again, and the engine coughed to life. He examined the diagram on the top of the gear shift then moved the knob to the left and up. As he let out the clutch the car started to lurch forward.

"No-no-no-no," his mom said. "You're not in reverse!"

He pressed down on the clutch pedal again.

"You have to push the knob down and over to get it in reverse," his mom explained.

Right, right, Henry thought. He remembered now. He pushed the knob down, over and up, and into reverse.

"That's right," his mom said. "Hang in there!"

She clapped her hands as Henry let out the clutch and the car eased out of its parking space. "Little more gas," she said as the engine started to choke. "Now let up on the gas pedal," she said as the car started to speed up.

The engine choked off, and the car came to a stop perpendicular to the parking space.

"That's all right. You just have to remember to push in the clutch when you take your foot off the gas."

Henry nodded. He remembered practicing that with his dad. He started the engine again, shifted into first gear, and drove slowly west, past the front of the Randolph Building, past Snoot's Gym, down the hill, past the practice fields, and out the west entrance.

"Look at you!" his mother said proudly.

Henry smiled happily at his mother. She smiled back but pointed straight ahead. "Keep your eyes on the road!"

As they drove, Henry told his mother about his struggles with Mackie, his first paper — an F! — and about Wobbly — poor Wobbly. He described the Cub season — all losses! — and his dislike of Rev. Deemer. He told her about how Gordon was worshiped by the new boys and how he'd been nicknamed "Chosen". He didn't tell her about Ken Bright. And he didn't tell her about smoking pot or getting beat up by Lawton.

The French restaurant was in a restored farmhouse outside of Charlottesville. Most of the walls on the first floor had been removed to create an open dining area, and a new kitchen had been built onto the back of the house. His mother said it was rustic French cuisine, but other than the French onion soup, Henry could make neither hide nor hair of the menu. His mother helped him place his order, and after the waiter brought his mother a glass of white wine, Henry asked, "You're still friends with the Faisons, right? Lawton Faison's parents?"

"Yes. Though we don't see them as much as we used to."

"What's his father like, Mr. Faison?"

"Lawton Faison?"

Henry nodded.

Lawton Faison Sr. was something of a sore subject in the Palmer household, and Grace Palmer didn't know how much she should share with her son. She knew Gordon—her husband—wouldn't want her to share a thing.

"Do you know Lawton well—Lawton Jr. I mean?" she asked.

Henry kept a straight face, as best he could. "Just a little," he said. "We're in the same advisee group, with Mr. Nightingale."

Grace Palmer nodded. She sensed that he might be hiding something also.

"Your father and Lawton's father used to be best friends. They were roommates at Randolph and at Princeton—but you know all about that, right?"

Henry nodded.

"I remember when Beth came back from Memorial Chapel in Cambridge—"

"Beth?" Henry asked.

"Oh sorry, right. Beth Coleman, or Beth Faison now. Lawton's mother. You remember Mrs. Faison?"

Henry nodded. He'd met her when he visited Sullivan's Island with Gordon.

"Beth and I were at Sweet Briar together. A group of us moved to Boston after graduation, and we would go to church every Sunday at Memorial Chapel to meet other Southerners. I remember Beth coming back from church one Sunday and saying she'd met the man she was going to marry."

She stopped there, considered the brass chandelier over their table, then shook her head sadly and laughed to herself.

"What?" Henry asked.

"Nothing," his mother said. "We were young."

Henry could tell his mother was trying to conceal something. She was no better at keeping secrets from him than he was at keeping secrets from her.

"That was Mr. Faison, right?" Henry prompted.

"Mr. Faison?"

"The man Beth was going to marry."

"Yes." Grace Palmer studied her son closely. "Why are you so interested in the Faisons? It's all ancient history."

Now it was Henry's turn to tiptoe around a subject. "I'm just kind of curious about Lawton, I guess."

Mrs. Palmer recognized the evasion in the way Henry's voice trailed off and he looked away at the end of his sentence.

"Who you know just a little," she said teasingly.

Henry blushed.

"Want to tell me about it?" his mother asked.

Henry shook his head. "Not really."

Mrs. Palmer decided not to press. She knew he'd tell her soon enough.

"Anyway, I immediately disliked him," she said.

"Who?" Henry asked.

"Lawton's father."

"Why?"

"I thought he was the most arrogant person I'd ever met. You might be talking to him and the whole time he's looking over your shoulder to see who's coming into the room. It really didn't matter to me, because I wasn't dating him, but I saw the way he treated Beth."

Mrs. Palmer picked up her glass, and a small frown came to her face as she looked over Henry's shoulder and took another sip of wine.

Henry remembered how pretty Mrs. Faison was, and how sad she'd looked.

"What is she like?" Henry asked.

"Beth was the smartest girl at Sweet Briar. I don't think she ever got anything other than an A, and it was effortless. I never saw her take a single note, but she remembered everything. Such a beautiful writer. I really thought that she would go to New York and work for a publishing house."

"Why didn't she?"

"It was a different time," Mrs. Palmer said. "Girls from Richmond didn't move to New York — at least not girls like Beth."

The waiter brought a small platter of puff pastries and crackers with chevre and capers. Mrs. Palmer helped herself to a pastry, and she watched Henry stuff two crackers with cheese into his mouth.

"Why don't you tell me about Lawton Jr.," she said.

Henry stopped chewing and wiped his mouth with his napkin — an uncharacteristic gesture, his mother thought; he's stalling.

"There's not much to tell, really."

"There's something," his mother corrected. "Otherwise, you wouldn't be asking me questions about the Faisons."

The waiter brought Mrs. Palmer a second glass of wine and Henry a glass of iced tea. Mrs. Palmer watched Henry put two teaspoons of sugar into his glass, squeeze the lemon, and stir the ice. Still stalling, she thought. When he looked over to her, she smiled. Henry shrugged. They understood each other.

"I guess you could say me and Lawton got into a fight."

Mrs. Palmer put down her glass of wine. She had not expected that. "Really? A physical fight?"

Henry nodded. "Only it wasn't much of a fight. He got me on the ground pretty quick, and it was over in no time."

"Were you hurt?"

"No. No. It was no big deal, really. He just got mad all of a sudden."

"What was it about?" his mother asked.

Henry wasn't going to open the door to all of that. He'd told her enough already. He waved one hand in front of himself.

"Stupid stuff," he said. "It's not important. Really. But don't tell Gordon."

"You didn't tell him?"

"No! I don't want people to think I hide behind Gordon."

"Okay. Well. It's not going to happen again, is it?"

Henry shook his head. "And don't tell dad either," he said.

"Why not?"

"'Cause he'd tell Gordon, and he and Mr. Faison are friends, right?"

Grace Palmer looked again at the brass chandelier. Ironic, she thought, that Henry should get into a fight with Lawton Jr. She'd been telling her husband for years to dump Lawton Sr. She imagined what her husband would say later that night if she told him she and Henry had spent the evening talking about Lawton Faison; he'd be furious. He always wanted to keep unpleasant facts a secret — even from his own flesh and blood. She felt her face flush. It was partly the wine, she told herself, but she knew it was mostly her anger over her husband's secrets.

"I don't know," she said. "They used to be friends — best friends. Lawton was your father's best man, and Gordon was Lawton's. But I think that's all over now."

Henry leaned forward. This was the most promising lead yet, he thought.

"What happened?"

Grace Palmer took another sip of wine. "Where to begin," she said quietly, as if to herself. "Lawton Faison has never given a second thought to another person — Beth included." She sighed. "You have to understand, the Palmers of McNeil County have nothing on the Faisons of South Carolina — plantation owners, governors, senators. Their hubris is on an entirely different scale. When he married Beth, I think he felt like he was adding another jewel to the family collection. A precious stone that sparkled in the light. And I imagine he now feels like he's been robbed — like one of his paintings has stepped off the wall and walked out the room. It's all of a piece to him — Beth, the house at Sullivan's Island — you remember going there?"

Henry nodded. His mother shook her head.

"I can't imagine what it's been like to live with Lawton for the last ten years, or five years anyway. I've known about it for five years. That's when Lawton came to Raleigh and told Gordon he needed a loan to save their cotton business. Short term. Two years max, he promised. Your father, like an idiot, gave him the money and Lawton gave him a deed of trust on the Sullivan's Island house. Promised it was free and clear. Your dad believed him, of course. 'He's like a brother, Grace,' he said to me."

Grace Palmer shook her head and emptied her second glass of wine.

"Turns out the Sullivan's Island house was already mortgaged to the eaves. The bank foreclosed on their cotton business in August and are foreclosing on the beach property now. This is the Fall of the House of Faison, and Lawton still owes your father two hundred fifty thousand dollars. We'll never get that money back — and Lawton probably feels cheated somehow."

She shook her head at her son.

"Your father would be furious if he knew I told you this, so I guess this can be our little secret too. The two Lawtons." She grinned grimly at her son now, and her bitterness came through. "I hope for the boy's sake, they're not two peas from the same pod."

Was that it? Henry wondered. Lawton's world was collapsing, and he wanted to take a Palmer down just like his father? That seemed weird, but something didn't quite add up—something Gordon had told him.

"Lawton told Gordon his parents are in Paris."

Grace Palmer gave her son a puzzled look. Hadn't she been clear? Wasn't he listening? "The poor dear. He's trying to keep a brave face. Lawton's parents separated last month. Beth is back in Richmond. She's rented a carriage house in The Fan."

Henry drummed the white tablecloth with his middle finger. "You think Lawton knows?"

Mrs. Palmer cast her eyes down to the table. "I talked to Beth last week. She said Lawton asked her not to come this weekend."

Mrs. Palmer pushed one of the pastries on the serving plate away from her, then drew little circles in the white tablecloth with her fingernail. Inadvertently, they had arrived at the real reason she'd wanted to take Henry out to dinner. She hadn't even realized it until now. Was it fair to broach the subject? Gordon, her husband, wouldn't think so, but she knew he had the advantage if she didn't tell anyone.

"It's funny. Me, and Beth, and Jane Oliver—we all moved to Boston that summer, thinking that we'd meet someone, get married, and live happily ever after. And look at us now. Beth's moved back to Richmond. Jane's divorced. And Gordon wants me to move back to Sand Hill."

Henry dropped the cracker and cheese onto the tablecloth. "What? Are you kidding me?"

"Your father says we need to move to Sand Hill to help your uncles with the family business."

"I don't want to live in Sand Hill!" Henry's voice was louder than he realized, and the people sitting at the tables nearby turned to look at them.

Mrs. Palmer lowered her own voice in an effort to calm her son. "Of course you don't. Who does? Whenever we take that turn in Aberdeen, I get a stomach ache."

Grace Palmer broke some bread off the loaf on the table and began tearing it into smaller and smaller pieces. "I honestly think I'll go insane if I have to live there. I told your father that and he just shakes his head and says, 'They need my help. I couldn't live with myself if I stayed here and let it fail.'" She dropped the pieces of bread onto the table. "It's a poor excuse," she continued, as much to herself as to Henry. "He doesn't have to do anything of the kind. If he'd just come out and say 'I want to live in the same town as my careless brothers,' I wouldn't be so mad, but he makes it out to be some kind of great sacrifice. Always the martyr!"

Henry had heard his mother complain about his dad before, but never like this. Never this harsh. Never so categorically. It alarmed him. It almost sounded like she was saying she might leave. Henry adored his mother, and he'd always had a strained relationship with his father, and God knows he'd never thought that the two of them were particularly well suited for each other, but still, he'd always assumed that they had an understanding that transcended their incompatibilities. They'd always managed to put on a good face at home and to the world — at least until now. They went to parties together. They gave parties. They seemed to know all the right people. Their life seemed pretty good from what Henry could see, and his dad had made all of that possible, or a lot of it anyway, since he was the one who had a job and made the money.

"You did kind of marry into this didn't you?" he said somewhat sheepishly. "I mean you knew about dad's family in Sand Hill and everything, right? It's not like Dad kept his loyalty a secret."

Grace Palmer realized that maybe she had said too much. She exhaled and felt her pulse slow. Although she had always seen Gordon Jr. as more her husband's child and Henry as more her own — both in temperament and natural affection — and although she had always sought succor in her relationship with her younger son — surely more than she would have had she also had a daughter, which she'd always wanted, — still, she had never wanted Henry to feel like he had to choose between his mother and his father. And she did not want to compromise Henry's affection for his father. She wanted Henry to be strong and natural in all of his feelings. But she also wanted to be honest with him and with herself.

"You're right. Your father has been a good husband and a good provider." She reached across the table and squeezed Henry's hand. The mother and son looked at each other. They held each other's gaze tenderly and without embarrassment.

"The only thing I'll add," Grace said, "and it's the last thing I'll say about it, is that sometimes I feel like he puts his birth family above our family."

She let go of Henry's hand then. He didn't fully comprehend what his mother had just said, but it didn't sound like she was getting ready to do anything too drastic, and it did sound like she was ready to change the subject, which was a relief.

"Tell me about your friends," his mother said.

LAWTON PAINTS THE WATER TOWER

WHILE HENRY AND GRACE PALMER discussed his family, Lawton Faison stood on a water tower platform one hundred feet above the grounds of the Randolph School. It was nine o'clock and most of the students were at the pep rally behind the Randolph Building getting fired up for tomorrow's homecoming game. He could hear the cheers in the distance and knew he had at least a half hour before anyone would be in the vicinity. The quarter moon was only beginning to rise, and Lawton wore the same black pants and black sweatshirt that he'd worn the night he ran into Henry and Mongo on the Lawn. He'd done a dry run by himself that night. Tonight, Billy Richardson stood on the ground with a flashlight.

Lawton held a quart of paint and a paintbrush and walked around the platform, eyeing Mortimer Hall to get his bearings. If he painted it here, he'd be able to see it from his dorm room in the morning, and everyone would see it when they walked to breakfast. He stepped to the other side of the tower. If he painted it here it would be visible from the football field and Mr. Endicott's house. He had planned on painting it only once, on the side facing the dorms, but as he stood here now, looking down on Endicott's house, he decided to paint it twice, because he wanted Endicott to wake up to it in the morning. The man was an autocrat — it's what Lawon admired most about him — but Lawton bore a grudge against him. Had Endicott wanted him on the prefect board, he would be on the prefect board. When Lawton called his father last Spring to break the news, his father hadn't said a word. At first, Lawton thought he'd lost the connection.

"Hello?"

"How did this happen?" his father had finally said. "I was a prefect. Thomas was a prefect. Every Faison who's ever attended Randolph has been a prefect. How could you let us down?"

"I don't know. I thought I'd be elected. Mr. Nightingale said he thought I'd be elected. Everyone I talked to said they couldn't believe I hadn't been elected. Gordon couldn't believe it — "

"Was Gordon elected?" his father asked.

"Yes," Lawton said reluctantly.

Long silence. "I don't understand it son. This is disappointing. To say the least."

Lawton knew his father was a dick. When he'd called home to tell his father he'd been selected head of Chapel Council, his father had sounded indifferent. Two weeks ago, when Lawton asked his father if he were coming up for Parents Weekend, the elder Faison had said he had to stay in Charleston for meetings but maybe his mother could drive over from Richmond. Lawton had called his mother and told her not to come. He didn't want to have to explain to people why his mother was there without his father — or why his mother lived in Richmond now.

At least his father would hear about the painting on the water tower from friends. He imagined his father asking him about it. "Yeah. It's pretty cool looking," he would say. "It was a sign used by early Christians so they could find each other. No one knows who did it, but they think it's a protest about how the school's abandoning tradition." His father would like that. Lawton wouldn't tell him he'd had anything to do with it. Not now. Not yet. Someday he'd tell him. When the time was right.

Lawton dipped his brush into the black paint. The water tower was painted a light silver color. Lawton was confident the black paint would be visible from campus. He felt a sudden pain in his back and realized he wasn't standing up straight. He stretched his arms above his head and rolled back his shoulders. He stared up at the uncouth stars. Billions and billions of galaxies? He didn't believe it. He held the brush out at chest level then painted a long arc that rose as high as he could reach and fell to a point below his waist as he walked around the water tower. He returned to the point of beginning and painted a second arc, this one falling to a height level with his knees and rising to a height above his eyes. Altogether the fish spanned a quarter of the tower — the quarter facing the campus. Then Lawton took several steps around the tower and repeated the process, so that the second fish towered over Endicott's house and would be seen from the football field tomorrow. Then in letters between the two fish, he wrote I-Ch-Th-U-S so that there would be no doubt about his meaning.

Lawton walked back to the ladder rungs and looked for Richardson but could not see him. He took a flashlight from his pocket and flashed it once down towards the ground; a few seconds later Richardson answered with a single flash. Coast was clear. Lawton left the paint brush and can on the tower platform, and climbed down the ladder. From the sound of things the pep rally was still going strong. If they hurried, he and Billy could make it there for the final cheer, so if anyone asked they could say truthfully that they were at the pep rally.

ENDICOTT WAKES TO FISH

THE NEXT MORNING Edwin Endicott tucked himself in at his breakfast table with six rashers of bacon, three eggs over easy, two English muffins, a pot of Maxwell House, The Washington Post, and The Sporting News. Because he still taught one section of AP U.S. History, he kept abreast of current events, but his passion was the Sports section. For twenty years Endicott had coached high school basketball, and while other men his age titillated themselves with distorted memories of past dalliances, Endicott's mind drifted toward the past triumphs — and catastrophes — of his coaching career. The mention of a familiar name in a newspaper story about the Pentagon was apt to remind him of an opposing player who had hit a winning basket or one of his own boys who had failed to convert the front end of a one-and-one in a close game. He had tried to continue coaching after being named Headmaster, but midway through his last season, after being thrown out of a home game for berating the official about an egregious no-call, the students had refused to stop chanting, "ED-WIN! ED-WIN!", and he'd realized he would have to resign. To this day, he attended every home basketball game, but if a game got too close or a referee's incompetence became too costly, he would leave the stands and watch the rest of the game through the small window of one of the gym's exit doors. There, he could curse as loud as he wanted and tell himself that no one could hear him.

Endicott's second great love was the Civil War. A proud graduate of the Virginia Military Institute, Endicott had, over the last five years, reconstructed a miniature Battle of Chancellorsville, circa 11 p.m. on May 2, 1863, when Stonewall Jackson was still alive and his Second Corps was bivouacked after routing the right flank of Hooker's Army of the Potomac. One hundred and thirty-three lead soldiers painted blue and sixty lead soldiers painted grey were stationed at various places in his backyard. Their numbers and locations represented the relative strengths and positions of the Union and Confederate forces at that fateful hour. A solitary equestrian figure, hand painted by Endicott, represented Stonewall Jackson astride Little Sorrel. The Stonewall figure was substantially larger than the others, because Endicott considered Jackson to be a towering colossus. Twice, Endicott had cleared the ground and laid out the battlefield again because of some new, and to his mind crucial, piece of information. Even today, one hundred and fifteen years after the great event, historians were still unearthing field reports or letters from soldiers with scraps of news about that momentous day.

Surveying the battlefield in his backyard, Endicott always asked himself, Why had Jackson paused his advance just shy of Chancellorsville after routing the Union's XI Corps? Was it only the light of the full moon that had lured Jackson out for a personal reconnaissance along the Orange Plank Road? How had Jackson's command post lost contact with the 18th North Carolina Infantry? Why had that infantry mistaken Jackson and his small group of officers for Union cavalry? On such small events, like Bonaparte delaying his advance on Moscow, hung the fates of nations and empires. Amateur historians famously argued that had Lee had Jackson at Gettysburg, Pickett's charge would never have happened, the rebel army would have taken Cemetery Ridge, and the Confederacy would have won the battle. But Endicott had a different, more reactionary theory. He believed that had Jackson not fallen at Chancellorsville, Gettysburg would have never happened, because

Lee would have pressed forward to Washington, laid siege to the Capitol, and forced a truce that would have secured the Confederacy its nationhood before Lincoln found Grant and before Sherman laid waste to the South.

Endicott carried his breakfast plate to the sink and looked down at the putting green of the Seventh Hole. Lefty Early, the school's alumni director, was lining up his putt. "Duffer," Endicott thought. He'd never seen Lefty sink a putt longer than ten feet. Early stepped back from his line and pointed up to the sky. He said something to his companion and the other man — a parent, Endicott thought, from the looks of him, well-dressed, nice golf bag — turned and looked up in the direction Early was pointing. Endicott glanced in that direction, and — what the hell? There were two long lines of paint on the water tower. Endicott dropped his plate into the sink and rushed outside. There it was — two intersecting arcs, connected at one end, heading in opposite directions at the other.

"What is that, Lefty?" Endicott shouted to Early on the putting green.

"It looks like a fish, Edwin. Or an arrow."

"Maybe a vase lying on its side," the other man said.

That's a relief, Endicott thought. For a moment he'd feared the worst: a penis. "Who's on duty? Mackie?"

"I believe so," Lefty said.

"I'll call him."

Endicott waved to the two men and rushed inside. It was too early in the year for the senior prank, he thought. This must be the work of a rogue student. Endicott picked up his phone and told the switchboard operator to connect him to Mr. Mackie. Years ago a boy had hijacked a farm tractor and driven it into Hayes Pond on Parents Weekend. Endicott had never caught the boy, but he'd chalked it up to hijinks. This seemed different, more sinister — symbolic even, heaven forbid. Endicott hated symbols — too provocative because too open to interpretation. Endicott liked facts — you couldn't dispute a fact. Good thing Mackie was the master on duty. He was the right man to decipher any clues and get to the bottom of things.

After two rings he heard the sharp, clipped voice of Terence Mackie answer the phone.

"Terry? Edwin here. Have you seen the water tower? ... Why didn't you call me? ... Okay.... What the hell is it? ... That's what I thought.

Have you called Frank? ... Not yet? Okay ... It's on both sides of the water tower? So you can see it from campus as well? ... God Almighty! Well, let's get someone up there right away and paint over it. It's just after 9 now. With luck we'll have it painted over before most of the parents get here."

Endicott hung up the phone. Why in the world would someone paint the sign of the fish on the water tower, he wondered.

HENRY AND KEN BREAK THE ICE

BY 9 A.M. WORD OF THE STRANGE painting had already spread on campus. As Lawton had predicted, most of the students saw it when they walked to breakfast. On B Dorm Mongo heard about it when Bone burst into his room.

"Dude! Wake up! You gotta see this!"

Mongo lay asleep on his side, facing the door. When he opened his eyes and saw Bone jumping up and down and panting beside his bed, he rolled over and faced the wall. Bone slapped his shoulder with a sweaty palm.

"Wake up! Wake up! Somebody painted a penis on the water tower!"

Knowing that Bone in his present state of excitement would not be able to leave him alone, Mongo got out of bed, put on a bathrobe and walked outside, barelegged and in flip flops. He and Bone stood on the patch of grass between the Randolph Building and Faison Chapel and looked up at the tower. Mongo was skeptical of Bone's penis theory. To him it looked more like a sperm or a squid.

"Naw, man. I'm telling you. It's like resting," Bone insisted.

"Resting?" Mongo wasn't fully awake and shook his body like a dog shaking water off its back. "Your dick sticks straight out when it's resting?"

"Maybe.... Sometimes." In his mind Bone contemplated his junk. He could see Mongo's point, but he wasn't ready to give up on penises. "Or maybe it's like lying on a table."

"Lying on a table? Why is a penis lying on a table?"

While Mongo and Bone debated the finer points of penis vs. squid vs. sperm, Ken Bright joined them.

"I don't know," Bone said sheepishly.

"And what are those two legs?" Mongo asked, pointing up at the diverging lines at the right side of the painting.

Bone thought about it. "Not sure." He frowned. His pet theory wasn't passing muster. Suddenly he brightened. "It's a vagina!" he cried out. "And those are the girls' legs!"

Mongo considered that. "Like she's lying on her side?" Mongo asked.

"Yeah. Yeah. Like that," Bone panted.

That could work, Mongo thought to himself. "What d'you think, Ken?"

Ken thought Bone was an idiot. He disliked Bone. "I say it's doggerel," Ken said.

"Dog-world?" Bone asked.

"Badly done. A botched job. Impossible to say," Ken explained.

Twenty yards away, beside the flagpole directly in front of the main doors to the school, Henry and Wobbly were having their own confab. They had heard about the painting at breakfast and had come out to take a look for themselves. Wobbly had been at the point of suggesting they go back inside when Ken Bright joined Mongo and Bone.

"That guy's weird," Wobbly had said.

Wobbly did not offer this observation to enlighten Henry about his ill opinion of Ken Bright — that was hardly news; he offered it in hopes of chumming up a like-minded sentiment from Henry. Wobbly had observed the recent cooling off between Henry and their next door neighbor, and he hoped that with a little encouragement Henry might toss the jerk overboard altogether.

Henry, however, did not take the bait. He was careful to take no notice as Ken walked down the front steps, and he turned his back on the group of seniors as soon as Ken joined Mongo and Bone.

"Want to head in?" Wobbly asked.

"Sure."

They had started to walk back inside when Mongo called out.

"Hey, Henry! Come over here!"

Mongo waved for Henry to join them. Henry headed in that direction and Wobbly followed.

"Not you, Wobby!" Mongo said.

Henry turned to his roommate. "I'll meet you back at the room," he said.

Wobbly scuffed his right shoe against the ground and briefly considered walking over with Henry in a show of spunk, but the sight of Mongo in his bathrobe got the better of him.

Ken and Henry nodded to each other as Henry joined the group.

"How's it going?" Henry said to no one in particular.

Mongo clapped Henry on the back with his heavy hand. "Bone's deadset on penis. I think it's a squid. Ken's not so sure. What d'you think, Henry? You get the final word."

"Strange penis," Henry said.

"Squid it is!" Mongo shouted. He grabbed Bone by the elbow. "You owe me five bucks!"

"What about a pussy?" Bone entreated Henry. "I also said I thought it was pussy."

Mongo winked at Ken and pulled Bone toward the front steps. "I'm going to take Bone inside and throw him in the shower," Mongo said. Bone laughed and they left together.

Henry and Ken were left standing on the patch of grass. It was the first time they'd been alone since that night in Ken's room.

"How's it going?" Henry repeated.

"Swimmingly," Ken said. "And you?"

"Hanging in there."

"How's Wobbly treating you?"

Henry thought of a half dozen things Wobbly had done over the last ten days that would have made Ken laugh, but he held back. "You know. No complaints."

"As broad-minded as ever?"

Henry smiled. "As ever."

Two questions had dominated Ken's thoughts. Would Henry tell anyone what had happened? And could Henry still be a friend? Ken had concluded that Henry had not told anyone, because he hadn't found himself the sudden object of disgusted looks or derisive comments. The only change he had noticed was Henry's standoffishness. Several times he had started to reach out to Henry, but each time his fear of encountering Henry's disapprobation had paralyzed him. This paralysis was so shameful that Ken had finally decided that Henry would have to make amends. And here Henry was, albeit not by his own choosing.

"Mongo seems to want to throw us together," Ken said.

"I guess." Ken seemed a little cold to Henry, but not unfriendly. He decided to take a chance. "I had another run-in with Lawton."

"Really?"

"Out on the Lawn. Mongo showed up out of nowhere and sent him packing."

"A knight errant," Ken said.

Henry pointed at the water tower. "I think he must have been doing a dry-run on the water tower."

Ken was confused. "Mongo?"

"No. Lawton," Henry said.

Ken shook his head. "I don't understand."

"I'm pretty sure Lawton painted the fish," Henry said.

"What fish?"

Henry pointed at the water tower again. "The fish on the water tower."

Ken looked at it again. He didn't see any gills, or fins, or even an eye. "What on Earth makes you think that's a fish?"

"I'm telling you it's a fish."

Ken tilted his head to the left and to the right in order to get a fresh look then shook his head. "I vote with Bone. Penis or pussy — at least that's funny. Especially Parents Weekend."

An awkward silence descended. Henry suspected Ken was being deliberately obtuse. That was okay, because Henry didn't want to try to explain himself anyway — the crazy shit Lawton had said the night he got beat up, the night Ken tried to nurse his wounds. He still didn't know what he thought about it, and he definitely didn't want to revisit it with Ken. At first he'd wondered if he'd imagined the whole thing; then he'd wondered if he'd misinterpreted the look on Ken's face. But if that were the case, Ken wouldn't have avoided him the way he had avoided Ken. Henry was sure it was what he thought it was. He just couldn't figure out what to make of it.

Just then Uly walked by carrying a quart of paint in one hand and a paint brush in the other.

"Uly!" Ken called out.

"Hi-i-i-i!" Uly waved at Ken and Henry.

Henry watched the small dog trotting beside him. Every few steps the dog would look up, expecting some comment or nod from its master.

"Hey Uly, what's your dog's name?" Henry asked.

Uly stopped, smiled at Henry, and looked down at his dog. He smiled even more brightly. "This is Maisie," he said. "Maisie and me have been good friends these last seven years."

The dog recognized its name and barked smartly as if in agreement. It looked at Uly, then looked at Henry and wagged its tail. Henry laughed.

"It's very nice to meet you Maisie." He looked at Uly. "My name is Henry, by the way. Henry Palmer."

Uly nodded at Henry. "Thank you, sir." Then he nodded at Ken and walked on in the direction of the water tower.

Ken took a step back and took the measure of Henry again.

"What?" Henry asked.

"Nothing," Ken said. "Just more surprises."

Ken smiled, and Henry relaxed.

"Hey, so guess what Mackie assigned for our next paper?"

Ken rolled his eyes in mock boredom. "Color symbolism in *The Red Badge of Courage.*"

"No. A Whitman poem."

Ken perked up. "Really? That was decent of him. Which one?"

"'O Captain, My Captain'."

Ken threw up his arms in mild protest. "Of course he'd pick that one! But better than *Red Badge of Courage* I guess."

"Yeah, it seems kind of obvious."

"There's lots better poems about Lincoln's dead body," Ken said.

"I was thinking about writing about that poem that's on your wall," Henry said.

Ken, who had been casually casting his eyes at the water tower, the flagpole, and the front doors in order to avoid seeming overeager of Henry's company, now turned to him in surprise.

"'*As Adam In the Morning*'?"

"Is that what it's called?"

Ken nodded. "It's a better poem, for sure."

"Do you think you might help me with it?" Henry asked.

Ken wondered if this was some kind of peace offering. It's not that easy, he thought. He can't just pretend that nothing happened. Ken shook his head. "You can figure it out. All I'll say is it's not about what you think it's about."

"I only read it once," Henry said.

"Then it's not what you will think it's about." Ken stepped around Henry and moved toward the front steps. "I got to go change. My mom's taking me to lunch before the game."

Henry had hoped his request would show Ken that he didn't hold anything against him, but as he watched Ken walk away he had his first inkling that maybe Ken felt like Henry had done him an injustice rather than the other way around.

As the two boys parted company, Uly climbed the ladder to the water tower platform with a can of silver paint and a paint brush. After he left Henry and Ken in front of the Randolph Building, he'd told Maisie everything he knew about Henry Palmer and his brother Gordon and their father, Mr. Gordon Palmer. Uly remembered when Mr. Palmer was a student, and he knew that he was now on the Board of Trustees and that Gordon was the Head Boy. He also remembered other Palmers who'd attended the school, just as he remembered other Faisons. "That's the first time any of those boys ever introduced themselves to me. Ain't that something, Maisie? Ain't that something!"

When he reached the tower platform, Uly opened the lid to the can of paint and stirred the paint with the brush. He recognized the Jesus fish from church, and he took a quick breath and crossed himself out of respect before painting over it. It only took him fifteen minutes to cover both fishes and the Ichthys. He tapped the lid back into place and climbed back down the tower. Maisie sat at the bottom of the ladder, looking up. As Uly got closer, her tail wagged faster.

HENRY GETS A WRITING LESSON

DAVID NIGHTINGALE SAT AT THE DESK in his classroom grading English papers. It was the last period of the day, and soon he would head to the gym to coach squash. For now he was offering gentle commentary to his students' mostly dull musings about *The Heart of Darkness*. He heard a tap at the door; when he looked up he saw Henry Palmer standing in the doorway with a backpack slung over one shoulder.

"Henry. Come in."

Henry hesitated. "If you're in the middle of something I can come back another time."

Mr. Nightingale replaced the cap on his fountain pen. "Oh no. I'm just grading papers. I welcome the interruption." He smiled at Henry and motioned to a desk. "Have a seat and give me a moment to finish marking this paper."

Henry slipped the backpack off his shoulder and took a seat in the chair closest to Nightingale's desk. He watched Nightingale write on the back of one of the papers. Henry hadn't noticed before just how large his hands were. Large and supple. He could imagine him holding a football or gripping a baseball, but he looked just as comfortable handling a fountain pen. Henry looked around the room. The numerous illustrations, photographs and quotations on the walls uplifted him, like the cliffside winds to the wings of a bird.

"What can I do for you, Henry?" he said at last.

"I was wondering if I could get your help on a paper. Not with writing it, or actually not with any paper in particular. Umm, I guess what I want is help with writing in general."

Nightingale leaned back in his chair and placed both hands behind his head. "I can try. What seems to be the problem?"

Henry fiddled with the zipper on his backpack. The confounding mind-boggle he experienced whenever he tried to put his thoughts and feelings to paper was hard to describe. Why was it so hard for him to say what he thought? He bit one corner of his bottom lip.

"The problem is that whenever I try to write anything I get turned around in three different directions until I'm stuck and can't figure out where I am, or how I got there, or where I'm going."

Nightingale leaned forward, placed an elbow on his desk and rested his chin on the ample palm of his hand. He considered Henry for a moment. "Sounds like maybe you're trying to say so much that you never get to the end of saying anything."

Henry nodded. "Maybe." He nodded again. "That sounds right." He drummed his fingers against his knee. "I don't know. I just got my paper back from Mr. Mackie, and it's not so much the grade — although that sucks — sorry."

Henry blushed. He already felt awkward enough coming to Mr. Nightingale for help, and now that he was sounding like an idiot.... Nightingale smiled to assure him no offense was taken.

"I got a C," Henry grimaced, "which is bad." He looked up at Nightingale and shook his head emphatically. "But I don't care about the grade so much as the fact that I can't seem to be able to get down on paper everything that I want to say."

Nightingale smiled at the boy and held out his hand. "Can I have a look at it?"

Henry opened his backpack and rummaged through his books until he found the paper in a crumpled wad at the bottom of the sack. He handed it to Mr. Nightingale and felt embarrassed as the teacher flattened it against his desk with a broad hand.

"'Down the River with Huck and Jim'. That's a good title," Nightingale said.

"Thanks. I wanted to write about what Huck learns — what Jim teaches him — on the river."

"I can see that," Nightingale said, as he flipped to the second page.

"But it's a complete shitshow —" Henry slapped the side of his head. "Sorry! — a mess, almost as soon as I get started."

Nightingale read the paper and put it down on the desk in front of him. "Why don't you tell me why it is that you wanted to write about —" he looked down to get the wording exactly right — "'a river of discovery' that Huck and Jim are on."

Henry fidgeted. "Well, Mr. Mackie said that *Huckleberry Finn* is the greatest American novel because it deals with slavery, which is America's original sin."

Nightingale smiled. "That is a big topic, very ambitious, and you mention that in your first paragraph, and that very well may be true — I won't try to dispute it — but I'm not asking you what you think

Huckleberry Finn is about. I'm asking why you titled your paper 'Down the River with Huck and Jim' and what for you makes the trip seem like 'a river of discovery'?"

Henry rocked forward and backward as he recalled how excited he'd felt when he came up with his idea for the paper. "It's because the farther down the river Huck goes the more he begins to think for himself."

Nightingale smiled and once again leaned back in his chair. "That's very good, Henry. What part of the story excited you the most?"

Henry thought about it. "Probably the very end, when Huck decides he's not going to go back with Tom or stay with the Phelpses but instead he's going to head out for the Territories with Jim."

Nightingale held out a forefinger and seemed to take aim at Henry's heart. "What did you like about that?"

Henry almost laughed with excitement. "It was like he was finally going to be his own person but a new person, because he was headed for the wilderness, and he was choosing to go with Jim because he realized Jim was his best friend, even though he's a slave, or was a slave."

Nightingale nodded as he considered Henry's response. "And does that have anything to do with learning how to think for yourself?"

Henry rocked back in his chair. "Well, yeah. I mean he wants to go to the Territories with Jim because he doesn't want to be told what to do — to be civilized — but wants to be his own person and do as he pleases, like he did all that time with Jim on the river."

Nightingale held his hands out, palms up, as if to say *voila!* "You've written your paper," he said.

Henry smiled. "Only because you asked me the right questions. When I'm by myself I start thinking and thinking and try harder and harder to say something important, and pretty soon I'm lost. The harder I try to say what I think, the less sense I make."

Nightingale had seen these symptoms before — but not often enough. A boy who tries to fly before he has fledged. The good news was that he was trying to fly at all.

"I congratulate you, Henry, for leaving home port and setting sail. Too many people never leave the shore."

Henry was relieved that Nightingale at least recognized he was trying. Still, what was the cause of his muddle?

"I feel like I'm supposed to find some great idea out there, and I keep reaching for it …. " Henry held out a hand and opened and closed his fingers on the empty air. "But I can't ever grab it, and I end up drowning."

"You're not drowning, Henry. You're swimming. Learning to swim. Learning to fly. Everyone should try it. Most don't."

Henry bit his lip. He knew that Mr. Nightingale was trying to help, and he believed that he was being encouraging and everything, but what he really wanted was some concrete advice about how to get beyond this dunderheaded wall that he was always beating his head against. He shook his head at what he was sure was a stupid question but asked it anyway. "How do I become a better writer?"

Nightingale recognized the yearning behind Henry's question, and he did not want to be hasty with his answer. He took off his horned rim glasses and rubbed his eyes. He picked up the pile of AP English essays that he had graded and shuffled their edges into a neat pile.

"I'd say there's two things. One is clarity—making sure your thoughts are communicated clearly. That's a formal thing that anyone can help you with so long as you practice. The other is honesty, and that's the harder thing. Lots of people are clear. Not many are honest. And by honest I don't mean not telling lies. I mean telling the truth, and not truth like it's some golden nugget or buried treasure that you discover, but truth about who you are and what you care about. It sounds trite, but it's not. To be a really good writer you have to be yourself. And only you can do that."

Nightingale handed Henry back his paper, and when Henry took it Nightingale smiled. Henry was pleased and then embarrassed.

"Thanks," he muttered.

"You are welcome."

"I'm not sure I understand everything you said."

Nightingale laughed. "I'm not sure I do either. We just do the best we can."

Henry stuffed the paper back into his book bag. He was thinking about what Nightingale had said about being honest about who you are, and he was thinking about his next writing assignment for Mackie, 'O Captain! My Captain!'. He zipped up his bag.

"There is one more thing," Henry said.

"What's that, Henry?"

"Do you mind if I ask you about a poem?"

Nightingale laughed. "Of course not. I love poems!"

"I have to write a paper about a Walt Whitman poem. Mr. Mackie assigned 'O Captain! My Captain!' It's not that it's a bad poem or anything. I mean I like it and all. It's just that I don't *really* like it, and there's another Whitman poem I like a lot more, and I want to write about it, because I feel like I have something to say, and you said just now, 'Be honest about who you are.' If I don't feel like I have anything to say about "O Captain! My Captain!", how can I be honest about who I am?"

"I think I agree with you," Nightingale said. "What poem are you thinking about?"

"'*As Adam Early in the Morning*'," Henry said.

"Really?" Nightingale was surprised Henry had read it; he'd never seen it anthologized.

"Yeah," Henry said.

Nightingale tapped the top of his desk with two fingers. "I love that poem. Definitely one of my favorites."

"I like it too, but there is some stuff that I'm not sure I understand."

"Do you have a copy?" Nightingale started to reach for his copy of Leaves of Grass on the bookshelf behind his desk.

"Uh-huh." Henry reached into his pocket and pulled out a scrap of paper with the lines of the poem written out by hand.

Nightingale pointed at the paper. "Did you copy it out?"

Henry nodded. "I couldn't find it in a book. Ken Bright had it up on his wall. He said you'd read it to them in English class."

"Yes I did," Nightingale laughed. "Small world."

Henry looked at the paper in his hand. "So I guess I was wondering—"

"Why don't you read the poem first. Then we'll talk about it," Nightingale said.

Henry held the paper out in front of him.

"I mean out loud. Read the poem out loud," Nightingale said.

Henry sat up in his chair and his eyes widened. "Okay," he said, and cleared his throat.

> As Adam early in the morning,
> Walking forth from the bower, refreshed with sleep,
> Behold me where I pass, hear my voice, approach,

Touch me, touch the palm of your hand to my body,
as I pass,
Be not afraid of my body.

Nightingale nodded. "That's good, Henry. You read that well. What do you make of it?"

Henry had liked the poem when he read it weeks ago in Ken's room but he had not thought about it again until Mackie assigned the Whitman poem. Ken had let him copy it but had refused to talk about it. All he'd said was, "It's not about what you think it's about." Henry wanted to figure out what he—Henry—thought it was about.

"I was kind of hoping you might help me figure it out," Henry said.

"It is a surprisingly knotty poem, isn't it? I always struggle with the last line, 'Be not afraid of my body'. What about the body is he saying 'be not afraid of'?"

Henry stared into the piece of paper like it was a looking glass, like he was seeing something in himself for the first time. Nightingale said nothing. He watched Henry and waited for him to ask for help.

"Touching it," Henry said. "He's saying do not be afraid to touch the body."

"Good. And why is someone afraid to touch another person's body?" Nightingale asked.

Henry remembered Ken touching him. He hadn't thought anything of it. It was like the nurse in Dr. Cohen's office or the time Mrs. Irving wiped his scrape with a damp cloth after lunch break in second grade. It was only when he'd seen the look on Ken's face that he'd been afraid.

"He's afraid of getting too close to someone," Henry said quietly.

"That's very good, Henry. And why do you think we are afraid of getting too close to another person?"

Henry opened his mouth, as if he were about to say something, but stopped. Then he moved his lips but no words came out. Nightingale had seen it before. The boy was teetering on the edge of his understanding. He needed more time, and, for now, a little help.

"Whitman did write homoerotic poems, or poems about homosexual intimacy, but many of his poems that are considered homoerotic are really about friendship. I think that's what this poem is about."

Henry looked back at the piece of paper in his hand and realized that he'd been the one who'd been afraid—not Ken. "It does say, 'Touch me'," he said hesitantly. "And he is talking about him touching his body."

Henry shifted in his chair and looked at the pictures hanging in the classroom. Nightingale slowly rubbed the back of his head and gave Henry a moment to settle his nerves.

"You know," he said kindly, "in Whitman's lifetime, men were far more affectionate with one another than they are now. They held hands. We have letters from men like President Lincoln and Alexander Hamilton in which they profess their love for their male friends. There's nothing homosexual about it."

Henry blinked. "But what if one of the people really is gay?"

"And the other's not?"

Henry nodded slowly and blushed.

Nightingale held up the fingers of one hand and pretended not to notice Henry's embarrassment. "Sexual intimacy, or *Eros*, is just one form of love," he said, and he brushed the pinky of his left hand with his right forefinger. "There's also friendship." He brushed another finger. "The love of a parent and child. There's selfless love, or what the Ancient Greeks called *Agape* — the love for the good of another. I think the Greeks had, maybe, six different words for love. Each of them described a different quality of what we call love. The fact that one person's gay and the other's not doesn't prevent you from sharing these other forms of love. Only fear prevents that. And what is there, really, to be afraid of? That, I think, is what Whitman is talking about."

The bell rang, and they heard classroom doors opening and boys pouring out into the hallway. Henry had basketball practice, and Nightingale had to coach squash.

"I hope that helped," Nightingale said.

Henry nodded and slung his backpack over his shoulder. On his way out the door, he pointed at one of the illustrations on the wall.

"What's this, Mr. Nightingale?"

Nightingale leaned to one side to see which picture Henry was pointing to.

"That's Adam and Eve," he said, "being expelled from the Garden of Eden in *Paradise Lost*. The moment they step out into the world of shadows, the world we all live in, to make their solitary way'."

"Is that Gustav Dore?" Henry asked.

"Yes it is. How did you know?"

"Ken Bright has an illustration by him of Dante crossing the River Styx."

"Ah yes. Passing through the Stygian darkness as we all must."

'As we all must' — Henry felt a sudden thrill…but he couldn't put his finger on why. He only knew that he was happy.

"See you later," Henry said.

Mr. Nightingale watched the boy walk out his door, and he nodded to himself. That one will turn out all right, he thought.

OWL

THE NEXT DAY, Ken sat in his green armchair with his headphones on, staring at his Ziggy Stardust poster and bobbing his head to *When the Whip Comes Down* when there was a knock at his door and Henry Palmer walked in.

"Palmer!" He fumbled with his headphones and almost dropped them before placing them on his receiver and turning off the music. "What a surprise."

"How's it going?"

Ken crumpled the sheet of notebook paper in his hand and tossed it to the floor beside half a dozen other wads of paper. "My *Lycidas* paper," he said. "Having trouble getting into the groove."

Henry started to turn back. "Should I come back later?"

Ken waved him forward and moved the *Norton Anthology of Poetry* from his bed to the floor. "Have a seat."

Henry hesitated as he remembered sitting there the night Lawton beat him up. Ken recognized his hesitation and muttered, "Oh fuck."

"No, no. It's fine," Henry said, embarrassed that he'd managed to call to mind the one thing he'd been determined to avoid. "I've been meaning to talk to you about something," he added quickly.

Ken inhaled, thinking that Henry might actually broach the subject. "Okay?" But Henry only took a seat, scratched a sudden itch at his elbow, and glanced around the room, seeming to take an inventory of the wall hangings.

"What's up?" Ken said, in an effort to coax Henry along.

"I feel like we kind of got sidetracked the other day. Last Saturday. Out there." Henry pointed towards the flagpole in front of the Randolph Building.

Ken nodded, but now he had no idea what Henry was talking about. "Uh-huh?"

"I was trying to tell you how I know Lawton painted the fish on the water tower."

Ken turned away from Henry and pretended to stare at something outside his window. He really didn't want to talk about Lawton Faison right now. "Okay," he muttered.

Henry misinterpreted Ken's body language as a brush-off and gave the back of Ken's head the finger. "It's because he wanted me to join his secret society," he said loudly, as if in protest.

When Ken turned around he was frowning. "'Secret society'?" he asked, using his fingers to put the term in quotation marks.

Henry rubbed the tops of his thighs. He couldn't tell whether Ken's irritation was directed towards Lawton or towards himself. "Yeah. To make Randolph more Christian."

"More Christian?" Ken scoffed. "Chapel, prayers before sitdown dinners — what 'more' does he want? Hair shirts? Hallelujahs?"

Henry breathed a sigh of relief and leaned back against the wall. "He said the board of trustees is going to insist that Randolph hire its first Jewish teacher."

Ken pursed his lips and arched an eyebrow. "That's bullshit. No offense, but have you seen who's on the board of trustees?"

"That's what he said."

"Well, did you ask your father?"

"No. I'm not going to tell him Lawton's started a secret society."

"I mean about the Jewish teacher."

Henry rolled his eyes and shook his head. "You don't know my dad. He'd suspect something was up and it's off to the races."

Ken stood up and kicked the balls of paper across the floor. "Lawton's full of shit," he said irritably.

"He is head of Chapel Council."

Ken turned suddenly to face Henry. "You mean Deemer's little band of Nazis?"

The anger caught Henry by surprise. "'Nazis''s a bit much."

Ken pointed his finger. "You're the one who said he wants to protest hiring a Jewish teacher."

Henry nodded. "That's fair."

Ken plopped back down into his chair and slapped his knee. It irritated him that he had let Lawton Faison get under his skin. "What does any of this have to do with the water tower?"

"It's the fish," Henry said.

Ken remembered Henry's fish theory from the other day. "You said that. I still like penis better."

"It's the sign of the fish."

Ken threw up his hands. "What does that mean?"

"Early Christians used the sign of the fish to find each other."

Ken shook his head like Henry was speaking gibberish. "Is this some kind of loaves and fishes thing, 'cause I'm not getting it."

"No. It's the Greek word for fish. Ick-something."

"Ichthys," Ken said.

"That's it — how do you know that?"

"Ichthyology."

"What does that mean?"

"It's the study of fish. From the Greek, Ichthys."

Henry laughed. "How do you know that stuff?"

Ken pretended to be surprised and pointed to his own face like Henry didn't recognize him. "Hey! It's me! I'm the word guy. Perfect 800 on my SATs."

Henry held his palms out and bowed to Ken in mock obeisance.

"That's the name of Lawton's secret society," Henry said.

"The fish? That's lame. No wonder you didn't join." Ken looked to Henry for confirmation, and when Henry didn't say anything he thrust out his hand. "You didn't join, right? You're not one of those anti-semitic creeps, are you?"

"No! I didn't join. And that's what I told Lawton. I said it sounded racist."

"Good boy. 'Cause you know I'm Jewish, right?"

"Really?" Now Henry was surprised. He couldn't think of another Jewish friend.

"Yeah. I mean, I'm not a practicing Jew — obviously." Ken pointed to the walls and ceiling of his room to indicate the world of the Randolph

School. "My family immigrated from Russia a long time ago—fled the Cossacks, before the Nazis. Bright means 'the one who is loved' in Hebrew. So I bear the stamp of my Jewish heritage at least."

"Does Lawton know you're Jewish?"

"I'm sure he suspects it."

"Why's that?"

"Because he's an anti-Semite, and he hates me."

"He hates you because he thinks you're Jewish?"

"I don't know if he thinks I'm Jewish. I don't go around talking about it—unless you bring it up. But yes he does hate me, and I hate him. It's a delicious bit of shared contempt."

"Why?"

Ken tapped his fingers against his forehead, and he was surprised to discover that he actually relished the opportunity to finally declare this animosity that he'd long kept to himself.

"It's not for the obvious reasons—that he's the most arrogant smug bastard at a school full of smug bastards. No, that really doesn't bother me anymore. I think the principal reason I hate Lawton Faison is that he is a gifted artist and he ignores his talent completely."

"What in the world are you talking about?"

Ken knitted his hands together and twiddled his thumbs. "I have sat beside Lawton the last two years in English—both with your Mr. Nightingale. Why they put him in AP English, I will never know, but anyway, as far as I can tell he never reads the books and he never takes a note. He does listen, and sometimes he does have good ideas—remarkable ideas, really, when you think that he never reads a single thing that's assigned to him. He's not stupid. He just doesn't give a shit."

"So what's his talent?"

Ken turned to Henry and smiled at the memory. "Drawing. He draws throughout class. Picture after picture, beautiful things. Last year we read *Othello* and Nightingale told us that Desdemona was his favorite female character in all of Shakespeare, and he brought in reproductions of paintings of Desdemona and photographs of an opera star singing her role. I swear to God during one of the classes Lawton drew the most beautiful face I have ever seen. I mean a gorgeous thing."

"Did he copy one of the paintings?"

"No. It didn't look like any of them. At the end of the class I asked him about it, and he slammed his notebook shut. He was furious that I'd seen it. He said, 'That's my mother. Mind your own goddamn business!'"

"But why do you hate him?"

"Maybe I don't hate him." Ken paused to give Lawton some more thought. "It's not hate," he said finally. "It's contempt. I hold him in contempt because he has talent and he ignores it. He squanders it. And for what? A morbid fealty to a degenerate idol — The Lost Cause and all that rubbish. The truth is I suspect Lawton hates all of it — everything about himself — which is weird, I know, because he's like the Southern Prince."

"The Prince of Darkness — that's what Tom Wales calls him."

"That new boy?"

Henry nodded.

"Short and pudgy?"

Henry nodded again. "Black guy."

"I know who you're talking about." Ken nodded. "I like that. 'Prince of Darkness'." He laughed. But the fish painting still didn't make sense to Ken. "I have trouble believing Lawton Faison would paint a stick figure on the water tower."

"It's a symbol," Henry said.

"Right. You said. Lawton's secret society."

"The Ichthys symbol."

"Ichthys, the fish. I got it."

"Yeah, but Ichthys also means Jesus Christ the son of God and Savior."

"What?"

"The 'I' stands for Jesus. The 'ch' for Christ. The 'th' for son of God, I think, and the 's' is for Savior, or something like that. Early Christians had to meet in secret, so one person would draw an arc, and if the other person drew the other arc they knew they were Christians."

Ken stamped his foot on the ground and flashed a smile at his young friend, pleased that Henry had taught him something for a change. "That's fucking brilliant!"

Henry laughed. "It is kind of cool, isn't it?"

Ken stared at the *Ziggy Stardust* poster on the wall directly across from his chair. He nodded, as if speaking to himself, then shook his head in disbelief. "So Lawton has started a secret society based on the early Christians to keep Jews from coming to Randolph?"

"To keep Randolph from hiring a Jewish teacher."

Ken shook his head, still staring at the wall. "A symbol of persecuted Christians used to persecute Jews—just the sort of retrograde perversion I would expect of him. The true grotesque." He turned to Henry. "Okay. I believe you."

Ken smiled at Henry, and Henry smiled back. Henry felt a burden lift from his chest, and his entire demeanor lightened and relaxed.

Ken saw the change in Henry and realized they'd surmounted their impasse. A wave a relief flowed from the top of his head to his heart. An ebullience bubbled up in him, and Ken's smile turned to laughter. He pointed at his Ziggy Stardust poster. "You know what Ziggy would want us to do?"

"What's that?"

"Start our own secret society."

"Of aliens?"

Ken slapped his hands together. "Exactly! The aliens and weirdos."

"Do I qualify?" Henry asked.

Ken pretended to take stock of Henry's khaki pants and blue button down. "We'll have to make you an honorary member—just don't tell Gordon."

"Definitely not," Henry agreed. "What will we do?"

"First off, we'll make fun of those fishy bastards, because that will drive Lawton nuts."

"How?"

Ken shrugged. "I don't know yet. We'll have to figure that out."

"And after that?"

"We'll laugh," Ken said. "Because how else can anyone tolerate his hateful bullshit?"

Ken was thrilled by the thought of poking Lawton Faison in the eye. Henry tried to match Ken's enthusiasm, but a part of him couldn't help but wonder whether he was stepping over an invisible line. A boundary between what and what he couldn't say exactly, and that only made him more uncomfortable.

Ken sensed his unease and slapped Henry on the back. "It's okay. You with me?"

Henry nodded slowly.

Ken cocked his head. "You sure?"

Henry smiled, then nodded with more assurance.

"Good," Ken said. He put his hand on Henry's shoulder in a gesture of brotherhood. "We'll call ourselves Owl."

"Owl?"

"They're Ichthys, which means fish. We'll be owl."

Henry sensed a hidden meaning but couldn't make it out. "Shouldn't we be like Osprey or some bird that catches fish?"

"What does 'Osprey' stand for?" Ken asked.

"I don't know. What does 'Owl' stand for?"

Ken smiled. "Oscar Wilde League."

"Oscar Wilde League?"

"Yes. O-W-L spells owl."

"I know how to spell Owl, but why 'Oscar Wilde League'?"

"Because Wilde eschewed ugliness in all its forms and still managed to make people laugh."

Henry hesitated. Was Ken ignoring the obvious for some reason? Was this a test? "He was gay, wasn't he?" Henry asked with some discomfort.

"Yes. Which makes it all the better. Being laughed at by a fat old queer will drive Lawton bananas." Ken's face beamed with delight.

That was true, Henry thought. It would bug the hell out of Lawton, for sure. "Who will be the members?" Henry asked.

"Of the club?" Ken put a hand to his chin and paced back and forth in mock contemplation. "It will have to be people with good taste and discretion, obviously …. Not many of those around here…." He stopped in front of Henry and laughed. "You and me for starters."

Henry rubbed the back of his head. He wasn't sure he was ready to join Ken as the sole members of a club named for a gay dude. "It's going to be secret right?"

"Of course. Unless you want to get kicked out."

"It's just that you said 'club'. You know like the Rod and Gun Club, or the Chess Club," Henry remarked lamely.

"Nope. We'll keep it as secret as his Ichthys — more secret even, because look at us talking about Lawton's 'secret society'."

"We should probably get at least one more person."

Ken caught the drift of Henry's discomfort. "Of course," he said, and nodded reassuringly.

"Just to bounce ideas off of," Henry explained.

"Sure. Who were you thinking?... Mongo?"

"I was thinking Tom Wales," Henry said.

Ken nodded. "That fits the bill."

"What do you mean?"

"A jew and a black," Ken said. "Two strangers in a strange land."

Henry felt a twinge of guilt. Was it just a coincidence that he'd chosen a black student to serve as the token member? He shook his head. Of course not. He couldn't think of another person better suited for this odd protest than Tom Wales.

"He's probably the smartest kid in our class," Henry said.

"I'm sure he is," Ken said.

"And he hates Lawton at least as much as I do."

"All the better," Ken said.

"Plus he can draw," Henry said. "He showed me an awesome drawing of Lawton as the devil."

"The Prince of Darkness," Ken said enthusiastically.

"Exactly!"

"You think we can get him to draw pictures for OWL?" Ken asked.

"What kind of pictures?"

Ken gave it some thought. "A picture of Oscar Wilde capturing Lawton's fish."

Ken started laughing at the thought of Oscar Wilde tormenting Lawton Faison, and he laughed so hard that tears ran down his cheeks. Henry soon joined in, carried away by Ken's joy.

HIPPIE JESUS

WALES ON B DORM

THE DAY TOM WALES RETURNED from Christmas Break, he moved into a single room on B Dorm. Once he'd finished unpacking and arranging his music and his books, he sat down on his bed and reconnoitered. B Dorm was louder, more cramped, and smelled worse than Mortimer Hall, and he was going to miss proximity to the Lawn: the many tall trees — especially the Locust that stood at attention outside his dorm window, the many squirrels rushing through the branches and rarely touching the ground except to retrieve acorns, and a certain mockingbird that would fly to the top of the Elm outside Jackson Hall and serenade the daybreak. These were perhaps his favorite things about the Randolph School, and yet he was certain he would be happier here, in his new room, for the simple reason that B Dorm lacked the cruel menace of Lawton Faison. Wales was congratulating himself on his good fortune when Bone, with a large, red pipe wrench slung across one shoulder, appeared on his doorstep.

"You want to buy some heat?"

"Pardon?"

Bone pointed to the cast iron radiator located below the one window in the room. "Stuff doesn't appear by magic."

Wales could hear the steam escaping from the radiator's antique valve. He could feel the dampness in the air. He could smell the stale stink. He touched the radiator and quickly removed his hand. "Seems to be working fine," he said.

"That's 'cause we turned it on first thing this morning, kind of as a welcoming present."

Bone smiled wetly at Wales, who in turn felt a mild stomach ache coming on. "Well, thank you, I guess," Wales said.

Bone took the wrench off his shoulder and held it with both hands across his chest. "Could shut it off just as quick."

When Wales said nothing, Bone stepped into the room, hoping an expression of genuine intent might do the trick, but this only excited Wales's interest. He was amused by the prospect of this fat, red-faced, small-handed boy wielding a plumber's wrench. Disappointed, Bone stopped short and put the wrench back across his shoulder.

"Twenty bucks today," Bone said. "Forty if you wait until tomorrow."

'Sounds like a sweet deal. Unfortunately I don't have twenty dollars."

"I'll extend you credit. As a favor."

"No thanks," Wales said.

Bone stared at him for a moment and tried to look angry. When Wales's attention waited on him calmly, Bone changed tacks. "You wouldn't have a Playboy by any chance?" Bone's eyes narrowed, and his tongue briefly flickered as his mouth twisted into a pervy smile.

Wales shook his head.

Bone lowered his voice and leaned in. "Some black porn, maybe?" He waggled his eyebrows in a revolting manner.

Wales shook his head, but Bone stood his ground. Experience told him that if he waited long enough a new boy holding out would give up some portion of his stash.

"I don't look at porn," Wales finally stammered with some disgust.

"Your loss!" Bone blubbered, and he put two fingers to his forehead, tipped an imaginary cap and walked away.

Wales cracked open his window to bring in some fresh air. What a pervert, he thought.

Before Christmas, Henry had asked Wales if he'd be interested in joining a secret society. When Henry told him that the only members were going to be Tom, Henry, and Ken Bright, Wales was flattered, and when Henry told him that the purpose of the secret society was to strike back at Lawton Faison, Wales was stoked. He'd told Henry that he'd love to join, and Henry had told him that the three of them would meet when they got back from the break.

Henry popped his head into the doorway just as Wales finished adjusting the locations of his speakers to fit the acoustics of the room.

"All moved in?" Henry asked.

"Just about. Some guy tried to sell me heat."

"Mongo?"

"No." Wales recognized Mongo. "Pudgy guy with a red face and red hair."

"Bone," Henry said.

"'Bone'?" Wales grimaced at the name. "Really?"

"I forget his real name," Henry said. "Did he ask you for titty pictures?"

"Yes."

"That's Bone," Henry said. "You didn't buy any, did you?"

"Heat?" Wales asked.

"Yeah."

"No. Didn't fall for that one."

"Good for you! Wobbly paid him forty bucks this morning." Henry pointed down the hall in the direction of his room and Ken Bright's. "You ready to meet with Ken?"

"Right now?" Wales said nervously.

"Sure. Bring that drawing you did of Lawton."

Wales opened his desk drawer and grabbed the spiral notebook he'd shown Henry in the fall.

"Let's go!" Henry said.

Henry stepped out of the door, and Tom followed him down the hall to Ken's room. Ken was sitting in his armchair, as usual.

"You know Ken, right?"

Wales nodded.

Henry pointed back and forth between the two boys. "Ken Bright, Tom Wales. Wales, Ken Bright."

Ken held out his hand to Wales. "Henry says you're quite the artist."

Tom reached out with his right hand before he realized that it was still holding his spiral notebook. He switched hands then briefly touched Ken's right hand with his own without making eye contact. He was an unusually self-aware, fifteen-year-old boy, but he surprised himself by how nervous he was. Ken had the reputation for being the smartest boy in the school, and he was an artist, like Tom, and not an athlete, again like Tom. When he'd seen Henry and Ken together in the fall, Wales had imagined trying to get to know Ken but had dismissed the idea as impossible. Now here Ken was, shaking his hand, apparently happy to see him. It felt weird. He wasn't used to another Randolph student taking it for granted that he was worth getting to know.

"Show him the drawing you did," Henry said.

Wales opened his notebook to his sketch of Lawton with horns and a tail and wearing a pin that said 'P is for prick'.

Ken laughed. "I like the Princeton touch," he said, pointing to the orange P that was drawn to mimic the Princeton University font.

"Thanks."

"So you know who Oscar Wilde is, right?"

"Yeah. He wrote *Salome*."

Ken looked at Wales, surprised. "That's a bit arcane. Have you read it?"

Wales shook his head. "No, but I've heard it."

"Heard it?"

Wales nodded. "The Strauss opera."

Ken's mouth fell open. For the first time since his arrival at Randolph he'd come face to face with a student with artistic tastes at least as esoteric as his own.

"You're an opera fan?"

Wales nodded, and Henry nudged Wales with an elbow.

"He's like a classical pianist. First time I went to his room he was studying a musical score."

Ken beamed with delight. "The perfect addition to OWL!"

Tom bowed. "Thank you."

Ken thrust one arm into the air above them. "All for one and one for all?"

Henry and Tom raised their arms and joined hands with Ken. "All for one and one for all!" They all laughed, then Ken poked through the books beside his bed until he found the biography he was looking for.

"Do you know what Oscar Wilde looks like?" he asked Wales.

Wales shrugged. "I have an idea, but I should probably study a photograph."

Ken handed him the book, which had a portrait of Wilde's face on its cover. "Don't study it too hard. I'm thinking four or five drawings of a bird with his face — not exactly like him. Just some suggestion, maybe, like his hair parted in the middle, or his dandy outfits. You know, just enough to make people guess. But we want to make it super gay."

Tom laughed. "Like wrapped in a boa?"

Now Ken laughed. "Yeah. Or earrings and a necklace."

"I got you," Tom said. "When do you want them?"

"I'm thinking this Sunday. At chapel service," Ken said.

Tom's eyes widened with excitement. "Oh man. That's going to bug the hell out of Deemer."

Henry held up his hand for a high five. "Bonus," he said.

BAT IN CHAPEL SERVICE

WHEN LAWTON FAISON ARRIVED at the chapel, a half hour before the start of service, he found a pen and ink drawing taped to the outside of the chapel doors. The drawing was of a bird with a fish in its talons. Strangely, the bird appeared to be wearing high heels, and the fish was the Jesus fish.

"What the fuck?"

Lawton ripped the drawing off the door and stuffed it into his pants pocket. He looked around to see if anyone was watching, or anyone who might have posted the drawing or seen someone post it. No one. Everyone was still at advisee dinner. He stepped into the chapel, turned on the lights and walked up the aisle. Nothing appeared amiss. He compared the posted hymn numbers against the numbers printed in the program — they checked out. The hymnals were in place. He walked into the sacristy. Rev. Deemer's vestment was hanging on the wall, and the robes for the choirboys were folded on the counter. The small window looking out on the golf course was ajar; Lawton closed it. He opened the cabinet that held the platters and cups for the bread and wine and found a second drawing. Again, the bird with the fish in its talons. This bird had a monocle and appeared to be wearing rouge.

"Motherfucker!" Lawton crumpled the second drawing and stuffed it into another pocket. He opened all the drawers to make sure there weren't more drawings, then stalked through the chapel, pausing to peer underneath the pews. He climbed up to the balcony to check there as well. Nothing.

As Lawton was searching the balcony, Rev. Deemer and Mrs. Deemer entered and found the church lights on. "Lawton?" Rev. Deemer called.

"Up here." Lawton walked to the front of the balcony and looked over the railing.

"What are you doing up there?"

"Just checking to make sure there are enough hymnals." Lawton didn't mention the drawings. He suspected they had been placed in the chapel for him in particular, and he didn't want Deemer or anyone else to make inquiries that might lead back to the water tower.

"Everything in order?"

"Looks good."

Rev. Deemer and Mrs. Deemer walked to the front of the church. Mrs. Deemer took a seat at the organ and arranged the music for the service. Rev. Deemer put a copy of his sermon on the lectern in the pulpit. He checked his wristwatch.

"I have quarter til. Go ahead and ring the bell for service."

Lawton stepped to the rear of the balcony and pulled on the bellrope hanging through a hole in the ceiling. It was heavy, and Lawton was only able to pull his hands halfway down his chest. He released his grip and let the rope slip through his fingers then reached up high above his head and pulled down a second time. This time, his hands reached down below his waist, and as he released the bellrope he heard the first, deep gong of the old brass bell in the steeple. The sound reminded him of the bell that tolled seventy-four times at his grandfather's funeral service. He wanted to keep on ringing this bell over and over like the bell that had rung that day, but he remembered that this ringing was only intended to serve as the call to worship, and so after the third bell ring Lawton held onto the rope and let it lift him off the ground to deaden the momentum overhead. He listened to the final clong ring down to nothing.

Very soon the boys started pouring out of the front doors of the Randolph Building en masse, and Mrs. Deemer began playing the church organ. In the course of walking to Faison Chapel, the boys fell naturally into groups of four or five or six friends, each catching up the others with the latest tales of one boy's stupidity or another's one-upsmanship. The din of laughter and catcalls reached its highest pitch halfway to the chapel, where the flow of boys gradually slowed before coming to a halt outside the chapel doors, which only admitted two boys at a time.

As the boys approached the chapel and came within greater earshot of the organ's mournful call to worship, they lowered their voices, and by the time they stepped through the chapel doors their laughter and good cheer were almost stifled altogether.

Bob Wobbly stood outside the doors of the Randolph Building waiting for Henry. When he didn't appear, Wobbly entered the chapel and waddled up and down the center aisle looking for his roommate. Not seeing him, Wobbly figured that Henry must have gone back to the room to fetch something after dinner, and he stepped back outside. The windows of their dorm room were dark, so Wobbly kept his eyes on the front doors of the Randolph Building while keeping his ears cocked to the organ music. When he heard the choir begin to sing the opening hymn he waved in the direction of their dorm room then rushed inside. He stopped at several pews in the back of the church and motioned for the boys to move over and make room, but they all rebuffed him with words to the effect of "Get lost, Wobbly!" and pointed toward the front of the church where there was always space. Wobbly started to retreat to the balcony but caught sight of Rev. Deemer glaring at him. Overawed, he ducked into a pew three rows from the front of the church and buried his head in a hymnal. Behind him Henry, Tom and Ken, sitting in the front row of the balcony, laughed at Wobbly's discomfort.

Following the hymn, Rev. Deemer offered some perfunctory words of welcome, and then nodded to Lawton Faison, who walked to the podium to deliver the scripture reading. Lawton ascended the steps, calmly regarded the sea of faces before him, opened the Bible to the appointed reading, and froze. There was another drawing of the bird with red lipstick and earrings, holding the Jesus fish. Lawton glanced at Deemer, who sat beside the pulpit waiting for Lawton to begin. Deemer raised his eyebrows, as if to ask, 'what's the matter?' Lawton cleared his throat, shook his head, then coughed into his right fist. As he did so, he slipped the drawing into his pants pocket with his left hand. The podium hid the maneuver from everyone in the congregation — everyone except those sitting in the balcony. Ken, Henry and Tom saw everything. From his seat next to the pulpit, Deemer also saw Lawton's sleight of hand. He frowned. Lawton fumbled his way through the reading and returned to his seat. Up in the balcony, the three members of the nascent OWL stifled their laughter.

Next, Rev. Deemer stepped to the pulpit and read a passage from the book of Matthew, in which Jesus tells the parable of separating the Sheep from the Goats. Deemer loved this passage because he thought it clearly proved that Jesus would judge the wicked and the just. As he read the word of God, Deemer's voice deepened and became more censorious, and by the time he closed the Bible he felt a passion for adjudication.

Wobbly, whose encounters with Deemer at Cub practices had left him in mortal fear of the man, kept his head down throughout the Scripture reading. He pretended to study the church program, turning it over and over, front to back and back to front again. So keen was Wobbly's sense of Deemer's disapprobation that he never would have looked up had the boy sitting next to him in the pew not nudged him with an elbow and gestured toward the front of the church with his chin. Against his better judgment, Wobbly's eyes followed the boy's suggestion and found Reverend Deemer looming over him like an exterminating angel.

"Are you a sheep or a goat?" Deemer thundered.

Wobby pointed a finger at his own chest, and mouthed 'Me?'—for the reverend's scowl seemed to be directed at him—and he was about to attempt an answer when Deemer lifted his gaze and surveyed the entire congregation. "I ask this question not in jest but because the word of God informs us that the just shall be granted eternal light and the damned shall face eternal punishment. Fortunately, the Son of God—"

Just then a whirling figure swooped down from the rafters above Deemer's head and hurtled zig-zagging towards Wobbly's face. For a split second Wobbly thought Deemer had called down a curse upon him, but then he caught sight of the pointed ears, black eyes, and the blur of teeth that snapped the instant that dark menace shifted direction and flew up and over and out of sight. When Wobbly ducked and screamed the attention of the entire school was diverted from the prospect of eternal damnation to a spinning demon with short, stubby wings beating fiercely and erratically, propelling its ball of black fur up and down above the boys' heads like a hairy yo-yo cast by a crazed carnival worker. Back and forth, to the left and right, frontwards and back again, zigzagging across and through the screaming chapel of boys, the bat desperately tried to find an open window or an open door or a hole in the ceiling to tumble out of, until finally, as it made another pass by the balcony, one boy rose up above the fray, swung a broom at the bat, like a baseball player swinging at a knuckleball, and whether out of pure luck or native skill managed to swat it to the ground, pin it against the carpet, and in one deft move open a window and drop it out into the clear night air. For a moment the silence of the chapel deepened into amazement until, almost in unison, the boys erupted in a roar of approval that the hero acknowledged, first by holding out his free hand as if to signal, 'Please, no, it was nothing', but then realizing himself the majesty of his performance, by raising the broom and both hands above his head, as the boys' cheers rose louder, "Ken Bright! Ken Bright! Ken Bright!" Henry and Wales looked at him in amazement because they felt sure that Ken had never swung at anything in his life.

Ken returned to his seat beside Henry, and before Henry could ask, said, "Badminton. I'm crazy good at badminton."

Lawton and the other members of Chapel Council skulked down the center aisle, barking threats of demerits in a futile effort to restore order, while Rev. Deemer stood silent in the pulpit, wondering whether the bat's intervention might possibly have been planned. By habit of mind, he was reluctant to chalk anything up to chance. Everything, he believed, had an explanation. But could anyone really bring a bat into church? Would anyone? No, he thought, the bat must have gotten in some other way. He made a mental note to ask the school's maintenance department to check the eaves and the belfry, and when the melee finally settled down he announced, "Please turn now to our closing hymn, Number 515." Mrs. Deemer plunked away at the organ, and all the boys gave a muddled rendition of "God of our Fathers", and the service ended early — to everyone's great relief.

As Ken left the chapel, several boys clapped him on the back. 'Didn't know you had it in you, Bright' was the general sentiment. Lawton, Billy Richardson and John Gillespie were responsible for straightening up after the service. Lawton tried to pawn the job off on his friends and leave early, but Deemer, standing at the front of the chapel, caught him before he could get out the door.

"Lawton, a moment please."

Lawton rolled his eyes at his two friends and followed Deemer into the sacristy. With his back to Lawton, Deemer removed his vestment and placed it on a hanger. He replaced the hanger on a hook on the wall. With his back still turned he put on his black coat and pulled on the front of his lapels to smooth the lay of the cloth across his thick shoulders. He fiddled with his shirt front to make sure everything was shipshape before turning to face the boy. "I couldn't help noticing that you found something in the lectionary."

"It was nothing. Just a scrap of paper."

Deemer pushed his wire rim glasses back up the broken ridge of his nose and held out his hand. "May I see it?"

"I have no idea what it's about," Lawton said in an offhand manner, and as he pulled one wad of paper out of his pocket a second scrap fell to the ground.

"What is that?"

"More of the same," Lawton said.

"Let me see."

Lawton handed him both papers.

Deemer considered first one drawing, then the other. "What in the world is this about?"

"No idea," Lawton said. "Just some random drawings by an idiot."

"Is this supposed to be the Christian fish?" Deemer asked with evident disgust. He pointed to the talons of the monocled, rouge-faced bird.

"Your guess is as good as mine."

Deemer leaned a little closer. "Does this have something to do with the water tower?"

Lawton appeared to be as surprised as the reverend. "Rev. Deemer, I have no idea what it means."

"Where was the second drawing?"

"In there." Lawton pointed to the cabinet beside Deemer.

"Do you know who's behind this?"

"No idea."

Deemer eyed Lawton suspiciously. "You'd tell me if you did."

"Of course."

"And the water tower?"

"No idea."

Deemer did not seem satisfied, but it was unclear whether his dissatisfaction was with Lawton or with the mystery of the drawings. He folded the drawings and put them in his jacket pocket.

"Very strange," he said. "Thank you, Lawton. That is all."

As Lawton left the sacristy he motioned for the other seniors to meet him outside. He took several steps away from the chapel doors to make sure they were out of earshot before turning around.

"Did you see Bright knock that bat out of the air?" Richardson said excitedly.

"It was awesome!" Gillespie agreed.

"We got a problem," Lawton said. He pulled the third drawing out of his pocket. "Someone is on to us. I found this stuck on the chapel door, and there were two more posted inside."

Richardson and Gillespie passed the drawing back and forth between them.

"Why is the bird wearing high heels?" Richardson asked.

"No idea."

Gillespie looked more closely. "It's a gay owl," he said.

"What are you talking about?" Lawton said.

Gillespie pointed to the vest the bird appeared to be wearing. "See? It's a dude, but he's wearing high heels."

"Why an owl?" Richardson asked.

"The ears." Gillespie pointed to two horns on the bird's head.

Lawton snatched the drawing out of Gillespie's hand. "Listen, guys. This was posted here because someone knows about us."

"It's funny," Gillespie said, laughing.

"It's not funny! We have to figure out what to do!"

"About the drawing?" Richardson asked. "We don't know who drew it."

Lawton rubbed the back of his left hand as he looked at the drawing again. Gillespie was right. It was a gay bird, and it was crushing the Jesus fish in its talons. Lawton looked more closely at the bird's face. It was smiling — it was laughing at him. They were laughing at him. He tore the drawing into pieces and wadded the pieces into a ball.

"It's Henry Palmer." Lawton spit out the name.

"Gordon's brother? Why him?"

Lawton slammed his fist against his thigh and stared blindly at them.

"He knows about us, and didn't you see him laughing next to Ken Bright and that pickaninny?"

ON MONDAY MORNING Deemer informed Terrence Mackie, the Dean of Students, about the drawings in the chapel. That afternoon the two of them met with Mr. Endicott in his office. The three men sat around a mahogany coffee table covered with recent editions of the school's glossy alumni magazine.

"They were posted at the chapel," Deemer said in response to a question from Endicott. He held up the two drawings he'd recovered from Lawton. "As you can see, in both drawings the bird is crushing the Jesus fish. I think the only conclusion is that some misguided soul is ridiculing our Christian belief."

Deemer had shown the drawings to Mackie that morning, but the dean had not examined them carefully. His first impression had not screamed blasphemy.

"May I look at those?" he asked Deemer.

"Of course." Deemer passed the drawings across the table.

"Where were these found *exactly*?" Mackie asked.

"One of them was in the sacristy and the other was inside the Bible on the lectern."

"*Inside* the Bible?"

"Yes. Lawton Faison got up to read the lesson and when he turned to the passage there it was."

Mackie looked to Endicott and raised his eyebrows to make sure that the headmaster recognized that he had uncovered an important clue. "So whoever put it there knew what the reading was."

"Apparently so."

"And how could that be?" asked Mackie as he leaned forward eagerly.

"He must have looked at the printed program," Deemer said matter of factly, unaware that he'd dashed Mackie's hopes of demonstrating his superior sleuthing skills.

"At least Lawton hasn't told his father yet," Endicott said. He motioned to the phone on his desk. "My phone's not been ringing."

Absent existential threats to the health and safety of the school, Endicott's primary concern was always alumni relations. With the upcoming installation of the new stained glass window, he had been in frequent contact with Lawton Faison Sr. and had come to the reluctant conclusion that the man's demands were more trouble than his likely future gifts were worth.

"Is the sign of the fish widely known among the students?" Mackie asked, taking up a new line of inquiry.

"I teach it in my New Testament class."

"And that's for fifth formers?"

"Yes."

"So any sixth former would know about it."

"Should," Deemer said. He couldn't in good faith warrant that all of his students paid close attention in his class. "Maybe," he added.

Mackie ran his fingers along the serrated edges of the papers. "This looks like paper out of any spiral notebook."

"Looks like it," Deemer agreed.

"And just a blue ink pen?"

"Looks like it."

Mackie touched the red marking, "Lipstick?"

"Crayon, I think," Deemer said.

Mackie scratched the lips with his fingertip and smelled the paper. Didn't smell like crayon to him.

Endicott grew inpatient with Mackie's gumshoe routine. The drawings by themselves were of no great concern to him. After all, Lawton Faison was the only student who had seen them. If they had been posted outside the dining hall, or the post office, or in any public space for that matter, Endicott would have been ablaze with indignation, for his constant fear was that some isolated spark of public protest, however small, would erupt into a conflagration of insubordination. The painting on the water tower was exactly the type of thing that Endicott feared and hated most — a flagrant and very public violation of decorum, a desecration of school property even — and on the morning of Parent's Weekend no less. As headmaster and *de facto* sovereign, he considered the act a personal affront, a big middle finger pointed directly at himself. Therefore, there was one thing, and only one thing, that could possibly be of interest in the present case: what light, if any, do the drawings shed on the water tower incident?

"Is our best guess that whoever did this was also behind the water tower?" Endicott interrupted. "Because of the sign of the fish," he added to clarify his logic.

Deemer was of two minds about the water tower. Clearly, it was a violation of the rules, but he couldn't bring himself to think of it as a desecration. Hardly. Whoever had painted the sign of the fish on the tower clearly intended it as a declaration of faith, a prophetic call to return to the essence of Christian heritage. In that light, erasing the symbol was closer to blasphemy. These drawings on the other hand ....

"Perhaps," he said slowly, reluctant to contradict the headmaster's lead.

Mackie consciously refrained from rolling his eyes. Apart from the repetition of the Jesus fish — a common enough symbol that by Deemer's own admission should have been familiar to at least a quarter of the student body — there was no reason to conflate the two incidents. In Mackie's experience, the simplest explanation was always the best. As far as he was concerned, they were dealing with two separate cases of rule-breaking, one of them considerably more consequential than the other, and he was going to follow the evidence wherever it led.

"I don't want to be too hasty," he said.

"Why not?" Endicott asked.

Mackie was reluctant to blurt out a theory that he suspected Endicott would dismiss out of hand, and so he held up one of the drawings and teased out the clues like an English teacher. "What are we to make of the lipstick and earrings?" he asked.

"Lipstick and earrings?" Endicott repeated with a mixture of excitement and alarm. He had overlooked those details.

Mackie passed him the drawings. "In one drawing the bird is wearing a monocle and rouge. In the other, red lipstick and earrings."

"Same bird?" Endicott inquired.

"Looks to be," Mackie said.

"What kind of bird is it?"

Mackie grimaced inwardly. The old man didn't seem to be taking up the scent. "Some kind of hawk or owl I'd say."

"Do owls hunt fish?" Endicott asked.

"Not that I know of," Mackie said, then added, in an effort to get Endicott to take up a different trail, "but maybe the artist didn't take care with such details."

"Hence the lipstick and earrings," Endicott observed with self-satisfaction.

"Exactly," Mackie said. Now that the old man was on the right track, Mackie looked at him, expecting a light bulb to turn on, but Endicott only continued to gaze at the drawings, apparently waiting for some additional clue from Mackie.

Deemer grew impatient and irritated. "It's disgusting, I think."

"What's that?" Endicott blurted.

"The lipstick and earrings. The bird is clearly male."

"A male?" Endicott said with astonishment. He looked to Mackie for some confirmation, then back to Deemer. "Why do you say that?"

"The monocle," Deemer said.

Endicott held up the drawings with skepticism. "But what do you make of the lipstick and earrings?" he asked.

"I think he's ..." Deemer hesitated to say the word. He looked to Mackie for help, but Mackie said nothing. "A homosexual," Deemer said finally.

About time, Mackie thought to himself.

"Really? Homosexual?" Endicott was clearly excited but still sounded skeptical. He examined the drawings more closely. "I see what you mean," he said finally, as if to himself. Then, after the thought had sunk in, Endicott turned to Deemer. "But what is a homosexual bird catching a fish supposed to mean?" he asked.

"Not just any fish," Deemer said. "The Christian fish."

"Right. The Jesus fish. What is a homosexual bird catching the Jesus fish supposed to mean?" Endicott repeated with a hint or irritation.

The three men cast their glances back and forth, like hot potatoes, one to the others.

"Sacrilege," Deemer said finally.

Endicott and Mackie looked at each other, each curious whether the other would concede this interpretation. Neither of them blinked. Endicott checked the clock; he had a two o'clock meeting with the school's development director.

"I think we've ventured about as far as we can for now," he said. "Let's report back if anyone has a new lead. I'll speak to Gordon Palmer and have the prefects keep an ear out. It's just a matter of time before something turns up. Boys have a way of blabbing — someone's bound to claim credit for the prank. Once that happens the whole school will know."

Mackie and Deemer stood up to leave, but Endicott motioned to Mackie. "Terry could you stay for just a moment? There's another matter that needs your attention."

Deemer excused himself, and as soon as the door to his office was closed, Endicott motioned for Mackie to take a seat.

"You don't think the bird is supposed to be Frank, do you?" Endicott asked

Mackie suppressed his laughter. "With earrings and red lipstick?"

"It's got a round face like Frank's. And is that supposed to be a clerical collar?" Endicott pointed to a few scribbled lines underneath the bird's head.

Mackie had considered those scribbles. Not much to go on. His best guess was a bowtie. He shook his head. "Frank is probably the last person I would suspect of being a homosexual," Mackie said.

"Well, yes. I know what you mean. The football coach and all. But you know what they say?" Endicott cocked his head and slurred his lips in his best attempt at a sly grin.

"That he's overcompensating?" Mackie laughed and shook his head.

"You're probably right," Endicott conceded.

"But maybe the person is trying to get back at Frank. Ridiculing the church and all," Mackie said.

"That makes the most sense so far." Endicott tapped the side of his nose with a forefinger and gave Mackie an emphatic nod. "Ask Frank if there's someone who has a special dislike for him. But remember the main point. I want to find the boy or boys who painted the water tower."

PERSIMMON WINE

TERRENCE MACKIE SAT AT HIS DESK in the Office of Student Affairs pondering the drawings from Sunday's chapel service. Two months ago Edwin had tasked him with solving the mystery of the water tower, and so far he'd gotten nowhere. He'd thought he had a promising lead when he learned that Uly had recovered a paint can from the tower platform. It's just a matter of contacting the local hardware store about recent paint purchases, he'd told himself. But alas, the maintenance supervisor told him the paint can had been taken from a utility closet. Since then, the trail had gone cold — until Sunday. These drawings were the best clues yet. They seemed to have something to do with the water tower — given the Jesus fish — but Mackie couldn't figure out what. The paper and ink could belong to anybody. The only possible lead was the red lipstick. Mackie had proposed that the school search every boy's room until they found a tube of red lipstick or someone confessed, but Edwin had nixed that idea. Endicott said he thought the boys enjoyed some modicum of privacy, but Mackie suspected he was concerned there might be blowback from parents — not many, but enough to make it not worth the trouble. For now Mackie was keeping an eye out for lipstick whenever he inspected a boy's room.

There was something else about the drawings that bothered him. He'd asked Frank if there was a student who might have a grudge against him, and Frank had said, "Why do you ask?" Mackie hadn't told Deemer that Endicott thought the bird in high heels resembled the reverend. He knew Frank was vain — Why? God knows, Mackie thought; the man was like a Neanderthal, with his wide, flat forehead and his stubborn, indomitable way of blundering forward no matter the circumstances. Instead he had suggested that perhaps a student had posted the drawings in the chapel simply to irritate the reverend. Deemer couldn't think of anyone with a grudge. Mackie had concluded that the bird in the drawings wasn't Frank — too pretty — but it did remind him of somebody; he just couldn't put his finger on whom. In one of the drawings it looked like the bird had hair that was parted in the middle — that definitely was not Frank, but who was it?

Mackie liked playing the detective. His father had been the court bailiff in a small rural county in southwest Virginia, and growing up he often sat in the courtroom to watch the criminal trials. He always enjoyed the prosecutor's direct examination of the sheriff's deputy and frowned whenever the defense attorney raised objections. His father had encouraged him to go into law enforcement, but Mackie had set his sights on law school. Middling grades and a poor test score had shut that door, but as Dean of Students he had found consolation in his prosecution of the school's disciplinary code. He opened the drawer to his desk and pulled out a magnifying glass. He passed the glass over the top of the head — definitely an owl. Over the collar — definitely not a clerical collar. He examined the earrings; hard to tell — maybe clip-ons like the ones his mother used to wear? He shook his head. Not enough to go on. He'd stared at the drawing so many times he was beginning to see things.

Mackie was tracing the outline of the bird with his long, bony finger when an orange drop of goo struck the paper on the bird's head. He looked around — his window was closed, no one had walked through his door. He looked up. There, directly above his head, was an orange spot on the ceiling. He squinted his eyes and saw a second drip drop. Mackie darted to his left, and the drip hit the drawing a second time, this time on the Jesus fish. Mackie wiped the ooze off the drawing and climbed up onto his desk. He rocked up onto his toes and touched the wet spot on the ceiling. He put his finger to his nose; it was sweet, like fruit jelly — not orange marmalade, not as tart, more like honey. Another case of home brew, he thought, and rushed out of his office. He bounded up the stairs to B Dorm two at a time. If he acted quickly he might catch the boy red-handed. It was third period, and the hall was empty — most of the students were in class. As he walked down the hallway he traced in his mind's eye the location of his office directly below. He stopped at Room 237 — Bob Coogan's single. Of course. Mackie smiled. Deadbeat stoner — Mongo indeed! Now I got you!, he thought.

Mongo had been in Mackie's English class two years earlier. The boy had failed every assignment thanks to Mackie's strict application of the "five grammatical errors is an F" rule — a rule that the English department had adopted at Mackie's insistence. Mackie had spent hours coaching Coogan to write sentences with an active rather than a passive construction — to no avail. He had come to believe the problem with Coogan's writing was not cognitive but existential, or even worse, willful — that the boy's grammatical proclivities were either an expression of his essential nature or an open act of defiance. Either way, it belied a character unsuited to a Randolph man. At the end of the term the English department had held a meeting to discuss whether to fail a student based solely on the department's rigid grammar rule. Mongo was their test case. Mackie was game; he told his colleagues that he'd done everything he could to save the boy and had finally concluded that Coogan was mocking him. He'd complained that although Coogan wasn't a bright student, he wasn't so stupid that he could not distinguish between 'The boy kicked the dog' and 'The dog was kicked by the boy'. As far as Mackie was concerned the boy deserved punishment rather than pity. When it came to a vote, David Nightingale, the department chair, had cast the deciding vote in favor of allowing Mongo to pass the course, thus emasculating Mackie's cherished grammatical standards. The so-called rule was now little more than a scare tactic to be deployed against new boys, mostly during fall quarter. Since then, Mackie's relationship with Nightingale, which was already distant but respectful, had become decidedly strained, and whenever he encountered Mongo's slack, oblivious face, Mackie would grind his teeth with the certain knowledge that the boy had single-handedly diluted the school's standards.

Mackie knocked on Mongo's door. No answer. He opened the door. No one was there. He walked around the room. Nothing amiss. He opened the closet—just clothes and shoes, and bandanas—a surprising number of bandanas. Nothing to suggest an explanation for the spot on his ceiling. He did a quick check for lipstick. Nothing. He stepped back into the hall. The leak was coming from somewhere. Next to Mongo's room was a storage closet. Mackie tried to open the door; the knob turned but the door did not budge. There was a deadbolt lock above the knob. Mackie frowned and took out his Master key. It didn't fit the deadbolt. His frown deepened. Then he noticed a funky odor, the same as the drip in his office. He leaned closer to the closet door and sniffed. There it was again, even stronger; it must be coming from inside the closet. Mackie pulled at the door again. Still stuck. He kicked it, and he would have sworn that the door moved slightly. He pulled at the door again with all of his strength. It didn't budge.

Just then Mongo himself came walking down the hall, hair down below his shoulders, towel wrapped around his waist, his broad chest covered with a thick forest of dark hair, and the vacant smile of a child with neither a care nor a thought in the world.

"Hi, Mr. Mackie!" Mongo said cheerfully.

"Why aren't you in class, Coogan?"

"This is my free period."

Mackie eyed the thick muscles arrayed like stone blocks along Mongo's hairy torso. The enormity of the boy offended him.

"Why aren't you wearing a shirt?" Mackie barked.

Mongo looked down at the towel around his waist. "I just got out of the shower?" he answered, as though Mackie had asked one of his trick questions.

Mackie's eyes narrowed. "What can you tell me about the smell coming from this closet?"

Mongo stepped between Mackie and the door to take a sniff, and as he did so his long, wet hair brushed against Mackie's face. Mackie winced.

"Smells a little bit nasty," Mongo said congenially.

"When was the last time you got a haircut, son?" Mackie seethed, as he wiped his face with his sleeve.

Mongo reached behind his shoulder, grabbed a handful of hair and examined it. "Looks like maybe a year ago?"

Mackie wanted to give the boy a demerit, but he knew there was no rule against long hair. He made a mental note to take that up with Endicott. "What's this room used for?" he asked.

"No idea."

"Do you have the key?"

"Is it locked?"

Mackie noted that the boy had sidestepped his question. "You see the deadbolt. I asked if you have the key."

Mongo adjusted his grip on the towel to free his right hand. He turned the door knob and gave it a hard yank. It swung open.

"Just stuck." Mongo stepped aside and held the door open, happy to help.

Ever suspicious, Mackie didn't offer any thanks. He peered inside. It was the size of a broom closet. The only thing inside was a trash bin filled to the brim with some sort of bubbling, orange ooze that was spilling over the top and pooling on the floor. Next to the trash bin, in the middle of the ooze, was a piece of cardboard folded in half and standing up like a sandwich board. Scrawled in black magic marker were the words, "Hello, Mr. Mackie".

Mackie inhaled sharply. "Do you know anything about this Coogan?"

Mongo, whose chin could have almost rested on top of Mackie, leaned forward. He shook his head, and his long hair flashed first over his right shoulder and then over his left shoulder, bestowing Mackie's head with a sprinkle. "Nope," he said.

Mackie wiped his face again and glared at Mongo, who maintained his stupid, mopey grin.

"We'll see about that!" He stepped into the broom closet and grabbed the cardboard. "Throw that away!" he said, indicating the trash can. "And clean that mess off the floor!" he barked. "And get a haircut!" he added for good measure.

Mongo watched Mackie storm down the hall and take the stairs down to A Dorm. He shrugged, shut the door to the broom closet and walked into his room.

Mackie marched directly to Endicott's office, gingerly holding the damp cardboard as though it were poison. He found the old man at his desk dictating a letter to Lawton Faison Sr. about the school's plans for the dedication of the stained glass window. Endicott turned off the tape recorder on his desk.

"What is it Terry?"

Mackie held out the slimy piece of cardboard.

"What in God's name do you have there?"

"I just discovered this in a broom closet on B Dorm."

"Good for you, Terry." Endicott said irritably. He didn't see why his day was being interrupted with this news.

"I discovered it because beer was leaking into the floor of the broom closet, through the ceiling, and onto my desk in the Student Affairs office."

"Beer?" At the very word Endicott dropped the tape recorder. "What do you mean?"

"It's some kind of home brew," Mackie said.

Endicott stamped his feet on the floor. This was clearly a sign of impending chaos. "Goddammit boys!"

"And there's a message."

"A message? What sort of message?" Endicott demanded.

Mackie held the cardboard up to eye level to demonstrate the act of reading. "It says, 'Hello, Mr. Mackie.'"

"Good God!" Endicott exclaimed. "It was meant to be found. Someone has thrown down the gauntlet!"

Mackie and Endicott reviewed the situation: water tower, bird drawings, and now beer. They agreed that none of this was a coincidence — even the bat in the chapel service might be part of some hidden scheme. Could a boy smuggle a bat? They didn't know, but things were definitely getting out of hand. Unless drastic measures were taken the center would not hold. The impossible would be possible. Dogs would be cats. And boys would be girls.

Endicott thrust his forefinger boldly up into the air. "I know what I must do," he said resolutely.

ENDICOTT CLIMBS THE FIRE ESCAPE

SEVENTEEN YEARS AS HEADMASTER at The Randolph School had taught Edwin Endicott that what boys need — crave even — more than anything else, is order. The certainty that the current state of the world would not change. A sense of permanence. The feeling that things were right side up. He had a nose for detecting when the world was out of joint and things were about to go awry, to slip the track, to slide into topsy-turvy. And he knew that the only way to set things right was to set an example, to thrust his staff into the ground and stand resolute against the buffeting winds.

To that end, Mr. Endicott left his office on the second floor of the Randolph School, just as dusk was gathering, just as the boys were leaving their dorm rooms or the gym and heading to the dining hall for supper. He'd changed out of his customary dark suit and dress shirt and into a pair of heavy canvas trousers, a blue chamois cloth shirt, a black check deerstalker hat with the ear flaps tied up, and a matching Harris Tweed upland field jacket. He looked like a British hobbyist detective in pursuit of a crime to solve. The only thing missing was a monocle and a full bent briarwood pipe. As it was, Endicott had forgotten to take off his reading glasses, and the extinguished end of a Dominican cigar stuck out of his jacket's breast pocket. He lingered in the front lobby, just long enough for the dozen or so boys there to behold him, then walked out the front doors, down the front steps and around the corner, to the bottom of the fire escape located at the backside of the Randolph Building.

The fire escape consisted of several flights of narrow iron steps attached in teeter-totter fashion to the side of the building. At every landing the window of a dorm room allowed egress to the fire escape; between landings the diagonal stairs bisected another window so that a person climbing to the top of the fire escape was afforded the opportunity to peer into multiple rooms. This was Mr. Endicott's purpose — not only to spy into boys' rooms but, more particularly, to be seen spying into boys' rooms. Mr. Endicott looked towards the gymnasium, where groups of boys were walking towards the dining hall, and then over towards the Lawn, where dozens of boys were making their way to supper. He reached into the outer pocket of his jacket and pulled out a flashlight. The sun still hung above the horizon and darkness was an hour away, but the flashlight served as a prop, highlighting his purpose for all who beheld him.

He clambered up the fire escape, keeping the flashlight in his outside hand. He walked stiff-kneed, with his toes pointed outward, like a sclerotic rooster on uneven ground. At the first window, just a few feet off the ground, he stopped and peered inside. The room's lights were off, so he switched on the flashlight and cast its beam into every corner. Finding no boys, he pressed on. Several boys coming from the gym stopped at the bottom of the fire escape and looked up. Endicott gave them a solemn nod, waved his flashlight in the direction of the dining hall, and summoned his most commanding voice. "Carry on!" he bellowed. The boys stifled laughs and scampered away.

At the next landing, the fire escape straddled two sets of windows to two different rooms. The first room was dark, and Mr. Endicott again probed its beds and corners with the beam of his flashlight. In the second room Lampton Childs, a new boy from Goldsboro who suffered from a horrendous case of teenage acne, had just put on a shirt and was combing his hair at a mirror. When he saw Mr. Endicott's face in the reflection, he hollered.

"No need to scream, son," Endicott said, raising his voice to be heard through the closed window. "It is I, Mr. Endicott."

Childs turned around to face the window. "Wh-what are you doing?" he stammered.

"I am searching for shirkers and layabouts. Have you seen any, ... boy?" Endicott couldn't recall the child's name.

Guilt-prone by nature, Childs put a hand to his heart to catch his breath. "But I'm in the school play," he stammered by way of explaining why he was still in his room and not making his way from the gym's locker rooms.

"That's neither here nor there. I asked you about shirkers and lay-abouts," Endicott commanded.

"Not that I know of, sir."

"Very good. Carry on."

Childs stood at attention, not sure what to make of 'carry on', as Endicott renewed his ascent.

Meanwhile, Mongo was sauntering from the gym towards the dining hall, humming *Shakedown Street* to himself, when he spotted Mr. Endicott's crabbed figure peeping into the dorm rooms. A sudden pang of buzz-kill dashed his spirits and, still dizzy with disappointment, he sat down cross-legged at the bottom of the fire escape to recover his equilibrium.

When Endicott reached the top of the fire escape, he leaned over to catch his breath then straightened himself and, with both hands gripping the outer rail, surveyed his campus like a minor potentate. He saw students gawking at him from the Lawn, and he had no doubt that boys sitting inside the dining hall were buzzing about Mr. Endicott being on a rampage and the school clamping down. He smiled smugly and congratulated himself on his superior understanding of boys.

"What ya doin' Mr. Endicott?" came a call from down below. Endicott looked down and saw Bob Coogan sitting at the bottom of the fire escape.

"What does it look like I'm doing, Mr. Coogan?" Endicott said imperiously.

Mongo tipped his head to one side. "Looks like you're trying to catch boys whacking off."

"Pardon?" Mr. Endicott did not trust his ears.

"Spanking the monkey!" Mongo called out louder. He placed his fist in front of his crotch and waggled it up and down. "You know, masturbating!"

"I know what you mean, Mr. Coogan. I was hoping you'd keep your filthy thoughts to yourself."

"I thought you didn't hear me —" Mongo said.

"I heard you fine —"

"Cause, pardon —"

"I understand," Mr. Endicott interrupted and held out one hand imperiously. "I misspoke. I should have said, 'Silence!'" He thundered the word, thrust his hand into the air, and looked to the skies for emphasis.

Mongo blinked once. Then blinked again to make sure he wasn't seeing things. Then laughed. He felt like he was watching a silent movie. "Where'd you get that hat, Mr. Endicott? It's cool."

Endicott chose to ignore the boy and started his descent. Mongo leaned back with both arms behind him and watched Endicott wobble his way down. His buzz returned.

Mongo was giggling to himself when Endicott stepped back to Earth. "You remind me of that detective on TV .... Who is it?... The case of, what's it called?"

"Sherlock Holmes," Endicott said dismissively.

"What?"

"You're thinking of Sherlock Holmes," Endicott repeated with unconcealed contempt.

"No. That's not it." Mongo stood up. He was at least four inches taller than Mr. Endicott. "Bald guy. Wears a hat but not as cool as yours. Lollipop in his mouth?" He grinned and tried to think of more clues to give Mr. Endicott. He pointed to the reading glasses on Mr. Endicott's nose. "He wears tinted glasses."

"I have no idea what you're talking about Mr. Coogan."

Mongo snapped his fingers. "Kojak! That's it! Kojak!" Now that he'd thought of the name he considered Mr. Endicott again. "No. Maybe not."

"That'll be four demerits, Mr. Coogan," Endicott said severely.

"What for? What did I do?"

"For insubordination."

"What does 'insupportanation' mean?"

"InsuBORdination! Showing a lack of respect," Endicott said angrily.

"No! No!" Mongo threw up his hands. "You don't understand. I like Kojak. I didn't mean anything bad." Mongo was entirely sincere. He thought Kojak was cool.

"Save me your protestations," Endicott said, and he leaned closer and lowered his voice. "And don't ever use the word 'masturbate' in my presence again."

Now Mongo was really confused. "That's what you were doing, right? Looking for somebody buttering his muffin, choking the chicken, punching the clown?"

"Eight more demerits!" Endicott shouted.

Mongo's face fell. The evening had begun so well, but this was a total bummer. "Then what were you doing, Mr. Endicott?"

"I was setting an example," he said with emphasis, and he waddled off in the direction of the headmaster's house, not waiting for a response.

"Fuck a duck," Mongo muttered, and headed for the dining hall.

MONGO PICKING MUSHROOMS

UP CAME THE SUN and showered its abundance on all of creation: the crowded street, the lonely bower, the towers of wealth and privilege, the obscure hamlet. Most of the inmates of the Randolph School were blinkered to its glories, awake, if at all, only to the daily call for breakfast and another roster of classes. But one resident was grateful for the sun's appearance. He'd already been up for over an hour, and now he faced the east with a hand above his eyebrows as the sun crested the hill and spilled its glory onto the field where he stood.

"Welcome!" he called to the sun. "Thank you!" He smiled at the day's daybreak, and the night's bright stars dimmed and disappeared. Looking down, he found that he could now see through the rough, tall grass to the ground, so he switched off his flashlight, bent over, and resumed his slow march across the cow pasture behind the school's auditorium.

Somewhere Mongo had heard that psilocybin were most potent if harvested in the early morning. Nothing in his guidebook, *Psilocybin Everywhere*, had confirmed this rumor, but he was sure that someone somewhere along his travels had shared this observation, and he had no reason to doubt its accuracy. Since six o'clock he had been crawling back and forth across the field behind Randolph Auditorium, like a digger of worms or a gatherer of eels, his flashlight casting a dim yellowish circle in front of him. Precious little had he found so far, but now that the morning light was upon him he could see the ground more clearly, and he crept forward, faster than before, stopping every now and then to pick a little brown mushroom, hold it up to his eyes for close inspection, and slip it into the fanny pack at his belt. By the time the chapel bell rang for first period a dozen cows, recognizing him from his night-time visits, had meandered in his direction and stood nearby scrabbling up mouthfuls of grass. One of them rubbed her neck against his brawny torso, either out of tenderness or for lack of a fencepost.

"Good morning, Gracie." Mongo laughed and leaned back against her as he wiggled his fingers through the tidy harvest of liberty caps in his fanny pack. That's enough for today, he thought, and zippered the pack closed. He pushed his way through the cows, affectionately swatting them on their rumps and calling them Isadora or Donna or Janis as the fancy struck him, then climbed over the pasture fence and headed back to campus.

As he approached the Randolph Building he passed students heading to class in the opposite direction. Mongo had decided to skip his classes today. Just yesterday he'd received a letter of admission to Virginia Tech, and he planned to celebrate by snarfing down a handful of liberty caps and let come what may.

NIGHTINGALE VISITS MACKIE

ON HIS WAY TO LUNCH that day, David Nightingale stopped by the Office of Student Affairs to touch base with Terrence Mackie. Mackie had requested to teach fifth form English next year. After speaking with the other English teachers, Nightingale had decided to maintain the current assignments. He knew Mackie wouldn't like this, but Nightingale had reservations about Mackie's pedagogical approach. Mackie was grading papers at his desk when Nightingale stuck his head in the door.

"Is this a good time, Terry?"

Mackie had been trying to make sense of a fourth former's sentence and was still frowning when he looked up and found Nightingale standing there. "Sorry!" He motioned for Nightingale to come in. "How can I help you?"

Nightingale stepped to the edge of the desk. "I just wanted to get back to you about class assignments for next year. I've spoken with everyone, and I don't think we'll make any changes at this point."

Mackie tapped the tip of his teeth with the blunt end of his marking pen. "Really?"

"Yes. I'm sorry about this, Terry, but we'll look at it again next year."

Mackie had been teaching at the school for eight years. For each of those eight years he'd taught two sections of Third Form English and two sections of Fourth Form English. He had little confidence that Nightingale would ever let him teach an upper level course. He grinned unpleasantly.

"Such a strange coincidence that you walked in just now. I just read your name in one of my papers."

"Pardon?"

Mackie put down his marking pen and picked up the typewritten paper in front of him. "Henry Palmer says you helped him with his paper."

Nightingale shook his head. "Henry Palmer?"

Mackie flipped to the second page and made a show of reading from the paper. "'I did talk to Mr. Nightingale about the poem before I wrote the paper, but the ideas here are mine.'" Those are his words. In the pledge.

Nightingale reached for the paper, and Mackie handed it to him. As Nightingale read the paper, Mackie said, "I assigned the class 'O Captain, My Captain', but Henry Palmer decided to write about some godawful re-imagining of the Garden of Eden."

Nightingale nodded as he read the paper and then smiled with approval when he got to the end. "Not a bad job of it, I think." He handed the paper back to Mackie. "Especially for a fourth former."

"So you put him up to this?" Mackie said irritably.

"Put him up to what?"

"To this nonsense about original sin."

Nightingale didn't find any nonsense in Henry's argument, but he chose to ignore Mackie's criticism. "No. As a matter of fact I don't think that came up. Henry gets all the credit for that."

"But you gave him the idea of—" Mackie turned back to the front page of the paper to make sure he got the title right, "'As *Adam Early in the Morning*.'"

Nightingale found Mackie's obvious irritation ridiculous, but he suppressed a laugh. "No. Again. Henry found the poem himself."

"How is it that you ended up helping him?"

Nightingale remembered Henry asking for help with his writing, but he decided not to mention that because he knew that would make Mackie even more defensive.

"Henry is one of my advisees," he said. "We were meeting about something, and he asked me about the poem."

"Did he tell you he was supposed to write a paper about 'O Captain, My Captain'!?"

"He might have." Nightingale tried to sound noncommittal.

"And?"

Typical Mackie, Nightingale thought. Always so prickly about his authority. "I didn't tell him what to write about Terry. I only asked him questions about the poem."

"You didn't tell him what it meant?"

Nightingale shook his head with disapproval. "No. I asked him what he thought it meant. And then maybe helped him better understand what he was saying."

"Well..." Mackie placed the paper back on the desk in front of him and poked it with his index finger. "This is terrible."

"Do you mean the paper, or Whitman's poem?"

"Both!" Mackie barked.

Nightingale shrugged and held his tongue. This was why he didn't want Mackie teaching Fifth Form English.

Mackie made a show of removing the cap of his marking pen, as if he were preparing to renew his grading. Henry's paper was in front of him, as yet unmarked. To the right of Henry's paper was a pile of graded papers; to the left a pile of ungraded papers. Nightingale started to leave when he noticed a sheet of paper with a drawing at the edge of Mackie's desk. The drawing was of a strange bird wearing a monocle.

"What's this?" Nightingale pointed to the OWL drawing.

Mackie looked sideways, in the direction Nightingale was pointing. "That's one of the drawings that was posted in the chapel."

"In January?"

Mackie nodded but kept his head down, hoping to speed up Nightingale's departure.

"May I?" Nightingale picked it up without waiting for Mackie's response. He remembered Edwin's description of the drawings, but he'd not seen them. He immediately recognized Oscar Wilde by the fat cheeks, the flop of hair and dandyish outfit. He laughed to himself at the likeness. Then he recalled his brief conversation with Ken Bright after a Hamlet class. Oscar Wilde and Walt Whitman — this poem, in fact, "As *Adam Early In the Morning*". He traced the Jesus fish with his finger. He remembered there'd been a nasty exchange between Ken and Lawton Faison in his class that day.

"Any progress in the investigation?" Nightingale asked.

"Just a bunch of dead-ends."

"Why the Jesus fish?"

Mackie looked up at the place in the drawing that Nightingale was pointing to. He smiled. "Frank thinks it's an attack on the church. Edwin thinks someone is making fun of Frank." Then he shrugged. "Your guess is as good as mine."

Nightingale didn't volunteer his guess. He handed the sheet of paper back to Mackie. "And what's likely to happen to the poor soul if you ever figure out who it is?"

Mackie deposited the drawing in his top desk drawer. "If we can tie it back to the water tower, we'll kick him out I'm sure."

"Banish him from the Garden, shall we?"

Mackie recognized the criticism in Nightingale's comment and grumbled. "You bet. Climb up the water tower and paint a big fuck you — on Parent's Weekend no less. You bet! You don't get to do whatever strikes your fancy."

Nightingale held up a cautionary finger.

> *I have said that the soul is not more than the body,*
> *And I have said that the body is not more than the*
> *soul,*

"What are you talking about, David?"

Nightingale didn't answer but continued with the quotation.

> *And nothing, not God, is greater to one than one's*
> *self is,*
> *And whoever walks a furlong without sympathy*
> *walks to his own funeral drest in his shroud*

Mackie stared at Nightingale and made no effort to hide his dislike of the man. He'd always suspected that Nightingale looked down on his background and his education and considered him a mediocre teacher. He knew that Nightingale was criticizing him now, somehow, and the fact that he didn't recognize the quotation made the criticism seem all the more condescending. He knew that Nightingale was waiting for him to say something, so he held his tongue. But then he really wanted Nightingale to get out of his office and leave him alone, and despite his misgivings, which he was sure were justified, he finally asked, "What's that?"

"That's Walt Whitman. That's why he didn't believe in original sin."

CAN'T FIGHT THE NICKNAME

EVERY DAY AT LUNCH the same group of new boys sat at the same long table in the same far corner of the dining hall. Not one of them could have told you how they all had ended up here in this out of the way spot, or why they remained there lunch after lunch; such is the blindness of habit. But even the humblest observer of human nature might have observed that their table was farthest away from the senior tables and out of sight of the faculty tables, and the same natural philosopher might even have hypothesized that some invisible hand or occupying army or process akin to natural selection had beneficently herded these new boys into a little ghetto all their own, where they were least likely to fall prey to a pride of bullies or a shrewdness of apes.

"Hey Pecker. Pass the salad dressing," Carter said.

Bobby Grimes ignored him.

"Pecker!"

Still no response.

Ward Carter picked up a french fry and threw it across the table. It sailed over Grimes's head and hit the portrait of Jay Mortimer, one of Randolph's dead masters. From the looks of old Mort's painting, this wasn't the first time he'd been caught in a crossfire.

"Don't be a dick, Pecker!"

Grimes grabbed the glass shaker of oil and vinegar and pushed it across the table. "Don't call me that."

Two boys said in unison, "Can't fight the nickname, Pecker."

Grimes hated nicknames. He'd originally been saddled with "Brokeass" in honor of his epic injury at the end of the first Cubs game, but after he pointed out that his father was the richest peanut farmer in southeastern Virginia, his teammates, who had an unshakeable respect for family wealth, abandoned that sobriquet. Not long afterward, Grimes had unwound his towel roll before football practice and found the typical tattered regulation t-shirt and a tiny athletic supporter marked XXS. He'd taken the jock back to the laundry cage where Billy Hicks, the school's pockmarked, mutton-chopped, barrel-chested equipment manager, chain-smoked cigarettes and passed out towel rolls.

Grimes tossed the athletic supporter onto the counter. "I need another jock."

Hicks groped the circumference of the cigarette with his thin lips and pulled it into his mouth as he inhaled. "That'n'll work," he said, and smoke sputtered out of his mouth with every word.

"I can't wear this."

Hicks shook his head. "That'n'll do for you."

Grimes reached through the window and slammed his palm on the counter. "I'm telling you, I NEED ANOTHER JOCKSTRAP!"

Hicks grinned, and a dry, scraping, emphysematic laugh burbled out of his mouth. "It's meant for a little pecker," he said, just as two of Grimes's fellow Cubs walked by.

When Grimes returned to his locker, still angry but clutching a beefier towel roll, Ward Carter greeted him with a sunny, "Everything okay, Pecker?" The rest of the team died laughing, and the name stuck.

Grimes reached across the table and pulled back the salad dressing. "How come Lampton doesn't have a nickname?" he whined.

Several of the boys looked to the pimply kid sitting across from Grimes, but at the sound of his name, Lampton Childs looked down at his plate. No one had bothered to stick a name to Lampton because no one ever seemed to notice him. He'd quit Cub football to try out for a minor role in the school play because of his crippling embarrassment about showering in front of his classmates. He kept to himself because he relished his privacy, and even the idea that his classmates might presume to know him well enough to rename him was deeply offensive. Lampton kept his eyes closed until the table's attention shifted elsewhere.

"And who nicknamed you L.D. anyway?" Pecker yawped at Ward Carter.

'L.D.' was short for "long dong". Carter waggled his eyebrows at

Pecker. "That is a deep secret," he smirked, and several boys burst out laughing.

"You should be grateful we don't call you 'L.P.'," Blair 'Fart' McMullen said to Grimes. McMullen's nickname referenced his penchant for bursting into boys' rooms, flopping onto his back, pulling his knees to his chin, and yelling, "Light me!" Despite Fart's prodigious flatulence, no methane explosions had ever manifested. "That's what Billy Hicks said, right?" Fart's secondary talent was as a mimic, and here he adopted a credible hillbilly accent. " 'It's meant for a Little Pecker'."

All the boys laughed, except Grimes and Childs.

"What is this crap they're serving?" asked Frank Braxton. Braxton's nickname was Waddles, owing to his short-stepped, hip-swaying manner of walking — though some boys mistakenly thought the nickname was Wattles, owing to the high likelihood that the boy would develop a double-chin in middle life. Waddles stabbed at the mysterious gray chunks floating in a puddle of white sauce on his plate.

"Chipped beef," L.D. said.

"It's disgusting."

"Why'd you choose it then?"

"I didn't. I was talking to Pecker when I got to the counter, and the next thing I know the lady hands me a plate of gravy. I thought it might be Welsh rabbit."

" 'Rarebit'," Henry said.

" 'Rarebit', 'rabbit', whatever. I didn't see how disgusting it was until I sat down with you guys."

"Want some of my salad?" Wobbly asked.

Waddles looked doubtfully at the rust-tinged chunks of iceberg lettuce on Wobbly's tray. "No thanks. Maybe I'll go back and get a hamburger."

The boys continued in the same vein as Waddles made his way back to the lunch line, where Lawton Faison, Billy Richardson, and John Gillespie stood at the counter surveying the offerings: a steam tray of chipped beef and the usual platters of hamburgers and hot dogs. A heavy-set woman in a white uniform and hairnet stood behind the counter and eyed the three sixth formers angrily. The woman had lost her hearing to a childhood case of the mumps but was able to read lips. She'd discerned these boys' cruelty more than once.

Richardson pointed at the hot dogs and held up two fingers. "One, hot, hamburger," he said loudly.

Lawton and Gillespie laughed. The woman bit her tongue and gripped the serving thong more tightly as she put a hamburger and bun on a plate and handed it to Richardson. Gillespie was next. He pointed at the hot dogs and said, "I'll have the same as him."

When they stepped into the dining hall, Richardson and Gillespie both turned toward the senior section, but Lawton checked them. "Hold on. Let's pay a visit to the Island of Misfit Toys," he said, nodding in the direction of the New Boy table. "I'd like to have a little symposium with Gordon Palmer's twirp brother."

Wobbly was the first to see the seniors approaching. In a low voice he said, "Don't look now but here comes Lawton Faison." Wobbly's right leg started bouncing up and down under the table, and he gripped the sides of his lunch tray with both hands.

Henry looked up from his plate and caught sight of Lawton sauntering across the dining hall with Richardson and Gillespie in tow. He had no doubt that Lawton"s sole purpose was to harass him, but he steeled himself and refused to look away. Lawton caught Henry's gaze and a thin smile curled across his lips.

"Well, if it isn't Henry Palmer," Lawton sang out as they reached the table.

John Gillespie put his hand on the back of Wobbly's neck, squeezed it and pulled down hard, to give him a rope burn.

"Oww!"

"You've been blessed by Rev. Gillespie." He laughed.

Wobbly rubbed the back of his neck and edged away from Gillespie. The other boys looked at each other with a mixture of relief that they were not the object of the sixth formers' attention and concern about what they might do to Henry. Lawton looked down at Lampton Childs who had an empty chair beside him. "Move over, Spam."

Instantly, Childs' neck and cheeks burned bright red, which only served to highlight his raging acne, but the others were too cowed to capitalize on his humiliation. Childs slid to the left and Lawton claimed the seat directly opposite Henry. Richardson and Gillespie rounded the table and motioned for Pecker and Fart to make room so they could flank Henry. Henry sat straight as a rod, anticipating the worst.

"I've been wanting to have a few words with you, Palmer." Lawton scratched the back of his left hand. "I've been wondering—does Gordon know you spend so much time with Ken Bright?"

"Why is that any business of yours?" Henry said, his voice an eerie mimic of Lawton's even tone.

Lawton smiled and leaned across the table. "Because I happen to know that Bright is the one behind those absurd drawings you posted in the chapel last month."

Henry noticed several of his friends shoot questioning glances at each other. As he suspected, no one knew anything about the drawings. There had been a lot of talk about the fish painted on the water tower, but no one had said anything about the OWL drawings.

"I don't know what you're talking about."

"Oh, I think you do. This is something that you and Bright cooked up to get attention, but it hasn't worked, has it?"

Lawton studied Henry's face for some betrayal of fear, but Henry met his gaze with remarkable coolness.

"I can't help you, Lawton, because I have no idea what you're talking about. Maybe you should ask your fishy friends."

Lawton nodded to his friends, who grabbed Henry's arms as Lawton stood up and in one swift motion pushed Henry's face down into his lunch plate. Henry felt the warm mush of his half-eaten burger and mustard ooze against his cheek.

"Let go of him!" Childs demanded.

Lawton turned and slapped Childs across the face. "Shut up, Spam!"

Childs yelped. Another boy jumped up, but Richardson grabbed him before he could dart away.

"Where you going, Squirt?" Richardson wrenched the boy's arm behind his back.

"Ow!"

"Sit down, new boy!" Lawton growled.

The other boys looked around for someone to come to their aid, but they were out of sight of most of the dining hall.

With controlled fury, Henry plucked the napkin from his tray and wiped the mess off his cheek.

Lawton leaned across the table and hissed. "Tell your hippie friend that we know what he's up to, and unless you're as gay as he is I suggest that you put some distance between him and you, if you get my drift."

With that Lawton stood up and the cold smile returned to his lips. He cast his maleficent gaze first at Henry, then across the whole table, as if bestowing a curse upon them all. "Nice talking to you girls," he sneered, then motioned to his posse.

As the three of them turned to take their leave they came face to face with Gordon Palmer, galumphing across the dining hall.

"Billy, John, Lawton, gentlemen, what's up?" Gordon's cheerful tone belied the set of his jaw. He eyed Henry, who looked a little worse for wear, just as Gordon had feared when he'd exited the lunch line and spied Lawton's proud head bobbing at the New Boy table. "What brings y'all to these parts?"

"Just catching up with your baby brother." Lawton feigned nonchalance. "Nice kid, when he's not mixing with the wrong crowd."

Gordon scanned the faces at the table. "Crowd looks alright to me."

Lawton moved closer and lowered his voice to its menacing register. "Have you noticed, Gordon, how much time your brother spends with Ken Bright? If you spent more time with Henry and less time with Mr. Endicott, maybe 'Chosen' wouldn't wander so far off the beaten path. I suggest you ask him about the chapel drawings." Lawton gave Gordon a knowing nod, and with a toss of his perfect blond head his crew set sail for the senior section of the dining hall.

As Gordon watched Lawton's posse move away, he wondered whether Lawton was fucking with him, or did Henry actually know something about the drawings. And Ken Bright? But he set those concerns aside for the moment to take pride in what had just happened. He'd saved his brother and the other new boys from Lawton's hazing, and he'd lived up to his expectations for himself as "Head Boy". This was important to Gordon. He knew how much the other students, especially the younger students, looked to him to set an example. At first he'd been embarrassed by how much attention he got—boys he didn't even know paid attention to everything he did—but as time went on and he grew accustomed to the role, it started to feel natural and even right that other boys should look up to him. He was worthy of their attention—that's why he'd been chosen "Head Boy"—and their admiration of him reflected well on them. Like the other boys, he now thought of himself as the paragon of the Randolph Boy, endowed with spirit and honor, and he wanted to live up to that.

The new boys at the table said nothing. Some of them were still stunned by the bullying; others were in awe of Gordon. The spell was broken by the return of Waddles, who had finally managed to secure a hamburger. Waddles noted the charged atmosphere and peculiar presence of the Head Boy. Had he not been holding a lunch tray, Waddles might have saluted; as it was, he nodded to Gordon as he slid past and resumed his former place among his friends.

"Wha'd'd I miss?" Waddles asked, chomping down on his burger.

After a brief pause, Wobbly said, "Spam got his face slapped by Lawton Faison."

Lampton Childs's heart sank.

"And I thought he was going to shit himself," Carter added.

"Who's Spam?" Waddles asked.

Wobbly pointed at Childs. "Our new boy, right here."

Waddles regarded Childs's pocked face and smiled, his mouth full of masticated beef. "Right on!" He swallowed, and held up a greasy palm for a high-five. "Spam, my man, welcome to the par-tay!"

As the group settled back into its natural rhythm Gordon, who stood like a sentinel at the end of the table, gestured to his brother.

"We need to talk," he said in a low voice. "Come sit down with me?"

Henry felt numb and didn't want to deal with Gordon. He suspected Gordon wanted to ask about the drawings, and he really didn't feel like lying to his brother right now.

"I don't have much time," Henry said.

"It won't take long."

Henry couldn't think of an excuse that wouldn't make Gordon more suspicious. "Okay," he said with a shrug.

Gordon moved away while Henry collected the mangled remains of his lunch.

"Good thing you got Big Brother to watch over you, huh Chosen?" Carter needled.

"Don't be a dick, Carter," Henry snapped.

"He's not a dick. He's a Dong!" someone chortled.

Henry joined Gordon at a nearby table. He sat across from his brother and pretended to take an interest in his food in hopes of avoiding the third degree.

"You okay?" Gordon asked.

"I'm alright."

Henry poked at a half-eaten french fry with his fork. Gordon leaned closer.

"What the hell was all that about with Lawton?"

"Just him being an asshole," Henry said in an offhand way, as if there were no particular reason for Lawton's assholery. He glanced at Gordon, to see how that landed, then returned his attention to the table and stabbed the french fry.

Normally, Gordon would have chalked up Lawton's hazing of Henry to his animosity towards himself, a sore loser's attempt to take his jealousy out on his rival's younger brother. But that didn't explain Lawton's comments about Ken Bright and the chapel drawings. Did Lawton really know something about the drawings? Did Henry?

"Has Lawton been harassing you lately?"

Henry laughed to himself. Gordon had no idea. He hadn't told Gordon about the episode behind the chapel, because he didn't want Gordon to try to fight his battles. Now that Lawton had introduced the chapel drawings into the equation he had even more reason to keep Gordon in the dark.

"No more than usual," Henry said, which happened to be pretty much true.

Gordon acted stupid. "What was all that about chapel drawings?"

The form of the question surprised Henry. Surely Gordon knew about the chapel drawings already. Wasn't that the point of being Head Boy, to know everything? "No idea," he said. "Seemed like he thought you knew what he was talking about."

Gordon noticed the surprise on Henry's face and suspected he was hiding something. "Why does he think you had something to do with the drawings?"

Henry shrugged. "I don't know. You'll have to ask him."

"I'm asking you. Did you have anything to do with drawings in the chapel?"

The sharpness in Gordon's tone reminded Henry of their father. He shook his head, no, and wondered where Gordon got off being so arrogant.

"But you know what I'm talking about," Gordon said.

Henry hesitated. Had he already admitted that he knew anything? He realized he needed to choose his words carefully. He felt his face getting hot as he shook his head again.

"You don't know about them?" Gordon pressed him.

"I don't know what you're talking about,' Henry said. "Are you investigating *me*?"

"Of course not. I — " Gordon stopped, shook his head and took a sip of his iced tea. "Look," he said. "Not many people know this, but that night the bat got loose at chapel someone posted drawings of a bird holding the Jesus fish — the one on the water tower. Lawton knows because he found them, but not many other people do. Mr. Endicott thinks that the person who posted the drawings is the person who painted the fish on the water tower."

"Okay, but what does that have to do with me?"

"I don't know, Henry. You tell me." Gordon felt his throat tighten, and he coughed. "Lawton seems to think it has something to do with you."

"Well you'll have to ask Lawton to explain that, because I can't."

Gordon reached out to wipe a smudge of mustard on Henry's cheek, but Henry grabbed the napkin out of his hand. Gordon pointed to the spot on his own face, and Henry wiped his cheek then checked the napkin.

"Thanks," he mumbled.

Gordon took a bite of chipped beef and wondered if Henry was hiding something. Something in his standoff manner didn't seem right.

"Listen. You can tell me if you know something. I'll take care of you."

Henry didn't want Gordon to take care of him and didn't like the way Gordon seemed to bearing down on him. "I don't know anything about it," he said.

"What's all this about Ken Bright, again?" he asked.

"What do you mean 'again'?"

"I told you not to spend time with that guy. He's a stoner, and ..." Gordon tried to find the right word.

"And a 'fag'?" Henry said, with obvious disgust at what he suspected Gordon was thinking.

"No! Why did you say that?"

"Lawton called him 'gay', so I guess it's not hard to figure where everyone's mind goes."

Gordon had been trying to come up with a word that captured the way Ken was both admired and reviled. Gay seemed about right, Gordon thought, but the fact that people were saying it out loud was surprising and, given Henry's proximity, kind of alarming.

"I'm not saying he's gay," Gordon clarified. "I'm just saying he's not the type of person you want to hang out with if you want to hang out with the right kind of people."

"People like you," Henry said, deadpan.

Gordon frowned. He felt like he was being rebuked by a toddler. "Yes, as a matter of fact. People like me. Why not hang out with people like me, Henry?"

All the disgust Henry had ever felt for his father, his father's family, the school — all of it — rushed to the surface and spewed out of his mouth in a vomit of words.

"I don't want any of this!" He spun his hand in a circle above his head to indicate the dining hall, the school, all of it. "I don't want the country club, or golf at Pinehurst, or marrying a Chi-O. I could care less about a beach house at Figure Eight or the Rams Club or god knows what. I'd rather hitchhike to California than go to college. Write a poem, than a stupid memo. Paint a portrait, sing a song, make a movie — do anything but sell my soul like you and Dad."

Gordon laughed; there was no way Henry really believed what he was saying. "I'm going to make a million dollars before I turn 30!"

Henry was appalled; he knew Gordon believed exactly what he said. "You'll be a hundred years old before you're 25!" he replied.

"What the hell is that supposed to mean?"

Henry refused to explain himself. He simply said, "I'm not spending my life grubbing after money."

Gordon wanted to reach across the table and throttle the brat. Who was he kidding? He wasn't any different. His friends called him 'Chosen', for Christ's sake. Gordon glanced at the new boys behind Henry. His friends were exactly who you'd expect them to be. Who was he fooling? He wasn't somehow better. Gordon closed his eyes until he knew he had control over his temper.

"This is not what I want to talk about," Gordon said.

Henry considered Gordon. He looked completely calm, like nothing had happened. Henry had expected Gordon to hit him; he'd kind of wanted Gordon to hit him. Henry had tried to puncture this mask that Gordon wore, but nothing fazed him. It was like Gordon really did believe he was this person he pretended to be. It was like the Gordon he'd grown up with, who was kind of uptight, sure, but basically a good guy, a good brother, a kind and caring person, was gone.

"Let's get back to those drawings," Gordon said. "Mr. Endicott thinks the person who drew them is the same person who painted the water tower."

Henry blinked; he was still processing this new idea of Gordon. "The drawings?" he mumbled.

"The drawings that were posted in the chapel were made by the same person who painted the water tower," Gordon repeated.

Henry picked up a fork and pushed the remains of a french fry across his plate. Okay, he thought to himself. Okay. Thank you, Gordon. That's useful information.

"What does Mr. Endicott know about it?" Henry asked, without lifting his gaze from the plate.

"I don't know. What do you know about it?"

Henry looked dumbly at his brother. "I told you. Nothing."

Gordon took another breath. They were going in circles again. He knew Henry was hiding something, but he didn't know what it was, or why. Hoping for some other way in, Gordon again focused on the remnant smear of mustard on his cheekbone. "What happened to your face, anyway?"

Gordon reached out again to wipe the mustard from his face, but Henry batted his hand away. "Don't touch me!"

"Jesus, calm down!"

Gordon pulled back, and Henry lowered his guard.

"Lawton gave me a close-up view of my lunch, OK?"

"Lawton is a prick." Gordon said.

"Tell me about it."

At least they had that much in common, Gordon thought. He smiled. "He's about to become completely unbearable."

"How's that?"

"You know they're going to dedicate a new stained glass window in the chapel next month."

"Oh yeah?" Henry looked up from his plate.

Progress, Gordon thought. "Yeah. A life-sized portrait of his Uncle Thomas."

"The guy the chapel's named for?"

"Yeah. Lawton's so full of himself. He keeps talking about some epic family resemblance, how his uncle looks just like him, or vice versa."

"So now we get to spend every Sunday staring at Lawton's face as well as Deemer's?"

Gordon laughed. "Exactly."

Gordon relaxed; he felt like a connection with Henry was re-established. But Henry stood up abruptly; he needed to talk to Ken.

"I have to go," Henry said, and in his haste he jostled Gordon's lunch tray and spilled his brother's iced tea.

"Dude! Take it easy!"

As Gordon swabbed up the mess on his tray, Henry wondered what Ken would think about the stained glass window.

"Give me your napkin."

Gordon moved his tray to one side and used Henry's napkin to wipe up every drop on the table. Henry suddenly felt sorry for his older brother, always wanting to do the right thing.

"I really have to go," Henry said, and he was gone before Gordon could say anything to detain him.

"Catch you later!" Gordon called out.

As Gordon watched Henry carry his lunch tray back to the kitchen it occurred to him that Henry had changed. He wasn't the same kid their parents had dropped off at school in August. For one thing, he was taller — almost as tall as Gordon now. For another, he had a sort of swagger and independence. Like his friendship with Ken Bright. Gordon couldn't imagine spending fifteen minutes with the guy; they'd have nothing to talk about. But Henry did. Apparently.

Gordon picked up his tray and headed for the senior section. He passed the teacher's table and the table for the drama geeks — no Ken Bright today — and the one where Tom Wales, Troy Lindsey and the other black kids sat. The stoners had a table, the misfits, the rich preppies who weren't jocks, and the rich preppies who were. Everyone had a place, and everyone knew their place. This was what bothered him about Henry and Ken Bright. There wasn't a place for them to be together. At least not one that Gordon could imagine.

KEN BRIGHT SAT IN HIS GREEN ARMCHAIR writing a letter to his mother. He had promised to write her once a month, and this letter, like most of the others, was late. He felt the pang of conscience. His mother had found a secretarial job with the Experimental College at Barnard, which sounded amazing, but she was still living with her mother in a two-bedroom apartment near Lincoln Center. She'd promised Ken that she would have her own place by the time he graduated, but he anticipated another lean, hot summer in the city.

> Dear Mother,
> It's finally March, but the branches are still bare, the grass is still brown, and the shadows are still long on the ground. Much like New York, I'm sure, except in essentials. There's an incredible, shallow sameness to this place. I feel like a Chekhov character, stuck in a way station, hoping for passage to a better world. Thank heavens I come home in two months!
> *Inherit the Wind* went off about as well as I could have expected. Mr. Nightingale told me it was one of the best school productions he'd ever seen — not a great accomplishment, I'm sure, but I was pleased. I still don't think I'm built to be an actor — too self-conscious always. Maybe a director? Or more likely a critic! Wouldn't that be fun? Going to plays three nights a week?
> How's Bapoo? Tell her I met someone who reminds me of her. Short, squat (don't tell her that part), quiet, a pianist, of course. He draws hilarious pictures — a little Thurber in the making! I think I'll ask him to draw a picture of Bapoo with a cup of coffee making a wicked comment about her Herr Schneiderman.
> I should hear from Yale and Columbia any day now. I'll call as soon as I do.
> Love,
> Ken

Ken was rereading the letter when Henry and Tom Wales burst

into the room. Wales, in particular, looked horror-stricken. He pointed to Ken.

"Tell him what you told me," Tom said to Henry.

Henry held out a hand to Tom in an effort to calm him. "Take it easy. It's not as bad as you think."

Tom shook his head in disbelief and turned to Ken. "Lawton Faison knows that you and Henry are behind the chapel drawings," he said. "And he told Henry's brother to look into it."

Henry waved his hand in the air. "Gordon's not going to do anything, and Lawton's just blowing smoke up our ass."

Ken slipped the letter and his writing board onto the floor beside his chair. "What exactly did Lawton say?"

"He said —" Tom started to speak but Ken held out his hand to stop him.

"Let Henry tell me. Sit down. Both of you." Ken motioned toward his bed, and after they took a seat, he turned to Henry. "Okay. So what happened?"

"Lawton just said he 'knows' " — and Henry waggled his fingers to put the word in quotation marks — "that you and I did the Owl drawings. He said the same thing to Gordon."

Tom looked to Ken. "How did Lawton figure out you two and the drawings?"

"He's not stupid — just lazy," Ken said. "Simple deduction."

Tom looked at Henry to see if he understood what Ken meant.

"He knows I know about the Jesus fish," Henry explained. "It was part of that secret society he wanted me to join."

"Is he likely to tell anyone?" Tom asked.

Ken scoffed. "And risk Henry exposing him as the person who painted the water tower? Not likely."

"He told Henry's brother," Tom said.

"He couldn't resist goading Gordon about Henry's connection to me," Ken explained.

"Yeah, well. And that worked," Henry said.

Ken grimaced. "Gordon been singing my praises again?"

"Why does he hate you so much?" Henry almost laughed.

Ken smiled. "You'd almost think he was gay or something." And he let out his terrible, high-pitched, nasal laugh.

Henry decided not to tell Ken that Gordon had, in fact, talked about him being gay.

"Lawton too," Tom said.

Ken stopped laughing and turned to Tom. "What did Lawton say?"

Henry would have kicked Wales if he could have done it without Ken noticing.

Tom turned to Henry. "You tell him what Lawton said."

Henry looked at Ken. He was now slumped in his chair and his eyes had narrowed into a tight, angry focus on Henry.

"Oh you know, he said you were a jerk and stuff."

"Tell me EXACTLY what he said."

Henry looked at the posters on Ken's wall.

"Well?"

Tom realized that he'd put Henry in an awkward spot, so he tried to make amends. "He said you were 'gay'."

Ken closed his eyes and imagined Lawton saying those words. He kind of liked the idea of Lawton talking about him. Poor Lawton, he thought. Someday he'll have to let his bird out of the cage.

Tom waited for Ken to say something, but he just sat there with his eyes closed. Tom looked to Henry. Henry shrugged.

"The guy's the biggest jerk," Tom said.

"He slapped Lampton Childs across the face," Henry added.

Ken still had his eyes closed, and Henry motioned for Tom to keep talking.

"Henry says his buddies smashed his face into the lunch tray."

Ken opened his eyes. "Quite the savage." He turned to Henry. "Any mention of Oscar Wilde?"

Henry shook his head. "I don't think they've figured that out." He remembered what Gordon had told him about Endicott's theory. "Gordon said Endicott thinks the person behind the 'bird' drawings is also behind the water tower."

"That doesn't make any sense, does it?" Tom asked.

"No one ever accused Mr. Endicott of being Sherlock Holmes," Ken said.

All three of them chuckled. The headmaster's fire escape frolic was now the stuff of legend, and not of the sort Endicott had hoped.

"So what do you two propose?" Ken asked, returning to the matter at hand.

"That's why we came here," Henry said. "To figure it out."

"Sounds like Lawton's a bit wound up and needs unwinding," Ken said.

Tom and Henry nodded.

"Well? Any ideas?"

"How 'bout a drawing of Lawton as Adolph Hitler? Leather boots. Little moustache. Goose step," Tom said.

"Not sure Lawton would mind that," Ken said sarcastically.

"Kind of over the top, isn't it?" Henry objected.

Ken laughed. "You think subtlety works with this crowd?"

"Just seems like people might think it's a bit much."

"Henry's probably right," Tom said. "Last thing we want is to make Lawton the victim."

They spit-balled various ideas — none garnered any enthusiasm — until there was a click and Ken's door swung open. Mongo stood framed in the doorway, his massive form clad only in a tie-dyed t-shirt and underwear. He took a step into the room and stopped, staring at the sunlight pouring in through Ken's window. He didn't say a word or move another inch. Henry thought he might be sleepwalking.

"Mongo? Are you alright, man?" Ken asked.

Mongo's head rotated from the window to Ken, and he blinked once as if coming out of a trance.

"Hey, man," he said slowly, and his voice was even lower than normal and seemed to echo in some deep place. "Do you have 'Dark Side of the Moon'?"

"Sure thing."

Ken thumbed through the pile of records on the floor beside his stereo. He held out the album. Mongo stared with unblinking eyes at the empty space between himself and the album cover for a long time. It was like he was trying very hard to figure out how to get from here to some imaginary there. Finally, he stepped forward and took the album from Ken and slowly turned it over and over and over and over and over in his hands. Ken leaned forward and put his hand on the giant's hairy arm.

"Hey, Mongo…. You in there?"

Mongo's head slowly rotated, until his eyes fell on Ken's hand, which he seemed to ponder as if he did not know where it had come from.

Ken spoke louder. "Mongo!" and Mongo's gaze slouched towards Ken's mouth.

"You with me big fellow?"

Mongo said nothing.

Henry leaned over to Ken and whispered, "I'm pretty sure he's stoned." He pointed at Mongo's fully dilated pupils. "It's like he's in a dark cave by himself."

Tom adjusted his position to get a better look, then quickly sat back. "That's crazy," he said in a frightened whisper. "Should we try to wake him up?"

Now it was Ken's turn to whisper. "I don't think he's asleep. Definitely stoned."

Mongo seemed to lose interest in Ken's mouth and resumed his close attention to the album cover.

"Keep talking," Ken said. "He'll snap out of it." He turned to Tom. "What were you saying?"

Tom's knee bounced up and down and he tugged on one of his earlobes. "Are you sure?" He still whispered.

"Go ahead," Ken said. "Mongo's cool, or stoned, or both."

Tom had never seen a person stoned before, and Mongo terrified him. He looked to Henry for some guidance, but Henry only shrugged. Although Henry had some experience with intoxicants, this was on another level entirely; Mongo's pupils were freaky.

Keeping his head down so as to avoid looking at Mongo, Tom said, "Okay. Well. Like Henry was saying, we don't want to be so over-the-top that people end up feeling sorry for him."

"How 'bout John Brown, or Abraham Lincoln?" Henry offered.

Ken made a face by screwing up one eyebrow and twisting his mouth. "But we admire *them* right?"

"You're right," Henry tapped his noggin. "Duh. I was thinking about bugging Lawton."

Ken drummed his fingers together, while Wales tapped out some rhythm on his thigh, Henry bit the corner of his lip, and Mongo stared at the album cover. Then with words spoken in such a distant and cavernous tone that they seemed to ring out from the bowels of the earth, Mongo said, "Turn him into a hippie."

"Yipe!" Tom started back in terror.

But Ken slapped himself on the knee. "Mongo! You're a man of brilliance! Mysterious brilliance, but brilliance all the same."

The behemoth did not acknowledge the compliment but simply stared at the black triangle on the Pink Floyd album cover as if it were a crystal ball.

"A hippie is perfect," Ken said to the others. "Lawton hates hippies as much as I do."

"You hate hippies?" Henry said.

"Well, yes, but not for the same reason. Lawton hates them because of their politics. I hate them because ...." Ken paused to consider the myriad ways he loathed the photos of lightly bearded men unwashed and uncouth laying about with stupid grins on their faces. "Because of their sham aesthetics," he said finally. "Tie-dye, peasant cloth, and B.O? Ugh, please. That's funny. It hadn't occurred to me until now that Lawton and I have that in common."

Tom held up his hand as if he were in class. Ken nodded at him.

"We could do a drawing of the Owl holding a tie-dye t-shirt that says, 'Lawton's a hippie!'"

"Too obvious. Methinks we must be subtler than that."

Tom held up his hand again. "A drawing of Lawton with a scraggly beard and a peace symbol around his neck?"

"Better," Ken said. "But not a knockout punch."

"Turn the Jesus into a hippie," Mongo said in that same, prior Olympian tone.

"What Jesus, Mongo?" Henry asked.

"The Jesus they're installing in the chapel," Mongo monotonized, as if he were reading lyrics from the back of the Dark Side of the Moon album cover.

"How do you know about that?" Henry asked.

Mongo slowly swiveled his attention, like a gigantic piece of artillery coming to bear on its target, from the album in his hands to the boys sitting on the bed below him. Tom Wales quailed.

"Billy and John say Lawton talks about it all the time," he said slowly.

Ken smiled at his companions. "Pays to know a stoner."

Henry slapped his knee. "Lawton thinks the Jesus in the new stained glass window looks like him!"

"How do you know that?" Ken asked.

"Gordon told me."

Mongo closed his eyes and nodded like a blind oracle. "Make Jesus look like Lawton look like hippie," he intoned.

"Fucking brilliant!" Ken said.

"A dirty hippie!" Henry said.

"Definitely dirty," agreed Ken.

"In the chapel?" Wales asked.

Ken and Henry nodded.

"Imagine the look on Lawton's face when the whole school sees that he's a stoner, not a savior." Ken slapped his slender hands together in front of his face.

"Deemer's head'll explode," Tom said.

"Bonus!" Henry said, and he once again held his palm up to Tom for a high-five.

Ken and Henry and Tom congratulated each other and then turned in unison to Mongo, the massive, mythical beast, who had materialized, *deus ex machina,* and spoken the Word.

"Hey Mongo," Ken said, speaking for all three of them, "How would you like to join OWL?"

Mongo, in underwear and bare feet, looming over the boys like a colossus — the uncanniness of his blackened stare only heightening the cosmic aspect of his bearing — slowly rotated his head from side to side.

"No," he mumbled. "I'll make the tie-dye."

BETH FAISON
———

BETH FAISON SAT AT A TABLE in the dining hall with her son, Lawton. The color of her scoop-neck linen dress matched her blue eyes and Lawton's eyes. The hall was empty — no shouts of laughter, no boys throwing food, just bright sheets of afternoon light pouring through the tall, arched, windows onto the dark dining tables and the dreary crimson carpet. She had suggested they meet here because she knew they'd have some privacy. The stained glass window honoring Thomas Faison was to be dedicated tomorrow; Beth had driven over from Richmond a day early in order to have a chance to speak with Lawton before his father arrived. She had not seen her son since Christmas break, and even then only briefly. Beth was not surprised when Lawton chose to spend the holidays with his father in Charleston — after all, most of his friends were in Charleston — but she had been disappointed and hurt when he refused her invitation to spend the night in Richmond before the beginning of winter term. She'd managed to see him at the Amtrak station in Richmond for an awkward hour before the school bus picked up the boys for the beginning of term, but he'd been sullen, had volunteered little, and had rebuffed her inquiries. Since then there had only been a few strained phone calls which had left her near tears.

Normally, Beth Faison had a kind, wholesome expression that made her appear ten years younger than her actual age, but today she seemed pinched. There was a shadow about her eyes, as if she had not slept well, and her mouth was set. She could feel her sons' legs bobbing underneath the table, but still she looked at him, longing for some gesture to remind her of that boy who used to cling to her neck at bedtime, begging for one more story or one more poem.

Lawton sensed her longing and responded with irritation. "What do you want, Mother? Why are you here?"

"I know you are upset with me, Lawton, and I didn't come here to defend myself, but if you have any questions — any questions at all — about what's happened, I will do my best to answer them honestly. But I don't want to burden you with things you don't want to hear. Or you're not ready to hear."

She watched her son spin a silver dollar around and under the fingers of his right hand. He had fine hands, like hers, and she remembered the first time she saw him do this trick when he came home the summer after his first year at The Randolph School. She'd asked him where he'd learned it, and he'd said, "I don't remember," and he'd gone on spinning the coin. Over and over. An Eisenhower silver dollar. Refusing to look at her. Ignoring her. The suddenness of the break had been shocking. It was like he'd just turned off a switch. Since then, the gulf between them had widened, and the divorce had made things worse.

"I'm good," Lawton said.

"Good?" she said doubtfully.

After a beat or two, Lawton fumbled the coin and it clanked onto the table.

"How's school?"

"It's okay."

"Almost done!" she offered cheerily.

"Almost."

"When do you hear from Princeton?"

Lawton reached into his hunting jacket and pulled out an envelope. Princeton University appeared on the return address.

"You heard?" Her face brightened. "What did they say?"

Lawton opened the envelope, unfolded the letter and handed it to her. She read it, and her shoulders slumped. She reached for her son's hand but he pulled away.

"Oh Lawton, I'm so sorry. I know you had your heart set on it. How long have you known?"

Lawton took the letter from his mother's hand and put it back into the envelope.

"I've been carrying this around for a week."

"Have you told your father?"

Lawton shook his head. Lawton's father had graduated from Princeton. The Class of 1956. For as long as Lawton could remember his father had told him, 'You'll be the Class of 1983.'

"You applied to UVa., didn't you?"

Lawton nodded. That was a lie.

"And?"

"Haven't heard yet."

"Where else? The Citadel?"

Lawton shook his head.

"Well," his mother said. "That's a phone call."

"I don't want to go to The Citadel," Lawton snapped. He stuffed the envelope back into his jacket pocket.

Beth Faison watched the expression on her son's face change from a proud, distant teenager's to a frightened child's. She recognized that look.

"What am I supposed to tell dad?" he asked.

Beth knew neither of them had any chance of living up to her ex-husband's expectations. He was the sort of man who regarded all the trappings of his domestic life, including his wife and child, as empty mirrors whose purpose was to reflect his self-regard. She'd given up on pleasing Lawton Sr. when she'd filed for divorce, but her son still chased that phantom.

"The truth," she said simply. "You should tell him the truth."

"He'll be angry."

"I suspect he will."

"He'll say I failed him."

Beth could hear Lawton saying just that. "Maybe, but that's ridiculous."

"It's what I always wanted."

Beth didn't believe that. That was his father talking. If Lawton really wanted to go to Princeton he wouldn't have such horrible grades. She'd wanted him to apply to art school. She'd seen his drawings. She'd seen him draw. It was the only thing he did for pleasure and without prompting. She'd mentioned it to Lawton — Lawton Sr. — and he'd dismissed it out of hand. He refused to consider any destiny for his son that he could not imagine for himself — especially one that reminded him of his wife.

"Have you really always wanted to go to Princeton?"

"Yeah. Like dad."

Lawton looked so unhappy. Beth hated to see him like this, but maybe it was a good thing. He was young. He had talent. He could be lazy, but that was to be expected from a kid who'd had everything handed to him. Better the setbacks come now, she told herself, when he still had room for change and time to grow.

"Well, I'm sorry. But maybe it's time for you to be like you."

Lawton slapped the table. "Is that what you're doing, mom? Being more like you?"

There it was, she thought. His father's bitterness and cruelty. She had failed to wean him of that. Another trial he'd have to endure. The drying out of privilege. His father had refused to face it. Lawton would not be able to avoid it.

"I'm doing the best I can," she said. She ran a hand across her thigh to smooth a fold in her dress and looked away from that Faison scowl on her son's face.

"What are you doing?"

"I got a job at St. Catherine's. I'm teaching seventh grade English next fall, believe it or not."

"That's ridiculous." Lawton started spinning the silver dollar around his right hand again.

"It's a good job. I love St. Catherine's."

"It's embarrassing."

"What's embarrassing about it?"

"I know girls at St. Catherine's. I'll be like some faculty kid, or worse — I'll be the kid whose mom took a job in the middle school because she got a divorce."

Her son didn't even look up at her; he just watched the coin spin around his fingers. Tears came to her eyes.

"Well it's a start, and I'm grateful for it. It's not easy finding a job at my age. If I could do it all over again I would have gotten a job years ago."

"Dad would've loved that. Being married to a career woman."

At their last mediation before the divorce was finalized, Lawton Sr. had said just the opposite; he had made a point of complaining that she'd never gotten a job. She'd been furious about that, but she let her son's comment pass.

"Change is always hard," she said. "Like it or not."

"I don't like it," Lawton said. In fact, he hated that his parents were divorced. It embarrassed him. He knew his dad could be a dick, but hadn't he always been a dick? Wasn't that the person she'd married? When his father told him, "Your mother has filed for divorce and is moving back to Richmond to 'find herself'," he'd suspected there was more to it. He assumed his father had screwed around. Lawton had seen the way his father talked to younger women. Looked at younger women. But was that reason enough for divorce? All he knew was that it had already caused him headaches — being alone with his dad over Christmas was no fun. He blamed his mom because she had always been the one that took care of things, and now things were fucked.

The sound of voices in the kitchen reached them, and a woman wearing a white apron rolled a cart of salad dressing and salt and pepper shakers into the dining hall. The evening crew was preparing for supper. Beth felt like she needed to get to the point. She placed her hands on the table in front of her and straightened herself in the chair.

"I need to tell you something that you're not going to want to hear," she said gently.

"Let me guess. You're divorcing dad again."

She recoiled. She was not surprised that her son blamed her for the divorce, but to have him insult her like this was a shock. She chose not to respond to that. She hadn't come here to justify herself or to condemn his father; she'd come here to try to help her son begin to face up to his present circumstances. It was obvious that his father had done nothing to prepare Lawton for what was coming. That also was hardly surprising; indeed it was exactly what she had expected. He refused to face the losses himself; how would he ever admit them to his son? Poor Lawton — her husband — had killed the family legacy through one lazy investment after another; now everything was coming due. Poor Lawton — her son — was going to have to find his own way, rely on his own talents, and she knew that nothing in his upbringing had prepared him for that.

"I guess there's been a lot of bad news lately, hasn't there?" she began.

"No kidding."

"I got a call last week from John Gillespie's mother," she continued. "She called to tell me how much John was looking forward to going to Sullivan's Island over Spring Break."

"That's the plan," Lawton said without looking up. "Him and Billy and me." He watched the silver dollar roll around and around his fingers.

"Lawton, listen to me …. Look at me." She reached across the table and touched her son's hand to get his attention. The silver dollar rattled to the table, and he looked at her irritably.

"What? What is it?"

"You're not going to be able to go to the Sullivan's Island house anymore."

"Why not?"

"We lost it."

Beth Faison watched Lawton rub the face of the Dwight Eisenhower with his thumb then drop it into the pocket of his hunting jacket. She thought perhaps he hadn't heard her.

"We lost the Sullivan's Island house, Lawton."

He placed his hands on the edge of the table and rocked onto the back legs of his chair.

"What do you mean you 'lost' it?" he asked.

"The bank took it."

"Why?"

"Because your father couldn't pay the mortgage. I believe the phrase is 'living beyond one's means' or 'delusions of grandeur'," Beth said, and now the bitterness crept into her voice.

Lawton stared blankly at her.

"Look, Lawton dear, the simple fact is your father is not the businessman he thinks he is. He took out loans he couldn't repay, and the bank took the house."

"When?"

"Last month," she said.

"And you're just now telling me?"

"I assumed your father would have told you. It was rather awkward when Betsy Gillespie called."

"Goddammit!" Lawton slapped the table with the palms of his hands. "What is happening?"

Beth Faison saw the mixture of anger and fear in her son's face. Maybe he was beginning to comprehend.

"Debts have to be repaid, Lawton, one way or another," she began in answer to his question, but before she could go further her son leapt to his feet.

"I gotta get out of here," he said, suddenly panicking. "See you later." And Lawton walked straight out of the dining hall, without looking back.

Tears came to Beth Faison's eyes again as she watched her son rush away. Just like his father, she thought. She felt like she'd failed him.

ON THE BACKSIDE of the Manor, invisible from the Lawn and the rest of the school, were three brick sheds dating back to the time when the Manor was the Randolph family home and the grounds were a small plantation. The three sheds were slave quarters then, built by slaves from bricks fired from red clay dug on the grounds. Two of the former slave cabins were now used to store farm supplies and old equipment: derelict tractors that were kept for parts, bags of fertilizer, pails of poison, picks, shovels, fence posts, and an old thresher that had not been used since the school stopped growing winter wheat. The third cabin was Uly's home: a small bedroom, a living area with a fireplace, and a bathroom. It had no kitchen per se, just a counter with a sink, a hot plate, and a wooden table with two chairs. The walls were bare, except for a framed clipping from the *Clarion*, the student newspaper, dated January, 1968, with the headline *Uly Saves the Day!* and a photograph of Uly smiling broadly and holding a tabby cat beside a ladder leaning against a tall oak tree on the Lawn. On the mantle above the fireplace was a framed photograph of Uly's wife and daughter, taken forty years ago. Beside it was a pewter cup given to Uly in 1952 on the occasion of his twenty-fifth year of service to the school.

Uly stood at the sink and placed the toothed cog of a can opener against the outside of a can of Campbell's soup and pressed the circle blade inside the lip. A drop of grease oozed out of the can and thinned into a line as Uly turned the handle and spun the blade around the can's circumference. The grinding sound of the toothed cog and the smell of fat excited Maisie, who hopped onto her back legs and pressed her front paws against Uly's pants leg. When Uly glanced down at her, Maisie barked and her tail flashed back and forth. Uly laughed.

"It's your favorite, girl. Chicken and brown rice. Plump and tender, not like those pullets in the barn."

Uly lifted the round blade just before it got entirely around the can and pried open the lid with his finger. He grabbed a metal spoon and carried the can to a small table and chair. He took a seat and scooped half the contents of the can into a white ceramic bowl that sat on the floor. Maisie, who had followed at his heel from the sink to her bowl, stood there looking up at Uly, wagging her tail and smiling so that her front teeth showed. Uly gently rubbed her ears, and Maisie leaned into his touch and closed her eyes with pleasure.

"Have you been a good girl today?" Uly whispered. "You waited outside Jackson Hall for me to finish cleaning the classrooms, didn't you?"

Maisie wagged her tail and gave Uly a single bark.

"You didn't chase Mrs. Mackie's black cat, though I know you wanted to."

Maisie cocked her head.

"I know you know what I'm talking about," Uly said. For a time Maisie had been in the habit of chasing the Mackie's cat whenever they came across him outside the faculty houses. For a while the cat had accommodated Maisie by running up a tree, but last week she decided she'd had enough, and when the chase reached the tree the cat turned on the dog and swiped her twice across the nose. Maisie had yelped and come running back to Uly.

"I saw you looking over your shoulder, wondering if that dang cat behind you."

Uly spoke with a mock tone of disapproval, and Maisie lay down on her stomach, with her paws straight out in front and her back legs straight back. She put her head down on her front legs and turned up two sad, brown eyes. Uly laughed, and Maisie's tail started wagging slowly. Uly knew that Maisie understood that he was only teasing her, but the sadness in her eyes still pained him.

"You're a good girl," he said. "Get your supper!"

In a flash Maisie was on all fours with her head in the bowl supping. Her tail wagged and the ribs of her taut dogsbody quivered as she ate. Uly smiled. He'd had the dog for seven years. Mr. Franklin, the farm foreman, had found her behind a stack of hay bales in one of the barns. The rest of the litter was dead. Mr. Franklin said a stray must have gotten in there. No sign of the mother; Mr. Franklin said she probably ate a poisoned rat. Why Maisie didn't die he had no idea. She was a little, mottled-gray thing, the color of a shucked oyster. Probably three weeks old. Uly had bottle-fed her at first. Then eggs. Then scraps from his plate. And finally canned food. Before Maisie, he'd only kept cats; wild things that he'd feed outside and never allow indoors. He didn't know why he'd taken in the little pup, probably because she'd appeared so helpless. Over time, she had become his best friend.

"I talked to Mabel yesterday. She said Thomas is going to graduate from the University of Illinois. Wants to become a doctor. I told her how proud I was, and that her momma would be proud too. Mabel always was the smart one. Johnny's smart too, but nothing like Thomas. She wants me to come to the graduation. I told her I'd try to make it. Hopefully it'll be after school gets out."

Maisie's eating soon ceased. She sat next to her bowl and waited for Uly to finish his own supper. When he looked down, she reared up on her back legs and placed her gentle paws on his thigh. She waited for Uly to tap his leg then jumped into his lap. She circled about three times to settle herself, then Uly lay his palm on her haunches.

"You never met Thomas. Shoot, you never met Mabel neither. Mabel hasn't been here since he was a baby. She says he looks like me. She says she wants to get a picture of me and him together at the graduation. She won't come back here, she says. I got to go see her."

Uly looked at the photograph on the mantelpiece. His fingers lightly stroked the dog. The light in the cabin gradually darkened. At first, Maisie breathed steadily with her eyes closed. Then she slipped into a deeper sleep and snored.

LAWTON FAISON SR.

THE WALLS OF THE HEADMASTER'S private dining room were lined with portraits of past headmasters, each wearing his own lugubrious expression. Edwin Endicott liked to use the room for meetings of the board of trustees, weekly meetings with senior faculty, and special occasions like today, when he was welcoming the guests of honor for the ceremonial dedication of the new stained glass window at Faison Chapel. Endicott sat at the head of the table, which was covered with a white tablecloth and set with silver-plated service. To his right sat Lawton Faison Sr., Lawton Jr., his Head Boy Gordon Palmer, and two members of the extended Faison family. To his left sat Mr. Nightingale, Rev. Deemer, and two retired members of the faculty who had been on staff when Thomas Faison was a student.

Lawton Sr. wore a smartly tailored suit, a light blue shirt and a pink tie. He was trim and tanned, and he wore his sandy brown hair longer than most men of his age and station. He had round, tortoise shell glasses, and when he deigned to laugh, he laughed loudly, showing off a perfect set of white teeth. He looked the part of fortune's favored son, and he believed without reservation that he deserved his good fortune.

"I remember the ball was thrown behind him and he had to twist his body and reach back with one hand to catch the ball, and when he turned upfield — 'Bam!' — an Episcopal player smashed him right in the face." Mr. Faison turned to Lawton and Gordon. "This was before players wore face masks — but he managed to keep his feet, somehow. I was ten or eleven years old. Daddy asked Mr. Snoot if I could stand on the sidelines, and he told the boys who worked the chains to keep an eye on me, and so I was right there when Tommy was hit. I thought for sure he'd go down but he hopped back two steps, kept his balance and got around that boy and took it all the way to the end zone. Fifty yards at least! It was the most beautiful thing I had ever seen, and I knew then that someday I would play ball for Mr. Snoot."

Mr. Faison, who had directed his anecdote to Endicott, turned to the rest of the table and bestowed a smile. He paid little particular notice to anyone other than Mr. Nightingale, his former teacher, whom he could remember admiring as a boy and now was pleased to grace with his attention. Nightingale nodded at the story. He had not known Thomas Faison, but he esteemed Mr. Snoot, both as a coach and as a colleague.

"That must have been near the end of Mr. Snoot's tenure," Endicott said.

Mr. Faison laughed. "Yes. He was a bit past his prime by the time I got here. I remember one game, against St. Matthew's I believe it was, we were down a touchdown, and Mr. Snoot started yelling, 'Nightingale! Where's Nightingale?'" Mr. Faison turned to his former teacher. "He was calling for you to suit up and save the day."

"Obviously, I hadn't made much of an impression on him as a junior faculty member," Nightingale said.

"You were a legend even then," Mr. Faison said.

"Legend?" Nightingale chuckled. "I just peaked early."

"Those days of wine and roses, eh?" Mr. Faison flashed his fine white teeth.

"Indeed," Nightingale said. "Gone with the wind."

Lawton Sr. flicked an imaginary piece of lint off his coat sleeve. "You played football at Carolina, didn't you?"

"I was always better at baseball," Nightingale said.

"But you played football, too, didn't you?"

"I did. Two years. Then the war came, and that was that."

"Where were you stationed? Germany?"

"Yes."

Mr. Faison nodded. "Tommy went to Korea. Didn't have to go. Daddy wanted him to go to business school, but Tommy enlisted."

Nightingale nodded. He knew lots of men who had managed to avoid the war by attending graduate school and postponing their military service. He was surprised that Lawton Faison's brother had chosen otherwise. "Your family must be proud of him," he said.

"I am. God knows, I am." He turned to Endicott at the head of the table. "That's why I am so glad to be here, Edwin. Today is a special day."

Endicott, who had pushed back from the table, patted his paunch and beamed. "Yes, it is. We are expecting several members of the Class of '46 to be here. Rev. Deemer has prepared a lovely service. We've asked young Lawton to say a few words, and then we'll unveil the new window. It's on days like these, when we make connections between our present and past, that I believe Randolph does its greatest good."

"I couldn't agree with you more, Edwin. And it means so much that Lawton, who never knew his Uncle Tommy, will be part of the dedication."

Deemer, who had been looking for an opening to speak to Mr. Faison, bulled forward. "I thought it fitting," he said. "Especially since Lawton is head of the Chapel Council."

Mr. Faison turned to his son, who had barely said a word since the dinner started. He frowned at the slumping figure and touched the boy's shoulder as if to wake him. "You know I was head of the Chapel Council my sixth form year."

The touch seemed to startle Lawton from a dream, and he glanced quickly around the table to get his bearings before turning to his father. "Yes. I know," he managed.

Mr. Faison squeezed his son's shoulder. "I was also on the prefect board, with Gordon's father." Lawton twisted free of his father's grip, and Mr. Faison turned to Gordon. "Gordon Palmer was Head Boy, which irritated me to no end." He laughed. "Your father used to tease me about that when we were at Princeton together, and even at my wedding.... He was the best man at my wedding. Did you know that?"

Gordon nodded. "I think so."

Mr. Faison turned to the rest of the table. "He made a toast at the reception, of course. He said, 'My name is Gordon Palmer, and I'm the only person here who Lawton has ever looked up to, but that's only because he had to.' He thought he was so funny."

He half-smiled at Gordon, and Gordon got the sense that Mr. Faison was daring him to laugh.

"At your parents' wedding a month later," he continued, now turning back to the room, "I got him back. I said, 'So last month, at my wedding, Gordon Palmer stands up at the reception and says, 'Hi. My name is Gordon Palmer. Did you know I was the Head Boy at Randolph?'"

Mr. Faison laughed and looked at Gordon.

"What kind of person does that?' Gordon was so embarrassed. He turned bright red...."

Mr. Faison regarded Gordon with a critical eye.

"I half expected him to call me last Spring when they announced that you were on the prefect board and Lawton wasn't. I thought of calling him when I heard you'd been named Head Boy, but I didn't want to give him the satisfaction."

Mr. Faison laughed again, and looked around the table to make sure everyone understood that he was joking. That smile. Those teeth. So white and straight and cruel.

Nightingale remembered Mr. Faison as a boy. Always the center of attention. Always cocksure of his place in the crowd. Always quick to laugh at someone else's expense. A mediocre student. He'd only been accepted to Princeton because in those days the school was a pipeline for the privileged sons of the old Confederacy.

"Sit up, Lawton!"

Mr. Faison slapped his son on the back, and the boy lurched forward. Lawton reached out to regain his balance and knocked over his iced tea. Lawton watched the brown floodtide flow across the table until Mr. Nightingale covered it with his napkin. The boy placed his own napkin on top of Nightingale's. "Sorry," he mumbled.

"No harm done," Nightingale said.

"Damn it, Lawton. Show some self-respect!" his father snapped.

Nightingale watched the boy shrink. He wasn't surprised that Mr. Faison had turned out to be an arrogant, careless man, but he was surprised by the callous public treatment of his son.

"Has Lawton shown you any of his drawings?" Nightingale asked.

"Drawings? No."

Lawton looked up from the tablecloth alarmed by this turn in the conversation.

"Lawton really is quite an accomplished artist—"

"How do you know what kind of artist I am?" Lawton interrupted.

Nightingale smiled at Lawton. "I've seen you draw things in class. I particularly remember a drawing you did of me during a discussion of Hamlet."

Lawton remembered that drawing. At the end of class Nightingale had said, 'Thank you, Mr. Faison, for paying such close attention.' No further comment, not even a wink or smile. He'd wondered at the time if Nightingale had seen his sketch.

"He gets that from his mother," Mr. Faison said. "Beth can paint a pretty picture."

"Well. He has a gift. Truly," Nightingale said.

"Hasn't helped his mother much," Mr. Faison retorted.

Endicott sensed the tension in the room and made a show of pulling out his pocket watch. "It's 6:15. We really should wrap things up here and give Rev. Deemer and young Lawton a chance to gather their wits."

He stood up, and the others followed. Gordon picked up his plate and Lawton's and looked around for a tub to bus the table.

"Leave that for the help," Mr. Faison said, shaking his head.

Lawton Sr. shook hands with Nightingale and thanked Endicott. He told his cousins that he'd meet them at the chapel. The others filed out, chatting as they went, until only the two Lawtons were left in the room, Mr. Faison turned on his son.

"Have you heard from Princeton yet?"

Instinctively, young Lawton considered how he might escape, and as if his father read his mind, Lawton Sr. took a step directly into Lawton's path to the door.

"Not yet."

Lawton had decided not to tell his father about Princeton today—no point in darkening his mood before the dedication. He wondered when his father would confess that he'd lost the Sullivan's Island house.

"I thought you said they were supposed to send out acceptance letters the first of the month."

Lawton avoided his father's eyes by looking down at the carpet, but as soon as he heard those words he knew that his father was toying with him. Like a cat with an injured mouse. He screwed his courage and looked up. "Should be any day now," he said, knowing that his father wouldn't believe a word he said.

Mr. Faison stared at his son for several seconds then shook his head. He reached into his coat pocket and pulled out an envelope. It was from The Citadel, and it was addressed to Lawton Faison, '83.

"What's that?"

"Open it," his father said.

Lawton opened the letter.

> *Dear Mr. Faison,*
> *It is with great pleasure that The Citadel extends to*
> *you the offer to join the Class of 1983 —*

Lawton turned to his father, who was smirking.

"I didn't apply to The Citadel."

"I know you didn't."

"So what's this about?"

"Despite your prevarication, I know that you have, in fact, had a letter from Princeton. Your mother told me this afternoon. Let's just say I saw that coming from a mile away. I've known all along that you were going to need a back-up plan, so I contacted General Graham and asked if he could make room for you."

Lawton looked back at the letter. "This is dated, March 15."

"Yes it is."

"So you've been holding onto it for a month?"

"I figured I'd wait and let the Princeton admissions department confirm what a disappointment you are … What did your mother say …?" He shifted into a high, feminine voice to mock his wife. "'He said he'd been carrying the letter around for a whole week.'"

"I'm not going to The Citadel." Lawton emphatically poked the dining table with his forefinger to prove to himself as much as his father the strength of his conviction.

His father laughed. "Well you're not going to Princeton, that's for sure. What are your other options, son? Drawing pretty pictures of Mr. Nightingale?"

Lawton handed the letter back to his father. His father pushed his hand away.

"That's not mine. That's yours."

Lawton couldn't bring himself to throw the letter onto the ground, so he put it into his jacket pocket.

"Where's mom?" he asked "She said she'd be here."

"She had to drive back to Richmond. She said she'd try to come up one of these next weekends."

Lawton didn't believe his father for a second. He was sure he'd asked her to leave.

"Okay, whatever," he said. "I gotta get to the chapel."

And his father stepped aside and allowed Lawton to leave the room.

THE HIPPIE JESUS

GORDON LOOKED FOR HENRY after dinner but couldn't find him anywhere. He wanted to tell him how big a jerk Mr. Faison was. When he got to the chapel he looked for him again but didn't see him. Maybe he was on the balcony? He glanced in that direction — not there. He'd talk to Henry later about skipping chapel. Conscious that the Head Boy always sets an example, he moved to the front of the room and took a seat next to some third formers. He noticed Mr. Faison sitting two rows ahead on the other side of the aisle. Even the way he lightly brushed his hand across the top of his head seemed haughty. What a dick, Gordon thought.

A black curtain hung on the front wall, hiding the new stained glass window. Gordon had heard Mr. Endicott gushing about it, and he was curious to see whether the Jesus really did look like Lawton. Lawton was already the vainest person in the school; he could only imagine what a resemblance to Jesus Christ would do to his ego. He spotted Lawton sitting on the platform at the front of the church. To Gordon's eye, he looked strangely miserable — even more so than in the dining room. Doesn't look much like a celebration for him, Gordon thought.

Lawton, meanwhile, was watching his father, who sat in the front row reading the program and smiling to himself. Lawton couldn't stand the idea of being at The Citadel for four years, the Corps of Cadets, those stupid uniforms, drilling, parading. What was the point? He didn't want a commission — God no! All the while his father would be there needling him with tales about his glory days at Princeton, the connections he'd made at his eating club, and how it had set him up to attend Harvard Business School. The son could never live up to that dream. Never had. Never would. But look at his father sitting there — so proud and so pleased, like nothing had changed, like everything was still perfect, at the memorial to his dead brother. So very like a cat he was, Lawton mused, a great cat, cruel and aloof and all but extinct — not a wild cat, but a panther at the zoo, like the Florida Catamount he'd seen as a boy, with his father no less, lying on a limb behind a piece of glass at the Atlanta Zoo, being fed and pampered to his dying days, oblivious of the cost, indifferent to the service. His father. The pampered panther.

All of these thoughts, and others, passed through Lawton's mind as he sat at the foot of the pulpit and waited for his turn to stand and deliver. He didn't bow his head during Deemer's opening prayer, and he did not hear Deemer's opening remarks and words of welcome, but when his father turned to look at him, then nodded to him once, then once again, Lawton heard Rev. Deemer clear his throat. He looked across the way and saw Rev. Deemer standing at the lectern, bobbing his head for Lawton to step into the pulpit and give his address. Lawton reached into his jacket pocket and pulled out a sheaf of folded papers, including the letter from the Citadel. He climbed the steps to the pulpit, and when he reached the top he thought he heard someone whisper 'Fraud'. He recognized the voice, but he couldn't attach a name or a face to the sound. He stared out at a sea of faces and expected to see an angry boy glaring at him or gloating, but all he saw was Gordon Palmer. Sitting there, right below him, flashing him a thumbs up. The voice wasn't Gordon's, he thought. Maybe it was no one. He placed the papers on the lectern and cleared his throat.

"I want to begin my remarks with a reading of a poem by Henry Timrod, native son of Charleston — my hometown and the hometown of my uncle, Thomas Robideaux Faison, whom we honor today."

There was a noise from somewhere near the middle of the

congregation, a soft whistling maybe. Lawton glanced up briefly, saw nothing or no one in particular, suppressed a frown and returned to the papers in front of him.

"This poem is entitled 'Ode Sung on the Occasion of Decorating the Graves of the Confederate Dead at Magnolia Cemetery, Charleston, South Carolina.' Magnolia Cemetery happens to be where my uncle is buried—"

Half the boys inwardly groaned, and several exhaled audibly. They could tolerate a little Bible reading in chapel, but poetry? Sitting in a high-backed chair behind the lectern, Rev. Deemer noticed the disturbance and cast a death stare at the boys to quiet them. Lawton cleared his throat again and began.

"SLEEP sweetly in your humble graves,
Sleep, martyrs of a fallen cause! —

Bone had already tuned out. He stared at the window to his left, the one with the Virgin Mary, who was kind of a fox when he thought about it. Meanwhile, Wobbly, a couple rows back, rolled his eyes and muttered, "Aw, God!" Lawton himself paused as an image of dead soldiers sleeping underground floated into his mind. He shook his head to rattle away the phantasm and glanced at his father. Lawton Sr. had a distant smile on his face—was he thinking of his brother maybe? Lawton wondered what Uncle Thomas would make of it—the chapel, the stained glass window. His father loved all the fuss over the family name, but his uncle? Maybe not. He'd enlisted to fight in a war after all. 'A stupid sacrifice' his father had called it. Lawton couldn't imagine his father volunteering to serve, or making a sacrifice of any kind for that matter. Lawton returned to the poem. He tried to conjure the splendor of those dead boys asleep underground, their resting places marked for all time by marble garlands and columns. Somewhere in his imagination something was waiting to be born.

"The shaft is in the stone! —" he read.

And someone coughed, or was that a snicker? Lawton looked up and noticed Bone elbowing Mongo. Jesus, that guy was a moron. No sense of duty. Lawton remembered going to the cemetery as a little boy and placing flowers on his uncle's grave—white hydrangeas from his mother's garden. It was summertime, and when they got home his mother had found a tick just behind his left ear. *"Always be sure to get the head out,"* she'd told him. And just then he heard a voice—not her voice; it was a boy's voice. The same boy. He looked up, and the whole room was staring at him. He glanced at his father again. His father was staring at the program, not smiling anymore. *He wasn't with us at the cemetery that day*, Lawton thought. *He usually didn't come with us; even on homecoming days he would make some excuse.* Lawton did remember going there once with his father. He returned his attention to the poem. This was his favorite stanza.

> "Stoop, angels, hither from the skies!
> There is no holier spot of ground
> Than where defeated valor lies
> By mourning beauty crowned. — "

The stooping angels, defeated valor, the earth sanctified by the blood of fallen soldiers. Lawton closed his eyes and concentrated on the thrill in his blood, the blood of his ancestors, of his uncle, the blood of honor and heroism. When he opened his eyes his father was smiling. Maybe he was thinking of that time they visited the cemetery together too. Standing in front of Uncle Thomas's tombstone, he'd looked up at his father who was holding a Gardenia blossom. "Did everyone buried here go to war, daddy?"

"Not everyone. But a lot of them."

"Did you go to war, daddy?"

"God no. What a waste." And he remembered his father tossing the flower down onto the grave.

Lawton slipped the page with the printed poem behind the pages with his speech and faced the room. He coughed again to clear his throat.

"A little more than a hundred years ago, not far from this spot, tens of thousands of brave young men gave their lives in defense of their homes and loved ones against invading armies, and though they were defeated they still live on in our memories as emblems of a greater cause, a cause built on the love of one's home, one's land, and one's brethren ...."

Mr. Nightingale sat near the back of the chapel and shook his head as Lawton read on. *The sins of the father*, he thought. He looked at the boys sitting in the pews around him, and from the looks on most of their faces, he was pleased to see that these ancestral voices appeared to be dying out.

On the other side of the chapel, Wobbly and Braxton sat in the middle of a pew halfway down the aisle. Braxton had started a game of Hangman when the service started. They passed a program back and forth between them. Wobbly had picked letters that spelled out L-A-W-T-O-N I-S A F-A-__ .

Lawton thought he heard someone whispering, and he looked up from his paper again. Was it the new boys next to Gordon? Or Gordon? — He could almost hear Gordon laughing about his commission at The Citadel. — But Gordon just stared back at him like a stupid cow.

Gordon was surprised by the hitches in Lawton's delivery and by the way he looked awkwardly around the room. He had thought Lawton would be more comfortable speaking before a crowd. He read often enough at chapel, for one thing. For another, he seemed to always assume the center of attention. Still, Gordon knew from experience how nerve-wracking public speaking could be. Try as he might, he always went hoarse when he spoke in public because his nerves choked him and he had to force out his words. He hadn't known that about himself until it happened. Maybe that was happening to Lawton now.

Lawton forced himself to return to his speech.

"My Uncle, Thomas Robideaux Faison, learned those lessons while he was a student here at the Randolph School, and he carried those lessons with him after he left here, attended Princeton University and then enlisted with the US 8th Cavalry Regiment.... "

Mongo passed his church program to Bone. Written in the margin was "What a prick." Bone nodded in agreement and pointed to the pencil in Mongo's hand. Mongo handed him the pencil, and Bone scribbled something on the program and handed it back to Mongo. Drawn above Mongo's message was a large erect penis, complete with a hairy ball sack. Bone tapped the penis, pointed at Lawton, and nodded in agreement When he noticed Deemer glaring at him, he folded the program and hastily opened a hymnal. Lawton droned on.

"Fortunately, because places like Randolph still exist, places that remember and revere their history, you and I and all of us can still learn the lessons of the past and carry them with us into the world. My uncle is an example of the best that the past has to offer, and we should all be grateful that from this day forward the students and sons of students at Randolph can come here to gaze on his likeness, to remember his example, and to reflect on his glory."

Lawton heard the sound of laughter and stopped. It was the sound of his father laughing at him, just like he had an hour ago. The blood rushed to his face. He stared at the page. He was afraid to look up, afraid that his father might see his shame. There was a slight cough behind him. It was Rev. Deemer, signaling that the speech was over. Lawton turned his head away from the gathered boys and glanced at his father. He was not laughing after all; he was nodding to Lawton in agreement. Lawton looked back to Rev. Deemer, who stood beside the black curtain. Deemer nodded to Lawton then pulled a cord, and the black curtain dropped to the floor.

At first there was silence, then a hushed murmur in the pews, then gradually the boys began chattering like ducks just before the sunrise. Instead of Christ the King arrayed in robes of celestial glory pointing up to the heavens, the Savior sported a duct-taped canvas hunting jacket, its sleeves outstretched on an imaginary cross. Peeking through the jacket's unbuttoned front was a red and green tie-dyed t-shirt, featuring an indigo blue peace sign. A daisy crown of flowers was taped to the Savior's head, a pair of khaki pants pinned to the jacket hung down in place of His legs, and a pair of topsiders were taped to His bare feet. Gradually, the name *Lawton* could be heard bubbling among the pews, as the boys recognized Faison's trademark hunting jacket and the uncanny resemblance he bore to the stained glass face in the window. As if to dispel any possibility that the icon might be an effigy of anyone else, a hand-painted Princeton pennant had been pinned to one of the jacket's front breast pockets, and sticking out of the other pocket was a drawing of an owl with a scraggly beard and round glasses, holding a skeleton's head. Suddenly, just as laughter started to break out, music began playing somewhere in the front of the chapel, in the vicinity of the installation. The sound of a rhythm guitar grew louder, then the melody on lead guitar, and finally a familiar voice:

> *Well the first days are the hardest days,*
> *don't you worry any more*
> *'Cause when life looks like easy street,*
> *there is danger at your door*

As the music swelled, Rev. Deemer staggered about the front of the church looking for its source, Mackie shouted out demerits left and right, and Mr. Endicott scrambled to his feet and flailed his arms above his head, in a vain attempt to silence the room. The boys teetered between cowering beneath the threatened rod and breaking free to bedlam. A rumble of laughter gurgled forth from the middle of the room, getting louder and louder, until the head and shoulders and torso of one Bob "Mongo" Coogan rose up with tectonic force and towered over all the other boys. Mongo shook his savage mane and with arms outstretched and booming voice led a chorus of,

> Woah-oh, what I want to know is, ARE YOU
> KIND?

And despite the increasingly violent remonstrances of all the Deemers and Mackies and Endicotts of the world, the room was lost to Jerry, to the music, and to the ebullience of Mongo, whose gypsy magic had transformed a dirge into carnival. The spirit was risen indeed.

Up above, at the front of the room, Lawton stood alone in the pulpit. He heard the music. He heard the boys' singing. He heard the boys' laughter. A different boy might have laughed too, might have given in to the boys, but Lawton was caught in the dreadful thrall of a morbid idea, a web of his own weaving, and stood stony silent, transfixed. He knew that the boys were laughing at him, and their laughter rang in the hollows of his ears like memorial bells. He watched Endicott turn red in the face while his mouth shuttered furiously and his body bobbled up and down on the toes of his shoes. He watched his father shake a fist in the air and yell something at Endicott. Lawton couldn't hear what his father was saying. Lawton couldn't hear what Endicott was saying. Lawton couldn't hear what the boys were saying. Lawton could only hear the sound of someone laughing. A boy. A boy he thought he knew. A boy who retreated farther and farther into some dark thicket of Lawton's mind.

THE QUESTION OF HONOR

HENRY WRITES A GOOD PAPER

MR. MACKIE SAT BACK in his chair and stared at the chestnut tree outside his classroom window. He had both feet crossed on the corner of his desk and a marking pen at his lips. He twirled the pen while he gathered his thoughts, then held it at eye level, like a gunsight, and aimed his next question at Bobby Grimes.

"So, Grimes, what are we to make of the Epilogue?"

Grimes was not aware that *Ethan Frome* had an Epilogue. He'd lost his book two weeks ago and had not bothered to buy another copy. He'd only read the Cliff's Notes through Chapter 9, because he thought that was all Mackie had assigned.

"Shit," he muttered, and leaned to his starboard and ventriloquized, "Help me out, Carter."

"Well," Grimes sputtered aloud, hoping to buy time. "Ethan and Mattie were badly injured in the sleigh accident."

"Yes …. We're done with Chapter Nine," Mackie intoned.

Mackie drummed the top of his desk as he waited for Grimes to make his point. Grimes had his head turned slightly away from Mr. Mackie, in order to make out what Ward Carter was whispering into his right ear.

"And?"

Grimes straightened up. "And Mattie and Ethan recover then Ethan divorces Zeena and …" Grimes's voice trailed off as he saw the expression on Mackie's face turn from boredom to deep annoyance and heard L.D. laughing beside him.

"What's so funny, Carter?" Mackie barked.

"Bobby's answer," Carter said.

"Care to help Grimes, Carter?"

"Sure thing," Carter. said. "The Epilogue confirms that Ethan Frome is not able to escape his fate, and that things only get worse as a result of their hare-brained attempt."

"Which is what?"

"Their decision to kill themselves by sledding into the tree."

"Very good."

Grimes gritted his teeth and muttered to L.D., "I'm going to kill you."

Mackie swung his feet to the floor and tapped the tips of his teeth with the blunt end of his marking pen.

"We've spent a good bit of time this year talking about irony. Who can give me examples of irony that appear in the Epilogue? Show of hands?" Mackie looked around the classroom for volunteers and, finding none, called on Wales.

"Ethan wanted to be with Mattie, and Mattie wanted to be with Ethan, but instead of running away together they end up trapped forever in the house with Zeena."

"Very good. Anyone else?"

Again no one raised a hand so Mackie called on Wobbly, who was staring into the middle distance and tugging on a single whisker that had miraculously appeared on the underside of his chin. On the best of days, Wobbly had a shaky mastery of the concept of irony. Sarcasm he was a master of—in fact he practiced it all the time. He knew that sarcasm was a form of irony because Mackie had made a point of calling that out in class one day when Wobbly had said to Braxton, 'Nice try, Einstein,' after Braxton had cost his team extra credit points when he'd failed to correctly identify the name of Holden Caufield's little sister. But Wobbly also knew that Mackie called sarcasm the 'cheapest form of irony'. Unfortunately, Wobbly did not understand why sarcasm was cheaper than any other form of irony. Indeed, Wobbly could not think of any other form of irony, though he knew Mackie had talked about it constantly over the course of the year. Wobbly pulled at his lone whisker until he felt a slight twang of pain at its root. Then he stopped, momentarily, lest he pull it out. Then he tugged at it again. Why couldn't he remember this? Wobbly had no explanation, other than his general dislike of English class and his special dislike of Mackie. Unlike Grimes, he had read the Epilogue of *Ethan Frome* — the book itself, and not the Cliff's Notes version. He tried to remember if anyone had been sarcastic.

After Mackie had amused himself long enough by watching Wobbly struggle for words, he said, "I'll give you a hint. At the end of Chapter Nine after the first sled run down the hill they are walking back to the top, and Ethan thinks to himself this will be the last time we walk together. What do we learn in the Epilogue that renders that thought ironic?"

Wobbly thought to himself. No one said anything about the sled ride in the Epilogue except for Mrs. Hale. But she wasn't being sarcastic, she just talked about what had happened. Wobbly was pretty sure that was not irony.

Growing impatient, Mackie said, "What does Ethan mean when he thinks in Chapter Nine that he and Mattie will never walk together again?"

Wobbly could tell that Mackie was exasperated, and he suspected that he was asking a trick question. "That she's going to be paralyzed by the sled crash?"

"No! They're walking up the hill together! He doesn't know that she's going to be paralyzed when he thinks that, does he?"

"No." Wobbly offered, but only because he was pretty sure that was what Mackie wanted him to say.

"He thinks they will never walk together again because he's going to drive Mattie to the train station and they'll never see each other again, right?"

Wobbly nodded.

"So how is that thought revealed to be ironic by what we learn in the Epilogue?"

Wobbly floundered. He knew that Mattie couldn't walk because she was paralyzed by the sled crash, but how was Ethan thinking earlier that they wouldn't walk together again 'ironic'? It was predicting the future. Wobbly was sure that was not irony.

"What's 'irony' mean again?" Wobbly finally asked.

Mackie threw up his hands and stared at Wobbly like he was the dullest lump of clay he'd encountered in his ten years of teaching.

"Because Mattie is paralyzed! She can't walk! So Ethan was right that they would never walk together again, but not for the reason that he thought. Irony is saying one thing but meaning another. 'Dramatic irony' is when a character says or does something that will have dramatic consequences that the reader understands but the character does not. This is textbook dramatic irony. What other examples of irony do we find in the Epilogue?"

Wobbly thought about what Mackie had said. Something did not seem right, but he couldn't put his finger on it. He still did not understand irony.

Henry Palmer raised his hand.

"Thank you, Palmer."

'I have a question."

"All right."

"I understand how it's ironic that Ethan thinks they will never walk together again because Mattie's leaving and it ends up the reason they never walk again is because of the sled crash, but how is that 'dramatic irony'? I mean we don't know yet that they are going to crash in the tree. In fact, I thought that she was going to die at the end of Chapter Nine. The reader doesn't learn that she's paralyzed until Ethan learns that she's paralyzed — in fact Ethan knows that she's paralyzed *before* the reader does, because the Epilogue takes place years later. So that does not seem like dramatic irony to me."

Mackie put the inkpen back into his mouth and returned his gaze to the chestnut tree. It was a Chinese Chestnut — not an American Chestnut. All the native chestnut trees on campus had died out in the 1940s due to chestnut blight, and this tree had been planted as a gift of the Class of 1952.

"Fair point, Palmer," Mackie said. "That's two points for Wales."

At the beginning of the year Mackie had split the class into two teams, dubbed Wales and Grimes. Whenever a class member correctly challenged anything Mackie said, his team scored two points; if he incorrectly challenged anything Mackie said, his team lost three points. Mackie did not keep track of the score, but the boys did.

"And isn't it actually *doubly* ironic that Ethan thinks that this will be the last time they walk together?" Wales asked.

Mackie had been happy to give Palmer two points for correcting what was really only a slip of the tongue on his part. He knew, and the boys knew he knew, the difference between situational and dramatic irony. But Wales's claim of double irony gave him pause. Wales was a clever student. If he said there was double irony, there probably was double irony, though Mackie couldn't think of what might be doubled at the moment.

"How so?" Mackie asked warily.

"Because Ethan thinks they will never walk together again because they will never see each other again, but in fact, they end up spending the rest of their lives together but never walking."

The boys looked at each other and looked at Mackie. This sounded pretty good, and Wales was the smartest kid in the class. When a smile appeared on Mackie's lips half the class burst out in cheers and the other half groaned.

"Two more points for Wales," Mackie said.

"Wales! Wales! Wales! Wales!" his team chanted.

Tom Wales blushed, but no one noticed.

The class bell rang, and the boys started stuffing their book bags.

"I have your papers here on 'O Captain! My Captain!'. You may collect them as you leave, all except Mr. Palmer. Palmer, I'd like a word with you."

The boys stepped forward to receive their papers then headed to their next classes. All except Henry, who was the last boy left standing in the room, near the door with his book bag over one shoulder. Mr. Mackie leaned back against his desk with Henry's paper in his right hand. He looked particularly sour, almost cross-eyed.

"Palmer, the assignment was 'O Captain! My Captain!', not 'As Adam Early in the Morning.' Did it occur to you to check with me before you chose a different poem for your paper?"

Henry nodded. He'd figured Mackie might be butt-hurt about his decision to switch poems. "I tried to write about 'O Captain!', Mr. Mackie, but I wasn't feeling it."

"You weren't 'feeling it'?" Mackie repeated. "What is that supposed to mean?"

"I couldn't get anywhere with it. I just didn't connect with it. It would have been a horrible paper, believe me."

"As opposed to the paper you wrote."

"I liked it." Henry smiled genuinely. "It's the first paper I've written this year that I liked."

"Well I didn't like it, Palmer. If I'd wanted to hear about your Pelagian theory of the Fall of Man, I would have assigned that."

"Pelagian what?"

Mackie waved a hand dismissively. "Never mind. How did you find 'As Adam Early in the Morning'? It's not exactly textbook material."

"A friend told me about it."

"A friend? What friend?"

"Why does that matter?"

Mackie leaned forward. "It matters because I asked you the question. What friend, Palmer?"

"Ken Bright."

"Ken Bright?" Mackie was surprised. "You're hanging out with sixth formers, are you? That's precocious."

"We don't 'hang out'. I live next door to him."

"On B Dorm," Mackie confirmed. He knew where Henry and Bright lived.

"Yes."

Mackie slapped Henry's paper against his thigh and studied the boy. "Did Bright help you write your paper?"

"No!" The question offended Henry. This was the first paper he'd ever written that he was proud of. "I wrote it by myself. Except Mr. Nightingale did help by asking me questions, like I said in my pledge."

"Well tell Bright not to interfere with my assignments in the future. Understood?"

Henry nodded.

"He's not doing you any favors."

Mackie held out the folded paper to Henry, and Henry stepped forward to take it. He grabbed one end of the essay and tried to take it, but Mackie held onto the other end. Henry looked up at Mackie's face, expecting him to say something more, but Mackie only held his gaze for a moment then let go and said, "Dismissed."

Henry left the room quickly to get away from the jerk but stopped halfway down the hall to reread his paper.

> BE AS ADAM EARLY IN THE MORNING
> *As Adam early in the morning,*
> *Walking forth from the bower refresh'd with sleep,*
> *Behold me where I pass, hear my voice, approach,*

Touch me, touch the palm of your hand to my body
as I pass,
Be not afraid of my body.

This poem by Walt Whitman makes me think of
what it must have felt like to be an innocent person,
without shame about my body, without fear of someone
touching me, without fear of being myself and encountering another person as myself and not being afraid of
letting another person see me as I am, naked. Can anything be more beautiful than that?

Whitman sets the poem in the Garden of Eden before the Fall, because I think he's saying that the Fall
never really happened, that we can all be like Adam in
the Garden if we only cast off that sense of guilt that we
all have. This sense of guilt is somehow tied up with the
shame we feel about having bodies. Why should we be
embarrassed about being naked?

The Fall has never really made sense to me. God created Adam and Eve and commanded them not to par-
take of the Tree of Knowledge and then, after they eat
of the Tree of Knowledge, banishes them before they
can also eat of the Tree of Life? Why would God not
want his creatures to have knowledge? Did God want
us to be his stupid slaves? I don't think Whitman be-
lieves in that kind of God either.

In the Bible Garden story God walks in the Garden
and knows Adam has broken his commandment because Adam hides from him. In the Garden story, God
asks Adam why he is hiding — why he is afraid to approach God — and the answer is that he is afraid of the
punishment he will suffer for disobeying God — punishment that is subsequently told in all of the ensuing
books of the Bible: war, death, famine, etc. In this poem,
the narrator (or Whitman) as Adam (not God) is invit-
ing me, the reader, to approach his naked body, to touch
him, and to be not afraid of his body. In Whitman's
poem, the source of fear is not a broken commandment

but a misconception about the body — a fear of the body. Clearly, Whitman is saying that if I, the reader, can overcome my fear of the body — mine and another person's — I can also be like Adam early in the morning, before the Fall, before guilt. This is not because the Fall of Man has been undone. This is because the Fall of Man never happened — it's a trick of the mind that has been played upon us by 2000 years of sick Christian dogma.

It's not a coincidence that the Poet as Adam invites me to touch him with the palm of my hand. Remember Christ after the Resurrection? He tells his disciples NOT to touch him because he has not yet ascended to Heaven and remains unclean. Even Christ in the Bible, who was supposed to have ransomed us from the Fall (our Original Sin) and made our salvation possible, does not fully vanquish the idea that this world is in some fundamental way filthy. Whitman, on the other hand, invites me to touch his body. He is telling me that the world is not filthy and can be made fresh again — not by the death and Resurrection and Ascension of Jesus, but by simply letting go of those foul ideas and seeing our fellow creatures as beautiful, as Adam, early in the morning, before the Fall.

I love this poem. It suggests to me that I can — that all of us can — be like the new Adam, like the new Christ, if we simply behold ourselves and our fellow creatures as beautiful instead of filthy. Imagine myself and my fellow man as being like Adam before the Fall — not after the Fall. This is not a trick of the mind; this is a faithful, honest and innocent encounter of another person.

Pledged. I did talk to Mr. Nightingale about the poem before I wrote this paper, but the ideas here are mine.

Henry Palmer

Mackie had written numerous comments in the margins with a

red pen: "I don't care what you think, I care about what the poem says." "'New Adam'? 'New Christ?' this is 'New Age' I grant you but hardly faithful to Christian dogma." "The 'trick of the mind' is this New Age thinking." "You have managed to discover Whitman's homoeroticism — congratulations! — but do you really want to embrace it?" At the bottom of the second page was his grade: C.

Henry smiled. He didn't care about the grade. He could tell by the comments that he'd managed to piss Mackie off and pop his self-important bubble. There wasn't a single comment about grammar (and Henry had no doubt there were grammatical mistakes) because he had engaged Mackie on the substance of his ideas. He'd finally managed to write about something he believed, and the fact that Mackie had objected to almost everything he had to say only made him happier.

LAWTON AND MAISIE

LAWTON STARED AT THE LIGHT FIXTURE on the ceiling of his room: a white globe hanging like an unlit moon in an empty sky. He turned to the window. Still dark. No color.

"*Yessir, captain.*"

He didn't look around anymore. He could hear Billy Richardson breathing in his sleep on the other side of the room. No one else was there. He'd been hearing voices for two weeks now — ever since the chapel service. At first he'd looked around to see who was talking and had been surprised to find no one there. He didn't recognize the voice. He no longer thought that it was his father or his dead grandfather speaking, but it was a man's voice. It sounded more like his own voice than anyone else's, but it wasn't him speaking to himself. It was someone else speaking to him. Snatches of interrupted conversation — the voice located just above his head and behind him, if he had to place it. Always behind him, where he couldn't see the man, or the boy. Always unexpected but never loud — the volume of a boy's voice, not a man's, from another room. Like the person was in another room, or like Lawton was in the wrong room. Usually like the person was mocking him.

Over the last several days the occurrences had become more

frequent. There wasn't a pattern to it. There wasn't a continuation of dialogue, at least not one that Lawton could follow. It had become frequent enough that it no longer surprised him; he no longer jumped or spun around to look. That first day back in class he'd spun around in AP English because someone had said his name, "Lawton!" Gordon Palmer, who was seated behind him, mouthed, "What?" Lawton's sudden movement had caught Mr. Nightingale's attention; he'd stopped his lecture to say, "What is it, Lawton?" Lawton had turned back around. "Nothing, sir." And the class had proceeded. After class Nightingale had asked to see him, but he'd made some excuse. He didn't want to talk about the chapel service or the stained glass window or anything at all. Not with Nightingale. Not with anyone. Over time this boy's voice, or maybe it was a man's, was the only one he cared to hear. He'd come to be curious about what he might say next. That the speaker might reveal himself. That it all might end up making some crazy sense.

Last night he'd barely slept. His head had buzzed like a light bulb getting ready to explode. He'd thought about taking a bong hit with Richardson after lights out, but he'd decided against it because he didn't want to lose touch with things. He felt like his grip was slipping already and feared the slightest nudge might topple him over. He turned again to the front window. They had a corner room, light from two directions — cross-breeze in the fall when it was hot. His mother had remarked how nice the room was when he'd finally let her visit. He'd gotten that perk anyway. The darkness was beginning to lift. He couldn't make out the Blue Ridge Mountains to the west, but he could see the water tower. He remembered the Fish that Saturday morning — he'd painted it so that he could see it from this room. Too bad it hadn't stayed up longer. He'd watched Uly paint over it. There was Snoot's Gym — old Mr. Snoot. His father had told him about a bus ride to Pennsylvania, to play the Hill School in football. Mr. Snoot was seated up front scribbling on a notepad. "What are you doing, Mr. Snoot?" "Counting the cars," he'd said.

"Faison's a big name here."

Maybe he should wake up Richardson. The dining hall opened at 7, and Richardson never woke before 7:30. He looked at the clock beside his bed. 6:11. Sun would be up soon. He got out of bed and dressed — the same clothes that he'd worn the day before. He put on his hunting jacket and checked the pocket. The letter from The Citadel was still there. He saw light strike the water tower. The morning sun must have cleared the hill behind the Rapidan.

"He never came from Savannah."

Lawton wondered who the voice meant. Sherman, maybe? Richardson snored lightly, like a baby sleeping on his stomach. He picked Richardson's sock off the floor and tossed it onto his body. Richardson stopped breathing, like a startled dog; then, after a few seconds, started up again. An endless machine, Lawton thought. Wasted. He picked up Richardson's shoe and tossed it onto the bed. Richardson rolled over onto his back.

"Wha?"

"Want to get some breakfast?"

Richardson looked outside and determined that there was still time for sleep. "You go ahead," he said. "I'll catch up later."

Lawton watched him roll back over and turn his face away from the window. Before long that rhythmic breathing started again. The boy had a gift for sleep. Lawton found his topsiders on the floor beside the bed and slipped them on. At the door he caught a glimpse of some specter in the mirror, a dark, horrifying shape, and he hurried out. Was that who was hailing him?

Outside, he heard an infernal whistling in the trees along the river. Birdsong? To him it sounded like the neverending whispering of boys. They were still talking about it, he was sure. Their murmuring mumblings, mumbling murmerings. How long had that been going on unbeknownst? He was sure that it was longer than he realized. How was it that his father didn't hear it? The last thing that Lawton had said to him was, "So will I see you at Sullivan's Island?"

"Been a change of plans, Sport. I'm having the house painted, so you better plan on coming home instead."

His father had smiled like it was the grandest thing, but there was a slyness to it. He'd seen it for the first time in that moment. The betrayal. The mendacity. The tell. Had it always been there and he was only able to see it now, now that he had been utterly humiliated? That was the difference between him and his father. His father embraced the lie, felt entitled to the lie, believed that everyone lied but that his lie was better because it was grander. Felt like it was part of his charm. Perhaps understood that others were in on the lie and would wink at him so long as he winked back. He was the better liar because his lie was bigger. A prince of lies. Whereas Lawton himself couldn't smile. Couldn't wink back. Felt like a clown, not a prince. A clown of history. A tragic clown. That's what Lawton believed that he'd become. Or a sad clown, not even tragic. Too pathetic to be tragic. Drowning in a sea of shame.

"Full fathom five thy father lies"

Lawton did snap around to that, but no one was there, or some boys were there but too far away to have spoken the words. He stood at the bottom of the steps to the dining hall. A half dozen boys were already standing outside the doors, waiting for them to be unlocked. Behind him more boys were approaching from the dorms. He looked for a friendly face — Gillespie, Claiborne? — and not seeing one he walked away. He didn't want to see them whispering, and he wasn't hungry anyway. He'd only want to find a well worn path and shuffle along a bit and trick himself into not thinking that he was trapped, or was not the pathetic brunt of someone else's joke. He was stupid for thinking that breakfast might do the trick. Too many boys. Too many eyeballs. Too many whispers.

The chapel bell rang seven o'clock. He followed the sound towards the chapel until the last toll died out, then turned down the brick path, walked past the faculty houses, to the Randolph Auditorium. No one would be here until later, no one to see him walk around the back of the building and hop the split rail fence and electrical wire that separated the cow pasture from the grounds. He walked in the dirt rut that the cows had trod along the fenceline and followed it across the pasture, into the trees, and down to the river. The path led to a low muddy spot along the bank where the cows waded into the water to drink. He walked downstream to a deep hole, surrounded by large rocks, where generations of boys had sunned themselves before diving in. Lawton hadn't been here since September. He took a seat on the largest rock and looked down at the river. It was a slow, muddy thing, brown like the pigs he'd seen on Johns Island. He couldn't see the bottom, but he knew where the big rocks were, there just above that eddy. There was a long scratch in the rock, running perpendicular to the river. Boys were always told to jump downstream of that line. There was the deep water. There, there was no danger of foundering on the rocks. Lawton smiled at the thought. Shelley had drowned. Or was murdered. Was it suicide? Were there pirates, or did he simply slip beneath the waves?

Awake him not! Surely he takes his fill
Of deep and liquid rest, forgetful of all ill.

Funny that that was all that he could remember of Shelley now. He took the letter from his pocket. "We are confident that you will be a fine addition to the Corps —

"One spot, two spot, three spot, four"

Lawton put the letter back into his pocket. He picked up a stick and drew in the dirt an imaginary mule, harnessed to a plow, in a field of stars that became the Milky Way. He threw the stick into the water and watched it wash downstream. He sat there for some time .... A long time .... Had he gone to sleep? The far side of the river was in full sunlight when he stood up and walked back to campus.

He did not see the dog until he almost stepped on it. It was asleep in a spot of shade cast by the trash bin outside the back door to the dining hall kitchen. He recognized the dog as Uly's, a brindled mutt, part chihuahua, part something that Lawton couldn't place. It had a blue collar around its neck, a braided nylon string that had been spliced so expertly that there was neither a buckle nor a seam. Lawton had often seen the dog with Uly. In fact he always saw the two together: Uly with dog, dog with Uly. He imagined the dog standing at the bottom of the water tower when Uly painted over his Fish. He was sure she'd been there.

Lawton leaned over and slipped his right index finger beneath the blue collar. The dog awoke immediately and barked in alarm.

"Hush, bitch!" Lawton said sharply.

But his tone of voice only frightened the dog more, and she kept barking and began shaking her head and pulling back to free herself. Lawton reached down with his left hand to muzzle the dog's mouth, and the dog nipped his finger.

"Ouch! You little shit!"

Lawton struck the dog with the hand that she'd bit, and the dog yelped, then barked, then kicked out wildly with all four feet as Lawton lifted her off the ground, grabbed her back legs, and twisted her body like a wet rag until she went limp in his hands. He dropped the dog to the ground.

"What — ?" It happened so fast that it surprised him. He nudged the dog with his foot; it didn't move. He picked her up, weighed her in his hand, and placed her in the game pocket of his hunting jacket. She was about the size and weight of the rabbits that he'd sometimes shoot when he went quail hunting on Johns Island. He rocked back and forth and felt her bump against the small of his back. He liked the feel of dead things in his jacket. The bell in the chapel rang eleven o'clock. Lawton decided to take the dog there.

The doors to the chapel were locked — a change instituted by Rev. Deemer and Mr. Endicott after the stained glass dedication — but Lawton had the key. He unlocked the doors and stepped inside. The air was cool and filled with the sweet smell of the lilacs that were blooming outside the open windows. Lawton walked to the front of the church and stood at the high altar underneath the new stained glass window. The altar was empty except for two large candlesticks and a silver plate. Lawton looked up at the face of Jesus and laughed. He really does look like father and me, he thought. He reached into the game pocket at his back and placed the dead dog on the silver platter.

"This is my body," he said. "This is my blood."

He laughed again.

Will you come with me won't you come with me
Woah-oh, what I want to know, will you come with me?

He placed both hands over his ears to stop the music. He looked about angrily, expecting to see the boys laughing at him, then closed his eyes until the panic diminished. When he felt like he could move again without stumbling, he picked up the dog, put her back into his game pocket and walked back toward the chapel doors, but instead of walking out, he climbed up into the balcony. The bell rope was hanging through a hole in the ceiling at one corner. Lawton opened the trapdoor and climbed up into the steeple. He untied the rope from the bell and let it drop through the hole in the floor. Then he climbed back down to the balcony, sat down on the floor, and tied a noose into one end of the rope.

MR. NIGHTINGALE STOOD in front of the class and quickly took roll. Everyone was present except Lawton Faison.

"Has anyone seen Mr. Faison?"

"He's on the Road to Damascus," said one boy.

"That would be the Apostle Paul, Mr. Claiborne," Nightingale said.

"He's at the Sea of Galilee," Gordon Palmer said.

Not very original, Nightingale thought. He never reported absences, although he was supposed to. He only took roll in case an absence might be a sign that something was amiss. He didn't care if boys skipped his class because they had something better to do; he just wanted to make sure they didn't skip because they were in trouble. Lawton Faison's absence triggered the concern he'd felt ever since the dedication at the chapel.

"He's taking down all the Princeton paraphernalia in his dorm room," another boy said.

"Enough of that," Nightingale said. "Let's talk about Book I of *The Waste Land.*"

The boys opened their books and Mr. Nightingale began the class.

When class was over Nightingale walked outside. He had a free period, which he ordinarily would spend grading papers, but he felt uneasy about Lawton's absence. He'd tried to speak to Lawton after the dedication service, but the boy had seemed so shell-shocked that Nightingale wasn't sure Lawton even recognized him. He'd only come to when his father walked up and angrily said, "What the hell kind of service is this? That boy needs to be horse-whipped." Nightingale had excused himself. He'd tried to speak to him again after yesterday's class, but Lawton had said he had to meet with Frank Deemer. Nightingale knew about Lawton's Princeton rejection, and he knew a little about his parents' divorce and the family's financial difficulties. He worried that the walls might be collapsing on the boy. He had never been particularly close to Lawton, but he was the boy's advisor, and he hated to see anyone suffer.

He stopped by Lawton's dorm room in Mortimer Hall, making a point of loudly announcing his presence on the hallway before knocking at Lawton's door. Billy Richardson, Lawton's roommate, was there with

John Gillespie. They were listening to Jimmy Buffet and looking at the Sports Illustrated swimsuit edition. Richardson had been accepted to U.Va. and Gillespie to UNC; both were already deep into their senior slide.

"Ah, Mr. Richardson and Mr. Gillespie. Sorry to bother you. I was hoping to lay eyes on Mr. Faison. Any idea why he missed class just now?"

"I saw him this morning," Richardson said. "Said he was going to breakfast. I assumed he was going to class."

Gillespie nodded in agreement. He had the centerfold spread out on his lap.

"Thank you. If you see him, ask him to contact me if you would."

"Sure thing."

Nightingale walked back outside. It was one of the school's salad days, when everything was green and seemed fresh and new. One group of boys tossed a Frisbee. Another group threw a lacrosse ball. Lawton played lacrosse, but none of the boys was Lawton. Where might he be? Nightingale decided to check Faison Chapel — maybe Lawton was taking in the stained glass now that it was no longer defaced. He walked past the Randolph Building, along the front drive to the opening in the boxwood hedge, and down the walkway to the front doors of the chapel. He peeked inside. No one. He wondered where else Lawton might be. Hayes Pond? Seemed unlikely. That little cow pond appealed to a different sort of boy: farmers' sons, boys from small towns who'd grown up swimming in lakes and rivers. But he couldn't think of anywhere else the boy might be, so he set off in that direction. As he rounded the back corner of the chapel, he saw a boy sitting against the trunk of the massive pin oak.

He recognized at once that it was Lawton, by the sweep and color of his hair and that hunting jacket that he always wore. He felt a surge of relief and was surprised to realize just how concerned he actually had been. He decided to say hello, just to let Lawton know that he was thinking of him, and as he approached he noticed a thing hanging from the tree. At first he thought it might be a rag or a scrap of paper, and he wondered why it was hanging from a rope. Then he made out one leg — perhaps it was a rabbit that Lawton had caught somehow? — but then he saw the tail and the blue collar and realized that the hanging object was a small dog. That in fact it was Uly's dog, the dog that followed him from building to building and always waited patiently outside for Uly to reappear. The dog that tolerated pats from strange boys and teachers, but always faithfully waited for its master, or walked beside him on campus, looking up to see if Uly was looking down, and wagging its tail and smiling whenever Uly dipped his head and said a word or two. Uly was always so glad to have his companion with him, so grateful that he'd been given a dispensation by the school to bring the dog to work, he and the dog serving as an example to the boys of companionship and the benefits of showing care and concern for another living thing. Lawton sat against the tree and stared at the dog's body. Either he did not hear Nightingale approach or he did not care because he did not turn to look up, even when Nightingale stood directly beside him.

The dog was hanging by a noose that had been fashioned out of nylon rope. One end of the rope was tied to the trunk of the oak tree, and the noose had been thrown over the lowest branch and then affixed around the poor dog's neck. Mr. Nightingale shuddered to think of what had happened to cause Lawton to do this. Lines from Blake came to his mind:

> Then cruelty knits her snare
> And spreads his baits with care
> He sits down with holy fears
> And waters the ground with tears
>
> The Gods of the earth and sea
> Sought through Nature to find this Tree;
> But their search was all in vain:
> There grows one in the Human Brain.

He leaned down and touched the boy's shoulder.

"Lawton? It's David Nightingale here."

Lawton looked up, startled, like he'd awakened from a nightmare. At first he did not seem to recognize Mr. Nightingale, or was surprised to see him there, or to find himself here sitting on the ground. But then he saw the dog swinging in front of him and recoiled. He looked at Mr. Nightingale, aghast.

"There was another dog on her. I saw another dog raping her, a bigger dog," he said in an effort to explain to himself what had happened.

Nightingale patted his shoulder. "It's okay, Lawton. It's going to be okay. Let's get up."

He entreated Mr. Nightingale to believe him. "It was a rape. And he was a different breed. They would have been mongrel pups. No one wants a mongrel, least of all from a nigger's dog on the distaff."

"No, no, Lawton," Mr. Nightingale said gently. "You mustn't speak like that."

Lawton grabbed Mr. Nightingale's forearm with both hands and pulled him down closer. "They said I'm to go back to the Citadel. Be the Cadet Major like grandfather was. It'll be like nothing happened. There'll be no debt to pay."

Nightingale shook his head. "Let's get up now Lawton. Come with me." He extended his right hand to the boy.

Lawton regarded Mr. Nightingale's face and drew back.

"It's okay, son."

"Mr. Nightingale?"

The man nodded. "It's me."

Lawton turned his head in shame.

"It's alright," Mr. Nightingale said. "It's going to be okay."

Mr. Nightingale continued to extend his hand, and eventually, Lawton took it, and Mr. Nightingale helped him to his feet. He held the boy by the shoulders until he was sure that Lawton had his feet under him. Lawton kept his head down and began to cry. Mr. Nightingale held the boy's head against his shoulder while he convulsed and sobbed. When the crying stopped, Mr. Nightingale stepped back and gave Lawton his handkerchief. Lawton wiped the tears from his face.

After a while, Lawton looked up at Mr. Nightingale. "Am I done here? Am I going to have to leave?"

"That's not for me to decide," Mr. Nightingale said. He put an arm around the boy's shoulder. "Let's call your mother."

Lawton nodded, and they started walking towards the Randolph Building. As they passed the dog, Mr. Nightingale said a silent prayer to beg the gods' forgiveness, while at the end of the rope Maisie's body swayed slightly, though there was no wind.

ULY WAS IN THE KITCHEN mopping the floor with disinfectant when the phone call came from the head of maintenance. His dog was hanging from a tree behind the chapel. He was told to fetch a ladder from the maintenance shed and take down the dog and the rope. Uly hung up the phone and rushed outside. She always waited outside the door when he did the cleaning; no Maisie. He whistled, looked around, and not seeing her, shambled as fast as his feet could take him to the chapel. When he rounded the back of the building he saw her hanging from the tree by the neck. Tears welled up in his eyes then streamed down his face as he touched her and found her eyes open and bulging from the pressure of the rope. He cradled her in his arms, removed the noose, placed his hand over her face and rocked her back and forth.

"It's gonna be alright Maisie. Pawpaw's here. Pawpaw's going to take care of you. Don't fret no more. It's alright. It's okay. No need to worry anymore about this cruel world. You're in a better place now. No one can hurt you now. Don't you worry about me. I'll be alright. I won't forget you, girl. You were a good little dog…. A good little dog…. A good little dog…. The best little dog…. I sure do love you."

He rocked Maisie in his arms and whispered to her. No one else was there. No one saw his gentle ministrations. No one saw him take the shirt off his body and swaddle her. No one saw him kneel beneath the tree and say a prayer. No one saw him lift her shrouded body off the ground and carry her, holding her in both arms in front of him like a sleeping infant child, from the tree behind the chapel.

More than a dozen boys were scattered about the Lawn when Uly carried Maisie back to his cabin behind the Manor. All of them and several masters saw Uly walking in a plain white t-shirt, carrying what looked like a small bundle wrapped in his uniform. A couple called out, "Hey, Uly!!" but Uly did not answer, which was odd, because Uly usually had a friendly word for everyone. But no boy or master thought to ask what he was carrying, or if something was wrong, or if he was alright. Later all of them heard how Uly's dog had died, but most of them didn't realize they'd witnessed Maisie's funeral procession. Those that did maybe remembered how the dog always walked beside Uly, and tolerated a scratch behind the ear, and even wagged her tail and showed her teeth whenever they stopped to talk, but none of them went to check on Uly, or called, or did a thing.

Gordon was among the boys who saw Uly walking across the Lawn that afternoon and thought it strange. He was one of the boys who shouted, "Hey Uly!" as he remembered seeing his father do on move-in day last August, and he did wonder, a little, when Uly did not acknowledge him but continued walking, looking down occasionally at the bundle he was carrying, but never in the direction of the hello. And when Mr. Endicott told him that afternoon that Lawton Faison had hanged Uly's dog, Gordon's first thought wasn't about Lawton; it was about Uly, and how lonely he must be, and sad, to lose his dog that way. But soon he and Mr. Endicott were discussing what to tell the prefects about the incident, and through the prefects the student body. And pretty soon Gordon was dealing with the matter at hand, maintaining student morale and student discipline, talking first to the prefects and then to Lawton's closest friends, and he forgot about Uly until that night, when he was getting ready to go to sleep, and he wondered what Uly might be doing at that very moment, and whether there was something that he himself should do. Gordon even tried to imagine Uly in his home, without his dog, but he quickly told himself that he had no idea where Uly lived or what Uly might be thinking, because he did not know Uly, and besides, Uly was so different from him. He went to sleep thinking there was nothing for him to do, that there was nothing he could do, and the next day Gordon hardly thought about Uly at all.

But David Nightingale didn't forget Uly. After meeting with Lawton and his mother, and saying goodbye to the boy, Nightingale walked to Uly's shed behind the Manor. He peered through the window and saw Uly sitting alone at the wooden table, with the little bundle containing the dog on a chair beside him. He knocked, and when Uly opened the door and saw him standing there he let out a soft cry, "Oh Mr. Nightingale," and they put their arms around each other.

"I'm so sorry, Uly. I'm so, so sorry."

And with Nightingale's help Uly chose a burial spot underneath the Locust tree outside his door, and they dug the hole together, and Nightingale bowed his head as Uly said a prayer and bid farewell to Maisie.

NEWS OF LAWTON KILLING THE DOG spread quickly. Some boys had seen the noose hanging from the tree before it was removed. Some boys had seen Uly carrying the dog back to his cabin. Some boys had seen Lawton's mother hugging him in the parking area in front of the school, just before supper, helping him into the passenger seat of her car, and driving away. Before nightfall everyone knew that Lawton Faison had killed Uly's dog and been allowed to withdraw from the school. No one could say how they knew the school had allowed him to withdraw — there'd been no announcement or posting; it was simply common knowledge. And it was true. After conferring with the family and meeting with senior staff Mr. Endicott had informed Lawton Faison Sr. and Beth Faison that their son would not be allowed to graduate with his class but that he would receive his diploma over the summer. Possibly Lawton had said something to Richardson or Gillespie before he left.

When Henry caught up with Ken in his room after study hall, Ken was pulling a dark hoodie over his head.

"What are you doing?"

Ken pointed to a can of paint on the floor. "I'm going to paint the water tower."

"Right now?"

Ken nodded.

"What are you going to paint on it?"

Ken handed Henry a scrap of notebook paper with a stick figure drawing.

"Hangman?" Henry asked.

Ken shook his head. "Lynching."

Henry looked at the drawing again. It was surprisingly crude. But there was a noose, and that was a black man. The whole thing seemed crazy to him. "Why?"

Ken snatched the drawing back and stuffed it into his pocket. "You've heard what everyone's saying, right?"

"About Lawton?"

Ken bobbled his head and mimicked a child's singsong voice. "'He snapped'. 'He must have been high on something'. 'You think he'll be okay?' 'Is he going to be able to graduate?' 'What's going to happen with college?'"

Ken kicked his bed so hard that it bounced against the wall and knocked over a stack of books on the floor. "It's disgusting!" he said. He stepped over the mess he'd made and rummaged through the bottom drawer of his dresser.

"It's not surprising that people are worried after he did something that crazy," Henry said.

Ken kicked the bottom drawer shut and turned on Henry. He held a flashlight in his hand. "He lynched the dog, Henry! Lynched it!"

Henry took a step back to give Ken room. "I'm not saying I'm okay with it, but it was a dog. That's not a lynching."

Ken held the flashlight upright in front of him and circled it with his right fist. "He tied a noose! Did you see the noose he tied?"

Henry nodded.

"Why a noose Henry? Why did he put a noose around that dog's neck?"

"I don't —"

"Do you think it's just a coincidence that it was Uly's dog?" Ken stared at him in disbelief.

"What do you mean 'coincidence'?"

Ken took a step towards Henry. "Do you think he would have hanged Mr. Endicott's dog?" he asked angrily.

"No."

"Or Boney's?"

"Probably not."

"But somehow it's okay in his mind to hang Uly's dog. Why is that?" Ken took another step forward, and Henry took another step back. "Well?" Ken pressed. "Why is that?"

"I see what you're getting at —"

"And with a noose!... And the school let him withdraw?"

"He's not going to graduate."

"But he'll get his diploma," Ken said.

"He's from a pretty big family."

Ken spat on the floor. "I don't give a goddamn about his family! If they're going to kick out a poor third former for cheating on a pop quiz they better damn sure kick out a rich sixth former for lynching a dog."

Henry held up his hands to calm his friend. "I'm with you, Ken! I'm with you! But why paint the water tower?"

"So the school will see it for what it is."

"Which is—"

"A lynching."

"Most people will think you're calling the school racist."

"Call a spade a spade. Remember, the Germans let the Nazis gas six million Jews. Lawton Faison's ancestors enslaved hundreds of African Americans—"

"How do you know—"

"He bragged about it! The school winks and nods about the slave cabins behind the Manor." Ken pointed in that direction.

"You can't change history," Henry said.

"I'm not trying to change anything! I'm just trying to make people see things for what they are. Lawton Faison gets away with hanging Uly's dog. The least I can do is make them see the ugliness."

Ken picked up the can of paint and brush, and Henry held out a hand to stop him. "It's not going to change anything."

"Probably not, but I'll feel better about myself."

"Why don't you wait until tomorrow? Just sleep on it," Henry said.

"Everyone's half-forgetting it now. By this time tomorrow it'll just be another unpleasant story that disappears like a stone dropped into a well."

Ken pushed past Henry's hand to get to the door, and Henry grabbed his arm. He knew there was nothing he could do to stop his friend and worried that in Ken's present state of mind he wouldn't be careful and might get caught. "I'm coming with you," he said.

Ken shook his head. "This isn't an OWL thing."

"I know. I'll keep watch in case someone shows up. Give me the flashlight."

On their way to the water tower they agreed that Henry would stand below and Ken would climb to the platform. One flash meant all clear. Two flashes meant trouble. There was a quarter moon, and it wasn't completely dark. Looking up from below, Henry was able to see Ken moving around the platform as he painted. A dog barked in the vicinity of the faculty houses, and Henry held his breath as he listened for someone approaching. After a minute he told himself it was probably a skunk getting into a garbage can. He looked back up at Ken, who had made it a quarter of the way around the platform. Henry could hear *Cheeseburger in Paradise* coming from one of the dorm rooms in the Randolph

Building. He laughed to himself when he thought about what Ken must be thinking. After twenty minutes he heard a whistle overhead. Henry flashed the light once and Ken climbed down.

"All done?"

"Yeah. It's not pretty, but it'll do the job."

Just then Henry heard hurried footsteps behind them.

"You boys! Stay right there!"

Henry saw a flashlight beam strike the ladder beside him. Ken dropped the paint brush and can and ran toward the golf course.

"Stop right there! Stop!"

The flashlight found Henry, and he did not move as the man approached quickly.

"Palmer?" It was Mr. Mackie. "What are you doing out here?"

Henry did not say anything, and Mackie flashed his light in the direction that Ken had run and then back onto Henry's face.

"I asked you a question, Palmer. What are you doing?"

"Nothing," Henry said.

"Nothing?" Mackie flashed the light on the ground and found the paint brush and can. He flashed the light up at the water tower and then back onto Henry.

"Were you painting the water tower?"

"Nossir."

"Who was that with you?"

Henry did not say anything.

"I said, Who … Was … That … With … You … Palmer?!"

Still, Henry said nothing, but his insides began tumbling like rocks in a hopper.

Mackie's thick glasses had slipped to the tip of his nose in his rush to the water tower, and he pushed them back up the bridge and eyed Palmer hungrily.

"Pick up that paint and brush and come with me!" he barked.

Henry followed Mr. Mackie back towards the Randolph Building. It was now 10:30, and he could hear boys yelling in the bathrooms as they got ready for lights out. Henry assumed that Mackie was the Master on Duty and that he was escorting Henry to the duty room next to the lobby on the second floor, but instead of taking the main stairs to the lobby Mackie turned up a side stairwell and climbed to B Dorm. Why is he taking me back to my room? Henry wondered. Henry followed Mackie down the hallway. They passed Wobbly with a toothbrush on his way to the bathroom.

"What's going on?" Wobbly asked.

Henry shook his head.

"Get ready for bed, Wobbly," Mackie said sharply.

Henry followed Mackie down the hall. Just before they reached Henry's room, Mackie stopped, put his ear to Ken's door, then opened it without knocking. Neither Mackie nor Henry expected to find Ken, but there he was, in a dark hoodie, sitting in his chair with a headset on. Ken looked up, surprised to see them, and removed his headset with his left hand. He had the music turned up loud, and the song was audible through the headset.

There's a starman waiting in the sky

"Hello, Mr. Mackie."

He'd like to come and meet us

Mackie nodded. "Turn the music down, Bright."

But he thinks he'd blow our minds

Bright held the headset out to Mackie. "This is good stuff Mr. Mackie."

There's a starman waiting in the sky

"David Bowie," Ken said.

He's told us not to blow it

"You should listen."

'Cause he knows it's all worthwhile

Mackie shook his head. "I'm not interested in your music, Bright. I want to know if you were with Palmer at the water tower just now."

Bright held the headset out further and nodded, indicating that Mackie should really listen to this part.

> *He told me*
> *Let the children lose it*
> *Let the children use it*
> *Let all the children boogie*

"He says we just got to boogie, Mr. Mackie." And Ken pronounced the *boogie* with Bowie's British accent so that it sounded nasty.

Mackie grew irritated at Bright's insolence and turned scowling back to Henry. "I'm asking you one last time, Palmer. Was Ken Bright with you at the water tower?"

Henry looked past Mr. Mackie at his friend. Ken's eyes got bigger and he raised his eyebrows as if to say, 'What's it going to be, old boy?' He didn't gesture for Henry to say 'Yes" or 'No'. It was more like he was excited and curious to see how Henry would respond.

Henry shook his head no.

La, la, la, la, la, la, la, la, la, la, la

Now furious, Mackie turned back to Bright, who again held out his headphones.

"Turn off that goddamn music!" Mackie stepped towards the turntable and would have snatched the needle off the record but Ken's right hand shot out from his hoodie pocket and removed the needle first.

"Don't touch that!"

As soon as his right hand reached the lifting arm of the cartridge, both Henry and Ken saw the black paint on his fingertips. Henry caught his breath and Ken's hand trembled as it lifted the needle off the record, causing a worble to come through his speakers.

"What's that?" Mackie asked.

"Just a little feedback," Ken said, and he returned his hand to the hoodie pocket.

A smile crept across Mackie's face and he pointed at the pocket of Ken's hoodie. "I mean the black paint on your hand."

Ken tried to look like he didn't know what Mackie was talking about.

"Show me your hand, Bright."

Ken hesitated. He looked at Henry and raised his eyebrows again — this time to say, 'Sorry old chap' — and pulled his right hand out of his pocket. Mackie turned to Henry.

"Show me the paint, Palmer."

Henry held out the paint can and brush. Mackie turned back to Ken.

"What do you have to say for yourself, Bright?"

Ken almost said, 'You caught me paint-handed,' but he checked himself. Why make it easy for them? Instead, he smiled and held out his hands, palms upward, in a gesture of 'What can I say?'

"That's a disciplinary offense for you," Mackie said to Ken, and he turned to Henry. "And an honor offense for you, Palmer."

THE PHONE RANG in David Nightingale's kitchen the next morning, just as he was pouring himself a cup of coffee. It was Edwin Endicott. He asked to see him in his office. Now if it was convenient.

When he got there, Endicott had just gotten off the phone with Gordon Palmer Sr., and he was frowning at his desk with his reading glasses perched at the end of his nose.

"It's about Henry Palmer," Endicott told his friend. "Bad news, I'm afraid."

Endicott informed Nightingale of the events of last night. About the painting on the water tower and Henry lying to protect his friend. He said Henry's honor hearing would take place tonight and Bright's disciplinary hearing tomorrow.

"Are you close to the boy?" Endicott asked.

Nightingale nodded.

"You should talk to him if you can. Get him to tell the truth."

"Will it make any difference?"

"Of course it will. He'll uphold his honor."

"But will you give him a second chance?"

Endicott scoffed. "You know my position on that."

Nightingale knew Endicott's position very well. Early on in his tenure, the school's board of trustees had complained that a certain long-haired, loosey-goosey relativism was creeping into the school's culture, and they gave Endicott a mandate to correct the course. Endicott had seized the wheel with enthusiasm and immediately announced a policy of no more second chances. "A boy knows what's right and what's wrong," he said. Soon the trustees were happy, the alumni were giving more money, and the parents were complaining less about drinking and drug use on campus. The only naysayers were a vocal minority, Nightingale among them, who worried that the school was giving up on too many boys and had lost track of the quality of mercy in its haste to mete out justice.

Nightingale touched the scar just above his right ear. "I remember one time my dear friend told a lie to protect me," he said.

Endicott leaned back and knocked the glasses off of his nose when he attempted to remove them. "This is completely different," he huffed.

Nightingale didn't say anything but raised his eyebrows doubtfully. "You hadn't broken any rules," Endicott said.

Nightingale rolled his eyes in a self-deprecating manner. "By getting blackout drunk?"

"You were an adult," Endicott said defensively.

"And missing classes the next day?"

Endicott waved both hands at his friend in an effort to dismiss the subject. "We understood the circumstances."

Nightingale nodded. "Yes. You told a lie to protect a friend." Nightingale watched Endicott's face grow hot with anger, and he quickly added, "I've never doubted that you did the right thing, and I have always been grateful for it."

Endicott started to say something but stopped himself. He massaged the top of his bald head with his fingers and leaned down to pick his glasses up off the floor. As he did so his eyes fell on the photograph of Winston Churchill. He turned to Nightingale, thrust out his jaw, and with his reading glasses beating time in the air, grunted his disapproval.

"When a master asks a boy about a disciplinary matter, the boy must tell the truth. It's as simple as that. There is no honor without truth!"

Nightingale recognized Endicott's Churchill impersonation. He'd seen him pull it out of his hat before, at times like these, when he felt threatened in some way. Nightingale had no illusions that he could change his old friend's mind. Edwin had always been stubborn to a fault, and in recent years he had only become more like himself. Still, he knew it bothered Endicott when they disagreed, and in this case he should be bothered.

"Sometimes, Edwin, friendship is the greater truth," Nightingale said.

Just then there was a knock on the door, and Gordon Palmer walked in.

"Oh, sorry," he said, when he saw Mr. Nightingale. "I didn't think anyone else would be here."

Nightingale kept his eyes on Edwin, and when he saw the old man's grimace, he knew that his barb had landed. He turned to the door.

"It's all right, Gordon. I was just leaving." He put a hand on the boy's shoulder as he passed by him. "Don't worry about being late. Take whatever time you need with Henry." And as he left the office he wondered whether Ken Bright would show up for first period class that morning.

Gordon had no idea what Mr. Nightingale was talking about. Coach Boney, the resident faculty member on Lauderdale Hall, had stopped by his room and said only that Mr. Endicott needed to see him first thing. He turned to the headmaster, who motioned to the chair near his desk.

"Take a seat, Gordon. And close the door behind you."

As Gordon crossed the room, Endicott shook his head in a futile attempt to spit the hook of Nightingale's parting remark. David always had a soft spot for the boys who got in trouble, but that's no way to steer the ship, he thought. He refused to compromise the honor code for the sake of a single boy. There were no free passes; he had the greater good to consider. He considered young Gordon. This was a tricky bit of business.

"I fear young Henry got into a bit of trouble last night."

"Henry?"

The old man nodded. "Terrence Mackie saw someone on the water tower and when he went to investigate, he found Henry standing at the bottom of the ladder and a can of paint on the ground next to him. Did you see the water tower this morning?"

Gordon nodded. "What is that?"

Endicott frowned. "Hard to say for sure, but I fear it's a black man hanging from a noose."

"That's what I thought. Henry did that?"

Endicott leaned back in his chair and laced his fingers together over his paunch. "No. We're almost certain Kenneth Bright painted it. Terry caught Bright in his room with black paint on his hand."

"So Henry is like a …" Gordon couldn't think of the word.

"An accomplice," Endicott said helpfully. "I wish that's all there was to it, but no. Terry says Henry committed an honor offense."

"An honor offense?" Gordon felt a sharp pain in his abdomen. "What did he do?"

Mr. Endicott described for Gordon the story that Mackie had told him that morning. Both Endicott and Mackie were more focused on Ken Bright, because they were convinced he'd also painted the Jesus fish on the water tower in the fall, but they couldn't ignore the honor offense. "Terry asked him if Bright painted the water tower, and Henry said 'no'."

What was Henry doing there with Ken Bright, Gordon wondered. How many times had he warned him? Why would he lie?

"I have to talk to him," Gordon said.

"Of course. Go ahead."

Gordon put his head in his hands and tried to think of a way out. Being a new boy was no excuse, especially in the spring. But there was still the disciplinary charge against Ken. "If I can get him to admit that Bright painted the tower, can he stay in school, assuming the prefects go along with that?"

Mr. Endicott tried not to show it, but he couldn't help but feel pleased with the boy. Endicott had already decided this was the course he would take. The case against Ken Bright was solid but maybe not a slam dunk; unlike most boys caught in the act, he hadn't admitted anything. Henry's participation would tie up that loose end. Endicott had already decided to let Henry stay in school, but only if he told the truth about Ken Bright. The delicate part was not appearing too willing to compromise the Honor Code, even with his Head Boy. He had expected Gordon to make a plea for mercy—it was only natural of a brother—but he had not expected him to offer the *quid pro quo*. Clearly, Gordon had grown up in the job. He really was a good Head Boy. Now the only thing left for Endicott to do was to feign indignation. He tossed his reading glasses onto his desk.

"I will not be put in the position of plea bargaining an honor violation," he said.

Gordon's head bobbed nervously. "I know. I know. I know. It's just that—" he broke off. He was going to say that he couldn't preside over Henry's hearing and uphold his oath to administer the Honor Code without fear or favor if the result was going to be kicking out Henry. Back in the fall Mr. Endicott had told him this day would come, but who would have predicted this?

"If I can talk to him I think I can get him to admit that he lied and to tell the truth."

"That would be better than the alternative, but it doesn't solve the problem," Endicott said.

The problem? Oh. Endicott meant Ken Bright, Gordon thought, not how Gordon could save Henry and still fulfill his responsibilities as Head Boy, which was giving Gordon pause. Bright. He *was* the problem....But maybe also the solution.

"If Henry tells the truth and turns in Bright and the prefects vote for censure instead of expulsion, would you go along with their recommendation?"

Mr. Endicott pretended to scowl at the boy's presumption.

"And as part of the censure," Gordon quickly added, "Henry can't be a prefect as a sixth former."

Endicott picked up his reading glasses by one arm and spun them around as he spoke. "I will not guarantee anything. The prefects have their job to do, and I have mine. Whatever the prefects recommend, I will certainly take into consideration and give great weight. That being said, if I believe that the prefects are not upholding their duty to the Honor Code, I will not hesitate to overrule them. I am not a rubber stamp. If, however, the boy testifies truthfully and is honestly remorseful, and if he does provide testimony that we need to determine that Ken Bright painted that disgusting thing —" he pointed his glasses out the window at the water tower — "then I can see that perhaps the prefects' recommendation along the lines that you describe might be justified, even though it perhaps is not in line with how I would decide the matter if it were only left to me."

Gordon started to say something, but Endicott, thinking that he wanted further clarification, held up his hand.

"It would have to be very clear that Henry's testimony led to Bright's expulsion. That's all I will say on the matter."

Gordon was so relieved, he started to hug the man, but he saw that Mr. Endicott was displeased. "Thank you so much. Thank you."

Gordon offered Mr. Endicott his hand, but the old man ignored it. "Go talk to your brother," he growled.

"I will. Right now." And he left Endicott's office to find Henry.

SNITCH

GORDON FOUND HENRY in his room on B Dorm. Wobbly had already left for first period, and Henry was still in an unbuttoned shirt packing his book bag.

"Gordon! I gotta —"

Gordon held out his left hand to stop Henry and put the forefinger of his right hand to his lips. He didn't want to talk here, next to Bright's room.

"Meet me in the Reading Room."

"Right now?"

Gordon nodded.

"Is it open?"

"I have the key."

Gordon left. Henry zipped up his bag and looked at himself in the mirror as he buttoned his shirt. He looked pretty much like every other white boy at Randolph. He mussed his hair — still too cute. He unbuttoned and re-buttoned the front of his shirt so that it was cock-eyed, with one button leftover at the bottom. That's better, he thought, and turned off the light as he walked out of the room.

Gordon had left one of the Reading Room's tall, paneled double-doors ajar. Henry pushed it open — it was heavy against his hand — and saw Gordon standing to the left, outside the four lines of tables that formed a square in the center of the room. Henry had tried to study here once but couldn't do it. He'd liked the high ceiling — at least twenty feet up — and the bank of windows that looked out onto the Lawn, but the names of all the Head Boys painted in a line along the perimeter of the ceiling had freaked him out, and he'd worried that all the boys studying there might think he'd only come to bask in his dad's name.

Gordon motioned for Henry to join him at the tables, but Henry hesitated at the door. A part of him wanted to tell Gordon what had happened and get his advice about what to do, but another part of him didn't want to talk to Gordon at all, because he knew Gordon would want to lecture him about what a fuckup he was. Plus, Gordon was Head Boy, right? So how much help was he going to be?

"Henry, come on. I don't have much time," Gordon said. He took a seat and pointed at the chair beside him.

Henry stumbled forward and shut the door.

"Mr. Endicott told me about the honor offense this morning," Gordon began, once Henry had joined him. "I can't get into the details of all that right now, because I'm on the prefect board, obviously ...." Gordon's voice trailed off, and he touched the tip of his chin with his forefinger as he gathered his thoughts. "This is really awkward, and I'm sorry, but if we talk about what happened then I probably can't be part of the hearing — the honor hearing's tonight at seven o'clock — and you want me to be there for reasons that I'll try to explain. You should sit down."

Henry had his book bag and was due in class in five minutes. "Should I skip first period?"

"What do you have?"

"Mackie's English class."

Gordon smiled. "You should definitely skip that."

Henry took a seat next to Gordon, and Gordon took a deep breath.

"So. The way it will go is Mackie will speak first, and everyone will get a chance to ask him questions, and after that you'll come in. I'll explain to you the charges and the procedure and then ask you to make a statement if you want to. After that, the prefects will ask you questions, and depending on what you say and what Mackie says, we may ask Bright to speak also. Then once everyone's had a chance to talk and have their questions answered the prefects will decide whether you committed an honor offense, and if so, the punishment."

Henry put his face down onto the table and stretched his arms straight out as far as he could. He had a knot in his back that he couldn't untangle. This was a freaking nightmare, he thought. He sat back up and asked Gordon the question that had kept him awake most of last night.

"If you find I violated the honor code you're going to kick me out, right?"

Gordon tapped one of his incisors with his index finger.

"Normally yes. But there may be a way to get around that, and that's really what I wanted to talk to you about."

"Okay."

The heel of Gordon's right foot bounced up and down on the carpet, and he drummed the side of his head with his fingers as he tried to figure out how to explain things to Henry without breaching Mr. Endicott's confidence.

"Look. From what I've heard it's clear that Bright was there at the water tower. Mackie says he had black paint on his hand, and who else would pull a stunt like that? It has Ken Bright written all over it. The guy hates the South. He probably had a hard-on the whole time he was painting the thing — what's it supposed to be? A lynching?"

Henry didn't want to say anything that might get Ken into trouble. He rolled his neck and listened to his vertebrae crack. He knew Gordon was trying to help him, but still .... "I'm not saying it's true or not," he said finally.

"Well you've already said once that it's *not* true, right? To Mackie?"

Henry just looked at his brother. This irritated Gordon.

"Look. I bet if Mackie had caught Ken with paint on his hand before he asked you any questions you would have said it was true."

Henry still didn't say anything.

Gordon got angry. "I'm trying to help you out, Henry .... As best I can."

"What do you want me to say? You said we shouldn't talk about what happened."

Gordon slapped his forehead and grinned sheepishly. "You're right." He nodded. "You're right. I'm sorry. This is just hard to explain."

Henry did not understand what was hard for him to explain. Was Gordon going to help him out or not?

"Look. Not many boys get a second chance. We haven't talked about it or anything, but I'm pretty sure the prefects will vote for a reprimand if you come clean. You won't be kicked out. You'll have an honor offense, but you'll be able to come back to school next year. You just won't be a prefect when you're a senior."

"What about Mr. Endicott?"

"What about him?"

"Doesn't he have the last word?"

Gordon pursed his lips. "Let's just say I think he'll back me up. He's so bent out of shape about Ken Bright that I think he'll let you come back if you turn him in.... Pretty sure.... Practically positive he'll let you come back."

Henry didn't like the sound of that. Ken was his friend, and the more he thought about it, the more he agreed with what Ken had done. It seemed righteous. Lawton had lynched the dog, and the school had let him leave without even a reprimand. No one wanted to admit that. Gordon stared at him.

"I'll have to think about it," Henry said.

Gordon cocked his head and extended the empty palms of his hands to Henry as if to say, 'Give me something!' He'd stepped way out on a limb with Mr. Endicott, he was on shaky ground with his promise to uphold the Honor Code as Head Boy, and all his little brother could say was 'I'll think about it'? He placed a hand on the back of Henry's neck and squeezed. "Listen to me, little brother. This is the right thing to do."

Henry shook off Gordon's grip.

"At least you'll be able to tell dad that you told the truth at the Honor hearing," Gordon said.

Henry had called home that morning. He'd wanted to speak to his mom, but his dad had picked up. He'd told his dad briefly what had happened. He could tell that his dad was furious by the way he kept clearing the bile out of the back of his throat. "I told you I'll think about it," he said again.

"Look. If you get kicked out, things will get really tough. This stuff can stick to you for the rest of your life. You won't get into Princeton — I know that seems crazy right now, but I'm telling you, it can have lifelong consequences. It could keep you from becoming a lawyer — "

"What makes you think I want to go to Princeton?" Henry interrupted. "You have no idea, do you? If I had to choose right now I'd hitchhike across the country and catch a freighter to Singapore before I'd grind away four years of my life at Princeton, just so that I can grind away the rest of my life like dad."

Henry pressed his hands against the sides of his face to keep his head from exploding. When he opened his eyes, he caught sight of all the names of all the Head Boys and followed them until he found their father's name, "Gordon Augustus Palmer, 1952". He pointed at it and laughed sadly.

"I guess they'll be scribbling your name up there too, huh?" Henry turned his sour gaze onto his brother. RIP Gordon, he thought.

Gordon ignored Henry's outburst. He told himself that Henry was scared and upset and didn't really mean what he said, but he gave up on trying to explain how Henry's decision could affect his future. He just needed Henry to understand that if he told the prefects the truth tonight — that Ken had painted the water tower — he probably wouldn't get kicked out tomorrow. He reached out to touch his brother's shoulder, but Henry drew back.

"We can get through this, Henry. Trust me. Just tell us tonight what happened at the water tower, and between now and then don't talk to Bright. It won't look good if the prefects hear you talked to Bright before the hearing."

Henry shook his head and looked away. "What time?" he asked.

"Seven o'clock."

Henry nodded. "I'll be there."

Gordon couldn't think of anything more to say. He'd do his best for his brother. He was sure Henry understood that. He checked his pocket watch and compared its time to the time on the clock in the Reading Room. He held the watch to his ear, shook it, and put it to his ear again. "Must have forgot to wind it last night," he muttered.

Henry just stared at him.

"I think I'll try to catch the last half of AP English," Gordon said after he wound his watch and adjusted the time. He stood up from the table. "You okay?"

Henry nodded again.

Gordon started to touch his shoulder but thought better of it. "Just tell the truth, Henry, and everything'll be okay."

Henry waited until Gordon had left the room, then he picked up his bag and shuffled to the door. The hall was empty. He had forty-five minutes before second period began. He decided to stop by Ken's room; maybe he'd skipped first period too. As he walked down the hall he dragged his knuckles against the wall's beadboard wainscotting. The carpet smelled like Wobbly's dirty laundry. He hadn't told Wobbly anything. Word had gotten out about Ken painting the water tower but not about Henry's honor offense.

"What in the hell was he trying to do?" Wobbly had said over breakfast.

"Call out Lawton for being an asshole, for one thing," Henry had said.

"Sure, but why do we have to look at that thing he painted?"

"Maybe 'cause we're assholes too."

Wobbly had laughed at that, and Henry had been too exhausted to argue about it.

When he reached Ken's room he saw through the transom window that the light was off. He tapped at the door and opened it — Ken wasn't there. His bed was made up. His David Bowie photograph hung on the wall. Everything was as it had always been. Henry knew that would change. If nothing else, they'd kick Ken out tomorrow for sure. He thought about Uly, and wondered how he was doing. Should he try to check on him? The idea seemed at the time strangely impossible, but in truth it was only as yet unimaginable.

Behind him he heard *Melissa* playing. Mongo's room, he thought. He pictured Mongo lying on his bed, staring up at the ceiling, the music louder than he realized, thinking about cows. He tried to imagine what Mongo's parents were like; he was sure they were proud of their son.

Henry was about to head down to the Mess then make his way to class when he noticed an envelope taped to his own door. Written on the outside in blue ink was his name. He opened it and found a hand-written note.

> *Henry,*
> *I was sorry to hear about the honor charge this*
> *morning. If possible I would like to speak with you*
> *before the hearing. I am free after my last class at*
> *2 p.m.*
> *David Nightingale.*

He must have come by while I was meeting with Gordon, Henry thought. He folded the note and put it into his breast pocket. He suddenly felt a little bit less alone.

HENRY MEETS WITH NIGHTINGALE

HENRY SKIPPED HIS LAST CLASS that day and was standing in the doorway of Nightingale's classroom at two o'clock. Mr. Nightingale stepped around his desk to greet him.

"Henry, I'm so glad you came. Please have a seat." He pointed to a chair beside his desk and closed the door to the hallway. "Mr. Endicott mentioned that there was going to be an Honor hearing tonight, and when he said your name my heart sank."

"You know what it's about?"

"Only in the briefest outline."

"I was at the water tower last night—"Henry began, but Mr. Nightingale interrupted him.

"You don't need to tell me anything about it, Henry, if you don't want to. I only asked you to come by to make sure you have the support you need."

Henry waved his hand at Mr. Nightingale. "No. That's fine. I'm glad you left the note. I've been trying to figure out what to do."

"Okay. Then how can I help you?"

Henry sat down in the student armchair closest to Nightingale's desk and dropped his book bag to the floor. He put his elbows on the desktop, leaned over, and rubbed the back of his head with both hands. Where to begin? Going to Ken with the water tower? Why he'd lied to Mackie? His conversation with Gordon? There was so much to say. It also occurred to him that if he got kicked out tonight, this would probably be the last time he'd ever see Mr. Nightingale, and he'd never have him as a teacher. He'd imagined having Nightingale for senior English ever since Ken mentioned him the day he moved in. Of course it wasn't a sure thing he'd get kicked out. Not according to Gordon.

"I guess I'm wondering if I should come clean tonight and tell the prefects that it was Ken at the water tower."

"Or if you shouldn't?" Nightingale said.

"Right."

"Because you want to protect Ken."

"And I don't want to be a snitch."

Nightingale tilted his head. "Well I don't know if telling the truth and being a snitch are the same thing."

"In this case they are. Gordon told me if I turn Ken in I won't get kicked out. I'd have a mark on my record, but I could come back next year."

"I see." Nightingale nodded. "So they've offered you a deal."

"Right."

"And that makes you a snitch."

"Right," Henry said. "Because I'd be protecting myself by turning in Ken."

Nightingale was surprised. Maybe his meeting with Edwin had made a difference after all. "Now I understand," he said. "But you know that telling the truth is still telling the truth regardless of whether you get some special benefit from it."

"Yeah."

"I mean we have an Honor Code so that we can have confidence in our trust of one another."

"Right."

"We don't have locks on our doors because we trust that no one's going to steal our stuff. We have take-home tests and unproctored exams because we trust that no one else is going to try to cheat to get ahead. We are like a family — or something close to a family — because we trust each other."

"Right."

"So even though you might receive some benefit by telling the truth about Ken Bright, that doesn't change the fact that you are upholding the Honor Code and protecting that trust — "

Henry raised his hand and Nightingale stopped talking. Henry didn't disagree with anything Nightingale was saying, but he'd already thought about all of that stuff.

"All that makes sense, Mr. Nightingale. My problem is that telling the truth about this does not feel like the honorable thing to do."

"Because you'd feel like a snitch."

"Not just that, but also because Ken is my best friend, and I don't want to do anything to hurt him. His friendship is more important to me than the Honor Code. I don't think telling the truth and honor are always the same thing — in this case telling the truth feels like cheating my friendship."

Mr. Nightingale had never had a boy express to him what he himself found most troubling about the school's policy of maintaining the Honor Code at all costs. It was an age-old dilemma, how to balance the competing demands of principle and compassion. Endicott's no second chance rule seemed wrong precisely because it was inviolable; it denied that any balance was necessary.

"You make a good point, Henry. The Honor Code is a compromise that we make because of our blindness. We cannot see a person's character — whether he is truly remorseful, whether he is malicious, whether he never will do this again or do something worse. And because we cannot see a person's character, we judge his actions. If he does certain things, he will be punished no matter who he really is. It's not perfect, but sadly, nothing is."

Henry shook his head. This wasn't about the Honor Code; this was about his friend.

"But I believe that I can judge Ken's character," he said. "He's the most honorable person I know. He tells me what he thinks. He's not looking over his shoulder all the time trying to impress somebody. Plus he was right."

"Right?' Mr. Nightingale asked.

"To paint the tower. It was the right thing to do. It needed to be done. What Lawton did was terrible. It was crazy. Maybe he was crazy when he did it, I don't know, but what the school did was wrong, and what Ken did was right, and my conscience tells me to stand by my friend. Does that mean I'm not honorable?"

Mr. Nightingale smiled. "No, Henry. I do not think you are dishonorable. I think that everything you say speaks of a very high character indeed."

Henry suddenly felt relieved. Nightingale had the reputation for being the toughest grader in the school. Ken had said, 'A B-plus in his class is worth more than an A in anybody else's.' And he respected and trusted Mr. Nightingale. If Mr. Nightingale said he was honorable, Henry felt like he could follow his conscience.

"Thank you, Mr. Nightingale. I think I understand better what I knew I had to do."

"I'm glad we had a chance to talk, Henry."

Henry leaned over and picked up his book bag, then remembered there was one other thing he wanted to ask Mr. Nightingale.

"Why did he do it, Mr. Nightingale?"

"Lawton?"

Henry nodded.

Nightingale had thought about it a lot. About Lawton. About Lawton's father. Even about Beth Faison. He'd taught Lawton for two years, and he had a sense of how desperately Lawton clung to an idea about his family. An idea much like Lawton Sr.'s idea. An idea that was no longer true. An idea that was a lie to begin with. He suspected that Lawton's idea about who he was and about who his family was had become so divorced from reality that when the truth did finally break through, he found that there was nothing left of his idea to sustain him.

"Who can say?" Nightingale said. "It was so strange what he did, and cruel. I doubt Lawton knows the answer to that question, and I don't know if anyone ever can really explain anyone else — why they do what they do. Sometimes I think the best we can do is try to find some lesson for our own lives."

"Have you found a lesson?" Henry asked.

Now Mr. Nightingale thought about Henry, and Henry's brother, and Henry's father, and even Grace Palmer. He knew them all a little.

"Everyone should try to draw their own lessons," he said finally.

"Sure. I know. But I was wondering what lesson you draw."

Mr. Nightingale smiled. "I'd say, try not to be your father's keeper."

Henry would remember those words years later. How prescient they were for his own life. For now, he thought about Ken, and about Lawton, and about that poor dog. He pulled one strap of his book bag over his shoulder.

"How is Uly doing?" Henry asked.

Mr. Nightingale blinked and leaned back in his chair. "Uly?"

"I know how much he loved Maisie."

Nightingale knitted his fingers behind his head and considered Henry. "You knew her name?"

Henry nodded. "He told it to me."

Nightingale smiled. "As a matter of fact I do know how Uly is doing. We buried Maisie last night. I expect — I know, he's very broken up, right now."

"Will you tell him I'm sorry?"

Nightingale felt tears come to his eyes. "I will."

Henry nodded. "What's his name, Mr. Nightingale?"

"Uly's?"

Henry nodded.

"Why do you ask?"

"I don't know. It just seems strange to only know him as Uly, I guess."

"Uly Horatio Randolph," Nightingale said.

"Randolph? Like the school's name?"

Nightingale nodded. "Exactly so."

WHEN HENRY GOT BACK to B Dorm, he went straight to Ken's room. Ken sat in his chair with a folder of papers on his lap. There were boxes on the floor and a suitcase on his bed.

"What are you doing?" Henry asked.

"I'm reading my papers from AP English." He nodded. "Not bad."

"I talked to Gordon. He said if I turn you in tonight, they won't kick me out."

Ken gestured to the gods in heaven and laughed. "I was wondering why they decided to hold your hearing before mine."

"What do you mean?"

"How can they find you committed an honor violation before they've found that I was the one on the water tower? It's the classic prisoner's dilemma."

"The what?"

"The prisoner's dilemma. The only witnesses are the people who were charged — you and me. The only way for sure to convict is if one person snitches on the other. If they both stay quiet they may not be able to prove their case. The dilemma is whether one of them will snitch. I bet Gordon told you not to talk to me, right?"

"Yeah."

"Classic prisoner's dilemma. Keep the prisoners apart and one of them will break."

"Mackie caught me at the water tower."

"Right. But they haven't charged you with a disciplinary offense yet, have they?"

Henry shook his head.

"Amateurs!" Ken put the paper he'd been reading back into the folder and pulled out another one. "*Lycidas*," he said and frowned. "Not my best work."

"Mackie caught you with paint on your hand."

"I can say I was painting a bookshelf."

Henry looked around the room. "But you weren't."

"Or a trunk, or whatever. The point is they're offering you the deal to get out of the prisoner's dilemma."

"But the dilemma is the prisoners', right? Ours. Not theirs."

"Right!" Ken tapped his noggin and pointed at Henry. "Smart boy. But in this case the dilemma is only yours. They've offered me nothing."

Ken smiled at him. Henry felt like he was being tested.

"I'm not going to snitch," Henry said.

Ken laughed. "Good boy. That's a helluva Honor Code they have, isn't it? Agree to snitch and we'll look the other way."

"Are you okay?" Henry asked. "You seem awfully happy-go-lucky for somebody with a hearing tomorrow."

Ken held his arms out and brushed his hands together. "Go ahead, Henry. Snitch away. I'm not showing up for their hearing tomorrow."

"What do you mean?"

Ken pointed at all the boxes around the room. "I'm catching a bus to New York City tonight. I pull into Penn Station tomorrow morning at nine."

"Really?"

"I'm not going to stick around to give them the satisfaction of kicking me out." He stood up and took down his Ziggy Stardust poster, smiled at that sexy intergalactic traveler, then rolled it up and placed it in a box.

"Does your mom know what you're doing?"

"No! I'm not going to tell her. If I do, she'll try to make me stay. This way, by the time I get there it'll be too late."

Henry sat down on Ken's bed, put his elbows on his knees and propped his head up with his hands. "Wow. Didn't see that coming."

Ken took down his Breugel print and admired it. "So go ahead and tell them it was me on the water tower — if you want to stay, that is. It won't make no-nevermind to me."

"My dad would want me to snitch," Henry admitted.

Ken laughed. "Don't listen to me. He'd want you to 'tell the truth'." He raised his hands and put 'tell the truth' in quotation marks.

"It doesn't feel right."

"Turning on a friend?"

"Yeah," Henry said. "That's what it feels like."

"Well I'm trying to make that easier for you. My fate is already decided, so you won't be putting a nail in my coffin." He moved about the room and started loading his books and albums into boxes.

"What are you going to do about graduation?"

"Don't know yet." He flipped through his Warriner's English Grammar and Composition then held it out to Henry.

"Want this?" he asked.

Henry shook his head. Ken tossed it into the garbage can.

"Haven't had that conversation with Herr Endicott."

"Maybe you'll get the Lawton treatment."

Ken swallowed a laugh. "Not likely. I'm no legacy, and he's pissed about the water tower."

"What about Yale?"

Ken stopped his circumnavigation of the room and smiled at Henry.

"I talked to Nightingale after class this morning. He knows people on the admissions committee and said he'd put in a good word. He also said — how did he put it?" Ken glanced at the ceiling and rehearsed the words in his head before mimicking Nightingale's baritone southern accent. "'I would be surprised if the committee would risk it becoming known that they had rescinded an offer of admission to a student because the student protested the lynching of a janitor's dog'."

"He called it a 'lynching'?"

"Yep." Ken held out his right hand, and Henry gave him a high five.

"You were right," Henry said.

"About what?"

"About a lot of things. About everything." Tears welled up in Henry's eyes. "I'm going to miss you."

"Aw man, don't do that. I'm no good with tears. Whenever my mom starts crying I leave the room."

Henry wiped his face on his sleeve. "Okay …. Well …." Henry shuffled his feet. He didn't want to stand around Ken's room with tears on his face. Ken extended his right hand.

"You're a good friend, Henry Palmer, and the best boy this school has to offer."

Henry brushed past Ken's hand, put his arms around his friend and hugged him tightly. At first, Ken held his hands above Henry's head, then let them fall and hugged Henry back. He felt tears rise to his own eyes and quickly patted Henry's shoulder and backed away.

"I'll send you a postcard," Ken said, avoiding Henry's gaze for the moment.

"Promise?"

"I promise," Ken said.

They nodded to each other then, and Henry laughed. He recognized the tears in Ken's eyes and Ken's awkward attempt to hide them.

"Get out of here, Palmer!" Ken smiled and pointed at the door.

"So long, Ken."

HONOR HEARING

THE HONOR HEARING TOOK PLACE at seven o'clock in the prefect room. Mr. Mackie spoke to the prefects first. After Mackie left the room, Henry was fetched. As Gordon had described, the twelve prefects sat around the table, with Gordon at the head and an empty chair beside him. Henry knew all of the prefects, but he wasn't friends with any of them. The air was stale with the odor of twelve nervous boys holed up in a close room. The light was strangely dim and yellow, like candlelight. None of it gave Henry a good feeling.

Gordon struggled to smile — or perhaps not to smile — when Henry walked into the room. Henry couldn't tell which. Gordon didn't say anything but only motioned to the chair beside him. As he crossed the room, all eyes on him, Henry's heart began pounding and he felt like he was going to hyperventilate. He sat down and closed his eyes, trying to catch his breath. He felt a hand on his arm, and when he opened his eyes Gordon offered him an awkward smile.

"You need a minute, Henry?" he asked.

"I'm okay," Henry stammered. One of the other prefects brought him a glass of water. "Thanks."

Henry took a sip and felt better. He looked at the faces of the boys around the table. They looked maybe a little kinder and more nervous than he'd expected, like maybe they didn't want to be there either. This thought calmed him a little bit, and he turned to Gordon.

"You ready?" Gordon asked.

"Okay." Henry nodded.

Gordon cleared his throat. "We're here because there has been a charge of an honor offense brought by Mr. Mackie against Henry Palmer. We've heard from Mr. Mackie, who claims that Henry lied when he was asked whether Ken Bright was with him at the water tower last night.

Henry, do you understand the charge?"

Henry nodded again.

"Do you understand that you will be speaking tonight, at this hearing, on your honor?"

Henry nodded again.

"And do you understand that if the Prefect Board finds that you violated the Honor Code that we will make a recommendation for what penalty should be imposed, up to and including expulsion?"

Henry nodded yet again.

"Is that yes?" Gordon asked. "You have to use words so we know what you're saying."

Henry was surprised by Gordon's formality. "Yes," he said quietly.

"Do you have any questions?"

Henry wondered if Gordon had told the other prefects what he'd told Henry that morning. He wondered if Gordon would vote with the other prefects or sit that out. He wondered if Gordon would stand up for him. He looked around the table. Everyone was staring at him, waiting. "No," he said.

Gordon nodded to Henry, then he stared at something just over Henry's left shoulder and his face turned serious, like he was thinking very hard, trying to make sure that he got what he said next just right. Henry felt the tension rise, and he was scared again. Gordon glanced at the other prefects and then turned back to Henry. He didn't smile. Henry had no idea what he was thinking.

"Mr. Mackie asked you if Ken Bright was with you at the water tower?" Gordon said.

Henry waited for Gordon to go on, but Gordon just looked at him. Suddenly Henry realized that Gordon had intended the statement to be a question.

"Yes," he said.

"And if he was the one who painted the water tower?" Gordon asked.

"I don't think Mr. Mackie knew about the painting yet," Henry said.

"Okay."

"He just saw someone running away," Henry said.

"Right. So he asked you if it was Ken Bright who ran away."

"Not then, but later."

"In Bright's room."

"Yes."

"And you said, 'No'," Gordon said.

"Yes."

"Was that the truth?"

Henry was surprised by the question—that Gordon had gotten there so quickly and that he was asking about truth instead of about what had happened. Of course it wasn't the truth. Gordon knew that; Henry figured all the prefects knew that; why ask that? If he said it was the truth he'd be lying, and Henry didn't want to lie about his own conduct. If he said it wasn't the truth he'd be turning in Ken. He wondered if Gordon was asking him a trick question. He didn't answer. Gordon watched him.

"Was Bright with you at the water tower?" Gordon asked.

Henry did not answer.

Gordon's eyes widened as it started to dawn on him that maybe Henry wasn't going to turn Ken in after all. He decided to try a different tack.

"You know that the painting was done with black paint," Gordon said.

"Yes."

"You know that Ken Bright had black paint on his right hand."

"Yes."

"You know that Mr. Mackie accused Mr. Bright of painting the water tower."

That wasn't right, Henry thought, but he hesitated to respond because he worried that Gordon might be trying to trick him into turning Ken in again. Finally he said, "Mr. Mackie asked Ken, 'What's that on your hand?'"

"And Ken said, 'You caught me paint-handed'," Gordon quoted.

"Yes."

Gordon thought that maybe now that he had pointed out that Ken had practically confessed, Henry would turn him in. "Was Ken with you at the water tower?" Gordon asked again.

Henry did not answer.

"There was someone with you at the water tower," Gordon said with irritation.

"Yes."

"Who was with you at the water tower?"

Henry did not answer, and Gordon rolled his eyes.

"Was Ken not with you at the water tower?"

Henry did not answer. Gordon slapped the table.

"If Ken was with you at the water tower, don't say anything."

Still Henry did not answer.

Gordon rubbed his face vigorously with both hands then turned on his brother angrily. "What the hell, Henry! It's obvious. Why won't you just say it?"

Henry did not answer.

"Are you not going to tell us?" Gordon asked.

Henry shook his head. "No, Gordon. I am not."

Gordon threw up his hands. "I can't help you, man."

Gordon himself was surprised at how quickly it was over. He'd been sure that Henry would follow his advice, and he'd practiced his questions to make it as simple as possible for Henry to turn Ken in. He thought he'd done everything he could to save his brother and keep him at the school.

Gordon turned to the prefects around the table. "Do any of you have any questions?"

There was a shuffling of feet and a shifting of bodies as the tension of the last minutes subsided. A few of the prefects shook their heads. Others looked at Henry with disapproval. One boy made a show of dropping his pen on the blank pad of paper in front of him. Another boy, his lips shut tight and mouth turned down in a frown, leaned forward on his elbows and looked incredulously at Henry. Despite their obvious disapproval, Henry didn't feel like he was being condemned. It was more like, 'Why didn't you play along?' No one said anything. Gordon stood up and ushered Henry out of the room. At the door he gave Henry a look that clearly indicated, 'What the hell?' but all he said was, "Wait here."

Henry collapsed onto a chair in the hallway. He had not expected Gordon to do all the questioning. He was surprised that it was all over so quickly. What happens now, he wondered. Was there a chance they wouldn't kick him out? He made fists with both his hands and punched his thighs. No. Who was he kidding? He looked at the clock — almost eight o'clock. Was Ken gone already?

The prefects decided that they did not need to hear from Ken. After Henry left the room, they asked themselves two questions. First: 'Did Henry Palmer lie to Mr Mackie?' Unanimously, they voted that he had lied. Second: 'Should Henry Palmer be expelled from the Randolph

School?' The vote was unanimous, with one abstention.

Henry was still sitting in the hallway when they all filed out. Henry looked up, but after the first of them avoided eye contact, he kept his head down. Gordon was the last boy out. He sat down next to Henry and started to touch Henry's shoulder but thought the better of it.

"I'm sorry, buddy."

Henry searched his brother's face for some glimmer of outrage, but all he saw in Gordon's grim expression was disappointment, or disapproval—Henry wasn't sure which. Probably both. Gordon reminded Henry of his dad. He brushed the bangs off his forehead and tried to show Gordon a brave face.

"That didn't take long."

"You made it pretty easy," Gordon said.

"What did you decide?"

"The prefect board voted to kick you out."

"I know that. I mean you." Henry pointed at his brother.

Gordon sat up straighter. "I abstained," he said quietly.

"You didn't even stand up for me?"

"I did everything I could," Gordon said, struggling to keep his temper.

"By not voting?"

"That's bullshit, Henry, and you know it! I gave you the chance to tell the truth and stay in school."

"To snitch, you mean."

"To uphold the Honor Code."

"Fuck you, Gordon!" Henry leaned over and dropped his head into his hands.

Gordon put a hand on Henry's shoulder, and Henry shook it off.

"Fuck off," Henry muttered.

Gordon sat up and looked down the hallway. The door to Endicott's office was open.

"It's going to be okay," Gordon said.

"No, it's not." Henry stared at the floor and shook his head. What did Gordon know about things being okay? He'd never fucked up anything. Everything worked out perfectly for him. Head Boy. Princeton. Toughest thing for Gordon was being brother to a fuckup. But just look at him, Henry thought. He'd handled that great, hadn't he? No blood on his hands. Thought he'd give me a way out. Just deliver Ken's head on a platter and everything will be hunky-dory — you just can't grow up to be a prefect. Fuck that. He sat up and faced his brother.

"Why didn't you vote to keep me?"

"That wasn't an option," Gordon said.

He spoke the words so matter-of-factly that Henry might as well have been talking to Mackie. "What do you mean it's not an option, You said it was, if I turned Ken in."

"Yeah. But you didn't do that, did you?" Gordon said smugly.

Henry took a deep breath. He remembered Ken calling Gordon a "tool' the first time they met. That definitely did not do justice to this betrayal. "No. I didn't," he said calmly.

"And why not?" Gordon demanded.

"Because I'd hate myself if I did," Henry said.

"You'd hate yourself for telling the truth?"

"If I turned in my best friend."

"Your best friend? Give me a break!" Gordon stood up and slapped the wall above Henry's head. "He got you kicked out! If he was such a good friend he wouldn't have taken you out on his little 'protest'!"

Henry didn't bother correcting Gordon, because what was the point? He didn't care about friendship. He didn't even care enough about his own brother to stand up for him. Henry had always been able to count on that — Gordon standing up for him — but now, when he looked at Gordon and Gordon turned his face away, Henry thought for the first time in his life that he and Gordon might turn out to be strangers.

Gordon felt numb. He'd done everything he could. It wasn't like Henry was going to be able to save Ken — that was clear. It wasn't like the consequences weren't clear — one strike and you're out. He'd done more than anyone could expect — gotten Mr. Endicott to agree, without saying it, that Henry could stay in school. All Henry had to do was tell the truth. He saves himself by telling the truth. How hard is that? No point in going over all that again. Not now. He'd said everything he had to say. Just had to try to make the best of it, he thought. He glanced down the hall. Mr. Endicott was waiting for him. Endicott. He leaned down and touched Henry on the shoulder.

"You want me to call mom and dad?"

"No."

"Okay, buddy." He took a breath. "I've got to meet with Mr. Endicott.

I'll swing by your room later."

"Don't bother," Henry muttered.

GORDON AND ENDICOTT

MR. ENDICOTT HAD WAITED in his office for the prefects' decision. His hope was that Henry Palmer would testify that Ken Bright had painted the water tower, that tomorrow the disciplinary board would kick Bright out, and that this little episode would resolve itself quickly. He was prepared to uphold, with stern reservations, the prefects' recommendation that the Palmer boy be censured but not expelled. When Gordon told him that Henry had not turned on Ken Bright, Endicott slapped himself on the forehead and knocked his reading glasses off his face.

"Why didn't he just tell the truth?" he said in disbelief. "It was the easiest thing."

"I don't know. I really don't know," Gordon said.

Gordon sat on the sofa beside Endicott's desk. He looked exhausted, and Endicott felt a spasm of sympathy for his Head Boy.

"I'm sorry it came to that, Gordon. I really am."

"Yessir."

"He should have said that it was Bright. I can't think the discipline board will find otherwise."

"I know. I told him that. He didn't listen."

"I'm sorry — not only because of you, but because of your father as well. He's been a great champion of the school."

"He's going to be really mad," Gordon said.

"I spoke to him a few hours ago. I told him that I thought Henry would tell the truth and that the prefects would recommend censure but not expulsion."

"I told him the same thing."

"He seemed relieved."

"I don't know what I'm going to say to him," Gordon said.

"He understands. Your father has always been a strong advocate for the Honor Code."

"No. I mean, why I couldn't get Henry to tell the truth."

"You did everything you could. I'm proud of you, Gordon. Not many Head Boys could have handled this as well as you did."

"Thank you, sir."

"The only reason the Honor Code has lasted this long is because of sacrifices like the one you made today."

"Thank you, sir."

Mr. Endicott patted Gordon on the knee, and Gordon felt a spasm of pride. Later that night, as he walked back to his room and heard the music coming from the dorm rooms and saw groups of boys laughing together, he thought he heard someone whisper something in his ear. He stopped and turned around. No one was there. He shook his head. It was nothing, he told himself. Just a qualm that he quickly suppressed.

NEW BOY

AFTER GORDON LEFT ME, I watched him walk down the hall, all the way to Endicott's office, without looking back. I watched Gordon knock on Endicott's door and step inside, without looking back. "There he goes," I said to myself. "There he fucking goes."

And I realized even then that Gordon had passed his test. He'd placed me on the altar. He'd bared the knife. And now he would receive his blessing. When that door shut, I knew the price Gordon had paid for admission. I also knew that Gordon had no clue.

I dreaded having to call my parents, but it had to be done. I walked to the phone bank in the basement of the building. I picked up the receiver to one of the phones on the wall and slowly dialed our home number. As the phone rang, I held my breath, hoping that mom would answer, but it was dad. I later learned that he had been sitting by the phone for over an hour, waiting for the call.

"Hello?"

I felt a pit in my stomach, and my head began to throb. "Dad. I've got something to tell you."

I spit out the news, as best I could. Dad was silent for a long time. "Did you tell the truth?" he finally said.

"At the prefect meeting?"

"Yes."

"Yes, I did."

"You told them about Ken Bright?"

I hesitated. "No. I did not."

"I thought you said you told the truth."

"I didn't answer their questions about Ken."

"It was Ken that was with you, wasn't it?"

"Yes."

There was a long silence. "I don't understand you," he said finally. Then there was another long silence, and dad cleared his throat several times. Finally he said, "Your mother wants to talk to you."

I heard dad grumble, "He's been kicked out," as he passed the phone off to mom. I could see them standing in the doorway to the kitchen, and dad turning his back on mom and retreating to his study.

"Oh darling. I'm so sorry about this," mom said. "I just heard about it this morning. How does this happen so fast? Are you okay?"

Her voice was a great relief, and for the second time that day I cried.

"Can you come get me, mom?"

"Of course I can. I'll be there by noon."

When I got back to B Dorm, Study Hall was still in session. The hall was empty. No music was playing. The boys were still in their rooms completing assignments for tomorrow. I wanted to just walk away from it all, call a cab, tell the cabbie, "Raleigh," and arrive home before breakfast tomorrow morning. I dreaded breaking the news to Wobbly and having him hover around me, asking stupid questions as I packed my things. I had no doubt he'd think I was crazy for not turning Ken in.

When I got back to the room I noticed that the light in Ken's room was on. Had he not left? My heart pounded as I opened his door.

The room was empty — no more books, no more sheets, no more Ken. The only thing left was his *Transformer* album hanging on the wall. Taped to the album was a folded piece of paper. I had a feeling it was for me. I pulled the paper off the album and opened it. Handwritten inside was, "Property of Henry Palmer, OWL forever".

The next morning Gordon and I sat in the waiting room outside of Mr. Endicott's office. Mr. Endicott had already said his goodbyes and expressed his disappointment to me.

"In all my years as headmaster I've never been more saddened by a boy's dismissal," Mr. Endicott had said.

I didn't believe a word. I almost blurted out, "I'm sure you lost a ton of sleep over it," but I checked myself. The man was a toad. Why argue with him? When he held out his hand for me to shake, I did at least have enough self respect not to take it.

Mom had called from the road to say she would be there by noon. My boxes and bags were packed and sitting in a pile on the patio outside the front doors. Rather than sit in the front lobby and have to answer people's questions, and repeat my goodbyes, I had followed Gordon's suggestion that we wait here. The window in the waiting room had a view of the front drive. I sat on the couch staring at my shoes while Gordon stood at the window and checked every few minutes to see whether mom was pulling up.

"Looks like they painted over Bright's masterpiece," Gordon said. He pointed at the water tower. "It's like it never happened."

"I don't doubt y'all'll forget about it as quickly as possible."

"Fucking crazy," Gordon muttered.

"What's that?"

"Painting a black man hanging from a noose."

"He made his point," I said.

"Which is?"

"The school's racist," I said matter of factly.

"Give me a break! How does Lawton killing a dog make the school racist?"

Gordon was all red in the face, like I'd called him a coward or something. What did he have to be angry about? Everything had happened just the way he wanted — except for me not ratting on Ken.

"Because they didn't kick him out. They let him withdraw," I said.

"That's because he was crazy as fuck."

"He was racist as fuck."

"Maybe. But that doesn't mean the school's racist."

"Lawton hangs a dog by a noose, and the school acts like it never happened, like you said, but Ken objects and they kick him out."

"Ken broke the rules."

"What rule? The one that says privilege is more important than principle?"

"Oh my god. You sound just like him."

"And you kick me out because I wouldn't turn Ken in. It's a sick joke."

"You lied! You admit you lied. Don't make this about me. I made it possible for you to stay here."

"All I had to do was rat on my friend."

"All you had to do was tell the truth."

"Maybe friendship was my truth."

I surprised myself with that outburst. Gordon kept gawking, and I turned my back. That didn't stop him from trying to have the last word. He stepped around the sofa to face me.

"The Honor Code's not a joke! It's been part of the school for a hundred years."

I stared at the floor. I couldn't bring myself to look at him anymore. "I wasn't the only one on trial last night," I said.

"What's that supposed to mean?"

"You had a choice too."

"Fuck you, Henry!"

Just then there was a tap at the door, and Mr. Nightingale put his head into the room. "Hello, Gordon. I wanted to see Henry before he left. Should I come back?"

Embarrassed that Mr. Nightingale had heard him lose his temper, Gordon cleared his throat and checked his pocket watch. "No. It's fine." Gordon said. "Mom should be here any minute. I'll go outside and get the car packed when she shows up."

As Gordon passed Mr. Nightingale he rolled his eyes as if to apologize for me, but Nightingale ignored him. He took a seat next to me on the sofa, and I noticed that he was holding a green book.

"I was sorry to hear the news this morning." He put a hand on my knee. "I want you to know that it was an honor getting to know you this year, Henry."

I was happy to see Mr. Nightingale — he was about the only person I wanted to see before I left — but I felt embarrassed and maybe even a little ashamed at being one of those fuckups who gets kicked out of school.

"Maybe you shouldn't be here, Mr. Nightingale. Gordon thinks I'm a disgrace."

He laughed. "I'll take my chances."

The window was open, and outside a group of boys threw a lacrosse ball back and forth. Occasionally a shout rang out as one of the boys took a shot on goal.

"I don't know what I'm going to say to my dad," I said.

"Tell him that you were loyal to your friend."

"I'm not sure he'll understand that."

"Maybe not, but it's the truth."

I looked at Mr. Nightingale to see if he was making a bad joke, but he was smiling kindly.

"I guess that's the least I can do, right?"

"I don't know about 'least', but you can do that much. As I told you yesterday, Henry, I think you are an honorable person, and nothing that's happened here has changed that. Everyone who knows you — who really knows you — will still think of you as an honest and honorable young man."

I nodded in the direction of the front patio where my brother was standing. "Tell that to Gordon."

Mr. Nightingale reached into his shirt pocket and pulled out a folded piece of paper. "This came for you this morning. It was delivered to me, and I was asked to give it to you."

I unfolded it. It was a telegram:

> *To: David Nightingale*
> *From: Ken Bright*
> *Please hand deliver to HP.*
> *"Only connect."*

"What does it mean?" I held the telegram out for Mr. Nightingale to read.

"It's Forster," he said. "I think you know what it means." He pointed to my heart. "Put that in your pocket. Keep it. Remember it. It's all you need to take with you from this place."

There was a shout from outside. I stood up and looked out the window. Gordon was standing on the front patio waving at me and pointing towards the front entrance. "Hey Henry! Mom's here."

I turned back to Mr. Nightingale. "Thanks again, sir. For everything."

"There is one more thing. I want you to have this." Nightingale handed me the battered green book he was holding. "It's *Leaves of Grass*. Funny that Ken should send you Forster. Whitman was Forster's American father, spiritually speaking. I believe you may have already discovered him for yourself."

"I wrote a paper about one of his poems for Mr. Mackie — the one we talked about."

"That's what I understand. You are well on your way."

Tears rose up in my eyes again, and I hugged the man hard. Mr. Nightingale hugged me back.

Gordon appeared at the door. "It's time to go. Mom's waiting."

Mr. Nightingale took me by the shoulders and looked me in the eyes. "Send me a postcard from the Territories, won't you?"

"I will, sir."

I left the room with Gordon. Tom Wales and Wobbly were standing on the front patio when we got there. Gordon pushed past them and started carrying my stuff to the car. The three of us stood there, helpless and embarrassed — me because I'd been kicked out; Wales and Wobbly because they didn't know how to say goodbye.

"Aren't you supposed to be in English?" I said.

"We skipped."

"Well if Mackie asks, blame me."

They laughed at that. I picked up a football that was lying in one of my boxes and handed it to Wobbly.

"Work on that five-step drop like we talked about, and there'll be a place for you next year on J.O. for sure."

I meant the comment as a joke, but Wobbly managed to take it as a compliment. He shook my hand firmly — just like his daddy had taught him — and promised to do his best.

When I turned to Wales, he had tears in his eyes.

"I'm going to miss you, Henry."

We hugged. I looked at my belongings — just bedding and towels left.

"Wish I had another football."

Wales laughed. "Me too."

"I won't forget you," I told him.

We walked down the front steps to the old blue Mercedes that was parked out front. Mom stood beside the open trunk wearing her blue sundress and espadrilles. She opened her arms to me and I threw my arms around her and buried my face in her neck. When I pulled back to look at her I saw tears running down her cheeks, but she brushed my cheeks and pulled me close again.

"Let's not talk about it now," she said. "We can talk about it as much as we want on the drive home."

I nodded against her shoulder, and when she let go of me I walked around to the passenger side while mom said good-bye to Gordon. I took one last look at the school, at the patio and the inscription over the front doors, and at the windows to my dorm room and Ken's. I glanced over at the chapel and the oak tree where Lawton had hanged the dog. I looked up at the water tower that was painted silver again. I looked over at the row of faculty houses and the lawn in front of them and saw Mongo sitting cross-legged in a patch of sunlight. He twirled a yellow dandelion flower beneath his nose. "Ferdinand," I thought. Beyond

Mongo, I saw Uly step out of Mr. Nightingale's house and start walking toward the Randolph Building. He had a mop over one shoulder and carried a bucket of cleaning supplies in his opposite hand. As he walked, he looked down at the ground beside him, as if Maisie were still there smiling up at him.

"Hey Uly!" I called out.

Uly stopped and looked around for the person who'd called his name. I waved both hands above my head.

"Hey Uly! Over here!"

Uly spotted me and he put down the bucket. He lifted his hand in reply.

"Take care!" I shouted.

Uly stood there, still, with one hand up in the air, not waving and not saying anything, as if he were waiting for me to finish talking. I struggled to find words. Finally, I said, "I'm sorry, Uly! I'm sorry about what happened to Maisie!"

Uly nodded. "Thank you." And he waved his hand now. "Take care of yourself, Henry Palmer."

I got into the car beside mom. She waited for me to buckle my seat belt then patted my knee and smiled.

"You okay?"

I nodded.

She looked back toward Uly, who'd picked up the bucket and was disappearing around the corner of the building. "Did you get to know Uly?"

I paused and thought about it. "Not really."

"How does he know your name?"

"I introduced myself."

She studied me for a moment, smiled, then started the car, put it in gear, backed up, and made a wide turn to the left. We headed down the front drive, toward the school's East Gate. As we passed under the iron archway beyond the tall boxwood hedge, she asked me about the book I was holding.

"Mr. Nightingale gave it to me. It's *Leaves of Grass*."

I flipped it open and noticed handwritten notes here and there in the margins. On the inside page was his name, David Nightingale, Old Well, Chapel Hill, NC.

"This is his personal copy. From college."

On the title page was an inscription:

> To Henry Palmer,
> "Walk forth from the Bower, refreshed with sleep."
> David Nightingale

And underneath that was a quotation:

> "To live is the rarest thing in the world. Most people
> exist, that is all."
> — Oscar Wilde

I laughed.

"What's so funny?"

"I wonder if Mr. Nightingale knew all along," I said aloud to myself.

"Knew what?"

"Nothing."

I wasn't ready to tell my mother what had happened — there would be plenty of time for that later. Now that I was finally in the car and leaving the school for good I only wanted to stare out the window and behold, as if for the first time, the wide world all around me.

www.ingramcontent.com/pod-product-compliance
Lightning Source LLC
Chambersburg PA
CBHW020532020726
47494CB00006B/1729